I0720545

THE NOVELIST

Charlotte Clarke – 19th Century Writer, Journalist and Sleuth

CRAIG A. GODFREY

Black Rose Writing | Texas

This is a work of fiction. Names, characters, businesses, places, events, and incidents are either the products of the author's imagination or used in a fictitious manner. Any resemblance to actual persons, living or dead, or actual events is purely coincidental.

ISBN: 978-1-68513-356-6
PUBLISHED BY BLACK ROSE WRITING
www.blackrosewriting.com

Printed in the United States of America
Suggested Retail Price (SRP) $22.95

The Novelist is printed in Garamond Premier Pro

*As a planet-friendly publisher, Black Rose Writing does its best to eliminate unnecessary waste to reduce paper usage and energy costs, while never compromising the reading experience. As a result, the final word count vs. page count may not meet common expectations.

INTRODUCTION

Port Arthur. Place of incarceration and hell on Earth for some. 1833-1877
Today Port Arthur is a picturesque historic village. A place to visit for the day, take in the peaceful scenery, learn of its dark history, hear stories of its cruel past as a prison for transported felons from Great Britain in the early 19th century, and enjoy a picnic amongst its 21st century manicured landscape.

Situated almost a hundred kilometres south-east of Tasmania's capital, Hobart, the penal colony of Port Arthur is one of the Australian Convict Sites now recognised as a World Heritage site.

Named after George Arthur, the lieutenant governor of Van Diemen's Land, as Tasmania was known until the mid-1850s, Port Arthur is the largest settlement of several built on Tasman Peninsula. Port Arthur is only accessible by sea or over a narrow isthmus called Eaglehawk Neck.

From 1833 until 1853 (when the *Cessation of Transportation Act* was passed) Port Arthur was a feared destination for even the most hardened criminals. Most of the inmates were convicts who had reoffended since being transported to Van Diemen's Land or those rebellious souls deemed unmanageable. Life at Port Arthur was nothing but a misery.

The prison system on Tasman Peninsula was closed in 1877. Almost immediately Port Arthur became a tourist attraction. Much of this popularity had been nurtured by a popular novel at the time, Marcus Clarke's *For the Term of his Natural Life,* published in 1874. Visitors came by ferry from Hobart on day trips to see the village of pain and suffering to walk amongst the deserted buildings.

The site soon fell into disrepair. The government at the time put the properties up for sale, however there was little interest until 1889. By the late 1880s and early 1890s the peninsula became increasingly popular for tourists. Yet the more decayed the buildings became, the more popular the destination grew. Land and properties started to sell. However, the new owners, rural settlers, demolished many of the buildings, wishing to distance themselves from the dark history of Port Arthur. After all, the location was picturesque and the farming land fertile.

Even so, tourism grew stronger. Port Arthur became the town of Carnarvon, also attracting boating, fishing and sports shooters.

Some entrepreneurial souls became guides, and for a few shillings conducted guided tours amongst the ruins, regaling dark stories of solitary confinement, pain and suffering.

Unfortunately, further destruction came in 1895 and 1897 with two bushfires. An even earlier fire in 1884 had already almost destroyed the church on the hill. The ruined church is today one of the iconic images of Port Arthur. By 1897 the church was overgrown with ivy, giving the building its Gothic appearance that many early Tasmanians identified with ruins back in the *mother country*, England. The 1897 fires, striking on New Year's Eve, were the most destructive of the settlement.

Marcus Andrew Hislop Clarke, novelist.
Born 24th April 1846, died 2nd August 1881.

Novelist and journalist Marcus Clarke's popular novel *For the Term of his Natural Life* was originally published in *The Australian Journal* from 1870–1872 as a novelisation of a convict's life in early Van Diemen's Land. However it was so well received it was published as a novel in 1874 – three years before the closure of Port Arthur. Marcus Clarke visited the prison on Tasman Peninsula to research his work. He interviewed prisoners, and his efforts paid off with his novel still in print today.

Marcus was born in Kensington, London, to parents London barrister William Hislop Clarke and Emelia Elizabeth Mathews Clarke. His mother died when Marcus was only four years old. Born with his left arm at least two inches shorter than his right, he was rejected as a recruit in the army in later years. In his school years at upper-class Highgate School, poetic-minded mates described Marcus as *kaleidoscopic, parti-coloured, harlequinesque and a thaumatrope.* He had difficulty applying himself to his studies, was considered charming and witty by some and spoilt, conceited and aimless by others. This was attributed to his father's Bohemian lifestyle. By 1863 he was an orphan. At the age of seventeen Marcus Clarke emigrated to Victoria in Australia where his uncle was a county court judge. On arrival Marcus was given employment as a clerk in the Bank of Australasia but showed no ability or interest whatsoever in banking. One year later he worked at a farming station in the Victorian country. Once again destiny had other plans for him. In 1867 Marcus joined the staff at *The Argus* and *The Australasian* in Melbourne. Immediately his talent was noted, especially for his descriptions of Melbourne's *low life* opium dens, brothels and gambling houses; all of which he personally researched. His popularity amongst readers grew.

In 1870 *The Argus* sent him to Tasmania to gain first-hand knowledge about the penal system and write about the convict period, as it was known then. This nurtured his interest in the dark side of servitude and the seeds to his famous novel were firmly sowed in his creative mind.

Marcus Clarke married the actress Marian Dunn, daughter of Irish actor John Dunn, in 1869. Sadly, in 1881 Marcus died of poor health and a bankrupt, aged just thirty-five, leaving behind a wife and six children, all under the age of eleven.

Women journalists.

As the 19th century progressed, magazines and periodicals increased tenfold in popularity. Many of these publications were *women only* publications specialising in society, the arts, fashion, feminism and women's suffrage. Due to the popularity of these publications, women were increasingly accepted by the traditional press, and by 1894 *the Society of Women's Writers and Journalists* was founded ...

Leaving the doors wide open for the likes of Charlotte Clarke, novelist and sleuth.

For
Marcus Andrew Hislop Clarke
Novelist
1846-1881

THE NOVELIST

CHAPTER ONE

Port Arthur. The last Friday of 1897, New Year's Eve.
High in the fork of a eucalypt, beneath its shaded canopy, a raven watched over her eggs, warm amongst her nest of sticks. Already she was aware. She smelt the air. Fire approached. She knew this was not the smouldering of one man's campfire, but an uncontrolled, deadly firestorm ... and it was headed her way.

Charlotte turned an anxious back on the raven's gurgling croak. She was immediately surrounded by burning embers. There had been little warning – just a hint of smoke and the crimson horizon. But now the wind picked up. The red sky was barely visible through the smoke. Thick, acrid, choking smoke accompanied by searing heat, like doors flung open to a foundry furnace. Charlotte's eyes tinged with blood, reddening like the setting sun.

'Run miss, run!'

Charlotte needed no command. Her guide Edward Culpepper raced ahead. Although he was local, his path was concealed by the thickening smoke. They rushed down the hillside away from the burning forest, in the direction of Port Arthur and Carnarvon Bay. Immediately a wall of flame the height of the trees careered across their path. Edward screamed a warning, but his words were snatched by the roaring fire. Edward saw a momentary window. Snatching Charlotte's wrist, he pulled her close. Together they rushed through the opening in the wall of smoke. But their only way out was up ...

'Jesus no!'

A gale force gush of broiling wind rushed downhill towards them. Edward turned on the spot. For the briefest of moments, the smoke parted. The fire seemed to backtrack.

'This way. Quickly.'

Neither saw the tree.

The massive eucalypt pounded the earth only feet before them. Dead branches splintered. The two were peppered with dirt and rocks catapulted from its gouged roots. They clambered through its smoking branches and managed another downward path when a boulder-sized fireball soared through the smoke close overhead. Charlotte had never witnessed such a phenomenon.

'The trees miss,' Edward shouted. 'They're full of oil.'

As Edward said this, the flaming ball of volatile combustible oil hit the ground. It exploded, spreading fire across the forest floor. They dashed through the flames. Charlotte struggled to breathe. Hot air burned her throat. The fire was all around them. The sound was a terrifying roar. Suddenly it changed direction, swarming across the ground towards them. Thick, acrid smoke disorientated Charlotte. She stopped briefly.

Edward? Where's Edward? Surely this is not how I die!

'Edward!' she screamed.

A dark figure appeared. 'Charlotte! Here!'

He took her arm once more and felt his way blindly, instinctively, downhill. The two escapees burst from bushland to an open field. But the maelstrom howled from the trees close behind them. It came after the two like a savage beast searching for its prey, chasing them downhill towards the cove. Immediately to the left another wall of flame charged across the tinder dry paddock. Dancing. Gambolling like the devil's demons, tussock to tussock. The Port Arthur settlement materialized. A building here, a building there through breaches in the wall of smoke.

Edward led Charlotte across a blackened field. The nearest building was the three-storey hospital thirty yards ahead ... a safe haven.

'Run miss ... run!'

Suddenly there was a powerful gush of wind and another wall of fire wrapped itself around the building. It stood no chance. Its wood-shingled roof ignited like kindling. The old stone hospital, recently occupied by two families, exploded in flames. Attacking the structure, sliding over sills and dripping to the floor like burning oil. The occupants burst from the front door and onto its arched veranda carrying what meagre possessions they could. They ran, frantic, towards the water's edge where other residents of the town gathered, ashen faced. Panicked.

Over the maelstrom Charlotte heard a foghorn. The 285-foot steel-hulled Union Steamship Company's SS *Manapouri* was docked at the wharf. Around midday, the ship had disembarked curious visitors to the re-tired penal settlement, an attraction to sightseers, and now it offered sanctuary. The entire settlement was on fire. Safety was two hundred yards away.

Heavy black smoke surrounded them once more. Charlotte lost sight of her guide. Only yards away, to her left, the Pauper's mess burned. The single storey brick building was belching choking smoke. Edward's face appeared through the haze. His eyes wide, red and awash with smoky tears.

'This way.' He offered a hand.

Charlotte managed a glimpse of Champ Street ahead. But between them and the harbour the huge four storey penitentiary was alight: its wooden floors, dormitories, spacious mess rooms and timber interior no match for the inferno.

The foghorn sounded another warning.

Through the smoke Charlotte caught sight of the passenger ship; her black hull dotted with portholes. The ship's red funnel spilling smoke from the boilers, her crew preparing to cast off to seek the safety of the bay. Through the cinder-peppered haze Charlotte saw anxious people clamber-ing up the gangway. Men, women and children running for their lives.

Organised chaos.

Charlotte stumbled across open ground towards Champ Street. But fire skipped after her, stalking her. It rushed across the dry unkempt grasslands surrounding Charlotte and her ankle length skirt caught fire. She tore the garment free, exposing pantaloons and her ventilated corset beneath her bodice. Edward appeared from behind.

'Thank god!' he yelled. 'There you are.'

Sparking embers threatened to blind them, flying towards them on a stiffening wind off the bay. Charlotte expanded her parasol, held it ahead of her like a flimsy shield, and ran.

It was terrifying. Yet Charlotte, ever the journalist, was living through her next headline. They hit Champ Street at the run. Instantly the conflagration created a vortex of dust, flame and burning ash along the gravel roadway. To their left, fire from the burning penitentiary clawed its way through gaping black holes in the collapsing shingle roof. Flames leapt from shattered windows reaching towards the heavens, purging dark corridors of its ungodly past. Cinders popped like firecrackers overhead. Interior walls crumbled. Sporadic explosions blasted unbearable heat back up the embankment. While the vortex of fire threatened to cut them off from salvation.

Surely, we'll burn to death.

The noise was horrendous. Edward spotted a window in the smoke. He yelled for Charlotte to follow. They passed the old Commandant's offices as the windows exploded. To their right was the old powder magazine with its castellated stone guard tower. Years earlier this was a store for munitions and explosives. Now, thankfully, it was empty, a deserted attraction. On the lee side of the tower Edward caught sight of the Commandant's House, now the Carnarvon Hotel. Charlotte's accommodation. The fire had passed close behind the single storey stone and brick dwelling, although outbuildings were on fire and all the fences destroyed. But Charlotte recognised a hotel maid ... and then other men. They were armed with buckets of water dousing the rear of the hotel. If nothing else, they could help save the hotel.

But the inferno had other plans.

A three-storey stone wall crumbled onto Champ Street. Their path was blocked. 'We'll have to head to the water.' Edward led the way north back through heavy smoke to where a rivulet ran into the harbour. The smoke worsened. The wind picked up. Burning gum leaves rained down on them, appearing with no warning through the blackened canopy all about them.

Mayhem hit the docks. The jetty ignited. Storehouses burned and the two vessels moored there, severed ropes to drift out into deep water.

Charlotte and Edward managed to backtrack to the corner of Champ and Tarleton. They stood at the intersection. Visibility was almost zero.

Edward heard a horse approaching, whinnying, panicked. A carriage approached at speed. Edward yelled a warning. Charlotte dived towards the gutter. The terrified horse loomed from the black cloud pulling an equally terrified driver standing at the livery seat trying hopelessly to rein in the horse. The carriage raced between Charlotte and Edward. There had been only a second to spare. The horse galloped over the embankment drawing red hot cinders and burning embers in its wake. The carriage followed. But one wheel struck a rock. The wooden spokes shattered. The carriage tipped. The driver cartwheeled and as the harness snapped free the horse plunged out of control into the rivulet. They rushed to help the driver. He was bruised and shaken.

'I'll live,' he said, badly shaken. The same could not be said for the horse.

Nearby oak trees exploded into raging fires. One tree igniting the next when a wind direction forced them to the harbour's edge. They watched spot fires dotting the landscape all about them. The village was ablaze. Cowering below the harbour seawall, the three climbed over slippery rocks to the Commandant's jetty where hotel guests and staff had formed a chain passing water buckets up the embankment to the hotel.

Charlotte appeared from a pall of smoke. She looked a shambles with her unruly spirals of red hair and blackened face like a theatrical minstrel. She was clothed in torn bodice, soiled pantaloons and muddy leather boots laced to the ankles. Somehow, Charlotte had managed to hold onto her cabbage tree hat. She yelled over the pandemonium. 'Any more buckets?'

A bucket was pressed into her bosom. Together Charlotte and Edward scooped up water and hurried back to the flames. Twenty minutes passed. An hour maybe. Charlotte hadn't a clue how long. But the hotel was saved. It was one of the few lucky buildings, with its whitewashed walls a beacon of hope, lit by flickering shadows and flames in the late-night sky.

Charlotte and Edward collapsed onto the front steps with a dozen other volunteer firefighters. They gulped tumblers of lemonade passed around by a grateful hotelkeeper, Mr Bentley Fairclough, whose wife Felicity fetched Charlotte a skirt for modesty.

The fire had passed them by while the darkness of night struggled to reclaim its territory. All about the survivors, fine ash settled like snow. Some glowing embers started spot fires that were smartly extinguished. But the truth of the matter was, there was little left to burn.

As Charlotte and the others watched in shock from the Carnarvon Hotel veranda, they could see that much of the infrastructure of the prison, once a 'home' of misery for thousands of desperate convicts, was destroyed. Although many fires moved on, the penitentiary blazed late into the night; in fact, it would continue burning for two more days.

All were exhausted. All were traumatised.

'Thank you,' Charlotte finally managed to thank Edward. She plucked specs of ash from the surface of her lemonade. 'I don't wish to go through anything like that again. Ever.'

Edward forced a smile. He stood and stretched. 'I must get to my father; he lives three miles from here.' He looked towards the fire's path of destruction and thought his father safe. 'I must make certain he is alright.'

'Of course.' Charlotte watched her new friend gather energy. She knew he had a three-mile hike ahead. Moments later her guide disappeared into the smouldering ruins, where he vanished like a ghost.

Charlotte's attention was drawn back to the activity on the bay. With the worst of the danger passed the vessels returned from deep water with their passengers. Charlotte watched people alight in silence. They too were all in shock and she wondered what her father would have done in this situation. Charlotte had travelled to Port Arthur in her famous father's footsteps. Marcus Clarke, the author of the best-selling novel *For the term of his natural life*, had visited Port Arthur twenty-seven-years earlier to interview prisoners and conduct research for his epic manuscript. Now Charlotte nursed ambitions to write a sequel to her father's novel. It was a long shot; she had no aspirations to become as famous as her father; well not outwardly so. Not yet. And with the Christmas holidays upon them, Charlotte had taken the opportunity to visit the old settlement. Now this! Who could have predicted such devastation?

Charlotte felt her emotions channelling her deceased father. *May as well turn a negative into a positive.* Suddenly Charlotte knew exactly what her father would have said. *You're a journalist girl. Do what you do best. Write. Write about the disaster also. You are here, a front-line witness. Write for your newspaper and research your novel also.*

Charlotte finished her lemonade and stood; aware her attire was in a shambles. She would need to change.

Down at the docks, many of Port Arthur's two hundred population who had boarded the passenger steamer SS *Manapouri,* or the trading ketch *Mary* were now back ashore. All were in shock. Most acted in an orderly manner. Many had lost all their possessions. Everything. Others would return to unscathed homes at the end of the night. Such was the nature of the fiery beast.

***

Around 10PM.

Two dozen or so had gathered at the front garden of the Carnarvon Hotel. Some sat on the steps. With the night sultry and the hotel steeped in smoke, hotel furniture had been carried outside. No one would sleep this night. Hotelier Bentley Fairclough set up lanterns, although continuing flames devouring the nearby penitentiary threw out an abundance of sinister light. They mingled in silence. There was little that could be done until the fire burnt itself out.

Constable Toby Hutton eventually appeared from behind the hotel. He looked forlorn, his exposed skin blackened with ash, his hair singed and slightly confused. He carried a tin trunk of police files. The twenty-seven-year-old policeman was well out of his league, forced out of the frypan into the fire one might suggest. He had been reluctantly promoted from village policeman to man responsible for law and order in a time of disaster. What a time for both his superiors, Sergeant Edison and Inspector Benbow, to leave him in charge as they did, to travel to Hobart with their families for the New Year's Eve celebrations. Already the constable was dreading informing Benbow that his cottage had been destroyed. However, the inspector's stables miraculously survived, along with his two prized horses. At least that was one thing to cheer about.

Hutton approached the gathering. They all stared. No one said much and those who did were mainly in shocked silence.

'Toby!' Felicity Fairclough hurried to his side. The sixty-year-old grandmother was genuinely concerned. She had always fussed over the young policeman, having lost her own boy in a tragic accident. 'Are you alright lad, you look a little lost?'

'It's gone,' he said meekly. 'The Police Office ... it's gone.'

'I know.' They all knew. The police office and station, a substantial stone dwelling close by to the old Commandant's House, was one of the first buildings to explode into flames. Mrs Fairclough had been only twenty yards away when woodwork at the rear of the building caught alight, quickly igniting the shingled roof. Seconds later Rose Cottage, used as a state school, and the Carnarvon Post Office residence next to that were ablaze.

'Sit,' the hotelier's wife signalled for Sarah Rose, the maid, to fetch a chair. But Hutton sat heavily on his tin trunk and looked up at Felicity with a tear in his eye. 'Mathew's gone.'

'Oh.' Felicity knew the constable talked of the ginger cat, Mathew, a nuisance of a cat around the hotel begging for food. However, the old tom did keep the rats at bay. 'Sorry to hear that.' Felicity didn't bother to mention they had lost their piggery and hen house. The pigs' squeals would give her nightmares for months to come. The sty was near the wash house and the bath house, latrines, and smokehouse. All were lost. Not that Toby Hutton would care.

'This is all I could save,' Hutton tapped the trunk on which he was sitting. 'Police records. Sergeant Edison's going to hit the roof.'

'You'll be all right lad.'

'Enough feeling sorry for yourself Toby,' Bentley Fairclough heard the tail of the lawman's conversation with his wife. 'You've got a responsibility son. We need to search the village in case anyone needs help.'

Felicity shot her husband a disparaging glance. But she knew her husband was right. Bentley was always right.

Constable Hutton knew the man was right also. He looked over his shoulder towards the dock where locals and visitors alike were still disembarking, walking about in silence. Their figures distorted through the haze and smoke and the reflective light of still burning fires. They were like spectres. Maybe they were, the constable thought. Either way they needed direction.

'Come on lad,' Bentley said. 'I'll give yer support.' With their hotel thankfully intact Bentley Fairclough left it in the capable hands of his wife. Immediately locals, Mr Armidale Anderson the school master, Craddock Harris and Mr Eldridge, and hotel guests Mr Cecil W Darley and his son Mr CW Darley joined them.

Constable Hutton took a moment to cast an eye over Charlotte. He knew the young red-headed woman had arrived on the steamer two days earlier and he had been keen to strike up a conversation with her. But now wasn't the time. That was the story of his life, *it never seemed the time.* Now here he was feeling sorry for himself. He needed to man-up as his colleagues would have said. *If they had they been here.* Resentful of his responsibility, the police constable had a sudden thought. He would use his authority to attract attention. *Toby,* his mother would say, *everything happens for a reason.*

'Do we know if anyone is missing?' Charlotte suggested before the searchers dispersed. Some of the latecomers, mostly the men, gave Charlotte a look … *Who the hell are you?*

'She's a writer for the newspaper,' someone whispered.

'What? Her?'

'Anyone missing? Good point,' the hotelier said. 'I'll go and ask the others.' He looked down the embankment towards the two vessels crowded with people. 'Maybe you'd care to join me, Father,' he asked the seventy-year-old clergyman, Father Dunne. 'You know all your parishioners better than me I'll wager.'

'Of course,' the old man stood arching his back, pushing out his belly, and with his bible in hand he followed the hotelkeeper down to the water's edge.

Charlotte watched the men spread out. She had sharpened her graphite pencil on a brick and now folded back the cover of her notebook to a suitable blank page.

'Does anyone know where the fire started?' she said aloud.

'It came from the north-east,' someone answered.

'That's correct. William Ferguson first saw the fire take hold on *his* land. Which is only 150 yards from the town'.

Leonard McShan found Charlotte busy making notes. She had already filled four pages interviewing the postmistress. McShan was Charlotte's thirty-three-year-old travelling colleague. A chauvinist in every sense of the word. He appeared from inside the hotel with a freshly bandaged arm from a minor burn. The matron, who had set up a first aid station in the hotel, followed him down the steps.

'There you are,' McShan's face was sour.

McShan's face was always sour, with his permanent downturned lower lip. Charlotte tolerated the man but promised herself this would be the last time she would allow someone chaperone her on business. She was twenty-seven for heaven's sake. Truth of the matter was, however, her editor Rupert Craddock at *The Mercury*, had insisted. Women journalists were a rare breed, his paper employed two in these modern times and the editor was fiercely protective of them.

'I can't allow you run about the countryside unaccompanied interviewing villains,' Craddock had told Charlotte. Charlotte Clarke had been pestering the editor to follow her dream of writing a subsequent follow-up to her father's most popular novel, *For the Term of His Natural Life*. A book as popular as Charles Dickens' *Oliver Twist*, or Victor Hugo's *Les Misérables*, so critics claimed.

'A follow-up story?' Craddock had asked. He was taken aback. Craddock had known Charlotte's controversial father well. He and Marcus had worked together in Melbourne nearly twenty years ago now. Charlotte's father had sadly died young – at the age of thirty-five – back in '81, another reason the editor took Charlotte under his wing. 'You mean you want to write a continuation of your father's novel? I'm not too certain Marcus would approve.'

'Not a continuation per-se, more of a story of survival.'

Craddock frowned. 'Survival?'

'Yes. What if the main characters in my father's book, Rufus Dawes and Silvia Vickers, did not drown in that shipwreck in the end? What if the two corpses found were so disfigured no one realised they belonged to two other lost souls?'

'You do realise,' Craddock said. 'That your father toyed with this theme in the serialisation of his novel.'

'Yes, of course.'

'So you're suggesting mistaken identity?'

'Exactly, and *that* is how their story continues.'

'Goodness me Charlotte. You have your father's imagination, no doubt about that.'

Editor Craddock still wasn't convinced. He was being charitable and studied the young lady who had proven invaluable to the newspaper these past few years. The attractive ... no, comely would be a more suitable description ... the comely five-foot five-inch redhead, with her spirals of curls to her shoulders, a little on the fleshy side, was a strong-willed and determined young lady. She was the daughter he never had. Charlotte would never take no for an answer, and he knew it. He loved her for it. Some of Charlotte's newspaper articles bordered on fantasy and were peppered with discreet exaggerations. Yet she attracted a large readership, and that sold papers. Yes, Charlotte had an eye for a good story alright. She had even been known to solve crimes the police department itself had difficulty solving, treading on the feet of authority in the process.

And Charlotte loved the endearing old man, her mentor and self-appointed guardian. She had a closer connection with Rupert Craddock than most people knew. He had worked with her father Marcus Clarke at the Melbourne Public Library before Marcus died from the bacterial infection erysipelas. For this reason, Rupert had assumed the role of protective figure with the fatherless young lady, when she moved to Hobart to live with her widowed aunt, Jocelyn Childers, another old friend of his. *An old flame, truth be known.* But the truth wasn't known.

'Writing another novel is all very well Charlotte, but what of your responsibilities?' the editor reminded Charlotte of her commitment to the newspaper. 'You have an unfinished article on the outcome of a current trial.'

'I'll have it on your desk tomorrow.'

'See that you do.'

There was also something else the editor considered. Now in 1897 Charlotte had had moderate success with her own debut novel, a romance, *The Very Coquettish Maisie Hill.* Rupert knew the young writer was destined for fame. But as her editor, mentor and principal, Rupert insisted she travel with a chaperone to Port Arthur to interview this old lag she had heard about. Hislop Seghill, an ex-convict, lived a hermit's existence in a bark shanty in the hills behind the township and it would not do for her to visit this man alone.

Charlotte's reluctant – and certainly unwelcome chaperone – Leonard McShan interrupted Charlotte's train of thought. He looked exhausted and if Charlotte was correct, he looked agitated, frightened even.

'Come, we need to secure a berth on the steamer if we're to get ...' McShan lowered his voice to barely a whisper. 'To get away from this hell-hole and back to civilisation on the morrow.'

Civilisation!

Charlotte reeled back, horrified. 'What on earth are you suggesting?'

McShan shrank, not one for confrontation. 'I have it on good authority that the *Manapouri* will be departing first light,' he said rather sheepishly.

Charlotte excused herself with the postmistress. She stood to confront McShan, but the man was six foot – albeit a scrawny six foot – and she was loath to look up to her colleague. Her eyes narrowed. 'I'm not going anywhere.'

'Y-you're not?'

'No. Here we are, journalists, witnesses to the greatest disaster to hit this peninsula, no, to hit Tasmania, and you want to scurry away to safety like a little field mouse. What kind of newspaper man are you?'

'I'm responsible for you ...'

'Humbug!' the redhead flared. Eyes turned. McShan flushed. 'I'm responsible for me. *Me*, Charlotte Clarke. I didn't ask you to come along and ... and follow me about like I'm some pet dog. Mr Craddock did.'

'Ah! Well, there you go, see,' Leonard said meekly. 'He's my employer also. And he ordered me ...'

'Go! I'm busy.'

'But...'

'I will have a firsthand headline and front page ready for you before you sail in ... what time is it now?'

McShan fiddled with a fob watch in his waistcoat pocket. 'Twenty-seven minutes past the hour of ten.'

'Fine. As the post office has been destroyed and much of the telegraph line with it, I will have a finished dispatch before sunup, and you will take it to Mr Craddock the moment you arrive in Hobart. I will sail back in a day or two.' And as an afterthought she added, 'With a follow-up story for the paper.'

The humiliated McShan was red with embarrassment.

'Don't worry about me Leonard,' Charlotte cooled her tone. 'I fear for old Hislop Seghill back up the hill in that burnt out forest. Edward Culpepper and I were on our way back down the hill after I interviewed him for my book when the fire attacked. I fear he may not have survived.'

'What are you going to do then?'

'I've asked Edward Culpepper to meet me here later this night. We'll inspect the destroyed buildings and I'll do my report. Then tomorrow, first chance, we will visit Hislop Seghill once again.'

***

Three hours earlier

Once the Carnarvon Hotel was safe from the flames, thirty-four-year-old Port Arthur visitor guide Edward Culpepper had left Charlotte to walk the three miles to his father's cottage north-west of Port Arthur.

Pa was safe.

Thankfully the area was spared the devastation. Now Edward returned in the dark, walking through the smouldering ruins. With the fire's passing, stillness settled over the village. Yet smouldering gum leaves still fell amongst the destruction, while an eerie haze hung over the township. Strangely the lamplighter, no doubt in shock, had lit several surviving streetlamps. Now, shining yellow and orange through the thick smoke haze, the streets reminded Edward of scenes in foggy London that he had seen in picture books, while here and there small fires picked up, fanned by the occasional fresh breeze.

Edward was exhausted, but the adrenalin still coursed through his veins. Passing the ivy-covered ruins of the church, destroyed by another devastating fire thirteen years earlier, Edward cut across the grasslands to avoid the acrid smoke. As he approached Carnarvon Hotel from the west his thoughts went to Charlotte. Edward had grown fond of Charlotte since she arrived on the steamer two days earlier. Following Charlotte's written instructions from their earlier correspondence, Edward had met her at the docks with a pony and trap borrowed from his neighbour. Once Charlotte and her travelling companion, Leonard McShan, had secured their accommodation at the Carnarvon Hotel, Edward had taken them to *interview*, yes that's the word she used, to interview his father Shipley Culpepper.

*****

Two days earlier.
'Father's now seventy-eight,' Edward told Charlotte – who was taking notes – as they rode to his father's cottage. "is memory ain't as sharp as it used to be but what he can't remember 'e makes up, usually twisting stories, told 'im by other ol' lags what 'ad been in the cells with him all them years ago.'
'Seventy-eight?'
'Aye, born in 1819.'
'What did your father do?' Leonard asked over his shoulder, from where his scrawny legs dangled from the back of the trap like an errant schoolboy's.
'To ... ah ... warrant being sent to the colonies.'

Edward fancied saying, *'e strangled a molly what was annoyin' him,* but said instead, 'Father was caught house-breakin' in Surrey. Got 'imself transported to Van Diemen's Land in '43.'

Charlotte executed some hasty arithmetic. 'He was twenty-four.'

'That's right. "e had a terrible time of it sailin' out 'ere all them years back, but I daresay 'e'll tell you his all.' The pony slowed on an incline and Edward gave the animal a flick with his switch.

Charlotte. 'What was his sentence?'

'Seven years.'

'You wrote me in one of your letters that your father wasn't released until 1856.'

'That's right.'

'Then why was he incarcerated so long?'

'Father was a rebel see, an' Port Arthur was where they kept rebels. "e was a repeat offender and didn't take too kind to bein' ordered about.'

Charlotte continued making notes.

Edward had taken the opportunity to study his passenger. It wasn't every day he had attractive company in such close proximity, squeezed next to him on the narrow seat. He smiled at her red locks bouncing beneath her cabbage tree hat and thought her white, simple ankle-length skirt, was a poor choice to be wearing on a dusty country road. Her grey shirt however, tied at the neck with a bow and tucked behind a leather brass-buckled belt at the waist, was a better choice. And although he knew short sleeves were the fashion now-a-days, Charlotte's lily-white and freckled skin was turning pink under the midday sun.

Charlotte caught Edward staring. Not that she wasn't used to men being indiscreet, and women too for that matter. But for some reason she was flattered, not offended. Although this local, a ruffian by the looks of him, was a few years her senior, she found some comfort in the attention. Maybe this was caused by her continuous feelings of repulsion in the company of Leonard *Insipid* McShan on the ferry from Hobart. Almost as if she read Edward's thoughts, Charlotte expanded her parasol to shield her from the sun.

'Everything alright?' she said, snapping Edward from his distraction as the trap veered to the verge of the dusty bush track.

Edward blushed.

'You better keep an eye on the road,' Charlotte smiled.

Edward pulled on the right rein and the old pony drifted to the right. 'Sorry Mrs Clarke.'

'If we're to work together a few days, please call me Charlotte.' And Charlotte meant it. Charlotte was a firm believer in the modern freedoms for women being touted these days. Only two years from the beginning of a new century, and, heaven forbid, there was even talk these days of women being given the right to vote.

'Alright then,' Edward looked Charlotte in the eye, 'I'll call yer Charlotte, an' you call me Ed if'n yer like.'

'I prefer Edward,' Charlotte answered. 'Ed sounds like a draught horse I know.'

'Well then, Edward it must be. An' may I say wha' a pretty name Charlotte is an' all.'

'Now you're being forward ... Edward.'

Edward blushed for the second time in as many minutes. 'I ... ah ... I didn't mean ...'

'I jest Edward.'

'Oh ... hah.' Edward decided to swing the conversation back to his Pa. 'Ah, where were we? Father. Yes. So, he received his *ticket of leave* that year, 1856, and a conditional pardon a year later. He was then thirty-six.'

'What a waste of life!'

'Aye. Anyways, 'e were determined to make somethin' of his life, what was left of it. He met me ma soon after. She were twenty-eight-year-old widow, Violet Jones. They married in 1858 and rented a cottage in South Hobart where they lived happily enough together, Violet and her two daughters, me half-sisters Mary and Alva. I came along in '58.'

'That was expeditious.'

'Yeh, well. No one seemed to bother that me ma were six months pregnant at the altar.'

If telling this to Charlotte bothered Edward, he didn't show it.

'So, when did Shipley Culpepper the ex-prisoner arrive back in Port Arthur as a guide for sightseers?'

"79.' Edward became sullen for a moment, serious even. 'Ma died in 1877 see, the same year the prison closed.'

'Oh, sorry to hear that.'

'Yeh, well. Consumption. She were forty-eight. Anyways father heard of all these visitors comin' here to look at the empty buildings. Ghouls 'e liked to call 'em, and 'e had the idea to guide 'em through, tell 'em stories, charge 'em a shillin' each.'

'And?'

'It's been most advantageous Missus. 'e dresses up in an old prisoner uniform and wears chains an' all. The visitors love it.'

'And now he's roped you in too, huh?'

'Aye. I come 'ere in '93 I did.'

'And do you dress for the occasion?'

'Dress?'

'Prisoner uniform and irons?'

'Of course.'

'Still lucrative?'

'Well, I don't go 'ungry,' a wry smile crossing Edward's his face. The final half mile along the track to the Culpepper cottage, hidden amongst thick bushland, was the most difficult, where the pony and trap tossed side to side over rocks and potholes made by rain.

'Here we are,' Edward pulled on the reins. The pony stopped and, for the first time, Charlotte felt a level of excitement. She was about to meet Shipley Culpepper, one of the few men still living, who had lived through the horrors of Port Arthur.

'You can wait here,' Charlotte spoke coldly to Leonard. It was clear to Edward, Charlotte had little time for her chaperone, a situation that quietly pleased him. In an attempt to save face, Leonard asked, 'And what would you have me do Mrs Clarke?'

'Please yourself,' Charlotte said. 'Go for a walk.'

The bushland surrounding the cabin looked most uninviting to Leonard, who looked to Edward for advice. 'Fill yer boots man,' Edward grinned. 'But watch out for them black snakes.'

Leonard repositioned himself on the cart, feet high off the ground.

'If'n yer don't mind me askin',' Edward said when they were out of earshot, 'I noticed that Mr McShan called yer *Mrs* Clarke.'

'That's because I was once married.'

'Oh,' Edward reeled back like he'd overstepped the line. 'Sorry, I didn't mean to pry like, I jus' ...'

'I'm widowed Edward. My husband, Charles Claiborne, was drowned in Storm Bay and his body washed up at Adventure Bay on Bruny Island.'

'Oh, I'm sorry to hear that.'

'Yes ... well. These things happen. It was nearly four years ago now.' Charlotte collapsed her parasol and buttoned the strap to hold it in place. 'We were married in 1890 and he disappeared during a storm, washed overboard, in '94.'

'How terrible for yer. Jus' four years, eh?'

Charlotte nodded. The memory was still painful.

'Any bairns?'

'No ... no children.' Charlotte recognised there was an unanswered question bothering Edward. 'You are wondering why I call myself Mrs Clarke and not Mrs Claiborne?' Edward's face said it all. 'It's because I chose to retain my maiden name. Having a famous father is a help to my career.'

Shipley Culpepper, in Charlotte's opinion, was a character from a Charles Dickens' novel. He was one of those old men who shrank with age; Charlotte imagined he would have been strapping in his youth, not unlike his son Edward. Hygiene was not a priority, his hair was matted and grey. He had large, wrinkled ears and a bald pate. His knotted ponytail was tied low at the back, like that of a seafarer from decades earlier. The old man's face was rugged and weathered, although once again, Charlotte could see remnants of a handsome face. Shipley's breath smelt of beer, but Charlotte expected this, Edward having mentioned how his father always had bread and beer for breakfast. This was an easy meal for an old man often alone, but it provided calories, vitamins and minerals, even though in these times of enlightenment the temperance movement was exhorting people to turn their backs on alcohol.

They sat inside at the kitchen table where the only illumination was natural light from the one window facing north. Four chairs surrounded the table. All were broken in one way or another.

'I can only offer yer beer fa refreshment,' the old man said. Knowing most people of his vintage still brewed their own small beer, Charlotte accepted, more out of politeness than the need for refreshment. Edward was impressed.

Charlotte enjoyed Shipley's humour, a natural raconteur with stories aplenty. With the old man's approval, Charlotte scribed notes, page after page, and congratulated herself on being a master at shorthand. And Shipley, now seventy-eight, was only too pleased to have company, in particular a young lady's company and even more so, the daughter of a famous author. Although Shipley had never read the book he had been shown a copy some years back. Three hours and several pints of small beer went in a flash. Outside, Leonard sulked and baked in the sun.

'Did you ever meet my father?' Charlotte finally asked, catching Shipley stifling a yawn.

'No lass, I never. But I know a lag what did meet your Pa an' 'e resides 'ere in Arthur.'

'Hislop Seghill?' Charlotte said.

'Aye, yer heard o' him then?'

'Yes, he was first recommended to me by a retired guard from the Campbell Street Prisoner Barracks and I was assured he met my father back in the 60s. He's reclusive I hear and avoids company.'

'Aye, the cranky ol' bugger'd shoot visitors if'n 'e had the chance.'

'Edward has offered to take me to him,' Charlotte said. 'We made correspondence earlier by messenger and Edward has arranged for me to meet Mr Seghill.'

'Yer, well. If'n anyone can get ol' Hislop's ear, it'd be me boy Edward.'

***

Afternoon before the fires. December 31ˢᵗ.

Hislop Seghill lived less than a mile from the village yet it was hard going – steep, rocky and thick bushland. Some areas deforested by the prisoners back in the settlement's notorious heyday had regrown with a vengeance. Wildlife was prolific and it was not uncommon to see a six-foot black snake every ten minutes or so.

'You stay away from them and they'll stay away from you Missus,' Edward said of the silent slithering reptiles as he hiked ahead of Charlotte. 'Just make plenty o' noise and they'll get outa yer path.'

'Oh, that's just dandy,' Charlotte said, poking the grass ahead of her with her parasol. 'They're poisonous aren't they?'

'Oh yer, deadly.' Edward sniffed the air. Smoke. He stopped. His face was serious.

Charlotte noted Edward's suddenly serious demeanour and asked, 'Everything alright?'

'Smell that?'

'You mean the smoke?'

'Aye.' Edward looked towards the sun, the haze in the air had made the sun appear like a fried egg, pinkish, with a distinct halo.

'Is it not a campfire close by?'

'No Missus. That be a bushfire and if I was to hazard a guess, I'd say it's northeast on the peninsula somewheres.'

'Is that serious?'

'I hope not. Best we continue.' Edward thought to change the subject. 'What's it like being the daughter of a famous novelist?' he asked, picking up the pace.

'It's no big deal, not really. Oh, don't get me wrong, I'm proud of my father's achievements, I really am. In fact, that is why I am here, but you know that already.'

'Yer wrote me in yer correspondence that yer want to meet Seghill because he met your father, but to what end?'

They stopped to catch their breath. Charlotte had never revealed her true motive in their correspondence, now she wondered if her guide was genuinely interested. She looked Edward in the eye. 'Promise me you won't laugh.'

'Aye. I promise.'

'I wish to write a continuation of my father's story, a second book, a sequel I suppose it might be called, an accompanying adventure to father's novel, *For the Term of his Natural Life*.'

'Write a book! You?'

'Yes *me*.' Charlotte looked irritated. 'And if you say anything about me being a woman Edward Culpepper, so help me …'

'Oh sorry. I didn't mean to upset yer; it just came as a bit of a shock.'

'Women are allowed to follow ambitions you know. We aren't all maids, cooks, servants, washerwomen or, god forbid, bed companions.' Edward's face turned scarlet. Charlotte's voice sweetened. 'Have you read my father's book?'

'Ah, can't say I have.'

'You can read, can you not?'

'Aye. I fetch the newspapers on weekends and read to me Pa. I've been thinkin' maybe I read one or two o' your stories in the past, Missus … Charlotte.'

'Do you purchase *The Mercury*?'

'Aye, and the Launceston paper, *The Telegraph*, on occasion.'

'Then you would most certainly have read articles written by me.'

'God's oath eh, an' here I am guiding you about.'

Twenty minutes further on they entered a clearing. The shanty was built of split timbers and bark. The walls, vertical boards. Seghill built his two-room *homestead* before the hill was levelled, for drainage purposes. This afforded him an elevated area at the front for a veranda, of sorts, with a roof of bark and a bark guttering to collect rainwater. This flowed into a fifty-five-gallon hogshead barrel. A single stone chimney served for cooking and for warmth in winter. But what really impressed Charlotte was the vegetable garden at the side and front, 'L' shaped and facing north. Everything was blooming and looking healthy, from tomatoes to beetroots, Brussels sprouts to cabbages, pumpkin, parsnips and radishes. An elaborate wicker fence surrounded the garden and tin cans dangling on string were rigged to frighten wildlife. 'This garden is very impressive.'

'Aye, Hislop sells them to the village. Thurmund Gill from the general store comes here with a pack mule twice a week.'

Hislop appeared to be away. The shanty was deserted. There was no answer to Edward's calls.

'Maybe he's out settin' traps for his next meal,' Edward said.

'Next meal?'

'Aye rabbit. Hislop eats rabbit everyday I'm thinkin'. Rabbit stew, just like 'is mama taught 'im to cook before 'e got caught poachin' the Queen's venison in the forest near Windsor.'

'Is that why he was transported here to the colonies?'

'Aye, that an' sellin' the meat. 'e were caught with several carcasses see.'

'Oh. When was that?'

'Well 'e's eighty-one now I believe, and was sent to 'obart Town as yer know it were called then, back in the 40s. Then he got caught reoffending, not once but three times. He also tried to escape with some other felons an' got caught. So 'e was sent 'ere to Port Arthur in the 50s an' was still 'ere when they closed the gates in '77.'

'Are you very familiar with him?'

'Well yes and no. 'e's a moody bugger ... sorry, moody cove. I've brought me dad 'ere a few times to reminisce with 'im but 'e keeps to 'imself pretty much. Unless o' course 'e's down yonder sellin' vegetables in the village.' Edward considered his most recent correspondence with the old hermit. 'This little meetin' today cost me a pound o' baccy.'

'Oh, I must repay you.'

'I didn't mean to ...'

'No, I insist. You must be reimbursed.'

Without warning a hunchbacked old man wearing kangaroo skins and what appeared to be a calico napkin exposing scrawny tanned legs with hobnailed boots on his feet, appeared like Robinson Crusoe from around the side of his cabin. His unkempt hair was tied back in a ponytail, with a knotted grey beard to his chest and if he had any teeth remaining, Charlotte couldn't tell. He held a blunderbuss at least as old as he was.

'Stand where yer are or I'll turn yer into a sieve.' With a blunderbuss filled with buckshot and pebbles, Edward had no doubt.

'It's me Mr Seghill, Edward Culpepper, Shipley's boy.'

'Edward,' Hislop's tired old eyes narrowed, finally focussing. 'So it is. Well I'll be. Ain't seen yer in years.'

'That's not quite true Mr Seghill, I was here last week remember and you agreed to talk to my friend here, Mrs Charlotte Clarke. Marcus Clarke's daughter.'

Hislop lifted his head to adjust his sight. Charlotte shifted into focus. 'Marcus Clarke's daughter. Well, I never.' Suddenly he grew serious. 'A load of claptrap that book … what was it? In a prison cell for life? Somethin' like that.'

'*For the Term of His Natural Life.*'

'Oh aye, that's it. Bloody claptrap.'

Edward reddened at his acquaintance's bluntness. 'Smell the smoke Hislop?' he asked the hermit. 'It seems to be gettin' worse.'

'Aye. I just been up yonder,' the old man waved the blunderbuss back towards the apex of the hill. 'Looks like a fire at Eaglehawk Neck.' He spoke of the narrow isthmus connecting Dunalley to the Tasman Peninsula a dozen miles as the crow flies, north-east. 'An' there's fire over on Fortescue. But that'll burn out at the bay, with any luck.'

'Aye. Let's hope it stays there.'

Hislop spat chewing tobacco at his feet. 'Well, I gotta take the weight off me legs.'

He sat in the shade under his veranda on his only chair, a bushman's chair made of dead branches held with leather straps and nails salvaged from the village.

'So then,' Hislop looked at Charlotte. 'Yer here now, so what d'ya wanna know about? Yer Pa, ain't it?'

Straight to business. Charlotte liked that. 'I was particularly interested in your meeting with my father. I was ten when he died you understand, and unfortunately I did not grow to know him as an adult. He visited Port Arthur in 1870, did he not?'

'Sounds 'bout right. I were a gardener by then, a lifer in me middle fifties. I was 'ead gardener for some time see.' Hislop alluded to his impressive garden. 'Green-finger the lags called me.'

'Yes, I noticed. Very impressive.'

'Yeh well, your pa and me talked for hours one day, askin' me about life in the cells, life in the prison system in general. 'e told me 'e were writin' stories for some newspaper 'e were writer for, in Melbourne I'm thinkin'.'

'*The Argus* and *The Australasian* were but two.'

'Were it? I can't remember.'

'Yes. But he wrote a serialisation of his stories first and they were published in the *Australian Journal* of which my father was editor, under the title *His Natural Life*. It was published as a novel four years after he spoke with you, in 1874.'

'I remember 'e was a pleasant enough cove to talk to, 'ad a bit of a stammer.'

Although Charlotte's father died sixteen years ago when she was ten, she remembered the stammer well. He had suffered it all his life.

'You read the novel, did you not?'

'I can't read lady.'

'But you said the book was ... claptrap's the word you used; I believe.'

Hislop pinched his lips tight, dreading what he'd said. But words can't be taken back and there was no doubt he used them. 'Look, I was jus' repeatin' what other lags 'ad told me.'

'Oh, like what?'

'Well, if'n you murder someone yer hang, plain an' simple. This fella in yer pa's book, what's 'is name ...'

'I think you speak of Richard Devine, also known as Rufus Dawes.'

'Aye, Rufus Dawes, that's' im. We'll 'e got sent to Van Diemen's Land. They would 'a hung 'im then instead.'

'If your friends *had* read my father's book, they would have discovered that Rufus Dawes was found not guilty of murder, but guilty of robbing a corpse. That is why he was sent to the colonies, for the term of his natural life.'

'Oh.'

Charlotte thanked Hislop for his candour none the less. Making herself as comfortable as possible, Charlotte sat on the veranda top step, positioning her parasol as protection from the fierce sun. She took her notebook from her satchel, turning to a page of questions listed to ask the old hermit.

'Were you ever given solitary confinement?' Charlotte started.

The old man nodded. 'Several times miss, especially when I was young an' rancorous.' Hislop described the loneliness, the fear of the dark, the cold. He described tasting the pain of the cat-o-nine-tails, as they called the medieval punishment of whipping; a punishment thankfully banned early in Hislop's confinement. Charlotte's questions brought back raw, dark memories, but the ex-prisoner seemed to be enjoying the young woman's company. Edward sat on a rock nearby, captivated by the determined journalist, her enthusiasm for her work and her thirst for knowledge. Many of Hislop's stories he had heard before, some backed by his own father's experiences. But unlike Hislop, Edward's father Shipley Culpepper bottled most of his memories, like a soldier returned from the battlefield.

An hour passed.

The hint of smoke intensified. Now a visible haze shifted through the trees, their branches and leaves disturbed by the increasing winds. Without warning a huge male kangaroo careered from the bushland. The panicked animal ploughed into the garden fencing with such force it ripped the plaited wattle barrier from its roots before entangling in tomato bushes. Another spooked wallaby rushed by.

Hislop stood awkwardly, his age disorientating him, snatching his blunderbuss. By the time he'd lifted his weapon to his shoulder the terrified animals were gone. But others could be heard thrashing through the undergrowth nearby. Rabbits, wombats, snakes – all in a mad attempt to escape.

'Fire!' Edward said, calm but anxious. 'That fire's moving faster than I expected.'

'Aye,' Hislop leant his firearm against the door frame. 'It don't smell too good neither.'

Already glowing cinders flew overhead as the wind picked up and the sky darkened.

Edward had one priority. Charlotte. 'Come. We've gotta move. Now!'

Charlotte was certain she heard the crackling of fire and tinder. The surrounding forest was certainly dry and heavy with fuel.

'Mr Seghill,' Charlotte ordered. 'You must come with us.'

'I can't leave!'

'You can't stay here.'

'Nar, it's coming from the north, it'll go by over the hill yonder.'

Edward hurried forward. 'Mr Seghill, it looks to me like it's headed this-a-ways. I don't mean to be rude but yer ain't no young buck no more, you'll be needin' a hand.'

Charlotte leant over taking the old man's lean weak arm. 'Take Edward's advice sir. Come with us.'

Hislop jerked his arm free. 'Don't be daft woman, I can look after meself.'

There was no arguing with a man so stubborn. Edward and Charlotte exchanged concerned faces.

'Then take care,' was all Edward could offer.

With heads down against the increasing winds, Charlotte folded her parasol and they ran back towards Port Arthur as the conflagration surrounded them with deadly determination from three sides ... and at high speed.

CHAPTER TWO

Eight hours later. 10:45PM, December 31ˢᵗ. Day of the fire.
The night was still heavy with smoke. Edward managed a shortcut through fruit trees. Many had miraculously avoided destruction. But the fruit had cooked on the branches where they hung. Edward stepped from darkness into the front gardens of the Carnarvon Hotel. Charlotte stood out in the crowd. She now wore a pink dress to replace the white garment snatched from her by the fire. Edward stopped in the shadows a moment. He felt a flutter in his chest. A feeling he rarely felt towards women. He had been unlucky in love; besides his lifestyle all these years living with his father, an ex-prisoner, hindered his situation.

Charlotte had her back to Edward. He paused. She was asking questions of Mrs Hyde the post mistress. Suddenly Edward realised that he, the voyeur, was being observed by a group of older women all smiling like Cupid's helpers. Flushed, he stepped into the lantern light. Edward removed the cap from his head, holding it with both hands before him, choosing a moment to interrupt Charlotte's scribbling.

'I'm back Missus.' Edward decided to keep his dialogue with Charlotte formal in front of the other women.

'Edward! … Your father? Do tell me he is unharmed?'

"e's fine. The fire didn't pass too close by.'

'Oh, thank goodness for that.'

'But I have other grave news I'm afraid.'

'Oh!'

'Hislop didn't make it.'

'No!'

'I was talkin' to folk on the way here. Hislop's property was totally destroyed, and they found his body next to the water barrel. Looked like he was tryin' to climb in when 'e were struck down.'

'Oh ... how ... how terribly awful. I am so sorry.'

'You and me, we tried to get him away, but ...' Edward's words trailed off. Charlotte closed her notepad, slipping it into her leather satchel slung over her shoulder. She turned to the post mistress. 'You must excuse me Mrs Hyde.' Charlotte twisted back to Edward, taking both his hands in hers, consoling. 'You did try Edward.'

'Such a terrible way to die.'

'But your father is safe. That is good news.'

'Aye.'

There followed a moment's silence. 'Give me five minutes,' Charlotte finally spoke. 'I'll quickly change.' Hitching up her skirt Charlotte mounted the hotel steps two at a time in a most un-lady like manner.

Six minutes later Charlotte reappeared in green trousers and wearing her cabbage tree hat. Edward suddenly burst into a smile. He didn't mean too. But he felt like a giddy schoolboy. As Charlotte walked towards him, he noted her britches were similar to pantaloons. At first appearance they looked like a skirt, but the two leggings were separate. Clearly Edward looked surprised. Charlotte twirled in a tight circle. 'How do I look?'

'You look ...' Edward was afraid of what he would say next, should he embarrass himself. 'You look ... ready Missus.'

'Call me Charlotte,' she whispered with a warm smile. 'I'd prefer you to call me by the name my parents gave me. Actually, anything rather than Missus.'

'Alright then. Charlotte.' Edward secretly hoped the nearby women heard. Feeling elevated from the humble son of an ex-Port Arthur convict, Edward added, 'So, you are ready?'

'Ready as I'll ever be.'

'Where are you off to?' the post mistress asked in a matronly tone, eyeing the pantaloons. 'That is, if you don't mind me asking.'

'We're going to help search for survivors,' Charlotte looked through the wide iron gates of the hotel that led to the main village of Port Arthur, now a smouldering ruin.

'But my dear, it's dangerous out there. Besides the men are already searching.'

The men! Charlotte's curse. *Always leave it to the men.* Off in the distance several small knots of men, their progress lit by spirit lamps, could be seen spreading out and searching the burnt-out buildings.

Charlotte retorted, 'My mother used to say many hands make light of the work ... or something like that.' And Charlotte hooked her arm through Edward's, turning her back and headed for the gates. If the old-fashioned post mistress didn't approve of a lady joining the men in such a macabre venture, too bad. Charlotte had an important story to write, a *scoop*, as she had heard American journalists call it. And that was her motivation.

'Here's your parasol miss,' Felicity Fairclough the hotelier ran after Charlotte. 'I had Rose clean it for you.'

'Oh, how considerate, thank you.'

'It was fortunate you didn't lose it. It's such a beautiful thing.'

In all the turmoil Charlotte had forgotten her precious parasol as she escaped to the hotel, less her skirt. She took her parasol and expanded the canopy for those around her to admire. The bamboo handle secured a cover of yellow silk woven with a pattern of pink cherry blossom. 'This was a gift from my editor,' Charlotte told those in ear shot. 'Mr Rupert Craddock.'

Someone said, 'How generous.'

'Yes. His elderly aunt sailed the Orient some years ago and brought it back as a gift for Rupert's wife. However, Mrs Craddock passed last year, and Mr Craddock insisted I have it.'

'You must be in the gentleman's good books.'

'I work hard Mrs Fairclough.'

'I'm certain you do.'

Walking out through the gates Charlotte and Edward returned to the devastation. It was sickening - the destruction was complete. To the right the penitentiary continued crackling and crumbling as flames devoured the settlement's largest building. It was futile to even contemplate putting out the flames. There was simply too much fuel to burn, and the intense heat forced them up the hillside away from the inferno.

'Here, this way,' Edward led Charlotte to steps behind the stone guard towers and powder magazine.

On the hill, before a devastated background of blackened eucalyptus trees, the ruins of several buildings still smouldered. It was a pathetic sight. And particularly sobering for Charlotte after arriving only days earlier on a warm sunny summer noon to a picturesque, very English setting, of stone buildings and manicured gardens – delightfully charming, even though the colonial settlement had a miserable past. Now, only exterior walls remained of many buildings. Miraculously some cottages had survived. Ahead, the hospital was a blackened shell. Charlotte watched six men manning a hand pump on a fire cart wagon, rapidly emptying the barrels of water. Their efforts were futile. There was nothing the two of them could do but watch.

Walking parallel to Champ Street, Charlotte and Edward arrived at Church Street, running diagonally and leading to the ivy-covered ruins of the church.

From up here on the hill Charlotte and Edward could see groups searching the buildings around the harbour, while others explored buildings to the north-east and southeast. Their voices carried through the stillness of night.

Otherwise, the two were alone.

Ahead, on the west side of Church Street in eerie total darkness were the attractive homes once occupied by the assistant surgeon, the Catholic chaplain, the medical officer, the commissariat officer and the Church of England's chaplain. All cottages had remarkably survived, except for the Church of England's rectory which was badly damaged.

Here in the shadowy gloom, not benefiting from the illumination of lingering flames, Edward lit his carbide lamp. The light from the burning acetylene reflected from the silvered dish, throwing hard-edged light into dark corners.

Shadows shifted. Altering shapes materialised in their peripheral vision. It was easy for Charlotte to imagine ghosts from decades past, gazing at her from behind a veranda column or staring down through a shattered dormer window. They searched methodically but there was no sign of life. Clearly the occupants of all the cottages had fled.

'What a shame,' Edward shone his light on the smouldering remains of the Church of England rectory. 'I always loved this 'ere cottage.'

He explained its significance to Charlotte. The porch cornice, columns, gabled ends and turned woodwork were burnt through and the porch had collapsed. Mysteriously the rear of the building had survived. With the front rooms destroyed, they were able to see into the main hallway where the roof and chimneys had fallen in. Edward concentrated his beam down the passage, now open to the stars. Immediately a dark shape flashed across the corridor. It crossed room to room at the rear of the cottage.

'Who's there?' Edward shouted.

Charlotte stiffened. 'What is it?'

'There's someone there.' Edward didn't want to admit it could possibly be a looter. He rushed forward stumbling over burnt timbers and loose bricks which had been sent skittling onto the front lawn when the roof collapsed. 'Ahoy there. Is there anyone there?'

No answer.

Charlotte used her parasol as a hiker's cane to follow Edward up the short embankment towards the front door. 'What was it?'

'I seen someone. At least I thought I did.' Edward called out. 'Hello in there ... is there someone there? It's Edward Culpepper ... Shipley Culpepper's boy.'

No answer.

'Are you certain you saw someone?'

'I ... I'm pretty certain. Let's move 'round the back.'

Charlotte smelt the stench of burnt flesh before she saw the gruesome body.

'Oh, sweet Jesus!' Edward gasped. 'Sorry. Didn't mean to blaspheme but ... oh god!'

Charlotte was more reserved. As an investigative journalist she had seen her share of cadavers and was no stranger to death. 'Who is it, do you know her?'

The deceased's head was twisted unnaturally against the bottom stair that led to the attic bedrooms. The feet stretched almost into the dining room. Although this part of the building survived the blaze, her right arm and abdomen had been charred by fire. A pool of blood spilled about the body, where it had clearly flowed from a gash in her head and Charlotte noted rigor mortis had already set in. The area stank of paraffin and burnt flesh.

Edward recognised her immediately. 'It's Annie, Annie Smith. She's Reverent Finch's maid.' Edward was suddenly aware of his *genteel* company. 'I'm so sorry you saw this Charlotte. It's not a pleasant sight for a lady. I'll take you back to ...'

'You'll do no such thing,' Charlotte straightened. 'What do you think I am Edward Culpepper, some milksop from a finishing school for young ladies?'

'No ... I ... ah ... I just thought ...'

'Well don't.' If it wasn't so dark Charlotte would have seen Edward's face glow red. Charlotte took a breath. 'There's clearly something you didn't know about me. I'm a journalist, yes. But I'm also a crime writer. As a journalist I write up crime reports, murders, kidnapping, violent robberies that occur in Hobart for my newspaper.'

'Oh ... I ...'

'And I'm certain I have seen a darn more dead bodies than you have.'

'Fair enough,' Edward tried to regain some credibility.

Charlotte inspected the body in detail, dedicating a fresh page in her notebook for the record. An oil lamp lay broken next to the body and it appeared the flame from the lamp had ignited her nightgown and chemise, burning them to her shoulders, so that she was almost naked but for her stockings. Nearby lay a broken medicine bottle labelled paraffin.

'Shine the light on her head please,' Charlotte ordered.

Changing angles of illumination shadowed eerie shapes, making the victim look gaunt; although Charlotte noted she carried several extra pounds for a woman her age, in her early twenties she guessed. 'This woman's been murdered!'

'No! What?'

'She's had her throat cut.'

'But … are you certain?'

'See for yourself.'

There was no denying the fine, yet deep puncture just below the chin where the jugular artery had been severed. The congealing blood and sheer quantity of it camouflaged the wound. 'Oh, Mother Mary. Jesus. Are you certain?'

'I'm certain. Done with a pointed blade of some description I'll wager.'

'Then I better go fetch Toby.'

'Toby the constable?'

'Aye, Toby Hutton.'

Charlotte only met the local constable an hour or so earlier, and she was not impressed with what she saw. 'Well good luck with that.'

Edward looked confused. He had grown to know Toby quite well since he was transferred from Launceston police headquarters to Port Arthur. 'I beg your pardon?'

'Well, he's not the sharpest pin in the cushion. We need an experienced policeman here, a detective policeman from Hobart. Or me, of course.'

'Me? Ah you?'

'Yes.' Charlotte thought a moment. She did not wish to boast but sometimes it was necessary. 'I've actually solved a crime or two that the police department have struggled with.'

'Really?'

'Yes, really. I'm a regular sleuth, even if I do say so myself.'

'Well, I never,' Edward was impressed anew. 'You never cease to amaze me. I would never have guessed. Why … look at you.'

'I beg your pardon?'

'Well, you're a woman.'

Now this was certainly not the first time Charlotte had heard this excuse. No wonder, she thought, Emmeline Pankhurst, the founder of the Suffragettes, was her hero. Charlotte chose not to be offended. 'I'm a woman, yes. So what?'

Edward felt he had clearly overstepped the line. Again. He looked sheepish but felt a necessity to explain. 'It's just ... well ... you don't come across as a ... ah ... the type to handle situations with villains.'

There you go again, opening your mouth to change feet.

'The type?'

Edward's face was the hue of a ripe tomato. 'I mean you're petite.'

Charlotte sighed, 'I'll take that as a compliment.'

'An ... and your fine apparel,' Edward continued to dig himself a deeper hole. 'And the parasol ...'

Charlotte planted her feet firmly apart. She twisted the grip of her parasol and quicker than a flicker from the lantern, she slipped a concealed stiletto blade from its sheath, hidden within the handle. With equal dexterity she placed the point to Edward's neck. His Adam's apple rose and fell as he swallowed hard.

'Gosh,' was all he managed. Charlotte stepped back, displaying the dagger briefly before re-sheathing it. 'I ... ah, stand corrected,' Edward said in a breaking voice.

'I'll take that as an apology for your, dare I say typical male chauvinist remark.'

'Touché!'

'Yes touché,' Charlotte was enjoying herself. She was growing fond of this tall lanky country lad. He conceded defeat without losing face. Yes, he was naïve, but she could tell he was an honest hard-working man. And he was different. Charlotte liked different. She was about to continue her examination of the body when a figure appeared at the rear of the building, stepping clumsily over smouldering wreckage. Edward turned smartly, shining the lamp directly into the figure's eyes, who raised a hand to shield his face.

'Who is that?' the man's voice intoned authority. 'What are you doing here?'

'Reverend! It's me Edward Culpepper.'

'Culpepper? Then lower that lamp man.'

'Sorry reverend.'

'What are you doing here?'

'We're searching for survivors.'

The lowered lamp illuminated the corpse at their feet. 'Oh dear god!' The reverend rushed forward. 'Is she … is that … oh no … Annie?'

'Yes sir.'

Reverend Sidney Finch dropped to one knee and made to touch the body when Charlotte intervened. 'Don't touch her!'

'What?'

'You must not interfere reverend, a crime has been committed here.'

'Who are you?'

Edward stood erect. 'Oh, this is Mrs Clarke from Hobart, she …'

'What the devil are you doing here?'

'I'm a journalist, I …'

Another figure appeared from the darkness of the back garden. 'Reverend,' the voice called out. 'Is that you?'

'Yes, Constable Hutton. We have a victim of the fires here.'

'Victim!' With only one other death recorded so far, this came as some surprise. 'Oh.'

'It's Anne Smith, my maid. Oh, dear god,' his grief returned. 'This is so sad.'

The reverend straightened, making room for half a dozen sightseers attracted to the scene by the excited voices and light. All were craning for a glimpse at the distorted, charred cadaver.

'Please, please,' Charlotte stood between the gathering curiosity seekers and the body. 'Have some respect. Can someone find a sheet or a blanket to cover her with?'

Everyone stood about, silent.

Who was this woman?

'Reverend,' Charlotte broke the silence. 'You sir, this is your cottage is it not?' The man of god answered with a dark look. 'Then surely, sir,' Charlotte persisted, 'you can find a suitable cover for the victim.'

'Who's she?' one of the older men asked the gathering.

'Charlotte Clarke.'

'From Hobart,' Edward said proudly. 'She's a journalist and detective.'

Constable Hutton found his voice. 'Detective?' he asked. He knew this woman was a guest at the Carnarvon Hotel the past two nights, but did not recall anyone speaking of a detective being in their presence.

Charlotte was uncomfortable with the title. *Amateur sleuth yes, but detective?* She shook her head at Edward before turning to Hutton. 'I'm a journalist, yes. An investigative journalist in crime.' Charlotte offered the constable a weak smile.

'Then what are you doing here?'

'Like you, looking for survivors,' Charlotte said. 'Look,' she was eager to direct the conversation away from her, 'this woman has been murdered.'

'Murdered?' the reverend called back up the hallway, returning with a large tablecloth to cover the body. 'Don't be absurd.'

Charlotte ignored the comment and looked to the only representative of law and order here this night. 'Constable Hutton,' Charlotte said. 'Look closely at the neck if you please.' Edward lowered his lamp. The constable leant over putting a hand to his nose and mouth to avoid the stench of cremated flesh. 'If you look closely, you can see the woman's throat has been cut.'

At this comment the surrounding group all vied for a better view. Hutton took in a cursory examination before straightening.

'Well?' Charlotte asked.

'I concede there is a cut to the neck. But I will not be rushed to a conclusion,' Hutton added. 'As I am certain you are well aware, Mrs Clarke, it is not for an officer of the law to make the assumption of death or the cause, no matter how obvious it is. This is a decision for the coroner to make.'

Of course, the constable was right. Charlotte sighed.

'Constable,' Reverend Finch interrupted. 'A word if you please.' The two made their way back towards the front of the cottage where they spoke intensely, quietly, in the dark a few minutes.

'Alright everyone,' Hutton returned to order the gathering. 'Outside if you please.' He swung open palms upwards, in a motion to herd the onlookers back into the garden. 'I want one volunteer to help Edward here wrap the body in a blanket and carry her to the doctors.'

The constable spoke of the doctor's cottage where the local morgue, built during convict occupation, was situated in the cellar. Immediately all sightseers were keen to depart.

'You too please,' Hutton ordered Charlotte.

'I think I should stay,' she said defiantly.

The constable shifted nervously. '*Please* miss.'

Charlotte turned to Edward who gingerly tipped his head towards the backyard.

'I'll go,' Charlotte shot the policeman a sobering glance. 'But I'll be making a full report to police headquarters when I return to Hobart.'

If either the constable or the reverend was angry at Charlotte's audacity, their faces were lost in the darkness.

Charlotte waited for Edward outside the old surgeon's cottage – home to medical personnel since the 1840s, and now the village doctor's residence. She stood still in the darkness of night, where smoke still hung about like an unwelcome visitor. Charlotte's inquisitive mind analysed the situation. Breaking down the facts. Her thoughts a collage of what, why, who and when. Charlotte glanced back to the reverend's residence, now fifty yards distant. While she watched on, the old cottage faded back into darkness, while the men carrying the lanterns moved on to search other ruins. Notably, standing tall amongst them, Reverend Finch led the group and Charlotte thought what a fine figure of a man he cut. Edward had mentioned the man of god was forty-three with a poorly wife suffering memory disease. Mrs Beverly Finch was forty-seven. The reverend's maid was young, in her early twenties. Had there been a romantic link?

Edward appeared with his lamp lighting their surroundings like a night circus. *Maybe that's what this is*, Charlotte had a strange thought, taking a last look at the retreating group of men. *A circus*. Charlotte took in the vista from where she waited for Edward. Although she was in the middle of a disaster zone there was a serenity surrounding her now they were alone.

'That was awful,' Edward said on the approach. 'Moving the lassie like that. She was ...' Edward considered his words carefully. 'She was stiff as a board. It were 'orrible.'

'It's called rigor mortis.'

'Aye, I've heard of it but never ... well never experienced it like.'

'You get used to it.'

'You seen it before then?'

'Yes, many a time. I'm an investigative journalist remember.'

'Aye. But still ...'

'In the hours following death the deceased's body goes through a number of phases,' Charlotte said. 'First is pallor mortis causing the skin to pale. The next stage is algor mortis when the body's temperature drops to that of its environs.'

'Environs?'

'Yes. Room temperature or wherever the deceased passed. Usually this means it cools down considerably but obviously in the tropics it may warm slightly.'

'Oh, never thought o' that.'

'And finally, the stage most are familiar with is rigor mortis, when the muscles tighten.'

'I heard the hair and fingernails keep growin' in death.'

'No,' Charlotte smiled at the old wives' tale. 'Rigor mortis eventually relaxes, and the body reaches a secondary flaccidity where the skin shrinks back. This is the fabled stage where people think just that, that the hair and fingernails grow after death but in reality, the hair and nails simply are revealed once more after being covered with skin.'

'You know all 'bout it then.'

'I should do, I've studied it long enough. What happened after I left you?' Charlotte asked.

'The reverend is claiming Annie has been depressed for months now.'

'So, what's he trying to say, suicide?'

'He hinted at it. He's also convinced Annie fell from the top of the stairs and as a consequence she has fallen all the way down.'

'And the puncture mark?'

'She's caught her neck on a loose steel brace at the bottom.'

'Poppycock! And Constable Hutton?'

'He agrees.'

Charlotte stepped back, allowing Edward's lamp light to spill onto his face. 'And what are your thoughts, Edward?'

'My thoughts?'

'That's what I said.'

Edward. 'Ah ... To be honest I dunno what to think.' Charlotte clearly did not approve. 'I reckon you know what yer talkin' about, I really do.'

'Well, that's a good start,' Charlotte said. 'So now, Annie lives in the rectory does she not?'

'Aye, she's the maid. Or was,' Edward added solemnly.

'So, there are two bedrooms upstairs. The reverend and his wife would occupy the front attic room I should imagine, and Annie the rear room.'

'That's correct. I know for a fact they looked after Annie well. She were treated like family.'

'Family huh?' Charlotte looked to the lamp, hissing in the silence of the still night. A large red emperor moth, attracted to the light, attacked the glass cover like an angry bat. 'Can you turn that thing down?'

'Certainly.' Edward tweaked the illumination.

'That's better. Now do you by chance have a cover?'

'You mean this?' And Edward presented a thick leather cover that masked the light. They momentarily blended with the darkness. Edward tweaked back the flap slightly and soft moonlight strength light leaked onto the grass at their feet.

'Excellent. Now you lead the way.'

'Where to?'

'Back to the rectory. I want to inspect Annie's room.'

'But miss ... Charlotte! We can't go back in there. It's private property for starters. It would amount to breakin' and enterin', now that we don't have an excuse to be in there.'

'Edward Culpepper. That girl was murdered. You saw her throat.'

'Aye, but ...'

'But nothing.'

With the faintest of light illuminating their path, to avoid attracting attention, Edward took the lead. Inside they took a wide berth around the pooled blood and approached the narrow stairway. Instantly they heard movement at the rear of the cottage. They froze. Edward covered the lamp. They listened in blackness.

Animals!

'That'd be the damned devils,' Edward whispered. 'They smell the blood.'

With the light masked, only blacklines suggested stair treads. Edward allowed minimal light to spill. Step by step they ascended. Shapes appeared in the gloom. Shifting shapes that morphed into spectral figures at the mercy of one's imagination. Edward was on edge. On the landing Edward permitted a little more light and the first thing Charlotte noted was the lack of any blood at the top treads or handrail.

'If Annie cut her throat here, you would expect to see some spilt blood, wouldn't you?'

Edward agreed. Charlotte lingered making notes in the semi-darkness.

'Would yer kindly make haste Charlotte? Reverend could return any minute.' Edward panned the light across the landing to Annie's bedroom door giving Charlotte no choice but to follow.

Inside was a cosy bedroom. Built for two small children originally, with a dormer window and a steep sloping ceiling where it followed the roof line. To one side was a single-door wardrobe of blackwood and pushed against the other wall was a narrow single bed of iron. A small table held a porcelain jug and basin toilet set with a floral design. Charlotte headed directly to a wood framed, leather lined trunk in the far corner. Resting her parasol against the trunk she tried the latch. It was unlocked.

Edward hissed in the stillness. 'What are you doin'?'

'Searching her things.'

'I can see that, but ... it's private.'

'Yes, it is. And the poor girl's dead. Murdered. I'm looking for clues.'

Edward shifted nervously, daring to look out the attic window into the yard. He thought he saw movement in the blackness, but then he told himself his eyes were playing tricks with him lately. 'Can yer make haste then?'

Charlotte moved quickly, but methodically. Indeed, the trunk was full of personal items, toiletries, under garments, two books, one a bible given to her by the reverend who had written inside; *For Anne, may this good book give you peace with God.* Signed *Reverend Finch. Sidney.* Charlotte put the books aside and reached for a bundle of letters tied neatly together with pink ribbon. The first letters she opened were mail from Anne's mother, in Bothwell. Charlotte, an experienced reader, cast a rapid eye over the contents and noted the usual correspondence; the weather, the pet dog, Cotton, missed her, the farm's doing well, father sends his love. But the second bundle, nine in all, had Charlotte flabbergasted.

'Eureka!' Charlotte cheered.

Edward stiffened. 'Please Charlotte ... keep your voice down.'

'Come Edward. I have what I want, lead the way downstairs.' And Charlotte stepped through the door with the letters in her hand. Edward knew there was no point arguing. He squeezed past on the confined landing and willingly ushered Charlotte outside.

'All right Charlotte Clarke,' Edward's confidence had returned. They stood in the nave of the ruined church fifty yards north, its roofless walls open to the heavens. 'What's yer got then?'

'Read for yourself,' Charlotte handed Edward the letter she had inspected in the bedroom, while she opened another. Edward paused. 'You *can* read can you not?' Charlotte said.

'You know I can,' he said, indignantly. 'It's just a bit private like, Annie's letters. I knew Annie, it don't seem right.'

Charlotte shook her head. 'Just read *some* of it.'

Edward held his lamp high and shook the folds in the paper flat with the other. He read aloud. '*My dearest Annie, the love of my life, sweet sweet Annie* ... I didn't know Annie had a ... friend ... not this kind ...' Private or not, Edward's curiosity peaked.

'Read who signed it.'

'Jesus Lord!' Edward looked about the roofless church seeking forgiveness for his blasphemous outburst. 'Sorry, ah … this can't be real. Can it?'

'Why not? It's signed Sidney and the only Sidney around here seems to be the reverend, Sidney Finch. It's not the first time a man in his position takes his maid as a lover.'

'No, but Reverend Finch and Annie!'

They read on together in silence. The love letters were explicit, and it appeared the reverend was smitten with his maid.

'There's enough material here to hang the man,' Charlotte said.

'You don't think he killed Annie, do you?'

'Why not? He's a prime suspect. These letters are several months old, check the dates. He may have fallen out of love. Maybe Annie was blackmailing him.'

'I find that hard to believe.'

'What about Mrs Finch?'

'Beverly Finch. She be a good woman,' Edward said. 'Attractive in her day. But she suffered from disease of the mind. The reverend's looked after her day and night, like an invalid. And Annie too of course.'

'And that's how the two became close. The older man attracted to the younger woman, and the young housemaid attracted to the man of position. Someone important in society.'

'But the reverend?'

'As I said, it's not the first time. Besides from what I saw of Reverend Finch, he is a most handsome older gentleman, fine figured, lean and muscular.'

'Now what do we do?' Edward asked.

'Do?' Charlotte thought hard. 'First things first. I must write the story of the fires for the newspaper and see that tiresome lap dog Leonard McShan onto the steamer to Hobart by sunup. Then I will stay on a few days to do the research I came here for in the first place.'

'Yer book?'

'Yes. But …' And Charlotte emphasized the word *but*. 'I will need your assistance Edward Culpepper, and together we'll solve this dastardly crime.'

'*We* will?' …

The ground shook.

Four-hundred-pounds of stone buttress hit the nave flagstones with a terrifying thud. It missed the sleuths by a matter of inches. Charlotte leapt aside crushing against her guide. Edward dropped the lamp. All about them turned to darkness. He snatched Charlotte, throwing her hard against the wall for protection. Their bodies pressed together. Edward looked skywards. There were stars where the buttress had been. Fine ash rained down. They froze in position, daring not move. Was this a rare act of nature or the act of a killer? Edward's face was barely inches from Charlottes and the two exchanged emotions from terror to pleasure.

'What just happened?' Charlotte whispered. Edward smelt her sweet breath with a hint of mint. Charlotte caught the scent of masculinity. She hadn't been in such close proximity to a man for many years.

'I ... I'm not certain.' Edward felt the need to be protective. He kept his body close to Charlotte in the darkness. He inspected the buttress at their feet. It had shattered the flagstones embedding itself several inches into the earth. Suddenly echoing footsteps resonated from the direction of the bell tower. A dark shape leapt through the arch, escaping through the north entrance to the nave.

'Hey!' Edward launched himself after the silhouetted shape disappearing into the night. But the figure was fast. Damned fast. Fast enough to lose Edward amongst the smouldering ruins.

'He got away.' Edward returned to Charlotte who had taken a defensive position in the shadows, her stiletto blade reflecting moonlight as she stepped from the church.

'Someone tried to kill us!' she said.

Edward was stone-faced. 'Aye, it looks that way.'

'Did you get a look at them, a man I take it?'

'Yes, a big devil and fast.'

'Then I feel we have upset a hornet's nest.' Charlotte re-sheathed the dagger into the parasol. 'I need to return to Carnarvon Hotel.'

CHAPTER THREE

There had been no New Year's Eve good cheer at Port Arthur. 1897 slipped into 1898 without celebration. Charlotte sat in her room, her most prized possession sitting on a walnut writing bureau before her. The portable black steel framed *Chicago Writing Machine*, Patent 1892, had set Charlotte back three months wages, but was worth every penny. Charlotte tapped and tinkered through the early hours. If her nocturnal determination bothered any of the other guests, she heard no complaints. Maybe everyone was weary. It had, after all, been one hell of a day ...

And now she typed her report of the fires and the destruction of Port Arthur for *The Mercury*.

***

6AM. New Year's Day, 1898.
Leonard McShan slept poorly. He had forgone New Year's Eve festivities back in Hobart just to accommodate Charlotte who insisted on taking this holiday period to visit Port Arthur. After all it was her only window of opportunity while the Mercury offices were closed for a couple of days. And Charlotte had been quite happy to travel alone, so if McShan was ordered by his employer to chaperone, so be it. Charlotte felt no commitment towards the man.

McShan grumbled his morning greeting. If one could call it a greeting. He wasn't happy. Then again, he was never happy. Charlotte sealed her eighteen-page report in a large envelope on which she had written, *Mr Craddock, Editor, The Mercury*. She bid her chaperone farewell and watched the SS *Manapouri* steam out of the bay, rounding Point Puer and heading south, before she crashed onto her bed, exhausted.

Some hours later Charlotte's mind drifted somewhere between sleep and consciousness. Her thoughts drifted to Edward. He had proven quite the gentleman. He was considerate, thoughtful, generous with his time and above all courageous. God knows, he had saved her life in the fire.

Charlotte heard voices. 'Wait here, I'll see if Mrs Clarke is available.'

Charlotte awoke. Was it the footsteps on the creaking floorboards walking down the hallway or was it the mention of her name? Either way Charlotte was now fully awake. The light tapping of knuckles on her bedroom door told her it hadn't been a dream.

Charlotte wrapped a shawl about her shoulders and opened the door. 'Mrs Fairclough. What time is it?'

'It's two in the afternoon my dear.'

'Oh, I slept in.'

'I'm not surprised. I heard you all night on that writing machine. Tap, tap, tap.'

'Oh sorry.'

'Well, you have a commitment to your newspaper, I guess ... ah, you have a visitor, Mr Culpepper is here to see you. I told him to wait on the veranda.'

For a man who had just walked three miles Edward looked bright eyed and fresh. 'You didn't leave on the steamer then?' he asked, hardly disguising his relief.

Charlotte warmed immediately to his friendly face. In truth she wanted to hug the man a greeting. 'No, should I have?'

'No!' Edward said a little too readily. He was so pleased to see Charlotte again, fearing she had returned to Hobart. 'Did you finish your report on time?'

'Yes, just.'

'Did you sleep alright, after that incident at the church I feared you might have nightmares.'

'I slept well thank you.'

Edward looked about. Their meeting on the veranda had caught the attention of some of the locals. 'Can we walk?'

'Walk?'

'Yes, along the foreshore maybe. I have news and it's private.'

'Oh, of course.'

Edward donned his peaked cap against the sun, leading Charlotte down towards the water's edge. Wisps of smoke still spiralled here and there. 'I spoke to Doctor Fowler this morning.'

'Yes.'

'He examined Annie's body at the morgue. She was with child.'

'No!'

'Yes.'

'The reverend's?'

'Well, here's the thing, see. I'm certain I have heard in the past that the reverend was incapable of having children. Always was.'

'Who else could it be then?'

Edward shrugged, then thought. 'Well, there's a few lads 'bout the village what would make good candidates, actually.'

Charlotte. 'I need to return to the rectory.'

'Do you think it's a good idea?'

Charlotte cast an eye back towards the hotel where distant eyes watched them with curious caution. 'If we want to find the killer, yes, it is.'

'But the reverend might be there.'

'Maybe not. I heard talk last night of the reverend and his wife being billeted at the home of a Mr Thurmund Gill, whoever he is.'

'Thurmund operates the local general store and pharmacy, up on the hill. His property survived.'

Charlotte now saw the damage clearly for the first time in daylight. Port Arthur was devastated. And with the westerly breeze the stench of destruction was borne across the hotel. It was a sickening and saddening sight. The nearby penitentiary continued to burn, there was still so much fuel within to feed the flames. Charlotte and Edward walked west along Champ Street in silence. Now with all the sightseers gone, only a handful of locals, most numb with shock, fossicked amongst the burnt shells of buildings, some salvaging whatever they could.

The rectory was much the way they had left it late the night before. The kitchen, pantry, scullery, bakehouse and latrine smouldered, however the main rooms, drawing room and attic were intact. Charlotte noted footprints leading in a side door that she could not possibly have seen in the dark; a door that was closed the night before. They were made by rubber-soled shoes with a distinct *horseshoe* heel.

There was no sign of Reverend Finch, his wife or any of the other tenants in Church Street. Although it was daylight, inside the rectory took on a macabre atmosphere. The stench of Annie's charred body lingered. Her pool of blood had darkened into a palate of black coppery sludge. Animal footprints and scats told a tale of the wild black Tasmanian creatures, the devils, that had been feeding on the blood.

'What exactly do you hope to find?' Edward asked, his voice low, looking over his shoulder anxiously.

'Don't know until I find it.'

'Clever.' If Edward sounded sarcastic, he meant to.

Suddenly a woman's voice came from the drawing room.

'Is that you Sidney?'

Charlotte and Edward stood rigid.

'Sidney?' Elderly Mrs Beverley Finch appeared at the end of the burnt-out hall, near the front door. She was silhouetted by the afternoon sun pouring through what remained of lead light panels either side of the door, surrounding the woman with a kaleidoscope of colours.

'Who are you?' The woman, suffering from lapsing memory, sounded frightened.

Caught red-handed Edward had no choice but to show himself. 'It's only me Mrs Finch, I've come to make certain you are alright ... after the terrible fires.' Edward turned slightly to Charlotte and whispered, 'So much for the reverend staying at Thurmund Gill's house.'

'Who is that with you?' the woman asked.

'Oh, this is Charlotte Clarke, Mrs Finch, a friend.' Edward walked along the passage. Charlotte followed. 'Is the reverend close by?'

'Who?'

'The reverend, your husband, Sidney.'

'Oh Sidney. He's ...' Mrs Finch thought a moment. 'He's here somewhere.'

'We better get going,' Edward told Charlotte, when Charlotte noted a hooked blade knife, the type used for leather work. Beverley Finch held a pear she had been peeling in her other hand.

'That is an interesting knife Mrs Finch, may I see it?' Charlotte asked. Mrs Finch handed it to her willingly. The blade looked recently polished, but Charlotte was certain she recognised specs of blood between handle and blade. She pointed it out to Edward. Immediately voices could be heard approaching.

The reverend.

'Must be off now,' Edward told the older woman, relieving Charlotte of the knife and handing it back. Out the side window they both caught a glimpse of Reverend Finch and Toby Hutton the constable. They were about to enter via the front door the moment Charlotte and Edward escaped out the way they had come.

Once at a safe distance Charlotte took Edward by the arm. 'I must have another look at the body.'

'The bo ... the body! No Charlotte, we can't just walk into the morgue.'

'Poppycock. Watch me.' Charlotte marched across the garden, entering a side gate into the doctor's cottage, unscathed by the disastrous fire. 'Where, exactly, is the morgue?' she asked looking about.

Edward ground his teeth. Protesting with a loud sigh, he capitulated. 'It's in the cellar. The entrance is separate to the cottage, on the south side.'

Charlotte looked back towards the rectory to be certain they hadn't been seen, before leading the way. A dozen stone steps saw them underground. They stooped to enter. The metallic smell of blood lingered. The door was unlocked, the room dark. They waited a moment for their eyes to adjust. Charlotte could barely make out the dark shape of the mortuary slab in the centre of the room, although some light entered from the stairway, washing over the floor. Edward fumbled in his pocket and Charlotte recognised the rattle of matches. One strike illuminated the cellar long enough to note there was no sign of the body. The match burned out. The morgue returned to darkness. Suddenly shadows appeared on the flagstones. There was nowhere to hide.

Reverend Finch spoke first. 'Just can't keep your noses out of it can you?'

Constable Hutton appeared alongside the reverend. 'You disappoint me Edward,' Hutton said.

Edward was lost for words. Charlotte stiffened. 'Where's the body?'

'Look,' Hutton said. 'You have no authority sniffing about, poking your nose into other people's business.'

'I'm a journalist,' Charlotte said. 'It is my responsibility to, *sniff about*, as you put it.'

'This is private property.'

'Annie was murdered,' Charlotte persisted. 'I'm certain of it.'

'Nonsense.' The constable felt his recently acquired responsibility was being challenged. 'I am satisfied that she was escaping the fire in a panic and fell down the stairs, probably broke her neck, and wounded herself in the throat on a steel brace loose on the bottom balcony rail.'

'That is ridiculous. Where's her body?'

'Annie's parents collected her body early this morning. They have taken her to Dunalley.'

Charlotte was angry. She fixed the reverend with a grim stare. 'Did you know she was pregnant?' Reverend Finch shifted nervously. 'Well, reverend?'

'Y-yes,' Finch said in a quiet voice. 'The doctor informed me this morning,'

'So, you didn't know prior to this day?'

'No-I-certainly-did-not.'

Charlotte held his gaze. Finch looked away, flushed. The man was lying. She just knew it.

'Mrs Clarke,' Constable Hutton contained his irritation. 'I must insist you leave Port Arthur at the earliest opportunity. The steamer is due to return in the morning and on board will be my superiors. It will then be departing late afternoon. Should you remain here I warn you now, you will be arrested and forcibly returned to Hobart under arrest. You will be charged and held accountable.'

'Steady on Toby,' Edward intervened. 'Yer bein' a bit heavy handed ain't yer?'

'And that goes for you too Edward Culpepper.'

'Edward Culpepper,' Edward mimicked the policeman as they walked away. 'This bit o' authority's gone to 'is 'e ad.'

Charlotte was in no mood. 'Doesn't that sound suspicious to you?'

'What, Hutton's attitude?'

'No! The removal of Annie's body so soon.'

'I suppose ... Maybe. But yer can imagine 'er parents ... how upset they'd be.'

'The knife,' Charlotte went on. 'Mrs Finch's knife, did you see remains of blood on the blade.'

'Didn't really get a chance.'

'Well, it looked like blood to me. It looked like the knife had been cleaned recently, but not thoroughly.'

'I'll have ter take yer word for it.'

'Where's the general store?' Charlotte asked, from out of nowhere.

'The general store?'

'Yes, I need a new pencil,' Charlotte half lied.

'I'll walk yer there. It's up on yonder hill next to the bakery, on the road to Nubeena.'

Edward led Charlotte through a forest of burnt trees to the top of a small hill on the village's northern flank. The fug of fire remained in the still air of the woodlands and the ground was still hot from the blaze. Huge black ravens, feasting on carrion, rose noisily for the high branches as the two approached. It was a pathetic sight. Singed carcasses of wildlife lay everywhere, hunted down, slaughtered and abandoned by the invading inferno as it passed over.

Sixteen-year-old orphan and store assistant Daisy Mather clearly had an eye for Edward. She looked to Charlotte with a level of envy, eager to catch Edward's attention.

'Mornin' Daisy,' Edward acknowledged the girl. She suffered from a miserable disorder doctors called a nervous absence of appetite, or anorexia nervosa as it was now commonly known as - an emotional dysfunction causing a desire to lose weight by refusing to eat. For many this proved fatal, which was so despairing to witness in one so young and pretty as Daisy. Her thin face accentuated large round turquoise eyes with naturally long eyelashes. But beneath her clothes, Charlotte thought, she looked skeletal. Edward introduced Charlotte. 'I'm so sorry about Annie,' Edward said. He knew the dead girl and Daisy were close friends. Daisy's eyes welled up and now Charlotte could tell the girl had been crying on and off most of the day.

'It was you what found 'er, eh?' Daisy said. Edward nodded soberly. 'Was she, did she ... do yer think she would have suffered, like was it quick?'

'Yes Daisy, I'm certain it was.'

Daisy looked to Charlotte. 'You was there too, wasn't yer?'

'Yes.'

'There's talk 'bout town yer reckon Annie was murdered.'

'From all my experience,' Charlotte answered honestly, 'it looked that way to me, yes.'

Although the general store survived the fire much of the stock was smoke infused to a certain extent. Out in the yard, store owners Thurmund and May Gill were busy hanging textiles on lines to air.

'You were close to Annie,' Charlotte asked, 'were you not?'

'Yes. We was best friends.'

'Did Annie tell you she was with child?'

'So, it is true.'

'Yes. Did she tell you about her relationship with anyone in particular?'

With quick short guileful steps Daisy slipped to the back window. When she was satisfied her master and mistress were busy outside, she hurried back. 'Annie were in a relationship with the reverend.'

'I thought as much.'

'Yes, she told me herself. It's been goin' on fer near on a year since the dirty ol' bugger's wife took ill.' Charlotte couldn't help smile at the girl's raw honesty. 'She told me things.'

'What things?'

'Well, he hit her, for starters.'

Edward stiffened. 'The reverend? Hit her? Hit Annie?'

'Yer. Took a strap to 'er, an' more than once.'

'Mongrel.'

'An' she tell me other private things ... like I remember once she said the reverend said to 'er things like what we 'ave been doin' tonight is condoned by the Lord, it's written in the scriptures, thirty-eighth chapter of Genesis. I've a good memory for numbers like. The church, you see, 'eard rumours months ago and confronted the reverend, but Reverend Finch always denied 'em. All the same they told him he wasn't to see Annie no more and she moved out four months ago, moving back into the rectory only recently.'

'So, is it possible she was having the reverend's baby?'

'Look,' Daisy leant in even closer to Charlotte. 'I don't wanna talk ill o' the dead, but I'm tellin' yer this cos I wanna help yer find the bastard what done it to 'er.'

'Oh? There was someone else?'

Daisy chose her next words carefully. 'Annie had a bit of a ... a reputation 'round the village.'

'With the men?'

'Yes.'

The back door flew open. Proprietor Thurmund Gill appeared. He walked into the room with purpose, wearing patched trousers and a stained shirt, sleeves rolled up, displaying the tattoo of a mermaid on his left forearm. 'Yer not slackin' are yer Daisy? There's a lot o' work to finish.'

'No Mr Gill. I was just answerin' some questions fer Edward 'ere and 'is friend Charlotte from 'obart.'

'Oh,' the man's eyes narrowed. 'What sort o' questions?'

''bout Annie.'

Thurmund Gill grew even more serious. He turned to Edward, standing with Charlotte near the window where the sun silhouetted their shapes. 'Ed,' he acknowledged Edward. 'And Charlotte, is it?'

'Charlotte Clarke, Mr Gill.'

'An' why would you be askin' questions 'bout poor Annie?'

Charlotte explained her situation.

Gill angered. 'Annie died in the bleedin' fire,' the proprietor said sharply. 'An' yer best be leavin' yer idle gossip behind yer, go back ter 'obart.'

Charlotte was far from satisfied. 'It is not idle gossip Mr Gill and Annie's death needs to be investigated.'

'Then let Toby Hutton do what he gets paid for.' Gill's face scowled. 'An' you get yer skinny arse to work Daisy, unless yer want an easier situation, like standin' in a field like a scarecrow and frighten the birds.'

'Mr Gill!' Charlotte felt her chest rise, her face reddened. 'That was totally un-called for.'

'Listen Mrs Clarke from Hobart,' Gill said in a mock, upper-class accent. 'The only reason I give Daisy 'ere work is cos she don't eat all me hard earnt profits. Look at 'er, skinny as a rake.' Daisy's bottom lip quivered. 'Bah,' Gill spat. 'I ain't got time fer this, good day ter yer.' He looked at Edward. 'Edward, is yer pa alright? The fires never got that far, eh?'

'He's fine.'

'Good. Then say hello ter him for me.' Gill left, slamming the door behind him.

'I'm sorry to have gotten yer in trouble Daisy,' Edward consoled the girl as the proprietor re-joined Mrs Gill in the backyard.

'That's alright. I'm used to it.' Daisy took a handkerchief from her apron pocket with spider-like fingers and blew her nose. 'You should know,' Daisy said defiantly, when she was certain Gill was out of earshot. 'Only yesterday Annie told me 'bout the baby, an' she were gonna tell me who the father was when she had second thoughts. She were scared. Real scared.'

'Who was it then?'

'Like I said, she never told me ... now she's gone.' The tears returned. 'But I know it was one o' the coves 'round town.'

Edward thought to ask. 'The reverend an' his wife slept 'ere last night did they not?'

'Yes. Bastard that 'e is,' excuse me language Mrs Clarke. ''e tried to touch me more than once. But I give 'im what for and 'e kept his distance since.'

Charlotte. 'The reverend would have arrived here late at night, is that correct?'

'Yes, although the reverend come 'ere earlier, when the fires were burning Port Arthur. I thought we was goners here at the store too, but the flames missed us.'

'Most fortunate. You said the reverend was here earlier, during the fires?'

'Yer. I thought it strange cos 'ere we was, fires all around us, and the reverend is out the back incinerating clothes on a backyard fire.'

Charlotte was furious. 'That reverend's guilty as sin itself I say.'

Edward joined Charlotte in her room at the Carnarvon Hotel while she packed her travelling case. The door to the passageway wedged firmly open. It might be 1898 and women afforded more freedoms than past decades, but still people loved to speculate at the expense of another's reputation.

'And poor little Daisy,' Charlotte said. 'She's an orphan you said.'

'Aye. She lives with an older sister near the general store. What are you going to do now?' Edward asked, wary of soft footsteps passing in the passageway.

'Well, there's naught I can do here right now, but I will be filing a full report with the police when I return to Hobart and I'll write a piece for the newspaper about Annie's death.'

'Well good luck.'

A hundred yards down the embankment at the dock the steamer SS *Manapouri's* whistle called the last of the stragglers to board for the return trip to Hobart.

'Oh, I nearly forgot.' Charlotte picked up a bible from the mantle from next to a copy of the *Book of Common Prayer*. She flicked through the pages.

'Here we are, 38th chapter of Genesis.' Charlotte's Christian upbringing was now reminded of the particular gospel Daisy at the general store spoke of. Charlotte read in silence. 'U-huh. It's a reference to Onan spilling his seed,' Charlotte said.

'Does that mean what I think it means?' Edward felt himself blush.

'It means onanism.' Charlotte returned the book to the shelf. Edward looked none the wiser. 'Self-pleasure,' Charlotte said, matter-of-factly.

Immediately Edward was keen to breath fresh air. He lifted Charlotte's travel case off the bed and hooked her portable writing machine firmly under his arm. 'I'll help yer to the steamer,' he said, stepping into the hall.

At the jetty Charlotte took a last look over at the smouldering village, reduced to a sad ruin by nature's wrath. On the dock Constable Toby Hutton gathered Inspector Benbow and Sergeant Edison's luggage. The two lawmen with their spouses and children had returned on the morning ferry, only to face to a devastated village. Hutton's taste of authority waned with their return. Now he was delegated to porter. Benbow's thirteen-year-old daughter Penelope tagged along, teasing the constable.

'Oh, Mrs Clarke,' Hutton walked over to greet Charlotte.

'Constable,' Charlotte answered curtly.

'I'd like to apologise for ... well my behaviour last night. I may have said some harsh words I now regret.'

'That's alright constable. You had a post to maintain.'

'I had no right ordering you to leave Port Arthur.'

'You were on duty and responsible through difficult times,' Charlotte assured the man, albeit impatiently.

The constable watched Edward carry Charlotte's luggage up the gangway, out of earshot.

'I was hoping we could meet again some time, on more agreeable terms. I'm really not a monster.'

Such a suggestion brought a smile to Charlotte's face. She was speechless briefly, seeing the policeman in a different light. He was certainly handsome, a year or two younger and maintained a trim healthy figure. He even appeared to have a sense of humour.

'I am still filing a report with police headquarters in Hobart,' Charlotte said, losing the smile.

'I seriously believe there is a killer loose in Port Arthur.'

'Do what you think best ... may I call you Charlotte?'

'If you must.'

'You may be correct about that Charlotte. I hope to prove you wrong. But it will be difficult as I am to transfer back to Hobart at Easter.'

'Oh,' Charlotte caught Edward waiting at the gangway and made to board.

'May I call on you some time?' Hutton asked. 'When I'm in Hobart.'

Charlotte was taken aback. 'I ... ah ...' She wanted to say *why* but knew the answer. 'I'm a very busy person Constable Hutton ...'

'Toby.'

'Ah, Toby. I don't know.'

The constable returned to the luggage trolley, placing his arm on young Penelope's shoulder, who had been observing the two of them. 'She's pretty,' the thirteen-year-old said. Together they watched Charlotte climb the gang-way. 'Do you fancy her?'

'That's none of your business young lady.' Hutton was about to call out a final farewell, but three sharp whistles from the bridge drowned his words.

'Well,' Edward said, suddenly awkward. 'Farewell then. Maybe we'll meet again one day.'

'Maybe.' Charlotte smiled warmly. She had grown fond of this hand-some and thoughtful guide. She felt safe around him. She felt something she hadn't felt since she first met her husband all those years ago.

'Maybe you'll return one day,' Edward said. 'An' you'll be famous like your Pa in yer own right with yer own novel.'

Edward knew he had fallen for this feisty redhead. He might be a little older, but they had so much in common. He felt genuine warmth around her that he not found with other women he had known. Now he felt an emptiness. The steward who stowed Charlotte's luggage returned as the fi-nal departing whistle ordered last visitors off the gangway.

'Goodbye,' Edward offered his hand as a farewell gesture. Charlotte took the hand and held it long enough to lean forward and, stepping up on her toes, she kissed him on the cheek.

'Au revoir,' she told Edward. 'Thank you for all you've done.'

The deckhand reached across to secure the gate. 'Sorry mate, you'll have to get off.'

'I'll write,' Charlotte called over the churning propellers. 'Keep you informed on the *you know what.*'

'You do that Missus.' Edward called back from the jetty. He felt his eyes moisten. Something knotted in his belly. *Could it be love?* Confused, Edward turned sharply on his heels and walked with purpose back towards the smouldering ruins.

CHAPTER FOUR

Over three months later, approaching Easter, 1898.
Agapanthus Cottage, Macquarie Street, Hobart.
Charlotte thought of Edward, now acknowledging there was something missing in her life and for the first time she wanted to fill that emptiness. For the first time in years, she realised how busy she had been since her husband Charles Claiborne had passed. Although her husband mistreated her in the last year they were together, he had proven his love in their early years of marriage. Charlotte did have *some* fond memories, but conceded she married too young for a woman with ambitions.

Recently Charlotte met Louise Mack, a young Hobart woman of similar age. Louise had had her first novel, *The World is Round*, published nearly two years earlier and had been a great inspiration to Charlotte, along with Vida Goldstein, pioneer of the Suffragette movement in Australia. Other mentors being the likes of Jane Austin and Mary Shelley.

Nowadays Charlotte consciously left behind the negative memories. She reverted back to her maternal surname. And, to be honest, the name Clarke opened more doors for her in the publishing world than her married name, Claiborne.

Since she was widowed Charlotte had chosen a life of celibacy. Now Charlotte was confused. Until recently she had avoided male company at all costs, but after arriving back from Port Arthur, Charlotte thought of Edward Culpepper day and night. Especially at night.

The front-door letter slot squeaked shut, resonating down the cottage hallway. This heralded the delivery of the day's mail. Charlotte was first to the door. Not that her fifty-six-year-old aunt, Jocelyn Childers, was slow. But Charlotte was expecting mail, namely a letter from Edward. It had been twelve and a half weeks since the Port Arthur disaster and Charlotte and Edward had been exchanging letters almost weekly.

'Your haste to the post never ceases to amaze me,' Aunt Jocelyn grinned. 'Why, you are faster than a striking cobra.'

Aunt Jocelyn was not a blood relative, but a close friend of Charlotte's mother who lived in Melbourne. Charlotte had grown up with the vivacious family friend and always called her aunt. Like Charlotte, Aunt Jocelyn also had curled red hair with sparkling green eyes and an effervescent nature and could easily pass for her mother. She had lived with Jocelyn and her twenty-three-year-old daughter Merrill since Charlotte's husband's body was found washed up on a beach over three years ago.

Charlotte plucked up the letters scattered across the polished floor-boards. Two addressed to Mrs J Childers and one to Miss M Childers. Charlotte sighed. She checked the floor hoping she had missed a letter, her eyes following the Persian runner back to Auntie's feet at the bottom of the stairs.

Jocelyn recognised disappointment. 'Nothing?'

Charlotte shook her head. 'What day is it?'

'Friday.'

'I always receive a letter Friday.'

'Maybe it's been held up in the postal service,' Aunt Jocelyn said hopefully. 'It might come tomorrow.'

Charlotte sat at her dressing table completing her grooming, ready for her twenty-minute walk down Macquarie Street to the newspaper offices. She studied her face in the mirror. Freckles. She hated her freckles, especially magnified in her hand mirror. Before her were Edward's letters. She had kept each and every one. Each letter seemingly more familiar than the last, although both parties were cautious of expressing their real emotions for each other on paper. Charlotte remembered her mother's words of wisdom: *absence makes the heart grow fonder*, and sighed once more.

Charlotte pulled on her knitted stockings held with garters, her chemise – wide-necked and, short-sleeved – and her pantalettes followed. Freckles might be out of favour, but Charlotte actually liked her breasts. They were full, firm and round. These she supported with her vertical stay corset; front hooked for convenience. After fitting a loose shirt over her corset Charlotte stepped into her skirt. She had just managed to lace her ankle high boots, when the front door bell downstairs rang loudly, being hard enough, it seemed, to haul the wire out of its fitting.

Charlotte heard muted voices in the hallway downstairs. Aunt Jocelyn and a deep male voice. Curiosity saw her move to the top treads to steal a peek. Auntie appeared at the bottom of the stairs. 'Oh, there you are dear. You have a gentleman visitor.'

***

Two days earlier, sometime after 8PM. Davey Street, Hobart.
The killer didn't hesitate. By the time his victim, seventy-nine-year-old Osbert Hambleton turned his tired elderly ears towards approaching steps behind him it was too late. The first blow to the back of the head sent the man into a spin. His eyes rolled back, his knees buckled, and he crumbled to the floor. Within seconds the retired professor, elderly scholar, historian and man of letters was struck twice more and lay unconscious, but still alive.

***

The next morning, 7.35AM.
Senior Constable Toby Hutton stared down at the deceased. He was careful not to step in the pool of congealed blood and soil his brand new, and shiny, black boots. He had, just this moment, joined Inspector Benjamin Boothman, who also stood in silence, trying to make some sense of what appeared a senseless crime. Boothman was a smart lawman who became an inspector at the rather young age of forty-three. Having served three years as prison

warder at the Campbell Street Prison, a tough post, he joined the police force at twenty-three. Now the no-nonsense police officer had little tolerance for lawbreakers and expected the same of his subordinates.

The victim, an old man, lay face down on the flagstones of the scullery at the rear of his Davey Street property; a six-bedroom two storey stone and brick mansion on a hill overlooking the growing township of Hobart, its harbour and the River Derwent. It was apparent the victim had been struck from behind. Two separate blows to the head were struck to ensure death. With the scullery door closed the atmosphere was uncomfortably oppressive.

'Wedge that door open for Christ's sake,' the police inspector ordered Hutton. 'Stinks like a morgue in here.' And in a sense, it was. Toby Hutton found a brick in the garden and propped the door open, before studying the crime scene once more. He experienced mixed emotions. He had recently been promoted to senior constable and transferred to Hobart. This was his first week in the new position and already he had a murder investigation on his hands.

'What do we know?' Hutton asked Boothman.

'He's been dead about twelve hours. Lived alone. He has a housekeeper call daily to prepare meals and clean. She found the body at six this morning.'

Hutton noted six sherry glasses on the sink ready to be washed and two blue and white plates, one with the remains of white bread sandwiches. He smelt one of the glasses. 'Sherry.'

'Hmm. Why six?'

'He had guests maybe?'

'Maybe.'

'No obvious weapon?'

'No. He has three distinct wounds on the head from a heavy object, probably metal. Maybe a jemmy or crowbar.' The inspector crouched to twist the head slightly. 'And a third severe blow to the throat. Note the neck,' Boothman pointed to an impact on the dead man's throat. 'His windpipe and larynx have been crushed. The poor old bugger has lain unconscious, slowly choking with his own blood pouring into his nose and mouth.'

'Jesus!'

'Yes. Jesus! Get the uniforms to search the gardens for a weapon.'

Forty-three-year-old Boothman liked Toby. He'd watched him grow up in Launceston, being his first cousin Mary's boy, and always saw potential in him as a lawman. So, when the inspector managed to have Toby transferred to Hobart to train as a detective, he was pleased for himself and happy to be able to help his cousin, who had been a battler most of her life.

Toby relayed the inspector's orders and returned to the murder scene. Door wedged open or not, the smell of death lingered. Toby found Boothman now in the kitchen next to the scullery, where the room was permeated with smell of the burnt remains of a chicken dinner.

'He was preparing his dinner before he was killed.' Although the fire in the oven had burnt out overnight, the blackened bird still smouldered. 'Hungry?' Boothman said with a wry smile, when something else caught his attention. 'Ah!' Boothman drew Hutton's attention to the fireplace. 'What's missing?' he pointed with his shoe to the poker stand sitting on the hearth.

Hutton noted the brush and shovel, but, 'No poker.'

'Exactly. I wonder if that is the murder weapon. Tell the lads outside to look for a poker.'

Housekeeper Eleanor Hark's tears smeared what little makeup she wore, namely rouged cheeks, for her mother always nagged her for looking pale. She was terrified. Terrified of the dead, terrified of superstition, of the unknown, and terrified the police would somehow implicate her in Mr Hambleton's death. With a grandfather who was shipped to Van Diemen's Land as a prisoner in 1838 she was paranoid. Either way, she was now out of service with her master dead, and at her age, her future looked bleak.

Boothman had walked into the dining room unannounced, where the housekeeper sat silently, her hands clasped before her, while staring at the floor. 'Mrs Hark.'

The woman jumped.

'Sorry to startle you. But I need to ask you some questions.'

The housekeeper made to speak, but her mouth was dry. Boothman had seen it all before. He walked to a drinks trolley and poured a sherry from a near empty crystal decanter. 'Here.'

The woman didn't hesitate. She gulped the contents and Boothman poured her another.

'How can I help you?' she finally managed, her throat lubricated with Spanish Oloroso.

'When you arrived this morning,' Boothman started, 'was the door locked?'

'Yes.'

'You have a key then ... to let yourself in?'

'Mr Hambleton keeps a key under a loose board on the back step. I'm the only one who knows about it. At least I think I am.'

'So, whoever the intruder was, they must have let themselves in and locked the door after they left.'

'Look,' the housekeeper was trembling. 'If I tell you something, real private like, will I get into trouble with the law?'

'Well, that depends. What sort or *something*?'

'Oh Lord, dear god, help me.'

'Speak Mrs Hark. If you have something to say, then say it.'

'It's Mrs Hambleton sir, she's crazy. I wouldn't put it past 'er to ... to, to do what happened.'

'I thought Mr Hambleton lived alone.'

'He does ... or did, sir. But Mrs Hambleton, Hyacinth, well she were here yesterday afternoon growling at her husband, they haven't lived together for years but she comes around from time to time to do work on the garden, maintenance like, she's a useful woman. Well, she was growling because he refuses to sell the house and move somewhere smaller, and she wants the money. Not that she needs it like.'

'How old is Hyacinth?'

'Seventy-two. I know because she had a birthday three weeks ago and I heard her telling someone.'

Boothman looked to Toby Hutton and was pleased to see he took notes.

'Last evening Mr Hambleton had guests for drinks, did he not?'

'Yes. He had meetings with scholars and like-minded academics from time to time. One of the group had just had a book published and they were here to discuss it. I made cucumber and watercress sandwiches and Mr Hambleton's favourite cheddar and chutney. I also prepared him a spatchcock dinner which he told me he would roast himself.'

'Do you know who the guests were?'

'No sir, I just know of Mr McQuade. He's headmaster at Hutchins School. Maybe he could tell you the names of the others.'

'McQuade ... thank you.'

Together the three checked the rest of the house, room by room. Nothing was disturbed. The house did, however, look short of furniture. There were some items of value in the bedroom and study. Small items easily carried by a burglar, but still in situ. A gold fob watch next to the master bed for one thing.

'The house is ...' Boothman looked at the housekeeper. 'Ah, a little sparse. There's not too much furniture. In fact, it looks rather tired and empty.'

'Mr Hambleton was struggling to make ends meet sir. I got no end of tradesmen hounding me for money. Me, for heaven's sake. It were awful embarrassing.'

'Hmm. Nothing else has been disturbed in the house then?'

'No sir.'

'If robbery's not the motive, what was?' Boothman asked Hutton. 'Who would kill such a harmless old man?

'Something personal? A vendetta possibly?'

'Possibly. We need to interview Mrs Hambleton.'

Hutton. 'As a witness?'

'Yes, and as a suspect.'

***

The following morning. Agapanthus Cottage, Macquarie Street.
Charlotte caught Aunt Jocelyn's last words. 'You have a gentleman visitor.' Hoisting her hem, she scurried down the stairs. Surely Edward would not

present himself unannounced. Aunt Jocelyn met Charlotte at the bottom. 'Where is he?' Charlotte whispered cheerfully bobbing her head about to see past her auntie.

'In the drawing room. Deep breath in my dear, or you'll have a seizure.'

Charlotte swept into the drawing room. She looked stunning in her day-wear, ready and willing for what she considered the best employment in the world – journalism.

'Mrs Clarke ... Charlotte. Good day to you.'

'Constable Hutton!' Charlotte's disappointment was barely concealed. 'What are you doing here?'

Constable Toby Hutton wanted to say, *well, it's nice to see you too,* but his confidence deflated. He said instead. 'I ... I finally got my transfer to Hobart. *Hobart*, Charlotte, they didn't send me back to Launceston.'

'Oh, good for you.' Charlotte looked less than enthusiastic, she froze in the doorway, one hand on the doorknob, the door remaining wide open to the passage where Aunt Jocelyn was joined by daughter Merrill, silently eavesdropping. Charlotte didn't hesitate to make her feelings known; she had never been all that capable at hiding her true emotions. 'So, what brings you here?'

'I have been promoted to senior constable,' Hutton said with an ex-pectant smile awaiting congratulations. He spread his arms wide putting himself on display. 'Plain clothes an' all as you can see. I'm to be trained as a detective.'

'No, I meant what brings you here to Agapanthus Cottage?'

Hutton looked even more deflated.

This was a kick in the guts.

'Oh ... I thought ... ah. I thought you might take tea with me one after-noon. High tea at the Orient Hotel maybe.'

'Constable Hutton ...'

'Toby.'

'Constable Hutton. I am very busy, now if you don't mind, I must get to the office.'

'The Mercury office huh, I'll walk with you ...'

'No!' Charlotte almost shouted. 'Ah, no thank you. I prefer to walk alone.'

'Then high tea?' The man was persistent. Thick skinned his mother always said. 'I'm free Sunday?'

'Well, I'm not. So, if you don't mind.'

Immediately there was a dark edge to the man's tone. 'Then when would it suit you, Charlotte?'

Charlotte had a sudden idea. It wasn't the greatest of plans, a total fabrication actually but the words spilt forth without thinking. 'I am betrothed Constable Hutton. To a man.' Out in the passageway Aunt Jocelyn stifled a cough, and not to subtly.

'B-betrothed? To whom?'

'Well, it's not really your business.'

'But ... betrothed?'

'Now good day to you constable,' Charlotte stepped away to allow the man pass. Auntie and daughter scurried off into the sitting room.

Hutton stepped back into the hallway, turning back to face Charlotte, he pulled his peaked cap tightly over his head while considering a different approach. 'I'm with the detective branch now ...'

'You said.'

'Yes, well, knowing how good you are as an investigative journalist, I mean you have a reputation as a bit of a sleuth, well I thought maybe we could work together on occasion. You could possibly teach me a thing or two ... and me you.'

Charlotte had had a minute to settle from the disappointment it wasn't Edward Culpepper standing before her. Maybe she had been a little harsh on the constable. The man was clearly smitten after all. And another side of Charlotte suggested it may be best to stay friendly with the lawman. Sure, keep him at arm's length, but he might prove invaluable in her own future investigations, an insider within the police force.

'Detective huh,' she said. 'You must be pleased with yourself?'

'Yes, yes. I am very excited. Actually, I arrived five days ago in time for the second verdict of Reverend Finch's trial.' The senior constable couldn't hide his feelings. 'The man has been acquitted.'

'Yes. Good news do you not think?'

'I'm certain you could guess my thoughts on the matter Charlotte.'

'Yes, well. I may see you around town,' Charlotte opened the front door and ushered the constable onto the street where Hutton walked away, a slight spring returning to his step.

***

The Mercury Newspaper Offices. Macquarie Street, Hobart.
Walking down Macquarie Street, Charlotte felt her cheek blush at the thought of Toby Hutton. She couldn't for the life of her think why the man had it in his head that she could even be remotely interested in him. She had never flirted with him nor had she made any indication in that direction. The blush dissolved and a cheeky smile replaced her memory of her fabrication, *I am betrothed. Golly*, she thought. Now that was blatant fiction and in a community the size of Hobart Toby would soon discover the truth. Charlotte shrugged off the deceit while approaching the corner of Macquarie Street and Elizabeth Street when she noted James Paton the owner of *The Clipper*, a weekly paper with Christian socialist leanings. The middle-aged editor stood outside his office in the two-storey brick and slate roofed building that he shared with another business, the *Brinsmead Piano Depot*. Charlotte smiled at a sign the full width of *The Clipper's* frontage reading *Largest Circulation in Tasmania*. A bold boast, she thought, with *The Mercury* office directly next door. Or the *Daily Davies* as Paton referred to his rival. He dressed in pinstriped trousers, shirt, tie and waistcoat and wore the leather apron of a compositor. It was *The Clipper's* print day Charlotte remembered. Paton was talking to children, no doubt giving the young tykes a spiritual ear full. Charlotte crossed the street to avoid the tiresome man.

'Ah, Mrs Clarke!' Paton called out. Deserting the children, he hurried through the front gate to cross the street.

Blow.

Charlotte braced herself. James Paton was forty but looked older. A lot older. He had lost his wife two years prior to a brain disease that caused her early death. These days he made it obvious he was a lonely man, *young*, and in the market, so to speak, for a new spouse.

'Charlotte, dear girl, how lovely to see you.' The editor tidied his drooping moustache with two precise strokes of the finger.

Charlotte stiffened. 'Mr Paton.'

'James, please.'

'James.'

'On your way to the newsroom?' he asked.

Clearly!

'It's just that I noticed you crossing the street. Thought you may have an appointment at Town Hall,' he said of Hobart's Town Hall directly across the street from their respective newspapers.

Charlotte sighed. 'What can I do for you, James?'

'Well, it's Friday,' the man said, his words matter of fact and confident.

'Goodness gracious me,' Charlotte replied, her voice laced with derision. 'So it is.'

'Well.' James clamped his hands together touching his chin. 'You know what Friday means don't you?'

'End of the week?' Charlotte knew exactly what the man was about. Friday was Victoria Sponge Day at the Tasmanian Coffee Palace next door to *The Mercury* building on the corner of Argyle and Macquarie Streets. And James Paton had been eager to have Charlotte join him for High Tea ever since she let it slip the light vanilla sponge filled with strawberry jam and double cream with powdered sugar was a favourite of hers.

'End of the week, yes,' James's eyes positively bulged. 'But also, it's Victoria Sponge Day.'

'Oh, of course. But I'm terribly, terribly busy and I'll be eating on the run today Mr Paton ... ah, James.'

'Oh, what a pity. Well, au revoir then, may the Lord be with you.'

Charlotte stepped off the pavement and, dodging fresh horse droppings, she hurried back across the road.

Charlotte dropped her satchel on her desk before spearing her bright yellow parasol into the office umbrella stand – a wrought iron figure of a black news boy crying out the daily headline. Made in America, so Charlotte was told. Charlotte hooked her coat onto the stand near the door, along with the hats and coats of those present. Two white aprons hung nearby, ostensibly for the use of the fairer sex. To protect their delicate skirts and blouse from ink stains, apparently. Charlotte's apron dangled where it had been abandoned from day one.

The Editor, Rupert Craddock's secretary Jeanette waited. 'Hail, rain or shine, that parasol goes everywhere you go. Isn't that right Charlotte?'

Charlotte loved her parasol with its hidden stiletto, and yes, it *was* handy against the sun on her white skin, the rain when wet ... and hail? Well, maybe not hail. Charlotte liked the editor's secretary, Jeanette, although she was fiercely protective of her position and occasionally, in an awkward situation, it could be like mediating with Attila the Hun. But Jeanette was outspoken and efficient and knew only too well how to handle men.

'Rupert wants a word.'

'Mood?'

'Too early to tell.'

Rupert might treat Charlotte like a daughter, but business came first. Charlotte knocked. 'Enter!'

Charlotte entered. 'Good morning, Mr Craddock.' Gauging the man's mood, mostly she called him Rupert. Today appeared to be a *Mr Craddock* day. The editor tipped his head forward to peer over his glasses; pince-nez that pinched the bridge of his nose with a leather strap knotted to one lens and hung on a strap around his neck.

'This Port Arthur business,' Craddock said of the Reverend Sidney Finch trial. 'We've got this unfinished story, a loose end. I don't like it.'

The reverend had been arrested and brought to Hobart for his trial. Following a hung jury, the judge ordered a second trial. 'Now the second trial was another hung jury,' the editor said, stabbing a finger at Charlotte's notes from the day before, where his prize journalist had spent valuable time, three days in fact, in the courtroom. The results the second time around – where eleven jurors voted an acquittal and only one voted him guilty – was another hung jury. The second appointed judge, Justice Gardiner, wasn't prepared to waste government expenditure on a third trial and set the man free.

Charlotte of course was ecstatic. She had concluded the reverend was innocent of killing Annie. Certainly, he was guilty of adultery, but murder. No.

'What was *your* verdict?' Charlotte asked, knowing the editor was loath to voice his opinion on such matters before any trial ended. Craddock stroked the dimple in his chin with his forefinger, rubbing at day-old whiskers. Although he was not overly tall at five foot seven inches, he possessed a strong face, square jawed with bulbous nose. Jowls added to his character, although he was hardly overweight for fifty-two.

'My verdict. I think the man's guilty as charged.'

'Poppycock!' To an outsider this conversation could sound disrespectful on Charlotte's part. But the two loved a good debate.

'There were the incriminating letters that you were in possession of and handed over to the police. The letter that mentioned Genesis chapter ... what was it, 37?'

'38.'

'Thirty-eight, yes. That was incriminating ...'

'There is no question the reverend and Annie were intimate,' Charlotte said haughtily. 'He was on trial for murder, not infidelity.'

The editor broke into a smile. This is what he loved about this fiery red head. Her fire!

'I think he sought to kill his mistress to save his own otherwise *perfect* reputation,' Rupert said. 'His wife was unconscious on laudanum administered by Finch the night of the murder.'

'She suffers from what we now know is dementia,' Charlotte retorted. 'Laudanum helps her sleep.'

'You saw her in possession of a knife with traces of blood on it.'

'Yes, animal blood. The reverend had prepared a duck for dinner with that knife only days before and had not cleaned it properly.'

'What about the clothes Daisy saw him burning at the rear of the general store the night of the fire?' Craddock persisted. 'Originally, he said he was burning worn old clothes that belonged to his wife. Why burn them – most suspicious. He was known to have four shirts, one for his employment, one for the wash, one for Sunday best ... the fourth he burnt. That's very suspicious.'

'The reverend confessed to burning a shirt splattered with blood, the duck's blood from preparing for dinner. He thought it would incriminate him.'

'Incriminate him, you can say that again. Besides, Charlotte, modern science could have proven his innocence.' One of the editor's interests was modern forensic science, like fingerprinting. 'Here we are approaching the twentieth century and modern analysis can discriminate between the nucleate red cells of birds or reptiles and the enucleate cells of mammals. Under the microscope the microscopic characteristics of human blood would have been identifiable from duck's blood. I suggest the reverend knew this and decided to burn his shirt.'

'We'll have to give him the benefit of doubt on that one,' Charlotte said.

'Benefit of doubt!' Craddock puffed out his cheeks. 'What of the broken paraffin bottle next to Annie's body?'

'Left by the real killer who tried to burn Annie's body but never managed to finish the act properly.'

'The real killer,' Craddock repeated Charlotte's words. 'That's the loose end I'm not happy with. Who did kill the poor girl then, if not the reverend?'

'The mystery lover, the one who got Annie pregnant.'

'And who might that be?'

'We don't know. There are dozens of potential suitors living in and around Port Arthur. There was talk of her having a relationship with one of the deckhands on the *Manapouri*.'

The editor ran his tongue behind his teeth in an attempt to dislodge an annoying crumb. 'You know Finch was most fortunate to have the best defence lawyer in Tasmania available to defend him.'

'It helps, I agree.'

They spoke of Orson Squires, paid for by the church, a witty, caustic, charming and contemptuous lawyer who was determined to prove his client innocent, and pity help any witnesses against his client who found themselves before him. They would be torn to shreds.

'His winding up speech was exceptional,' Craddock said, who had a copy of the transcript on his desk. 'You know the second jury took four and a half hours to come to a decision. And to what end? Another hung jury. Amazing.' Craddock's mind was running hot. 'What on earth would a young lady of twenty-one see in a man of forty-three, a man of god no less?'

'She was seduced by his power,' Charlotte said. 'His authority, and for him it was lust, an age-old recipe.'

'Now there's your headline ... *an age-old recipe for disaster*. There's been a lot of interest in this case. It's helped sell newspapers.' Rupert Craddock leant back in his chair. It was time to alter the direction of this conversation. 'How's your book coming along?'

'I've started, if that's what you mean.'

'I'll look forward to reading it. Only Marcus Clarke's own flesh and blood could attempt writing a follow up story to *For the Term of his Natural Life*. What are you calling it, by the way? Do you have a title?'

'I'm thinking *Beyond the Seas of Tyranny*.'

'I like that.'

Finally, Charlotte could share a smile with *Rupert*, their differences now aired. 'I'm trusting you will edit it for me?' she asked.

'It would be an honour.'

Craddock recognised traces of Charlotte's father in the feisty young lady. Marcus Clarke, also a journalist, had occasionally lost interest in certain stories and had to be pressed to complete them, like Charlotte with this damned Reverend Finch trial. And the editor hoped Charlotte would not succumb to her father's Bohemian ways also. She was already shaping up as a unique individual with a taste for adventure.

'Your father and I were good friends, but you know that,' Craddock had discussed their relationship when Charlotte first moved to Hobart from Melbourne. 'He was quite the character.'

'So, I believe.'

Craddock knew Charlotte was only ten when her father died and although he was good friends with Marcus, he had only met Charlotte once when she was five. He smiled at the memories. 'Much to the chagrin of some pretentious gentlemen of Melbourne, all frowning beneath their shiny beaver fur top hats, your father always wore his beloved cabbage tree hat, which, I have noticed, is your headwear of choice.'

'Well, they are so practical.'

'I agree.'

Made from the leaves of the cabbage-tree palm, the zigzag woven and plaited straw-coloured hats had a high domed crown and a wide flat brim, perfect for the Antipodean sun. 'My older brother Rowley, in Melbourne, still has Papa's hat,' Charlotte said.

'Marcus had his made for him by a prisoner at Pentridge Gaol,' the editor said. 'When he was researching an article for *The Australasian*.' Craddock thought a moment. '*Two months at Pentridge* the story was titled. I remember it. He always wore that hat defiantly on the back of his head'.

'You and Papa worked together at the Melbourne Public Library for some time, did you not?'

'Yes ... you know your father liked to smoke cigars. So, when he arrived at work in the morning – your father was Secretary to the Trustees at first – he would leave his half-finished cigar in the mouth of a metal lion halfway up the library steps.' Charlotte smiled. 'This became a signal that your father was at his desk. But I'm afraid he took his library duties lightly.'

Charlotte. 'Yet he became the sub-librarian.'

'Yes, a few years later, in '73. He applied for the head librarian position but didn't make it.'

'Did you meet at the library?'

'Well yes and no. I had met Marcus socially out on the town prior, when we were in our twenties. We were both the same age you know.' Craddock thought a moment before speaking, 'I don't know whether I should be telling you this, but ... well I'm certain you have heard stories.'

'Please, feel free.'

Craddock loved nothing more than to regale his youth. 'We enjoyed drinking to excess, we loved absinthe and sometimes we tried drugs. Your father and I did not live a virtuous life, Charlotte. Mornings were spent scribbling, afternoons smoking tobacco, and, in the evening, it was dinner, then theatre – Burlesque preferably – then gaslighting.'

'Gaslighting?'

'Patronising clubs. I remember your father writing somewhere once, *we were utterly useless beings, but then, well, we had good digestions and did not bother ourselves with high resolves and sentimental lovemaking.'* Craddock hoped he hadn't overstepped the boundary with his raunchy rhetoric, but Charlotte was only too keen to hear more. 'Someone told Marcus absinthe will drive a fellow mad,' Craddock chuckled. 'So, he drank it to find out.'

'You mentioned drugs.'

'Yes. Marcus was keen to try many narcotics. You must understand that because of your father's Dickens-like hunger for knowledge and worldly experiences he liked to experiment. I remember he was introduced to opium by a less than scrupulous Chinese detective named Fook Shing who took him to opium dens in Little Bourke Street in Melbourne.'

'Goodness! Opium.'

'He tried opium and liked it. He also enjoyed hashish enough to write an article about it for the *Colonial Monthly*.'

'You mentioned clubs?'

'Yes. We all joined the exclusive Melbourne Club, but it was excessively expensive, and we were living higher than we could afford, accumulating debt along the way. It was then that we poor journalists banded together and formed the Yorick Club.'

'Yes, I've heard of it. It became the centre for Melbourne's Bohemian population.'

'That, it certainly did.'

'Named after Shakespeare's character in *Hamlet* – "alas poor Yorick, I knew him well".'

'That's correct. Your father even brought a real skull along to the club where I remember it rested on the fire mantelpiece watching over the eccentric behaviour within.' Craddock focussed on the past, smiling. 'But primarily we shared a love of books.'

Charlotte stepped back into the Literary Department, as the journalist's office was better known. The fifty-year-old building, built to house the Bank of Australasia originally, was showing its age. Now, occupying the area once used by bank tellers, the elongated room, rather like the stateroom on board a large passenger ship Charlotte fancied, had walls of stone with tall narrow windows facing east allowing generous sunlight to spill into the room. That was on sunny days of course. The wall on the western side was an interior wooden wall, tastefully, yet surprisingly, wallpapered with a pattern similar to a fleur de Lis. Either side of the internal entrance, filing cabinets and horizontal chart cabinets crammed with documents and papers indicated a productive office. Alongside each desk, cork boards were pinned with clippings and notes of ongoing stories. At the far end near the editor's office, more filing cabinets overflowed while a moderate fire smouldered in an iron grate. A mustiness in the office hinted at a stubborn leak in the roof somewhere and the forty-year-old parquetry flooring was lifting causing problems for the fashionable higher heel, now worn by many.

Six leather-topped blackwood desks serviced four male journalists and, god forbid, two female journalists. The desks were in two orderly rows, each serviced by wicker-based teak swivel chairs with cast iron mechanisms for elevating or lowering its user. Each desk had an individual pigeonholed filing stand and a desktop *Underwood* writing machine. (Charlotte was fortunate to possess her own portable Chicago Writing Machine in addition to her office writer, or typewriter as they were becoming popularly known.) But that is where any tidiness in the office ended. Each desktop was strewn with paper documents, the incomplete labours of likeminded scribes, their unfinished articles and in general, productive literary chaos.

Outside grew dark. Inside even darker. Rain was on its way.

The south door opened and in walked Leonard McShan. He rattled a box of matches with an air of importance. Although the building was wired with electricity many kerosene lamps remained. These brass and floral-patterned frosted glass lamps hung on their pulley chains from hooks in the ceiling. There were four of these in the journalists' area alone.

Leonard had noted Charlotte leaving the editor's office. Charlotte tried to ignore the tall, scrawny, insipid man. He was as painful company as James Paton of *The Clipper*. Her skin crawled. Leonard's desk was nearest the editor's office. Leonard *was* also an all-rounder, quite useful actually, and one of those persons who could put their hand to anything, well almost. Ever since chaperoning Charlotte to Port Arthur, at Rupert Craddock's insistence, Leonard had become even more obsessed with her. He was also thick skinned, for Charlotte's attitude towards him was notorious within the building.

'Good morning Charlotte,' Leonard started. 'Everything all right?'

'Why shouldn't it be?'

'You just had a meeting with Mr Craddock. I was just wondering ...'

'Well don't.'

'You have mail in the office.'

This was unexpected. 'Me? Mail?'

'That's what I said.' Leonard didn't mean too, or maybe should have been more discrete, but a lascivious eye scrolled down Charlotte's body. Charlotte shivered. 'It was post marked Port Arthur,' he noted.

'How did you know ...?'

Leonard opened his mouth to speak but it wasn't worth waiting an answer. Charlotte hitched her skirt above the ankles and rushed across the passageway to the front office, opening the door with such enthusiasm the door banged against the wall. Never one for discretion, Charlotte had thrown the door open only to be confronted by a debonair socialite, poised at the hat stand, beaver fur top hat in hand. He automatically smiled; a libertine's reaction whenever confronted by a woman who took his fancy. He stood between Charlotte and her mail.

'Oh,' Charlotte was short of breath. 'Please excuse me sir.'

'You're excused.'

Charlotte made to step around the gentleman, but he stabbed his walking cane into the rug at her feet. 'You're in a hurry.'

'Yes ... ah sorry. But I need to collect some mail.'

'Mail eh. What's your name?'

Another womanizer, Charlotte had seen enough. 'Excuse me.' She pushed past. This rejection only cemented his determination. 'My name's George Davies,' he called after Charlotte who was now standing at the front desk, her back facing him. Molly the receptionist passed Charlotte her letter. Molly pulled faces, vying to convey an urgent message to Charlotte. '*George Davies*,' Molly whispered urgently, standing in a position to mask herself from the line of sight of the gentleman in question.

Of course, George Davies was the grandson of *The Mercury's* founder, John Davies. George was a heavy-set masculine figure, a handsome sportsman, an eligible bachelor and at twenty-nine he was two years Charlotte's senior. George had recently returned from London, training as sub-editor at the prestigious newspaper, *The Times*, at the bidding of his father – John George Davies, the current proprietor and heir of *The Mercury*,

In for a penny, in for a pound, Charlotte thought. Too late now. Besides the letter was far more important. At a glance Charlotte could see that the correspondence was indeed from Edward. With a smile that could have been misconstrued by George Davies, Charlotte scooted across the floor towards the door to the passage.

'Nice to meet you George Davies,' she said in passing, and returned the way she had come, leaving the prodigal son rather chastened.

Dear Charlotte, the letter started ... the news was bitter yet sweet. Edward's father, Shipley Culpepper had died suddenly of heart failure at the age of seventy-nine. Edward went on to explain, life as a Port Arthur guide had never been the same since the fires, and he was returning to find employment in Hobart or its environs. Edward wished Charlotte well and hoped to visit her in the near future, as soon as he could tie up his father's affairs, his funeral arrangements and deal with his meagre possessions.

Charlotte, the letter continued. *I do hope this here correspondence does not apear to forward of me, but in lite of our correspondence I wood like to call on yu on my arrival on the sixth day of April,*
Yor most humble servant,
Edward Culpepper

Charlotte checked the date the letter was posted. 23rd March. She stepped from the passage back into her office. 'Today is the 6th of April is it not?' she asked her nearest colleague.

'Yes.'

'Then why is it,' Charlotte demanded to know, 'that I receive a letter from Port Arthur post marked 23rd day of March and it arrives here at the office, and not my Macquarie Street address, and on the 6th day of April?'

The colleague stared at Charlotte as if she had been caught with her hand in the biscuit barrel. 'I ... ah ... I don't know Charlotte.'

A loud bell disturbed their conversation. It was the telephone exchange from which one line fed into the editor's office. *Such innovation* the editor had crowed, *isn't it wonderful*? The contraption was connected recently and registered; one of hundreds of telephone numbers listed in the Hobart telephone exchange directory, which started operating in '83. The modern innovation had created new employment positions, like *leg men* responsible for phoning the latest news to the editorial department and *rewrite men* who transcribed the information for the newsroom.

Such an event in the office turned heads. The four journalists present in the room watched Rupert Craddock through the interior glass windows. He listened intently to a receiver held to one ear and spoke into the mouthpiece to someone, somewhere, maybe miles away. Finally, he stepped from his office. 'Charlotte, you're still here, good. A word if you please.'

Charlotte closed the editor's door behind her. 'There's been a murder at a Davey Street address. Osbert Hambleton. Do you know the name?'

'Can't say I do.'

Craddock looked pensive. 'I knew of him. He was a scholar, a retired professor.'

'Oh.'

'My informant just told me his seventy-two-year-old wife is a suspect. This is right up your alley.'

Charlotte saw a bonus dangled before her. 'Thank you, Rupert. Leave it with me.'

***

Hutchins Boys School. Macquarie Street, Hobart.
Senior Constable Toby Hutton was chuffed. Inspector Boothman had given him the responsibility of interviewing Mr McQuade, one of Osbert Hambleton guests the evening before he was murdered. He was also headmaster of Hutchins, a private boy's school in Macquarie Street. McQuade

was not surprised to see the lawman on his doorstep. 'I've been expecting you,' McQuade told Hutton.

'Oh, news travels fast.'

'Indeed, it does. Come into the office.' Whilst the schoolmaster was keen to draw the policeman from the school corridor away from prying eyes, he did not offer Hutton a seat. 'What would you like to know?'

'Well sir, to start with you had a meeting with Mr Hambleton at his home did you not?'

'Yes.'

'Followed by a light supper?'

'That is correct. Mrs Hark the housekeeper made watercress and cucumber sandwiches, extraordinarily delicious, I think it's all the butter.' McQuade patted his stomach as if to say ... *butter, my fat belly doesn't need.*

'But did anything out of the ordinary happen? Was anyone vexed or antagonistic towards their host?'

'Not at all.' McQuade thought briefly. 'Unless you want to include Osbert's wife Hyacinth. Crazy woman.'

'Oh?'

'Yes. She's quite eccentric. I'd go even further and suggest she is mad.'

'In what way?'

'Well, she does work in the garden from time to time. Hyacinth wanted Osbert to sell the house you see, she wants her share of the money, but Osbert wouldn't have a bar of it. So, while we are standing about deep in discussion of Marybeth Saunders new book, *Tasmanian Wildflowers*, Hyacinth rolled the window sash up from the garden and gave Osbert a blast about water damage in the cellar. Then later, half an hour maybe, I saw her shadow out in the passageway, she was spying on us. Yes, the woman is quite strange.'

'Would you go as far to say Mrs Hambleton hated her husband?'

'Not so much hate. They tolerated each other. But I suppose you could say the relationship has always been stormy.'

'What time did you leave?'

'8.30 approximately.'

'Did you leave together?'

'Yes, every one of us.'

'Anything else come to mind?'

'It smelt like he was roasting chicken for his dinner.'

'Mr Hambleton did not appear well off for a resident in such a large property.'

'He wasn't.'

'Yet he hired a housekeeper.'

'Yes, but only minimal hours. So, with little money coming in from his pension and few royalties from book publishers the house was deteriorating. They fought over their divorce settlement. None of this improved the old man's temper.'

***

Meanwhile at Davey Street.

Charlotte had learnt from past experience that neighbours were the best source of information. The house next door to murder victim Osbert Hambleton, the sandstone residence of a dozen rooms, with three sides of the building covered in ivy, was easily approachable via a side gate. A rose-lined pathway led around to the rear of the property. Charlotte approached the servants' entrance. She paused a moment, about to tug at the bell handle, when she thought to rehearse her story. Charlotte had made previous enquiries. She had been warned, should she meet the disagreeable cook, beware. Mrs Makepeace was a hardened old woman with over forty years baking, roasting, boiling and steaming for her master. And she was fiercely protective.

But good fortune shone on Charlotte this day. As she poised to tug at the bell the door opened and the young housemaid stepped hurriedly into the yard. She carried the master's bed pan for emptying.

'Oh!'

Not expecting a visitor on the doorstep, the maid stopped suddenly. The pan slopped. Charlotte jumped sideways.

'Dear me. That was close. Sorry.' The maid was mortified.

Charlotte introduced herself. 'I didn't mean to surprise you.'

'Are you 'ere to see Mrs Makepeace?'

'No!' Charlotte said only too readily and improvising 'I wanted to see you actually.'

'Me?'

Charlotte explained the tragedy that had taken place next door.

'You know about it then,' the maid said. 'Awful innit. Poor old bugger bludgeoned they said.' Charlotte was momentarily distracted by the maid's morning chore and put a gloved hand to her nose. 'Oh, wait 'ere will yer while I get rid o' this down the privy.'

The maid returned two minutes later now smelling strongly of turpentine, where she had cleansed the pan.

'I believe his body was found by his housekeeper, what's her name ...?' Charlotte lingered on her last word as if the name was on the tip of her tongue.

'Eleanor,' the gullible girl answered.

'That's her,' said Charlotte. 'Eleanor ...?'

'Hark ... Eleanor Hark. I only met 'er a few times but she's a good egg.'

'Don't suppose you know where she resides?'

'No sorry ... oh 'ang on a mo'. She used to talk about pickin' 'er grand-daughter up from Ragged School. Jackie 'er name is.'

'Ragged School.' Charlotte knew the Ragged Schools well. Schools for the poor and neglected. 'Which one? Wapping?'

'No Missus. Cascade Road.' Banging pots nearby warned that Mrs Makepeace was back in the kitchen. 'I better get a wriggle on,' the maid said. 'An' I jus' remembered. I didn't open the master's bedroom window like I been told.' She leant across in a conspiratorial manner to whisper, bedpan in one hand and the other hand up to her mouth for discretion. 'Cos it needs airin' real bad.'

The walk from affluent society to poverty was less than twenty minutes, a fact that always disturbed middle-class Charlotte. Like it or not, there would always be a divide between the social groups of Hobart. And in most places for that matter. Charlotte found Cascade Road Ragged School in the rooms attached to the Baptist Church. She stepped through the gate in a white picket fence, attracted to children singing ... *Oh Lord my god, how great thou art.*

'Mrs Hark lives in Gore Street,' the volunteer teacher was only too happy to help. 'It's a small cottage with a lemon tree in the front garden taller than the roof. You couldn't possibly miss it.'

'Is little Jackie here today?'

The teacher pointed out a scrawny young girl, about eight, mousy hair sheared short. 'Did you want a word?'

'No. Why does her grandmother pick her up, and not a parent?'

'The mother is ... well I hate to say this, but often she is incapable. And there is no father I know of.'

Gore Street was only another ten-minute walk. Charlotte found the cottage easily enough, with its twelve-foot tree groaning under the weight of lemons. The dwelling was a tidy timber paling cottage of four rooms, boasting an outside lavatory with a roof.

Charlotte knocked. The door opened. 'Mrs Hark?'

'Yes.'

Charlotte introduced herself. 'My name is Charlotte Clarke. I am a journalist at *The Mercury* Newspaper.'

'Oh! You're here about Mr Hambleton I should imagine?'

'Yes.'

'It were awful. I found him lyin' on the floor, there was blood everywhere.' Eleanor Hark had a thought. 'Journalist you said?'

'Yes.'

'I've already spoken to the police.'

'Yes, I know,' Charlotte guessed she had. 'I am an investigative journalist; I aid the police.' Although this last comment was largely a fabrication (Charlotte shared information with the police when it suited her) it seemed plausible to the fifty-nine-year-old housekeeper. Mrs Hark studied Charlotte briefly before looking past Charlotte towards the street.

'Did you come 'ere alone?'

'Yes.'

'Well come into the kitchen, I just made a pot o' tea.'

Charlotte followed the woman down a dim passageway and into her kitchen full of light off the yard and through a window in need of a good clean.

'How do yer like your tea luv?' the woman asked, pouring more hot water from a large brown enamel kettle into the tea pot.

'With just a little milk thank you.'

Charlotte made a quick observation of her surroundings. A cooking range sat in the fireplace, built into the chimney, with an oven one side and an open built-in cupboard the other, half full of firewood. A small pine dresser displayed the woman's crockery, mostly blue and white or plain white. All looked chipped. Charlotte smiled inwardly; a biscuit barrel sat on the top shelf where the children couldn't reach it.

Charlotte sipped her tea, realising how thirsty she was. And it was strong and hot, the way she liked it. Mrs Hark finally stopped fussing and sat opposite, both hands about her cup as if she had cold fingers. Charlotte took her time, measuring her questions carefully.

'Would you mind telling me what you told the police Mrs Hark?'

'Call me Eleanor, luv.' Eleanor told Charlotte exactly what she had told the police.

'The guests that evening,' Charlotte asked. 'Do you have any names?'

'Like I told the police. I only knew one man, Mr McQuade, I knew him as the headmaster at Hutchins School.'

'McQuade.' Charlotte made a note.

'Do you know where I may find Mrs Hambleton.'

'Why yes, she lives out at Richmond.'

***

The township of Richmond,
15 miles north-east of Hobart across the River Derwent.
Charlotte was optimistic, hopeful she could reach the victim's estranged wife before the police, on the account the woman lived several hours from Hobart.

The first steamship built in Hobart; the 110-foot vehicular paddle steamer *Kangaroo* was already over forty years in service. It provided a service between Sullivans Cove and Bellerive. Charlotte and her hired liveryman Mr Timbals, along with Reggie the pony and his two-wheel buggy, boarded the ferry. The thirty-mile round trip to Richmond from Bellerive, and the return river crossing would occupy the remainder of the day.

Of course, this wasn't Charlotte's first visit to Richmond. She knew the village was initially established as a farming area for feeding the young colony from the early 1820s. But Richmond soon became a police district with its own gaol during the years of convict transportation. Now in 1898 Charlotte found the village a pleasant change from Hobart. Typically English, visitors would say, and a prosperous farming country.

Charlotte found the property, *The Oaks*, one mile past the Richmond Bridge, heading east on Brinktop Road. At first glance, between gaps in an untamed part of a hedge, *The Oaks* looked small compared to the family mansion in Davey Street. Charlotte had heard from the housekeeper that Hyacinth had moved out of the Davey Street property many years ago, although the Hambleton's remained bound in an unhappy marriage.

Mr Timbals left Charlotte at the front door before parking the carriage near a water trough where Reggie availed himself of refreshment. Having heard the visitors, the door swung open and by all accounts it appeared to be Mrs Hambleton herself.

'Yes, yes,' the woman sounded scatty. 'And what might you want young lady?'

She sounded terribly English for a colonial. Charlotte, parasol hooked over her arm, introduced herself, adding that she worked with the police in an investigative journalist position ... *whatever that meant.*

Immediately Charlotte had the notion that maybe, just maybe, this woman knew nothing of the murder and the police were yet to interview the estranged wife, now widow of the deceased, Mrs Hyacinth Hambleton.

Charlotte was invited into the front room of what was a modest stone homestead built in 1834, according to the carved lintel over the front door. Inside was crammed with antiques, silverware, paintings and furniture too grand for a smaller homestead.

'You're here about my husband's untimely death I take it?'

Charlotte breathed a sigh of relief. *So, she did know.*

'I'm not surprised,' Mrs Hambleton said. 'Letting riffraff into the house willy-nilly discussing his silly books.' There was no remorse, no pity, no despair.

Their voices in the front room attracted the Hambleton's adult children. The older son, maybe a few years older than Charlotte, stood next to his mother. All eyes looked to Charlotte. 'Who's this?' the son asked his mother. Charlotte may as well have been a mannequin.

'This is Charlotte …' Hyacinth looked at Charlotte. 'Clarke, wasn't it?'

Charlotte went on to explain her visit to the siblings: Ashley and Phillipa – holding a pathetic hairy rat-like dog – and Ashley's wife Adelaide D'Boville. Adelaide was a most attractive young Flemish woman with fashionable short curly dark hair. None were too impressed with Charlotte's presence. The dog growled. Charlotte made the most of what time she had.

Her first surprise was the collective lack of empathy for their father, who had been bludgeoned to death only hours earlier. The second mystery was the amount of furniture crammed into the room, and from what Charlotte could ascertain, they filled other rooms also, all the way down the cottage passageway. Life-size family portraits in magnificent, gilded frames, were propped against the walls. The mahogany extension dining table was stacked with crates of crystal, glassware, and decorative porcelain. But a typewriting machine particularly caught Charlotte's attention, sitting on a bureau. She recognised the Remington as a later model with a shift key to switch from lower case to capitals. A bundle of letters sat neatly next to the machine. One envelope was stamped *Langley House, New Town*, an institute Charlotte immediately recognised as a government institution for the elderly. An old people's home for the destitute. This was out of character for a family clearly wealthy judging by their material possessions, and in stark contrast to what Charlotte had heard about the interior of the deceased husband's house, a dwelling with minimal furnishings.

'Are you in the process of moving?' Charlotte asked.

Ashley Hambleton stiffened. 'Look, we are not prepared to talk to the newspapers now or any time soon. I really must insist you leave Miss Clarke.'

'Mrs,' Charlotte corrected. The family stared back. What an eccentric bunch Charlotte thought. She made to leave, positioning herself near the bureau. '

Goodness me,' Charlotte feigned excitement. 'Is that painting by Haughton Forest?' She stabbed her parasol in the direction of a large seascape out on the hall wall. The family turned. Charlotte scooped up the top letter on the bureau. Four pairs of eyes twisted back. 'I very much admire Haughton Forest,' she said. 'He's an exceptional artist.' No one responded.

Ashley opened the front door. He stood a moment blocking the entrance in what could be portrayed as a menacing manoeuvre, when Charlotte caught a whiff of what she thought was rotting fish. At first, she believed it might be soiled clothes, but it was familiar. Then Charlotte remembered she had a distant cousin with this rare skin affliction, known as Rotting Fish Syndrome; an inherited problem that causes the body to produce a fishy odour released into sweat, urine, breath and other fluids. It was a most unpleasant odour that suited the man's disagreeable nature. Ashley finally stepped aside to allow Charlotte to leave.

'Good day to you then,' Charlotte said, stepping from the gloom back into fresh air and sunlight, hurrying to her transport before anything appeared amiss.

Ashley watched the horse and trap leave the property. 'Bloody irritating woman,' he said, twitching the drape back into position.

'*Language* Ashley ... please.' Hyacinth Hambleton abhorred obscenities.

'Sorry Mum-mar. But why did you invite her inside in the first place?'

Hyacinth's lips pursed, raising her chin in defiance. 'I did not *invite* her in,' she spat. Which wasn't exactly true. 'I opened the door and she barged in like she owned the place.'

Ashley sighed. There would be no extracting the truth from mother any time soon. There never was. 'Well, all the same, the woman had no right to come here. I've heard talk about her before.'

'Oh?'

'I've heard acquaintances in the town speak of this Mrs Charlotte Clarke from the newspaper. Stubborn as a mule, I believe were the words they used. I fear she is a nuisance.'

Ashley Baxter Hambleton – fair hair, blue eyes and thick moustache – was the first born of Osbert and Hyacinth Hambleton. Ashley had had a troubled youth. He was spoiled as a child. As an adolescent he was given five shillings a week pocket money, far too much, but not enough for one so greedy. He stole one of his father's chequebooks, forged his signature and drew money from the account. By sixteen he had influence over a female companion whom he involved in his fraudulent activities. Only his father's contacts and wealthy great-aunt Genevieve Sayer's money saw him evade a gaol sentence. The female companion involved wasn't so lucky. In his mid-twenties his father found him a position as an investment broker.

But Ashley lost heavily in the collapse of the Van Diemen's Land Bank in '91. With access to clients' funds, he fraudulently transferred money for his own personal use, living the high life. But this could not last. With the court unable to prove his guilt, he once again avoided gaol time.

Orphan Adelaide D'Boville (Married title now D'Boville-Hambleton) had been twenty-two when she met Ashley. She had travelled to Hobart from Evandale in the north of the island – where she lived with her guardian – to spend the Christmas holidays with a friend and her family. She met Ashley at a dinner party organised by mutual friends. Attractive, with large guileless hazel eyes and a wide sensual mouth, Adelaide had lived in Australia since she was nine. Her English was fluent and her manner vivacious. The two fell in love. Ashley soon discovered Adelaide was in line for a large dowry from her wealthy guardian; but not until she married. He proposed only days later. Unfortunately, the marriage did not have the blessing of Ashley's parents, so the two married secretly.

Osbert Hambleton was wary of his new daughter-in-law from the beginning. But having been a teacher, he himself had married above his station. Hyacinth was from a moneyed pioneer family. So, as a rule, Mr Hambleton had kept his thoughts to himself – thoughts like Adelaide was no more than a continental hussy. Now, four and a half years later, the marriage showed signs of fraying. Ashley had grown bitter and envious of others. He had aged and become pot-bellied from drink. He neglected Adelaide and the twenty-seven-year-old Flemish beauty began taking notice when other young men made discreet passes at her.

Now Ashley was concerned. Father's death would attract unwanted attention. 'Come,' Ashley ordered the three women. 'We need to store this lot in the barn,' referring to the excess furniture blocking the hallway.

'I think you are over reacting Ashley,' Hyacinth said.

'Oh, do you Mum-mar. Do you really? I might remind you, father's gone and got himself killed. We need to move this lot ... before the police arrive and ask questions, or, heaven forbid, the bank auditors. So, quickly now.'

***

The Mercury Office. Hobart.

With a sense her visit to Richmond had been worth the time and the ten-shilling investment of a carriage fare, Charlotte alighted outside the newspaper office feeling good about herself. There was more to the Hambleton family, she just knew it. *They're hiding something,* she thought. Marching absentmindedly through the front door of the Macquarie Street building, Charlotte clumsily ploughed into ...

'Edward!'

'Charlotte!'

'Wh-what are you doing here?'

'Lookin' for you.'

'Goodness me ... and now you have found me.'

'Did yer get me correspondence?'

'Yes, this morning.'

'This mornin'! I mailed that at the post office in Carnarvon ... must be nearly two weeks ago. I wondered why I never 'eard back.'

'Yes, it was post marked 23rd of March and here we are, nearly Easter. Your letter must have gone astray.'

'Yeh ... well ... I ...'

'Edward, I'm so sorry to hear about your father.'

'It were quick. Heart failure, 'e just dropped to the floor.'

'I'm so sorry.' Charlotte genuinely felt for Edward. 'Were you ... were you with him, when he ...'

'Aye. There was naught I could do. He passed immediately.'

Suddenly aware they were both holding each other's hands in greeting, Charlotte stepped back to take in the man.

'Well ... look at you. Looking rather elegant.' Charlotte's compliment came automatically but immediately she thought it forward of her. She blushed slightly. But it was true, Edward Culpepper had dressed for the city and looked handsome in his shirt, waistcoat and jacket with tapered lapels – short and narrow sleeved to reveal the cuffs – light, tight fitting trousers with pinstripes and a bowler hat.

'Thank you. They're all brand new,' Edward said with pride. 'I got of the steamer yesterdee an' went straight to Henry Cook's tailoring Shop.' Edward plucked at his lapels. 'They all came off the rack, ready-made,' he said unabashed.

'These are good times in which we live, eh?' Charlotte smiled.

Conscious they were being observed by the front desk staff, Charlotte looked past Edward to the office wall clock. It read twenty minutes before five. 'Come, let's have high tea at the Imperial.' Charlotte spoke of the Imperial Coffee Palace in Collins Street. 'I'm famished. I've not eaten lunch.'

The three-storey stone building with its modern cast iron columned balcony would not look out of place in London. Inside was warm, bright and filled with the wonderful aromas of sweet and savoury pastries, iced cakes, steaming tea and fresh brewed coffee. Charlotte and Edward found a table by the window on the ground floor and they were served smartly.

'That was most fortuitous,' Charlotte said. 'Meeting up like that.'

'Most fortuitous, yes. Another minute an' I would 'a been gone.'

Charlotte's attention was momentarily drawn to the three-tiered stand before her. Neat sandwich wedges, small cream cakes – latest recipes from Paris – petit fours and baby pies. Realising she had missed lunch Charlotte took a chicken filled pastry and bit into its crust. Steaming sauce burst onto her lip and she found herself in a most un-lady like position, juggling the hot pie from one corner of her mouth to the other. Edward watched on with a wicked smile. How he had missed this woman. True, he had only known her a few days before she returned to Hobart after the fires, but their exchanged letters since, hinted to Edward that she felt about him, what he felt about her.

Charlotte managed to finish the pastry and sip her tea, unfazed by her performance. She *was* famished after all. Her eyes hovered over the sandwiches and Charlotte plucked a curried egg from the middle tier. 'Aren't you eating?'

Edward grinned. 'I was enjoying watching you.'

'Stop it.' Charlotte said playfully. 'You better start, or I'll eat the lot.'

Edward stared at the tower a long moment. He had not long eaten, having taken a late stewed mutton and potato lunch at his hotel. After a moments deliberation he took the top salver, slipping it from the stand, complete with pastries and sandwiches. Charlotte laughed, not certain whether to tell the man etiquette dictated he take one item at a time, using the tongs provided. Edward stuffed a pastry in his mouth.

'That's the way,' Charlotte said, aware of pursed lips and wide eyes at neighbouring tables. 'So, where are you staying?'

'I've taken lodgings at the Caledonian Hotel ... in Elizabeth Street.'

'Yes, I know it.' Charlotte knew the address as a single man's lodgings. 'You said in your letter you've decided to move to Hobart permanently.'

'That's right.'

'Then we will have to find you more permanent lodgings. You can't afford to stay at the Caledonian.'

'Yer not wrong. Two bob a night.' Edward spilt gravy on his jacket and, reprimanding himself, he tucked his starched napkin behind his shirt collar, fanning it out over his shirt to avoid another accidental stain. This attracted more frowns from etiquette savvy diners. Edward was oblivious; he crammed another sandwich into his mouth and started talking. 'So, where've you been today then, if'n yer don't mind me askin', turnin' up in hired transport out the front like you was a princess?'

Charlotte told her friend about the mysterious murder and the events to date. 'Please keep this information to yourself,' Charlotte finished with a warning.

'So, have yer got a story for yer paper?'

'Not yet. There's more to this family than meets the eye.' Charlotte had a thought. 'You'll be looking for employment?'

'Aye.'

'Look, I'll have to talk to my editor, but the newspaper could do with a messenger and I just had a thought, perhaps you could also assist me.'

'Assist you?' Edward used his knife to spread jam on a scone, before licking the excess from the blade.

'Yes.' Charlotte didn't know whether she was smiling nervously at Edward's lack of table manners or the fact that all and sundry around them were now staring. 'You can ride a horse can you not, and I know you can drive a buggy?'

'Of course.'

'The newspaper owns two buggies for office personnel, but we are short one driver. That's why I had to hire Mr Timbal today.'

'You don't mean a stable-hand I trust?'

'Golly no, you'd be a liveryman. Oh, there might be some stabling …'

'I don't know Charlotte.' Edward looked horrified. He didn't come to Hobart to work in stables forking muck. Charlotte laughed. Edward sat upright. 'What?'

'You should see your face Edward. No, I wouldn't expect you to work in the stables, we have a regular boy, Jim.'

'Good. Then I would be interested.'

'I'll see you have other duties also, helping journalists from time to time.' Charlotte dropped her eyes innocently to the salmon pastry on her plate. 'And assisting me of course,' she said, picking up the pastry with a gloved hand.

Edward felt a warmth he had rarely experienced with other women. He felt comfortable with Charlotte. There was no pretention. *What you see is what you get.*

'I've read the book by the way,' Edward said out of nowhere, steering the subject in a new direction.

'Book?'

'Your father's book, *For the Term of His Natural Life*.'

'You did?'

'Yes. It took me a while, but I finally finished it last week.'

'Well,' Charlotte was surprised. 'I'm impressed. What did you think?'

'That Sir Richard Devine was a mongrel, that's wha' I think. But I thought yer Pa got the life and times in servitude pretty good, but the endin' was disappointing.'

'Oh?'

'Yer, when Richard and Sylvia died in that shipwreck.'

'Well, that's interesting you should say that, because that's where I have started *my* book, the continuation I told you about. To continue my father's story.'

'How can you possibly continue their story, if'n Sylvia and Richard both died?'

'You'll have to wait and see.' Edward wasn't convinced. 'No,' Charlotte agreed, and sighed. 'I don't know myself yet.'

Edward took another sandwich. 'Yer know, I can't stop thinkin' 'bout Annie Smith, poor lassie. An' the filthy ol' bugger what spoilt 'er.'

Charlotte wondered how much Edward had read of the court case. 'You know Reverend Finch is a free man.'

'Aye. I read your paper don't forget.'

'Yes, well spoil her he may have, but I don't think he killed her?'

'I know. An' we haven't a clue, do we?'

'No, we don't. But I'm like a dog with a bone Edward. I'll solve the mystery someday.'

Edward looked long and hard at Charlotte and wished his Pa could see him now in such genteel company, wearing his fine new clothes and in this fashionable establishment.

'If'n yer don't mind me askin',' Edward finally spoke. 'What exactly happened to yer husband? I mean, yer had difficulties yer told me, before he drowned, didn't yer?'

Charlotte took a moment. She had mixed feelings. She rarely talked about her marriage to Charles Claiborne. She was twenty-two when they married. She was in love with the horse trainer. But not two years into their marriage he changed. He grew surly and difficult to live with and occasionally abused her. Edward was aghast.

'What happened?' Immediately Edward realised his question was personal. 'Sorry, I didn't mean to pry.'

Charlotte was silent a moment. The memories were painful. 'He fell off a horse,' she finally said. 'He was breaking-in a new mare when he was thrown, landing on his head. He was lucky he didn't break his neck. However, he was a different man after that. He started drinking, staying out all night, all the usual hallmarks of a philanderer.'

'Oh, I'm sorry.'

'That's alright. I need to talk about it sometimes.' But Charlotte was strong willed, ambitious and would not tolerate Charles's indiscretions. She told Edward everything. 'He was like that doctor in Robert Louis Stevenson novella, Jekyll and Hyde,' Charlotte said. 'He had twin personalities. One minute he was a gentleman and the next a monster. Then, amongst all this he lost a thousand pounds in the financial crash of '91.'

'Thousand pounds!' Edward whistled.

'He helped train *Dunlop* the horse that won the 1887 Melbourne Cup and Mr Jonathon Donavan the owner gave him a thousand pounds of the winnings as a bonus.'

'A thou-thousand pounds,' Edward whistled. That was a sum difficult to imagine, especially as a gift. 'That was very generous.'

'That's what Charles thought. However, he invested it, unwisely as it turned out, and along came the financial crash.'

'You said he changed, started drinking. Did he ever ... ah ... like beat you?'

'Only once did he lay a hand on me.'

'What did you do?'

'Gave the wretch a black eye.'

Edward coughed a laugh. 'Good for you.'

'Not long after that he went on *that* fishing trip with his best friend Thomas. Thomas owned a small cutter and was an experienced sailor. They went often actually. But this day they ran into a storm and the cutter was badly damaged. Charles body was found washed up on Bruny Island, a mile from the wrecked cutter. Thomas's body was never found. It was awful, I had to identify him at the morgue.' Charlotte was silent a moment, the dreadful memory flooding back, casting a shadow of darkness over the room.

'I'm sorry,' Edward managed to whisper.

Charlotte took a deep breath. It suddenly seemed therapeutic to talk about it. 'Charles was a mangled mess. It was awful, his face shredded where the body had been dragged over rocks in the storm.'

Edward swallowed hard. 'I'm so sorry.'

'Don't be. Like I said, he was a monster. I told him I was leaving him only days before, and he threatened me.'

***

Morning, the Next day

Charlotte sent a message boy to The Caledonian Hotel.

Dear Edward, your position as liveryman and general assistant at The Mercury has been confirmed, applicable immediately.
I will expect you at the office by noon,
Your friend
Charlotte

Edward arrived an hour before noon, dressed in his new outfit from Henry Cook, the Tailor. With his attire and friendly beaming smile Edward was immediately accepted by Charlotte's colleagues. Everyone that is, except Leonard McShan who knew Edward as the poorly spoken country boy from Port Arthur.

The office stables were accessed from Argyle Street along a cobbled lane to an area at the rear of the newspaper building, opened back in '54,

Charlotte informed Edward. Jim the stable-hand appeared like a grubby apparition from the shadows offering Charlotte a hand to climb aboard the four-wheeled buggy, his hands stained with grime, or was it a tan common amongst those who spend most of their working days outdoors?

'Thank you, Jimmy,' Charlotte politely shied away from the offer for assistance. 'But I'm not an old maid, yet.'

Charlotte mounted the buggy step, landing on the seat. Edward steadied the horse, stroking its nose before climbing onto the seat next to Charlotte. He was still grinning.

'So, you've met Billy then,' Charlotte said of the horse.

'Aye, me and Billy'll be jus' fine,' he flicked the horse lightly into a walking pace canter down the narrow lane. 'So, where to Mrs Clarke?'

'Save the *Mrs Clarke* for when we are in the company of my seniors in the office.'

'Then where to, Charlotte?'

'New Town. Have you heard of Langley House?'

'Aye. I've heard talk of it at Port Arthur. It's an asylum for the elderly and destitute.'

'That's correct.' Edward nosed the horse and buggy onto Argyle Street, strapping the horse into a trot heading north. 'There's an old woman there, Mrs Genevieve Sayer. She is the aunt of Hyacinth Hambleton, the woman living in Richmond that I told you about yesterday.'

'Yes, and?'

'Well Genevieve is a wealthy woman. She is very old, late eighties I do believe. So, what is she doing left to die in a government institution? I smell a rat Edward.'

'And how did you come by this information?'

'I'm glad you ask. You and I will get along just fine. Here.' Charlotte showed Edward the letter and envelope stamped with the Langley House heading. 'While I was at Richmond, I borrowed this.'

'But it's addressed to Mrs H. Hambleton.'

Charlotte nodded a smile.

'Then you took it?'

'I borrowed it. She can have it back.'

'All right. So, what does it say?'

'It's a letter from the institution explaining Mrs Genevieve Sayer is terribly ill and she is not expected to live much longer. Now,' Charlotte leant forward to look Edward in the eye and make certain she had his attention. 'I made enquiries and paid a visit to the legal offices of Mr Murdoch, Mrs Sayer's solicitor, where I just happen to have a confidential contact who assures me Mrs Sayer is a very rich woman. Her husband was a shipbuilder and bequeathed her a fortune when he died. She has no children, no heir to inherit her property, except a niece who lives in the Cape Colony. Further investigations taught me that Mrs Hambleton is insolvent. Her home in Richmond is under threat of being foreclosed upon by the bank. Now here's the tantalising bit. Mrs Sayer developed senile dementia and her niece, who by the way hadn't been in contact with her for over a decade prior ...'

'You mean Mrs Hambleton?'

'Yes ... well she suddenly appears on the scene insisting her aunt come live with her. The house in Bellerive is boarded up with all its contents. Over a period of months, the aunt deteriorates further and is eventually bundled off into the institution, to die. Meanwhile, I surmise, Mrs Hambleton and her children have been visiting the house in Bellerive and slowly removing, or, a better word, stealing, all her possessions.'

'How's that?'

'Remember I told you the homestead in Richmond is crammed with fine furniture, fine artworks, crates of porcelain and silverware, antiques even.'

'An' you reckon they pilfered it from Bellerive?'

'I'm certain of it.'

'Can you prove it?'

'Not yet. But I will.' Charlotte was looking pleased with herself.

'So why are we travelling to New Town.'

'I would like to talk to the matron in charge, and hopefully see Mrs Sayer.'

As Charlotte and Edward were at first mistaken as distant relatives, their presence in the institution was frowned upon. 'No Mrs Bloodworth,'

Charlotte assured the matron. 'I am a journalist, and this is my assistant, Mr Culpepper.'

'Oh, what's a journalist doing here?'

'Well, I was hoping I could meet with Mrs Sayer.'

'Good Lord, you don't know then.'

'Know what?'

'Genevieve Sayer passed away two days ago.'

'Oh. That's a little awkward.'

'Pardon?'

'I meant … ah, I wasn't aware.'

'That's why I thought you were relatives, come to sweeten the old lady up in the hope of personal gain. She was quite wealthy I found out recently.'

'So I believe. When was the last time her niece Mrs Hambleton paid her a visit?'

'That dastardly woman. Demanding this and demanding that. I have only seen her here twice in eight months since Genevieve was committed. Both times she forced Genevieve to sign papers.'

'But Genevieve's mind was diseased. She suffered memory loss.'

'That did not stop the persistent woman from extracting a signature or two.'

'I was right,' Charlotte told Edward, hitching her skirt hem and climbing onto the buggy seat. 'That Hyacinth Hambleton has been up to no good and I'm going to prove it.

'Where to now then?'

'Savings Bank of Tasmania, in Murray Street.'

***

The Oaks Cottage and estate, Richmond.

Adelaide D'Boville-Hambleton had tried to hold her marriage to Ashley Hambleton together, for financial reasons if for no other. At first, she had bought sheet music and entertained her new husband and his family with piano soirees. She had the voice of an angel, so she was told. Adelaide learnt needlework and prepared samplers for each member of the family and in particular she groomed and walked Ashley's Irish Wolfhounds; and she purchased veterinary and pharmaceutical books so as to treat the dogs for any illnesses. But all to no avail, her stubborn father-in-law, the now deceased Osbert Hambleton, had taken a dislike to Adelaide from the beginning.

It was during this time that Hyacinth and Osbert decided to live apart. Hyacinth moving back into the family cottage-homestead and estate, *The Oaks*, while Osbert remained at Davey Street, a large family home they had purchased decades earlier. The only family member Osbert missed was Phillipa, his youngest.

Adelaide was never happy with the move to Richmond. Her dowry had long been spent by Ashley on a lifestyle they could ill afford and on poor investments in the ailing stock market. As the months passed by, Ashley became morose, while his unwise investments deteriorated. He was never savvy as a financial broker. He made bad judgements, trying to bounce back by investing heavily with misappropriated client funds – another reason for the move into the country where he could avoid confrontation.

Hyacinth Hambleton struggled also. Adelaide lived with the arguments. Her husband and his mother fought often. Always about money. Osbert Hambleton, meanwhile, enjoyed his bachelor life. Cared for by his part-time housekeeper Mrs Eleanor Hark, who baked him pies and left cold roasted meats for the days she wasn't at the Davey Street property. And it was this property, Adelaide knew, that also caused many of the financial woes. Hyacinth wanted her husband to sell. He could move into the cottage at Richmond. But Osbert was having none of it.

Meanwhile life at *The Oaks* became boringly repetitious and frugal. Adelaide became more and more despondent, aloof from the corrupted blood line of the Hambleton's.

***

The Savings Bank of Tasmania, Hobart. Just before Easter.
A flirtatious smile from a pretty young woman goes a long way in the male dominated world of banking. The second smile saw Charlotte sitting before

Cecil Winthrop at his desk in the general manager's office of The Savings Bank of Tasmania. The bank was finally clawing its way out of the pit of the depression that had affected so many businesses early in the '90s.

Cecil Winthrop had all the time in the world. He was content to entertain Charlotte while they waited on the clerk to bring Mrs Genevieve Sayer's file from storage. Files that Charlotte convinced the man, may lead to embarrassing discrepancies the bank knew nothing about.

Winthrop's office was comparatively small, Charlotte thought, for the office of a major bank. Small, yet tidy and neat with a strong scent of recently oiled furniture. All Tasmanian blackwood, she noted. Even the hatstand was blackwood, where the manager's shiny top hat hung at a rakish angle on the top peg. The sixty-year-old bank manager's conservative old school, dovetailed coat hung beneath it. Like her editor Rupert Craddock, Mr Winthrop relied on pince-nez to bring his daily world into focus. The man was overweight with a walrus moustache, curled and waxed, reminding Charlotte of a vaudeville magician. Winthrop made polite conversation. 'Do you like dogs Miss Clarke?'

'Mrs.'

'Pardon?'

'Mrs Clarke.'

'Oh, do forgive me, Mrs Clarke.'

'Dogs. Why yes, I love dogs.

'I have a Pomeranian myself, Toots.' Charlotte wanted to laugh. 'Yes, I know,' Winthrop cringed. 'My wife named him.'

A knock at the door killed their conversation. The clerk entered, placing a file on the desk. 'Thank you, Humphrey.' Winthrop tipped his head back, the better to read the bookwork before him through his thick lensed glasses. 'Here we are. The balance sheet for 1897 to '98.' The manager read a moment. Finally, he looked to his visitor who had drawn his attention to what potentially could be a liability to the bank. Weighing up the situation Winthrop decided Charlotte could possibly be of use.

'My, there have been some large withdrawals these past months.' Sudden concern furrowed the man's brow. 'Large amounts here have been transacted from Burns Auctioneers, the jeweller Kohen Ariel ... here's one from Clyde Brewer for six hundred and eighty pounds.' Winthrop became animated, scrutinising page after page. 'Several transfers for varying amounts in rather large sums have been paid into the account of Mr Ashley Hambleton.'

'That's Mrs Hambleton's son, he's about my age.'

Immediately the bank manager was sickened. Had forgery and deceit been practised under his nose? He read on. Nine hundred pounds had been transferred from Sotheby's; Charlock Stockbrokers one thousand two hundred pounds; two thousand two hundred and thirty pounds from Anderson & Craig purveyors in realty; four hundred and five hundred pounds from Franklin Gallery, Dealers in Fine Art, Sydney. Cecil P. Winthrop broke out in a fine sweat.

'But there are letters here signed by Mrs Sayer approving all these transactions,' he said, his voice quivering doubt. 'Here.' Winthrop passed Charlotte a handful and she noted many were neat and professional using modern typing machines.

'I'm no expert Mr Winthrop but I would like to compare these signatures of Mrs Sayers with Mrs Hambleton's handwriting.'

'These are serious accusations Mrs Clarke.'

'They are indeed.'

'Oh, dear me,' Winthrop looked positively pale.

'I implore you to be discreet sir, until I can prove my suspicions correct.'

Instantly Winthrop became defensive. 'You aren't going to publish these discrepancies, if they prove to be discrepancies, in the newspaper, are you?'

'I'm an investigative journalist Mr Winthrop. More than anything I would like to see justice done. This woman, this Hyacinth Hambleton, needs to be made accountable.' Cecil Winthrop had turned a sickly shade of grey. 'But to answer your question sir, no, I certainly would not be party to making public accusations until the woman is charged accordingly.'

Charlotte pondered the severity of the situation a moment. Before her, on the manager's desk were dozens of documents and letters. She needed proof and now she had the bank manager, a prominent Hobart citizen, thoroughly spooked. Raised voices at one of the teller windows drew the man's attention. Humphrey was doing his best to defuse a situation with a dissatisfied customer who was becoming increasingly boisterous.

'This is most irregular,' Winthrop's grey face flushed pink. 'Please excuse me a moment.'

Charlotte watched the bank manager join the fray, puffing out his chest from the safety of the teller's cage, doing his best to quell the uncouth customer.

She would have to be quick. Charlotte chose three letters – folded then in half and half again before slipping them into her satchel. If she looked slightly guilty on the manager's return, she wasn't suspected of skulduggery.

'It's been a pleasure meeting you Mrs Clarke.' Winthrop remained standing. He took another look at the documents and sighed. 'Now if you will excuse me, I must bundle this lot off to our legal team.'

***

The Mercury offices.
Edward wheeled the buggy over the cobbles, parking the vehicle in the red brick stables at the rear of *The Mercury* offices. Stable-hand Jim, who had heard them approach, forked hay for Billy into the stall from the loft overhead, before scaling down the vertical ladder like an experienced seafarer in the rigging.

'Ol' Billy got the job done orright Missus?' Jim asked of the horse. He was about to offer Charlotte a hand to alight, before thinking twice.

'Yes Jimmy. Thank you.' Charlotte and Edward watched Jimmy a moment. He unhitched Billy, fastening him to a short leather halter in a stall where the horse would remain stabled, awaiting its next duty on the streets. Neither were aware they were being observed from a first-floor window.

'Some cove were 'ere lookin' for yer,' Jim said casually forking more hay, now mixed well with oats, into the stall.

'Who?'

'Dunno Missus, wouldn't say. 'e were 'bout your age 'n a bit nettled.'

'Oh?'

'Aye. I'm thinkin' 'e were a lawman.'

Charlotte hooked her satchel and parasol over her arm before looking up at the rear of the offices. A figure stepped back from the window.

'I have to write up my notes,' she told Edward. 'Enjoy the rest of the afternoon. I'll see you here tomorrow.'

Charlotte crossed the small yard between the stables and offices, where she walked into a verbal ambush. Senior Constable Toby Hutton hurried down the stairs skipping the last three treads in one leap. 'What do you think you're up to Mrs Clarke?'

Mrs Clarke?

'Constable Hutton!'

The lawman hooked his hands onto his hips. 'Senior Constable Hutton.'

'Fine. What are you doing here?'

'Who do you think you are, interfering with the law?'

Charlotte's eyes narrowed. 'What?'

'You were in Richmond recently.'

'So, what if I was?'

'You were there specifically to poke your nose where it does not belong.'

'If you are talking about Mrs Hambleton, then I have as much right to talk to the woman as you do.'

'Not when you arrive before the police, asking all those questions, getting the woman riled.'

'Riled. The woman is a thief!' The moment Charlotte said this in heated argument she bit her tongue.

'What did you say?'

Charlotte thought she best be careful, or she will have a lawsuit on her hands. Charlotte dropped her voice. 'Mrs Hyacinth Hambleton is hardly the sad recent widow, nor is she exactly honest.'

'And how did you deduce that, Sherlock?' Hutton said with unmeasured sarcasm.

'Don't Sherlock me.' Charlotte took in a deep breath. 'Did you not take notice of all the fine furniture, art works and silverware packed floor to ceiling like it was a warehouse?'

Hutton looked a little defeated. 'I wasn't afforded the luxury of being invited inside; no doubt the woman was wary after your visit.'

'I can't be held accountable if I am on the ball and you are not, Senior Constable Hutton.'

The policeman chewed his bottom lip. He had an alternate axe to grind. 'What's that hick doing in Hobart anyhow?' he finally asked, having watched Edward from the window.

'If you speak of Edward Culpepper, then I suggest you do not slander the man. He has integrity, unlike other acquaintances I know.'

'Integrity! Huh. He's just the son on a convicted felon. Edward's father *is* the thief ...'

Charlotte's face reddened. She was angry but thought it wise to tread carefully. 'You finished?'

'Finished. Me finished? Why I haven't even started yet.' Hutton dared step within a breath of Charlotte. If she didn't know any better, she may have thought the man had fallen for her. *He was jealous! Yes, that was it.* Toby Hutton was jealous of Edward. 'You mark my words Charlotte ...'

'Mrs Clarke!'

'Mrs Clarke. You mark my words. You tell that ... that *hick*, to keep his nose out of police business.'

'Mr Culpepper is employed by the newspaper. He works for me.'

Hutton's face was scarlet with anger. His eyes black and radiating bitterness. 'You've been warned,' he seethed, turning on his heels.

CHAPTER FIVE

April 10ᵗʰ Easter Sunday, 1898

Cole Sawyer was already in the mud and shit deeper than he anticipated. But the swampy paddocks directly north of the abattoirs on Hobart's waterfront – near where the stinking town rivulet passed through Wapping before spilling into the harbour – were lucrative. For it was in this wasteland that the resilient rag and bone man eked a living. Today though, recent rains turned the ground into a quagmire. Sawyer's hobnail boots – salvaged from the morgue – squelched in the muck as the hundred-and ten-pound vagrant searched for anything he could turn to farthings and pennies. He was feeling reasonable about himself this morning. Slung over his back, his hessian sack was heavy with glass marble bottles. These cordial bottles, with the marble stopper in the neck, were returnable to their original breweries, breweries like Kelly and Co., Weaver and the Cascade Brewery. The only downside was the bottles were heavy. Bloody heavy.

But at a penny for every dozen collected ... why he must have a good sixpence coming his way this day.

But fate had other plans.

Half a mile west, Hobart's GPO clock struck six in the morning. One minute later something rather special caught the old man's attention. A woman's shoe. White and brown leather. *Quality*. Pleased with his find he searched for the other, finding it a yard away. A pair of ladies' shoes was a great find. Why, he'd probably manage a shilling for the pair. Like anyone who finds a coin on the footpath, Cole Sawyer looked about for anything else of value when he saw the owner of the shoes.

'Jesus Lord!' the old man blasphemed aloud. 'Oh, Jesus!' She lay face down in the mud, semi-naked and clearly dead. Dumping his bag where he was, the bagman turned for town and, crossing back over the railway lines, he made his way as fast as possible to the watch house.

Senior Constable Toby Hutton waded through the mulch to the crime scene where a doctor and what appeared to be a nurse stood over the body. Cole Sawyer sat on a dry patch of ground nearby.

'Is that the man who found her?' Hutton asked the night watchman first on the scene. The man had been guarding the site for an hour now and was keen to retire for the day. 'That's 'im guv'nor.'

'Name?'

'They call 'im *The Landlord*.'

'The *Landlord*?'

'Aye, cos 'e's a vagrant and lives anywhere 'e fancies.'

'Do you happen to know the name his mother gave him?'

'Yes sar, Cole Sawyer.'

Hutton watched the old scrawny vagrant for a moment. He sat on a rise in the swamp busy cleaning muck off the glass bottles he'd collected before placing them back into a sack. Sawyer had already told the watchman he hadn't seen anyone acting suspiciously in the area this morning, so Hutton decided to leave him be, when he heard voices approaching.

Inspector Boothman and three uniforms trudged carefully towards the crime scene, all wearing Wellington boots, or wellies as they were called. Hutton looked to his own messed shoes and wished he had thought to do the same.

'Wait there,' Boothman ordered the policemen. He walked over to Hutton. 'You got here smartly then.'

'Yes sir, I arrived early at the watch house just after the alarm was raised.

The inspector nodded towards to the doctor and nurse. 'Have you spoken to them?'

'No sir, I haven't had a chance.'

'Do we know who the victim is?'

'Don't think so.'

Boothman sighed. Noting the doctor's footprints, he approached the body step for step so as not to confuse the crime scene. 'She was deceased when you arrived, I trust?' he asked the physician.

'Yes. We came immediately from the hospital the moment the watchman sent for us.'

'She's been attacked,' the nurse said, clearly shaken. Boothman nodded. 'And violated,' she added.

'Any identification?'

The doctor shook his head. 'Not that we can see.'

'Thank you,' Boothman said. 'You can leave now; the coroner has been notified. Make certain you take the same path out.' Boothman pointed to their original tracks. Hutton now joined him.

The two men studied the corpse. Her naked back was lacerated. Her skirt and petticoats had been ripped off and her tan coat rucked up under her breast. Pantaloons were missing and underclothing twisted about her ankles.

'She has scratches on her head and wounds to her back. I would suggest she was throttled, strangled, managed to get away and then stabbed trying to escape,' Boothman said. Hutton swallowed hard.

'See the undergarment,' Boothman continued. 'It is snagged and shredded.' You,' Boothman called to the three uniforms. 'Leave the stretcher for the coroner, he will be here shortly. Spread out and look for anything unusual. You are looking for a murder weapon, a knife most likely. You too Toby, I want this dung heap thoroughly searched.'

***

Hobart Morgue, Davey Street. Later that morning.
Francis Francesco had the darkest feeling. She had heard of the body found in the swamp. News travelled quickly in a small community. She had returned from the Easter Sunday service at St Mary's Cathedral to loose lips and accusing eyes. Her niece Rosa Esposito had not returned home from an

evening out. Rosa was sixteen but acted and looked older than her age. She was somewhat a wild child, difficult to handle. Rosa's mother and father, Maida and Paolo Esposito, lived in Melbourne and had sent their daughter to live with her aunt Francis eight and a half months earlier, hoping Maida's older sister Francis, a devout Catholic, would be a stabilising influence.

Coroner and divisional police surgeon Doctor Edwin P Jones, an American practitioner from Philadelphia now settled in Hobart, dreaded personal contact with grieving relatives. An atheist, he was a middle-aged man with hazel hair, oiled and combed flat with deep-set dark brown eyes. Eyes that had stared death in the face on many an occasion. Today he worked on Rosa's body, although often he would appoint another surgeon to conduct the autopsia, as he preferred to call the examination. 'Post-mortem sounds so uncouth,' he would tell his colleagues. 'Some call the procedure necropsy, but that is in effect just the dissecting of corpses. Autopsia better describes the science, I feel.'

Today he was to be assisted by medical officer Doctor Claude Argyle, as it was always best two surgeons conduct the autopsy, to avoid errors.

Francis Francesco walked into the medical examiner's laboratory on the heels of a young inexperienced student, not certain of the protocol in this awkward situation. Rosa's body was laid out on a marble slab with a shallow gutter running the full perimeter for collecting blood and other bodily fluids that might escape. The cadaver's womanhood was covered for modesty, otherwise the victim was naked. Although electric lighting was connected, large rectangular windows from waist height to the ceiling flooded the coroner's laboratory with ample daylight. Opened shutters at the top allowed odious odours escape. Generous wooden benches running the full length of both sides of the room were busy with numerous items normally found in laboratories, like microscopes for identifying the presence of blood in comparison to other substances, as well as hair or fibres adhering to a murder weapon or on the body. The slab was surrounded with dissection equipment; scalpels, tweezers and scissors. And for examining internal organs requiring removal, like the stomach, Doctor Jones found a photographer's developing tray ideal.

Francis Francesco's wailing could be heard throughout the morgue, confirming the identity of the victim.

Boothman was summoned and met the grieving woman in an interview room at the coroner's office. He arrived to console her twenty minutes later.

'She was just a baby,' Francis cried. 'My sister bambino, I not know how I can tell her thees news.'

'I know this is difficult,' the inspector said. 'But I must ask you some questions if I am to piece together what happened to Rosa.'

'She baby,' the woman sobbed. 'She so young.'

'Please tell me about her.'

Francis blew her nose, wiping tears from her cheeks. 'Rosa, she strong. Rosa think she's a woman. *Aunt Francis* she say, *Rosa look after herself. Rosa a woman now* she say. She worry me bad. Sometime she go away and not tell me.'

'Oh, go where?'

'She leave school without permission, and go swimming, with boys I'm thinkeen. One night she stay away till morning. I angry. Angry, worry and sad.'

'Where was she last night? Did Rosa tell you where she was going?'

Francis looked ashamed. 'She with boy.'

'Do you know this boy's name, where he lives?'

'Samuel. His name Samuel.'

'Samuel who?'

'I don't know these things.'

'Do you know where we can find him?'

'He work at Gas Company. He what they say … stoker … si, stoker Rosa say.'

***

The Mercury Offices, Macquarie Street.
Charlotte heard of the murder early afternoon Easter Sunday when Aunt Jocelyn returned from the Sunday service at St David's Cathedral on the corner of Murray and Macquarie Streets. Making suitable excuses not to

join Aunt in church, Charlotte had spent her morning studying the legal letters she had misappropriated from bank manager Cecil Winthrop's desk.

Comparing signatures would have to wait until she could confirm an expert opinion of Hyacinth Hambleton's handwriting for comparison. However, of particular interest were the typing anomalies Charlotte noticed as she floated her magnifying glass over the print. Some capital letters appeared blotched as if worn, while other lower-case letters were either over-inked or even slightly damaged. It suddenly occurred to Charlotte that maybe typing machines could be like fingerprints, each with their own distinct or subtle differences. If so, she may be able to identify the machine used, and in doing so, incriminate the owner for forgery and misappropriation. For now, though, the news of the body of a girl in the swamp was spreading about Hobart like a nasty influenza.

Although the newspaper offices were closed, by 6PM Charlotte had visited the crime scene, interviewed policemen who were left behind to keep ghouls at bay, and already had enough information for a front-page story. Enough anyway, for a headline and four paragraphs. Now Charlotte worked in solitary in the Literary Department, although in a separate cramped building at the rear of the property the compositing and typesetting team continued late into the night. She worked alone, so Charlotte thought.

George Davies, son of John George Davies the newspaper's owner, had slipped into the room silently, leaving the door ajar, watching Charlotte in silence, secretly. He had been attracted to the journalist's office by the tap, tap of the lone typewriter, having already held back the production of Monday's *Mercury* in preparation for Charlotte's story. Now the print room waited. George lingered until Charlotte extricated the page from her machine. She proofread her article.

'Well, well,' the voyeur finally approached from behind. 'So, it's you!' he feigned surprise, closing the door noisily behind him. Charlotte jumped. 'Sorry to surprise you,' he said.

Charlotte had been in deep concentration. 'Oh ... I thought I was alone.'

'No, good old George is here with you, keeping you company in the twilight hours.'

Twilight hours! Charlotte suddenly realised night had settled in. She looked at the wall clock. 7.45PM.

'So, you're the enthusiastic journalist covering the murder? I must commend you on your dedication.'

'Oh ... I ... well when I heard of this ... this awful murder, well, I just couldn't help myself.'

'Don't you have a man in your life? It's Easter Sunday.'

'No.' Immediately Charlotte thought her answer too hasty. 'Ah, well.' She changed tack. 'I'm too busy for ... for that.'

'For that?' George smiled at the word. *That.* He was silent a moment holding Charlotte's eye. This woman was pleasantly comfortable in figure. George liked that. Tall long-legged women with slim waistlines and generous in the breast were not really his cup of tea. Certainly, he had bedded a few, well truth be known he had bedded more than a few. But Charlotte had an intelligence about her and a history. Research within the building had taught him Charlotte was no spinster. She had been married and lost her husband in a boating accident. At least she was a woman of the world. And if he was honest with himself, he had a penchant for petite redheads.

'Here,' Charlotte broke them from their reverie. 'All finished.' She passed George the paper. 'I must be getting home; I didn't realise how fast the time had flown.'

'All finished huh?' he took the paper and studied it. 'Half a column. Perfect. Say, are you hungry?'

'What?' Charlotte was taken aback. Strange question. She was famished and just realised she missed Auntie's Sunday roast. 'Sorry, I meant pardon?'

'Are you hungry? Would you like to join me for dinner?'

'Dinner?'

'Yes. I dare say you haven't eaten, and I'm famished. The Customs House Hotel serve meals until nine, care to join me?'

'I ... ah ...' this was so unexpected.

'My treat.'

It all seemed so surreal all of a sudden. 'Your treat?' Charlotte smiled back before thinking things through. 'Then how could I refuse?'

'Excellent. I'll fetch my coat and take this to the lads in the newsroom.' George waved Charlotte's manuscript before him. 'And be back in two shakes of a lamb's tail, what.'

***

The Customs House Hotel, opposite Waterman's Dock and Parliament House. Maree was one of Hobart's finest publicans, an articulate, intelligent entrepreneur and attractive older woman who had maintained an excellent reputation through sober habits and Sunday church attendance. And pity help any patron who stepped out of line. Drunkenness or profanity would see you out the door. The no-nonsense hotelier was a rare breed, a rare breed indeed, where most female publicans around the docks were also madams who ran bordellos.

'Show Mr Davies to his usual table,' Maree ordered the waitress. Being Easter Sunday business was winding down earlier than most nights. The publican barely took notice of Charlotte, another of the newspaper heir's indiscretions, she thought quietly.

With only the choice of two dishes on the menu available after a busy evening, George ordered beefsteak and mashed potatoes for them both. To drink Charlotte ordered a sarsaparilla, while George ordered a bottle of French Bordeaux, two glasses.

Service was sharp. The taproom was emptying and Maree's grandson, earning a few shillings washing glasses in the scullery, was making more noise than necessary. George poured both glasses, insisting Charlotte try the full-bodied red wine with its earthy aromas of blackcurrant. After a mouthful of sarsaparilla Charlotte found the wine's tannins mouth-drying. The second mouthful was more agreeable.

George Davies felt the effects of the alcohol on an empty stomach course through his veins. The meals arrived and they started eating immediately.

'If I may be so bold as to ask,' he said. 'Why is such an attractive woman as yourself alone in this word?'

'Alone sir?'

'Please call me George.'

'I'm not alone.'

'No?'

'No. I have many friends, some of them gentlemen.'

'Oh. And suitors?'

'Golly, now you *are* being bold si' ... George.'

The wine was exposing the libertine. George's eyes were hardly discreet. Whilst Charlotte thought the man quite handsome, debonair and athletic, she found this indiscretion unnerving, if not flattering. 'Well?' he persisted, his glassy eyes wandering.

'I have suitors, yes.' Charlotte ached for silence. She just wanted to eat, and the beef was really very good, well cooked and tender with plenty of gravy.

'Suitors!' George's reply sounded doubtful. 'Do you really?' Was he suddenly jealous? George noticed Charlotte blush and reigned in his rhetoric. 'Your father was Marcus Clarke the novelist I heard.'

'Yes.' A measure of enthusiasm returned with the change of subject.

'He died when you were quite young, is that correct?'

'I was ten when Papa died.'

'Ten, how awful. How old was your father ... when he passed?'

'Thirty-five.'

'Goodness, that is too young.'

'Yes. Papa enjoyed life to the full and died young in the process. His fame came later.'

'It seems to happen to many artists,' George said. 'Posthumous fame. Are there royalties?'

'Very little with five siblings to share it with. Besides my father, like his own father, died a bankrupt.'

'How strange.'

'As I said, Papa enjoyed life; there was no chance of him accumulating wealth, no likelihood of him ever amassing a fortune.'

'Any other family here in Hobart?"

'All my relatives are either living in Victoria or back in England.'

'Your father was quite the character I am told. A Bohemian by all accounts.'

'Yes. Like his own father, my grandfather, William Clarke. He was a barrister in London. Unfortunately, Papa lost his mother, Emelia, when he was four, so his father brought him up. Papa was a lone child, and my grandfather was also Bohemian, as you put it, leaving my Papa to grow up with nannies while he was enjoying the nightlife London offered. This upbringing taught Papa expensive habits that later in life he could ill afford.'

'Interesting.'

'Papa was under financial pressure when he passed, he had filed for bankruptcy for the second time, in '81, the year he died.'

'That's so sad. So young. He was ill was he not?'

'He suffered pleurisy, and this developed into congestion of the liver and finally erysipelas which killed him within a week.'

'Erysipelas?'

'It is a serious bacterial infection that affects the skin. Otherwise known as St Anthony's fire due to the intense rash associated with it.'

'How awful.'

Charlotte had a quiet moment of contemplation. 'Yes, thirty-five-years-old. He left behind a wife and six of us children all under the age of eleven.' Charlotte had a more positive thought. 'He also left behind an unfinished opera libretto titled *Queen Venus* but I am happy to say the work was completed a few years ago by Henri Kowalski as *Moustique* and premiered on stage in 1889.'

'An opera?'

'Yes, he was versatile. Papa wrote many short stories also, plays and satires, as well as novels, collections of stories and performances for the theatre.'

'*For the Term of His Natural Life* was one of his best sellers I believe?'

Charlotte. 'Have you read it?'

'No, sorry. I don't read much.'

'And you are a newspaper man?' Charlotte wanted to add, *shame on you.*

Her host seemed to take this personally. 'I can't possibly read everything, I edit, proofread. Reading can become quite tedious sometimes.'

Charlotte altered the direction of the conversation. 'You recently returned from London?'

'Yes.'

'What's it like?'

'London? It's big. Actually, I'm finding Hobart rather like a little village since I returned. A little claustrophobic.'

'Yet I am certain there is an abundance of single women there, for a bachelor I should imagine.'

'Now *you* are being presumptuous.' This comment with a smile.

Charlotte was enjoying her meal too much to spoil the mood so soon. 'Well?'

'Well, what?'

'You don't have a lady in your life?'

'I was betrothed, in London.'

'Oh, and what happened?' *That was the wine asking.* 'Ah ... I mean ... if you don't mind me enquiring.'

'Her name was Bethany, Bethany Cordelia Cadbury.'

'As in the chocolate?'

'No. At least I don't think so. We ... our relationship finished rather abruptly.'

Charlotte forked a larger piece of meat into her mouth than intended and felt gravy dribble over her lip. George reached across and dabbed her chin with his serviette. Charlotte felt surprisingly comfortable, while George had *that* look in his eye once more.

'Well,' she said, her full mouth disguised behind her own napkin.

'Well, what?'

'Miss Cadbury?'

'She ... she was caught seeing another.'

'Another man?'

'Another woman actually.'

'Oh golly.' Charlotte started to laugh.

'It's not funny Charlotte. Have you got any idea what that does to a man's ... ego?'

'No. Another woman huh?' Of course, Charlotte had heard of such in-discretions between two women but had never met any women lovers. 'My apologies. It must have been devastating.'

George filled both glasses. 'It was. It was humiliating.'

Charlotte was thinking *your manhood was at stake, that is what really hurt.* The wine *was* actually really good. Charlotte went on to explain her plan to write a novel to continue her father's story. A sequel, of sorts. But George Davies felt more comfortable talking about himself. Finally, meal over, they stepped onto the docks where they were greeted by a sharp late evening chill in off the harbour.

'You live in Macquarie Street do you not?' he asked.

'Yes.'

He summoned Charlotte a single horse fly, one of four parked on the docks awaiting business. 'Thank you for your company, Charlotte.' George leant forward, ever so slightly. He took Charlotte's hand to assist her onto the seat, only to steal a kiss, his wine wet lips caressing the back of her hand.

It was approaching 10.30PM. In fact, the grandfather clock in the passageway chimed the half hour not long after Charlotte let herself into Agapanthus Cottage. All else was silent, when Aunt Jocelyn called down the stairs from the first-floor landing. 'You're home dear?'

'Yes Auntie.'

'Good, now I can sleep.'

'Yes, go back to bed.'

Aunt Jocelyn had been a mother to Charlotte, and she loved her dearly. But she was twenty-seven. *I can look after myself,* Charlotte thought, and as if to prove a point she extracted her stiletto blade an inch or two from the parasol handle, admiring its shiny steel three-sided blade, before placing her protector alongside other umbrellas and walking sticks in the hall stand.

10.45PM

Charlotte was too enlivened from her dinner engagement and red wine to sleep. The house was quiet. *Good time to do some writing.*

Charlotte brushed her teeth with John Gosnell's Cherry toothpowder, her favourite with the portrait of Queen Victoria on the pottery lid and propped an extra pillow at her back to sit up comfortably in bed. She looked at her manuscript on the bedside table. Her sequel to her father's famous novel was well under way. Charlotte re-read a paragraph here, a paragraph there. She was pleased with her efforts. But the fact remained: walking in her father's literary footsteps was a daunting prospect. She had her main protagonists, Richard Devine and Sylvia Vickers who, in *For the Term of His Natural Life*, had drowned in a shipwreck. But Charlotte had 'resurrected' them as survivors. In her novel, titled *Beyond the Seas of Tyranny*, the two actually survived the storm, and the bodies found were those of other passengers on the doomed ship.

Charlotte wrote for over an hour. The wine was wearing off. Old grandfather downstairs chimed midnight. Charlotte extinguished the flame in her spirit lamp and lay in darkness a moment wondering if and how she could write George Davies into her story. Lately she had thought of Edward as she wrote about Richard Devine. But George would make an interesting character also …

Edward, George …

Pleasant memories of both men were soon clouded by darkness and Charlotte was borne into a deep sleep.

CHAPTER SIX

The Oaks Cottage and estate, Richmond. Easter Monday morning. Early.
Adelaide D'Borville was up early and in the dairy, milking the estate's one remaining cow, China. China as in pottery, named because of her predominantly white hide. Only two servants remained employed at the property, now that times were lean; Maryanne the housekeeper come cook come cleaner, and the yard-hand Frank, who had grown old and lazy. This morning Adelaide fetched the milk while Maryanne baked.

With the door propped wide open to the dairy the welcome morning sun spilt across the flagstones. Adelaide sat on a squat stool and milked. Minutes passed. The milk bucket was less than quarter full when China tugged at her rope. The old Friesian attempted to look behind her. She smelt a stranger. At that same moment a man's shadow unfurled across the dairy floor. Adelaide jumped.

'Sorry there Miss,' a deep voice apologised. 'Didn't mean to scare you none.'

'Who are you?'

The good-looking, tall, fair stranger whipped the weathered slouch hat from his head in a clumsy, yet gentlemanly manner. 'Morton Dunbar. Jackaroo.'

'Jackaroo?' Although Adelaide spoke fluent English, this was a word not in her vocabulary.

By now Morton Dunbar recognised her accent. 'French huh?'

'Flemish. What is a jackaroo?'

'All-rounder hired help miss. I can and will do anything.'

'What do you want?'

'Is the master about, the missus maybe?'

'I am the missus and my husband is in the house.'

'Oh, my apologies mam. Good lord, you're the missus huh? Well, I never?'

'Never what?' Adelaide grew haughty.

'Never seen such a lovely sight.' Dunbar leant rakishly on one shoulder against the door frame and crossed his arms. 'The missus of the house on a milkin' stool.'

The cheek!

Adelaide cast a chary eye the length of the man's physique. He was certainly a fine specimen of a man. He was muscular beneath tight-fitting khaki shirt and trousers. *Had he been a soldier maybe?* Realising she had been staring, Adelaide continued milking. 'So, what are you doing here?'

'Looking for work.'

'We have none here?'

'Oh? I saw fences that need attending to on the way here. I ...'

'We can't afford you,' Adelaide said sharply. When she thought she may have been a little too harsh she added, 'Look, money has been a little short around here of late. We simply don't have the extra funds to hire a ... well someone just to repair fences.'

The wealth misappropriated from the Sayer Estate was a frustrating secret at the moment and Adelaide knew, at all costs, it must be kept that way. For now, anyway.

'Oh, to be honest with you, mam, I'm a little strapped myself,' Dunbar said. 'But the fact is, I'll work for a bed and grub.'

'Grub?' Adelaide queried, standing to stretch her aching back. 'You mean food?'

'Yes mam. Just a week or two would help me on my way.'

Morton Dunbar's affable smile won Adelaide over. He was certainly a handsome man and now in the light she noticed his eyes were different colours, one blue and one brown. This was rare condition she had heard about but had never observed. The jackaroo had nailed her vulnerability. 'Here mam, let me do that.' And Morton sat like a milk maid, tugging at China's teats two at a time, draining the udder in a masterly fashion. Adelaide watched on; a smile appeared on her face. For once she had thoughts outside her failing marriage. A fantasy even.

***

Easter Monday. Agapanthus Cottage.
Charlotte woke early, a little groggy. She conducted her toiletries, dressed and prepared her own breakfast – oats cooked in hot milk, sugar and black-berries – while the remainder of the house slept. It was barely 6AM. Charlotte had a story of misadventure to complete for *The Mercury*, another crime to solve. She owed it to Rosa Esposito, the victim found dead in the swamp. The night before, Charlotte gave Jimmy the stable-hand a sixpence along with a message, for Nellie Nichols at the police station. Nellie was an archivist in the police record office and a valuable acquaintance with a strong sense of freedom of information. Besides, her clandestine gathering of information for her journalist friend had aided and abetted the capture of several criminals in the past.

A good policeman, a professional detective, once told Charlotte the most crucial times for solving a murder, were the first twenty-four hours, before the trail of clues ran dry. No wonder Charlotte was incredulous when Nellie told her, 'Most of the police assigned to the case are having Easter Monday off.'

'Why?'

'The general line of reasoning is that the murdered girl was just another statistic, that she should not have been roaming around on her own in the first place and ...'

'And that she asked for it!' Charlotte spat. 'Balderdash.'

The two had met one block from the police station, and intentionally early, before the entire world awoke. Nellie, wearing a beret coquettishly an-gled over her jet-black hair, looked about uncomfortably. If she were to be recognised with Charlotte, she would lose her position at the Police

Department immediately. Although it was a general holiday for all, prying eyes were still about. 'Can we go somewhere, somewhere private?'

Charlotte knew the proprietor of Warner's Tea Rooms next door to Pool's Boot Palace in Elizabeth Street. Here, private booths in a back room were often occupied by discreet lovers. They waited on the west side of the street for the Number 2 double decker electric tram to pass before crossing. The main street was busy for an Easter holiday and a horse-drawn four-wheeled buggy passed the tram on the blind side at a gallop, causing a family to run for the footpath. Yelling attracted attention.

'Come,' Nellie said, slipping behind onlookers and into the tea rooms.

'That imbecile could have killed someone,' Nellie said, once inside, shaking her head. 'Doesn't he know vehicles must only travel at a cantor along the main streets?'

A rather frumpy wench with a floury apron met them. 'If'n yer be wantin' a hot breakfast the stoves ain't really hot yet.'

Having already eaten breakfast, Charlotte ordered a pot of coffee and two cups before taking a seat in the back room where they were alone. 'Sometimes I wish I had the authority to arrest people like that,' Nellie went on, still cranky about the speeding rider.

'*You* become a policewoman?' Charlotte tutted. 'Good luck with that.'

'You never know Charlotte. There's talk of women getting the vote soon.'

'So, what do you have for me?'

'Which case first? The Hambleton's or the girl in the swamp?'

'The girl in the swamp.'

Nellie opened her over shoulder bag taking out pages of notes. 'I copied these from Boothman's report last night.'

'Boothman!' Charlotte repeated the inspector's name. This was great news. 'Well done Nellie.'

'Please be discreet Charlotte. If I were to be caught, I imagine Boothman would reintroduce *drawn and quartering* after I was hanged.'

Charlotte read quickly. 'So, Rosa Esposito was sixteen ... living with her aunt, Francis Francesco ... address, Wignall Street North Hobart ... mother, Maida, lives in Melbourne ...last seen with Samuel ... Samuel who?'

'Doesn't say.'

Charlotte read on. 'But he works for the Hobart Gas Company.'

'Look at the next page,' Nellie told her friend. 'I copied down Boothman's notes at the crime scene.'

The pot of coffee arrived at the table and the young waitress, probably as young as the victim Rosa had been, hurried back to the kitchen to fetch cups. Immediately Charlotte had a rapport with the dead girl. A physical and very alive comparison with their waitress. Aware she was being scrutinised, the waitress dropped the china cups clumsily onto the table and scurried away. Charlotte read on in silence.

'It rained Saturday night, quite hard too, before 11 o'clock I remember. It says here the body was dry, lying on wet ground which meant she was killed, and her body left, after the rain.'

Nellie nodded, pouring coffees. 'Huh!' Charlotte grinned. 'Here's a report from my old friend Toby Hutton,' she said with a level of sarcasm. Charlotte read that Boothman sent Hutton to question publicans in the area Sunday afternoon. The publican at the Hope and Anchor told him a regular, who had made an obscene pass at one of his bar maids, came in late Easter Saturday for a drink. He seemed agitated. He was a garbage collector who owned a cart and often dumped at the swamp. His name is Bible Bob and he's about forty ... Bible Bob?'

'Yes, it is a derogatory sobriquet. The man is a well know heathen. His real name, I believe, is Bob Green.'

'Hutton has noted in his report here that this Bible Bob fellow has a record for breaking and entering.'

Nellie. 'Yes, but that doesn't make him a killer.'

'It doesn't help his case any ... Hutton's written here, *witnesses said they saw him with cart and horse on the Queen's Domain near the swamp late Saturday night*. Now if that's not suspicious I don't know what is.'

'Read on.'

'So, good old Hutton hauled him in for questioning,' Charlotte noted. 'I bet he had plenty of help,' she added. 'Says here, he had a scratch down his cheek and said he got it shaving. Sounds to me like they've got their man already.'

Nellie lifted her cup to her lips to blow at the surface of her hot coffee. 'Keep reading.'

'Mrs Green swears on the bible that her husband Bible Bob was at home before 11PM.'

'An alibi! This wouldn't be the first time a woman has lied to the police for her husband.'

'There's an interesting witness report on the next page.'

Charlotte read that a man who works at the coach offices and depot for Page Coaches near the Tramway Hotel in Macquarie Street saw a girl who fits the murdered girl Rosa's description. She came into the coach depot. 'And the Hobart Gas Company, where this Samuel works, is only across the road.'

'Huh-hu. Read on.'

'She was talking to William Jacks, a mechanic who works for the coach company.' Charlotte looked at the blank space beneath the name. She turned the page. 'Nothing else about William Jacks?'

'No, apparently he was off yesterday, and Hutton couldn't locate him. But this Jacks fellow is back to work today ...'

'And Hutton's enjoying a holiday.'

'Something like that. Another senior constable was assigned to talk to Jacks but I'm certain no one did.'

Charlotte sipped her own coffee. There was more to read but the back room was filling with patrons. 'Do you have anything more on the Hambleton case?' Charlotte asked. 'I desperately need to get my hands on Mrs Hambleton's handwriting. A signature would be helpful.' Charlotte explained why.

Nellie surreptitiously slid another file on the Hambleton's across the table. 'I thought these would make you happy.'

'Excellent. Can I keep these?'

'I made copies for you especially,' Nellie looked a little anxious. 'Put them away huh.'

'Thank you, Nellie. I'll pay for the coffee.'

'I should think so.'

***

Twenty-five minutes later. Page's Coach Workshop.
'The turnin' wheel, which we sometimes call the fifth wheel, which is connected to the front axle, well it's been jammin' see, an' the king pin's almost worn through.' The head mechanic at Page's Coach workshop was keen to explain to Charlotte why their top mechanic, William Jacks, was lying on his back beneath a ten-seater coach. 'It's a recipe for disaster, that is … ain't it Will?'

William looked out from under the chassis at the pretty redhead staring back down at him. 'What'd yer say?'

'I was jus' tellin' this 'ere young lady that this 'ere coach was an accident waitin' to happen. Until you, Will my son, got under there an' fixed it.' William looked on, his eyes questioning. 'Come on out a moment, Mrs Clarke 'ere is from the newspaper an 'she wants to ask yer some questions.'

"bout what exactly?' William asked. 'I don't mean to be rude Missus but I'm busy.'

'I can see that,' Charlotte said. 'I just wanted to ask you a few questions about the young lady you were talking to here on Saturday evening.'

'Don't know who yer talkin' about.'

'Well someone, a witness, went to the police and said you were seen talking to her, only hours before she was murdered nearby.'

'Oh Jesus, you can't blame that on me.'

'You knew she was murdered. Why did you lie, and say you didn't know who I was talking about?'

'Why do yer reckon? I don't want nuthin' to do with it, it's awful I know. But I ain't stickin' me neck out for no one. Murder! Jesus!'

'Well then, what were you and the girl talking about?'

'Look, I was here workin' all night. There's other's here what can vouch for me.'

Charlotte looked to the head mechanic. 'You must work long hours here?'

'Yes, all night sometimes, and all day too. We have coaches to service; passenger safety is one o' the company's priorities.'

'How many mechanics work here?'

'Five Missus.'

'Alibis or not, Mr Jacks,' Charlotte told the young mechanic. 'The police will be here to talk to you.'

'Her name was Rosa,' William spouted, red faced.

'I know that. What were you talking about?'

'She were lookin' for Jason. But he wasn't working Saturday. You a journalist?'

'Yes. Can you come out a moment?'

Immediately he became defensive. 'Like I said, I'm busy.'

'Look I'm an investigative journalist; I aid the police in their enquiries. I want the killer caught as much as anyone.'

'Look Missus ...'

The head mechanic was having none of it. 'You come out from under there William, that's an order.'

William crawled from under the coach, his hands black with grease. 'What do you wanna know then?'

'You said she was looking for Jason. Who's Jason?'

'Another mechanic, he's an apprentice, 'bout the same age as the girl. I told her he weren't here.'

'Then what?'

'She hung about a minute or two. I thought ... well ... she were a good lookin' lass and I thought she might ... you know ...'

'No, I don't know.'

'Well, I thought she might 'ave taken a shine to me like.'

'So, she hung about a while, as you said, and then?'

'Well, I seen her talkin' to another cove, smartly dressed 'e were. 'e walked in off the street. I've seen him around before. I've met him somewhere, but I can't think where. They talked a while over in the corner near the street an' seemed to know each other, or they got on alright anyways. Then she comes over to me an' asks if'n I got some paper to write on. Apparently, this bloke wanted to give 'er a note of some sort.'

'His address maybe ... you said they were known to each other.'

'I said they *seemed* to know each other.'

'Can you describe him?'

'Twenty-five-ish. 'e looked Scandinavian like, from Sweden or somewhere like that, with long white hair, tall an' slim an' I think 'e had blue eyes.' The mechanic thought a moment. If the police were coming for him, he now wanted everything out in the open. 'He had a fancy pen.'

'Pen?'

'Yer, one o' them new fancy pens with a tiny ball in the end what gets inked up as you put nib to paper.'

'Ball point?'

'That's the one.'

'So, you gave him paper?'

'Yer, I give 'im one o' the paper pads what we use for writing down orders for parts, odds and ends for the coaches.'

'Pad? Can you show me?'

William Jacks looked at his superior who jerked his head towards the mechanic's glass windowed office, designed to observe the workshop. William returned, handing Charlotte the pad.

'Is this the same pad?'

'I'd say so,' the head mechanic rubbed his chin. 'Yer can see Will's greasy paw marks all over it.'

Charlotte. 'Has this been used since Saturday?'

'It's one of three pads in use Missus, I doubt it.'

Knowing that a ball point pen needs pressure to write, Charlotte angled the page to the natural light pouring through a skylight. She took a lead pencil from her satchel and rubbed gently over the shallow indentations preserved on the page beneath the note, the note the mystery man wrote for Rosa. 'Do either of you gentlemen know a Jarl Haugen?'

'Haugen! I've heard that name,' the head mechanic said. 'I remember, cos it's a funny name.'

There was more written on the page, but Charlotte tore the sheet from the pad, filing it into her satchel. She would study that later. 'Who is he then?'

'I met him around 'er once. Your brother introduced me to 'im,' he said to William. ''e was sellin' odds an' sods.'

'Odds and sods?'

'Things what I don't believe were 'is to sell.'

'Like what exactly?'

'Clothing.'

'Do you know where I can find him?'

'Will's brother'd know, eh Will?'

William Jacks grew serious.

'What's your brother's name?' Charlotte asked.

'Jonathan.'

'Where can I find him?'

"e lives in Wapping, Sackville Street. But 'e won't talk to yer.'

'I should warn you,' the head mechanic said. 'He has a bit of a reputation Missus, does this Jonathan Jacks.'

'Reputation?'

The older mechanic turned his back on William and whispered, 'He gets violent.'

Charlotte retreated back out onto lower Macquarie Street. She had an address in Wapping for brother Jonathan and wondered how she would approach him. *She might need help.* Across the street and fifty yards further on, the Hobart Gas Company's brick chimney spewed burnt coal waste into the clear morning sky.

Samuel.

Yes, Samuel, employed by the Gas Company, Charlotte thought. *Friend of Rosa Esposito.* It was still early, 7.20AM in fact, but worth a try.

Even the interior of the Gas Company's administration buildings felt grimy with the fusty spoil from burning coal and its by-product, gas for lighting the streetlamps of Hobart. Although Charlotte knew the Gas Company would be producing single phase electricity later this year, whatever single phase meant. Charlotte caught the attention of the night watchman whose replacement for the day shift had turned up late, causing angst for the older man.

Charlotte. 'Do you have a Samuel working here?'

'Who wants to know?'

'My name's Charlotte Clarke ...' Charlotte explained her position.

'We have three Samuels working here.'

'This one would be around twenty I should imagine.'

'I reckon you're looking for one of the stokers, Samuel Maynard, unreliable cove. Like someone else I could mention.' The nightwatchman looked at his colleague, buttoning his jacket ready for duty. 'Samuel hasn't turned up for work yet. Supposed to start at six. He be drunk somewhere, you mark my words.'

'Would you do me a favour please? When you see him do not mention anyone was here looking for him.'

'What's he done then, got some lass expecting?'

'Something like that.'

Charlotte noted an office clock. It was 7.50AM. She had already arranged to meet Edward at *The Mercury* stables at 8AM. Keen to investigate *the girl in the swamp* murder further, she took the page from the coach mechanic's notebook, spread it out and rubbed a pencil over the remaining message. Besides his name, Jarl Haugen, only three words were revealed amongst what appeared to be a very rough map. *Austin's Ferry Inn.* Charlotte studied the map, careful to be certain she had fully exposed the indentations, and there, north of the inn alongside what she now realised was the upper River Derwent, was marked a crude X.

So, Charlotte smiled to herself, *X* does *mark the spot.*

'Good morning, Mrs Clarke.' James Paton, the founder of *The Clipper* newspaper, stepped through his front gate and onto the footpath with serendipitous timing. Charlotte, deep in thought, turned to face the man hurrying towards her waving Monday's *Mercury* in his hand. She stifled a groan, but sagging shoulders gave away her reluctance. 'Mr Paton.'

'James ... please,' he insisted. 'We're all colleagues after all, spreading the news.' The man was fifteen years Charlotte's senior with the hide of a rhinoceros and frustratingly annoying. Charlotte stood firm. '*The girl in the swamp*,' Paton read Charlotte's headline out loud. 'This is your article I believe?'

'Ah, yes.'

'Brilliant. I just knew it was your writing, so eloquent, so well crafted. You are at the top of your game my dear.'

My dear! Charlotte cringed, managing to remain polite. 'I'm glad you liked it.' She made to return to her office when the editor took her arm. 'You should come and work for me ... jump ship so to speak. At *The Clipper*.'

'Oh, I don't think so Mr Paton.'

'James.'

'James.' Charlotte pulled her arm free. 'I don't think Mr Craddock would appreciate me deserting him. But I thank you kindly for the offer.'

'I'll be moving into bigger premises in Collins Street soon,' Paton was persistent, if nothing else.

'Yes, so I heard.' Charlotte knew the site of *The Clipper* and *Brinsmead Piano Depot*, known as Lord's Corner, where Elizabeth Street and Macquarie Street traverse, had been purchased by the City of Hobart. Here, the building of the new General Post Office was to commence in the next year or so.

'Tell me,' Paton's cunning emerged. 'A little birdie told me there are plans afoot to build new *Mercury* premises also?'

'I wouldn't know Mr Paton. I am but a humble servant.'

But Charlotte knew only too well that plans for a new and much larger building to house the successful newspaper were well under way.

Charlotte found Edward waiting at the stables. 'Mornin'.'

'And a good morning to you Edward.' Charlotte reeled back to study Edward's neck. 'Goodness, that's a nasty scratch on your neck.' Edward was coy. 'What did you do to yourself?'

'I fell Missus.'

'Fell! You must have landed heavily.'

'Yes, well I tripped.'

Charlotte noted bloodshot eyes and a small tear on his jacket cuff. It also appeared Edward had tried to sponge the jacket clean. 'Had you been drinking perchance?'

Edward looked sheepish. 'Aye, I cannot lie to yer Mrs Clarke.'

'Charlotte!'

'Charlotte. With you not requirin' me services yesterday I went to an inn Saturday night, met an old acquaintance I ain't seen in years, and … well … one think led to another and I fell in the street.'

Charlotte laughed. Edward returned a wry, wary smile. 'I can't imagine you intoxicated Edward.'

'Aye. It is not somethin' I make a habit of.'

'Maybe you should wrap your neck in a bandage.'

'I rubbed Holloway's ointment onto it. It'll all be good miss … Charlotte. Me Ma always said fresh air is good for cuts.'

Charlotte cosied up next to Edward on the short narrow seat. 'Where to then?' he asked.

'Austin's Ferry. You know of the inn?'

'Austin's Ferry Inn? Aye.'

'There is a man living nearby whom I must see before the police get to him.'

'Before the police huh?' Edward shot Charlotte a generous smile over his left shoulder. 'I like yer style Mrs Clarke,' he said, tongue in cheek. *Investigative* journalist.'

***

Austin's Ferry Inn. Eleven miles north of The Mercury offices.
Edward settled their horse at the water trough outside the old inn, an elongated hollowed sandstone trough *deep enough for a man to bath in*, Charlotte thought. And some men more than likely had done so in the past. The inn was now a residence, although it was unoccupied.

They were alone. There was only one property halfway up a hill to the north of the old inn: a four-bedroom homestead on a grant of land given to settlers by Governor Macquarie almost a century prior.

X marks the spot.

If nothing else on the crude map, the homestead was right where it should be. Charlotte looked to the River Derwent. A trading ketch under full sail in a fair breeze was heading to New Norfolk, a village further upriver. Charlotte had seen a painting of the ferry crossing here at Austin' Ferry in its heyday, before the Bridgewater causeway further upriver opened back in the '40s, making travelling across river more convenient. Today, it was not difficult to imagine the punt loaded with cattle and carts making the crossing.

'What exactly are we looking for?' Edward asked.

'You wait here. I'm paying a visit to that homestead on the hill.'

Edward stepped down to stretch his legs and fill a pipe with tobacco. Charlotte never ceased to amaze him. As he watched, she hitched her skirt, mounted the wooden split-rail fence and leapt to the paddock on the other side like a true woodsman's daughter.

Mrs Haugen battled to secure freshly laundered bed linen on a line, the sheets being particularly stubborn as the wind picked up. On the upside, the woman thought, the sheets would dry quickly. Suddenly movement caught her eye between the fluttering laundry. Disturbed cattle scattered. The older Swedish woman's eyesight wasn't what it used to be; *was that a woman approaching across her paddock between her dairy cows?* She called for her husband Hans, a handsome man his early sixties. The Haugens rarely had visitors. Being foreigners, they were left to their own means mostly. But an attractive young woman crossing their field did not seem a threat. Hans Haugen met her at the gate.

'Mr Haugen,' Charlotte said, short of breath after climbing the hill.

'Ja.' Hans looked at Charlotte with a combination of incredulity and curiosity. Mrs Haugen reappeared from the house looking about for unknown accomplices. She propped the single barrel shotgun against the veranda post.

'Vot you do here?' Hans asked.

Charlotte felt tension. She stopped at the gate. 'Ah ... Mr Haugen ... Mrs Haugen. I am looking for your son Jarl.'

'Jarl? Vy?'

'Is Jarl here?'

Mr Haugen looked at his wife, worry lines accentuating his brow. 'Vy you ask?'

Charlotte saw no point in wasting time. 'I have ridden from Hobart. Is Jarl here or not?'

Mrs Haugen stiffened. 'Vy you ask? Who are you?'

'I am Charlotte Clarke,' Charlotte explained the situation.

'Jarl is goot boy. He no do no trouble to no ones.'

'Mr Haugen ... Mrs Haugen. Your son could be in grave danger.' For all Charlotte knew Jarl Haugen could be the murderer. 'Is he here, yes or no? I am here to help ...'

'I am here.' Jarl stepped onto the veranda from the front door. 'What do you want with me?' he called out.

Charlotte looked to the closed gate between her and the Haugens. The shotgun hadn't gone unnoticed. 'May I enter?'

Hans opened the gate and they gathered at the bottom veranda step. 'You say Jarl, he in trouble,' Hans said. 'You explain to us now.'

Charlotte had to acknowledge, Jarl Haugen, the twenty-five-year-old son, did not look like a killer. And certainly not a rapist. The man was dev- ilishly handsome and fine figured and would have women chasing *him*. She explained the situation and her role as a journalist.

'So, as you can see," she told Jarl, 'you were the last person to see Rosa alive and it will only be a matter of time before you are taken in by the police for questioning.'

'Taken?' Ingrid Hausen was fighting tears. 'Taken where to?'

'To the watch house.'

'Jarl.' Hans Haugen took his son by the arm. 'Vot you say? You know thees, thees, Rosa?'

Jarl looked to his parents and swallowed hard. He said nothing, then turned to Charlotte.

'Can we go somewhere to talk? In private.' The man's English was de- void of the strong accent of his parents.

The parents were aware enough to capitulate. Hans nodded. Charlotte followed Jarl to the milking sheds a hundred yards away, where she insisted on remaining within sight of the homestead just in case she had totally misread the young Swede.

'I don't want my parents to hear what I have to say,' Jarl started.

'I understand.'

Jarl's face was ashen. 'Rosa, how did she die?'

'She was stabbed several times in the back.'

'Oh god! Was she ... had she been ...'

'Violated? Yes.'

Jarl looked genuinely sickened and Charlotte had to concede, unless the man was a great actor, he did not appear to be a killer.

'As far as we know, you were the last person to see Rosa alive. What happened?'

'I was passing by Page's coach depot in Macquarie Street when I saw Rosa at the entrance. She looked lost.'

'What were you doing there?'

'It was Saturday night and I had been out drinking around the wharves.'

'That's a rough place for a dairy farmer to be visiting.'

'Yes. It was my friend's idea.' Jarl looked across the field to his parents who waited on the veranda, looking forlorn. 'We look for girls you understand. I stay with my friend at his cottage in West Hobart.'

'What's his name?'

'You will not get him into trouble, will you?'

'No. As long as he hasn't done anything he shouldn't have.'

'His name is Ryan O'Sullivan. We have been friends since school. Well Ryan met this girl at the Hope and Anchor and ...' Jarl looked embarrassed. 'He went to her home in Wapping.'

'Was she a street girl?'

'Yes. So, I went for a walk, we agreed we would meet in an hour at the Steam Packet Inn.'

Charlotte shuddered at the thought. Another rough and ready inn. If only his parents knew.

'So, you saw Rosa?'

'Yes. I knew her from before. We had met with mutual friends. Anyway, she said hello and I stopped to talk to her. She was a nice girl; I was surprised to see her near the harbour.'

'Did she tell you she was there to see an apprentice mechanic named Jason?'

'I don't recall. I had been drinking.'

'You gave her a map. That's what led me to you here at Austin's Ferry.'

'But I threw that map away.'

'Yes, but I found a copy.'

'How?'

'I am an investigative journalist remember, a sleuth. And pretty good at it by my reckoning. Why did you give her the map?'

'She told me she was unhappy. She lived with her aunt and she was very strict with her.'

'She was only sixteen.'

'Sixteen?' Jarl appeared genuinely surprised. 'I thought she was older.'

'Well in your defence I was assured she did look and act older, eighteen maybe.'

'So, I gave her the map. Told her to come and see my parents. My sister married recently you see, and we have a vacant room. My parents were talking about taking a lodger and I thought Rosa could work in the dairy.'

'So, what happened?'

'Pardon?'

'Why did you destroy the map?'

'Like I said, I had been drinking and although Rosa was a nice girl she wasn't exactly ... well ... she wasn't exactly a virgin. I knew a boy she was intimate with and I thought ... well ...'

'You thought you could bed her.'

'Yes.'

'Did you?'

'No!' If Jarl *was* a good actor this was not his time to shine. He looked guilty as hell and knew it. 'Yes.'

'You *did* bed her?'

'Yes.'

'What happened?'

'She walked with me to the Steam Packet Inn and we drank for maybe one hour, in the parlour mind. The taproom was full of loud men.'

'I can imagine.'

'My friend Ryan didn't show up, so Rosa and I took a room at the Phoenix Hotel nearby.' Charlotte knew about the Phoenix, popular with casual lovers with rooms rented by the hour. 'I paid two shillings for two hours.'

'So, the map?'

'After ... after we ...' Jarl blushed uncomfortably. 'After we ... you know ... Rosa fell asleep, and I had second thoughts about introducing her to my parents, so I took the map from her bag and destroyed it.'

'What bag, a handbag?' Charlotte knew there had not been a handbag found.

'Yes.'

'Can you describe it?'

'It was brown leather, quite large, with pewter clips and a long strap.'

Charlotte made notes in shorthand. 'Do you know a stoker employed by the Hobart Gas Company named Samuel?'

'No. Should I?'

'Apparently, she was seeing him also.'

'Really? Like I said, she was hardly a virgin.'

Jarl had a thought. 'She did talk about a man named Ahab.'

'Ahab who?'

'She didn't say, or else I can't remember if she did. I only remember the name because it's so unusual. Rosa said she had met him before, and he was really nice to her.'

'How nice?'

'I can't say. Apparently, he bought her drinks. She met him again Saturday night, sometime before she met me. He offered to keep her company, but she declined. Said he was too old, and she thought him a little simple.'

'Simple?'

'Slow of speech and immature. Actually, I do recall she said he was off a ship.'

'A sailor?'

'I think so. But he'd been to Hobart before because, as I said, she had met him before. I think he's off a coastal trader.'

Charlotte. 'My, this Rosa was a popular girl.'

'What happened when your two hours were up at the Phoenix?'

'I woke Rosa and promised to see her soon. Which was a lie. I wanted to get away from the situation as soon as I could, especially if she looked in her bag and missed the map. I bid her farewell and left her, while she dressed.'

Charlotte sighed. The man may be a typical Saturday night reveller, out for self-pleasure, a typical male she thought, in many ways. But she did not see him as a killer.

'Are you going to write about this in the newspaper?'

'No. But I must warn you the police will soon find you. Tell them the truth. Secure your alibis and you would be wise not to tell them you have spoken to me.'

Edward was where Charlotte had left him. 'What is it with you men?' If Charlotte sounded disdainful, it was because she felt it at this moment. 'That you have to drink too much and chase women.'

Edward prickled. 'Not all men are like that.'

'Oh, aren't they?'

'No. Like I said, I happened upon an old friend. We were celebrating and ...'

'And you drank too much and lost control of yourself.' Charlotte stepped back, crossing her arms before her, to study the man she thought she knew better. A man, if she were to be honest with herself, she was possibly having feelings for. 'Well?'

'Well, what?' Edward displayed defiance she hadn't witnessed before.

'Well did you succumb to the company of women? Maybe bar wenches throwing themselves at you?'

'No, I certainly did not.'

Charlotte cooled. 'Have you *ever* had a lady friend?'

'Aye. I was betrothed at one time, but the lass ran off with another.'

'Oh, I am so sorry.'

'Don't be, I was better off without her. And there was a lass at Port Arthur I was quite fond of for a while, Samantha. But, well ...'

'Well what?'

'She became a little too possessive. The friendship wore off.'

'Did you break it off?'

'Aye. Her Pa weren't too pleased though.'

Charlotte laughed.

Edward. 'What?'

'I'll wager her father was cranky.' Charlotte mounted the carriage. 'Losing a hard-working handsome devil as yourself for his little princess.'

Edward was amazed at this revelation. Was this woman flirting with him? He removed the chaff bag from a contented horse, securing it, before joining Charlotte on the seat. There was a spark between them, he just knew it. Holding the reins, he stared at the road ahead a moment.

Handsome devil, handsome devil ...

Edward so wanted to continue this conversation. Ask if she meant it. Lean over and kiss her, even. But his nerve deserted him. Instead, he clicked his tongue and the horse started off. 'Back to the newspaper?' he asked.

'Take me to the Phoenix please.'

'The inn?'

'Yes.'

Eartha Atwater remembered the couple well. The Phoenix publican was busy polishing the brass rail around the taproom bar preparing for a lunch crowd when Charlotte asked about Jarl and Rosa.

'How could I forget, they was such a handsome couple. Couldn't keep their hands of each other. Room seven they took, overlookin' the Gas Works, not that they wanted a view, if'n yer knows wha' I mean.'

'Do you remember what time they left?'

'Well, the young man paid for two hours but I seen 'im leave a bit earlier than that, so I'd say about half an hour after ten. It was raining for an hour or so 'bout then, but the young lady waited and left after the rain stopped.'

CHAPTER SEVEN

The Oaks Cottage and estate, one mile east of Richmond. Easter Tuesday.
Their love making was intense. Stolen love. The wanton fornication so badly missing in Adelaide D'Boville's life. Jackaroo Morton Dunbar had the Flemish beauty pinned to the barn wall, her legs wrapped about him, her ankles locking their passion. Completely uninhibited. Sex with husband Ashley had never, ever, been as great. In fact, the soppy man hadn't touched her in months. Morton locked his fingers beneath her snow-white flesh and showed his new mistress just how handy this jackaroo really was.

It was day three since Morton had been accepted into a spare room in the servant's quarters of *The Oaks*. As promised, he worked tirelessly. Long days of twelve hours. Adelaide's husband Ashley Hambleton was friendly enough yet kept his distance. For now, Morton was content. But for the price of three-square meals and a bed, he wanted more ... a lot more.

It was mid-afternoon. Earlier in the day Ashley had taken the covered cart to Bellerive where Morton helped his master load furniture from a deserted mansion. The property was well boarded up. It had been empty for some time. But Ashley had a key to a side entrance. Morton noted a brass nameplate on an arched trellis over the front gate, it was barely legible. *Domus Casandra. Whatever that meant?*

Domus Casandra was a substantial home, in what Morton recognised as faux Tudor, black and white. He guessed there were twenty or more rooms, many with views across the River Derwent to Hobart. Ashley was secretive, in fact he had barely spoken to Morton all day. The two men loaded what the cart would hold, Morton simply doing as he was ordered, and asking no questions.

They had returned from Bellerive an hour or so earlier. The round trip had taken most of the day. Once the furniture was unloaded from the cart and hidden in the barn Ashley continued on to the township of Richmond, taking with him his sister Phillipa, to purchase groceries and medical supplies. Hyacinth Hambleton, the matriarch of the family was busy in the cottage scullery, polishing silverware accompanied by a glass of Geneva, a refreshment she seemed to be consuming in increasing in volume these past weeks.

In the barn Adelaide and Morton's lovemaking was exceptional.

Morton lowered the semi-naked Adelaide onto the hay where they kissed and hugged, before laying side by side, exhausted. Morton lay on the straw staring up at the beams, deep in thought. Adelaide took his hand and squeezed gently. 'I ... I ...' she started.

'Yes?" Morton squeezed her hand back. 'Don't keep me in suspense.'

'I think,' Adelaide whispered, 'I'm falling in love with you.' The young woman's voice purred in that desirable accented English that Morton found so seductive.

He propped on one elbow and turned to look Adelaide in those large dark eyes. 'Nothing,' he said, 'nothing could describe how I feel about you right now my love.'

'Really?'

'Really.'

Adelaide grew morose. Deep in thought.

'What's the problem?' he asked.

'I want you. I want you so badly. I want to run away with you . but ...'

'But what?'

'I am trapped in a loveless marriage.'

Morton wasn't ready for this. This wasn't a part of his plan. It had all unfolded so rapidly, but his feelings for the young lady were genuine. 'We better dress,' he said, collecting his trousers. Adelaide looked at her wristwatch lying next to her coat and skirt that she had thrown aside in insouciant lust. 'We have an hour yet.'

'Oh?'

'Ashley always has a brandy at The Crown.' Adelaide reached for Morton, taking him in her hand. His arousal was instant. Never had he experienced such insatiable ardour. There was no turning back. Adelaide had the man where she wanted him, mounting him a second time.

Grinning like naughty school children, they finally dressed. After brushing herself down Adelaide straightened her attire and combed her hair before tying it back in a chignon. She admired herself in a cedar framed mirror sitting on a large Huon Pine chest of drawers, looking so out of place in the barn.

'What's the story about all this furniture stored in the barn?' Morton finally found the opportunity to ask.

'Oh, nothing really.'

'Nothing really!' Morton mimicked, smiling at the piles of old furniture and crates in storage. 'This stuff should be stored in the house.'

'The cottage isn't large enough, you know that.'

'Yes ... but ... here?'

'We're just storing it for a friend,' Adelaide said, evasively. 'It's only for a short time.'

'A friend huh? What, have they gone away or something? I mean ... ' Morton's words were smothered with another passionate kiss. Adelaide pulled away and shuddered. The woman was voracious. 'I must go,' she said pushing Morton away, and with a giggle she hitched up her skirt and ran off across the field towards the homestead.

***

Earlier, just after 8AM, Easter Tuesday.
Police Headquarters, Liverpool Street, Hobart.
Today was the second time garbage collector Bible Bob was dragged into the police interview room for questioning. Bob, who had turned forty-one in February, was a simple man with unfortunate habits that shadowed him

everywhere, like his record for breaking and entering, and his reputation for moral degeneracy.

Most recently Sally Donald, bar wench at the Hope and Anchor, had made a complaint to her proprietor, innkeeper Jack Fry, that Bible Bob – Bob Green, had not only made obscene comments towards her but placed his hand under her skirt.

'You've got a bit of form Bob,' Senior Constable Hutton harangued the garbage collector. 'Touching the ladies like that.'

'She ain't no lady.'

'Still doesn't give you the right to play hanky-panky with her.'

Bible Bob looked miserable. He was unkempt with a week's growth of whiskers peppering his face like carpenter's abrasive paper. His receding hair was greasy, his clothes soiled and patched, and his second-hand boots holed. And Hutton and the other police present all agreed the man smelt disagreeable.

'You never explained properly like, what you were doing on the Queen's Domain late Saturday night,' Hutton said. 'About the same time a young lassie was murdered and raped.'

'Jesus Lord, yer can't be pinning that on me.'

'Well, what were you doing out so late?'

'I told yer before. I was cartin' rubbish from the Franklin Pharmacy fire. Ol' Theodore Franklin gave me ten shillin' extra to empty the burnt cellar before Sunday.'

Hutton knew there had indeed been a fire in the cellar of the pharmacy. 'But why would the chemist require your services at night?'

'Cos 'e had carpenters comin' in early mornin' to rebuild.'

'On Easter Sunday?'

'Aye. He were losin' money bein' closed, 'e told me.'

'So, you what? Dumped the rubbish at the refuse site and then what?'

'I went home.'

'Over the Queen's Domain?'

'Aye, it's quicker.'

Bible Bob struggled with claustrophobia and tears. Locked in a tiny holding cell at the watch house he had to sweat it out while the swamp was checked. However, at least three cart loads of burnt fused glass, and other blackened chemist paraphernalia had been recently dumped where Bob said he left it. Pharmacist Theodore Franklin was questioned and confirmed he paid Mr Green thirty shillings in total to cart away the contents of his burnt cellar. Ten shillings being a bonus for continuing on into the night. A police constable sent by Hutton to the Collins Street pharmacy also confirmed four carpenters were well and truly underway with repairs.

Five hours passed before a relieved Bible Bob was reprimanded for his behaviour in the Hope and Anchor and finally set free, only to face the wrath of his wife.

***

Noon

For the price of a pint of porter Edward managed to secure Samuel Maynard's address, the seventeen-year-old stoker who worked at the Hobart Gas Company and the young man who apparently led Rosa astray.

The small cottage in Goulburn Street was two doors from the Peacock Tavern. In fact, at the crossroads of Goulburn and Barrack Street, where the drinking culture boomed with a public house positioned on each corner. A young lad around the age of eight or nine opened the door onto the street. Samuel's younger brother screamed down the passageway and a mother appeared from the kitchen, where the steaming aromas of stewing meat reminded Charlotte of how hungry she was. After hasty introductions Charlotte asked for Samuel.

'What d'ya want him for? We're 'bout to eat.'

'My apologies madam, I did not realise the time.'

'Well?'

Charlotte explained her position.

'The police 'ave already spoke to Sammy.'

'Oh?'

'That damned Italian woman, what's 'er name, Francis?'

'Francesco.'

'Aye. Francis Francesco. She gone tell the coppers that ... that that ... I don't wanna talk ill o' the dead ... but that little scrubber Rosa was with my boy the night she got killed, an' Sammy was home here with me and little Freddy.'

'Freddy? That's your youngest?'

'Aye. Sammy come 'ome straight from work. 'e were on a late afternoon shift. 'e walked in this door and went straight to Freddy's room and read him a bedtime story. Sammy loves 'is little brother.'

'So, what time did he arrive home?'

'Bit after ten.'

'And you told the police this?'

'Bloody oath I did.'

A man's voice called from the kitchen. A hungry voice. 'You comin'?'

Mrs Maynard yelled back at her husband down the passage. Charlotte saw a figure appear. A large man in trousers held with braces over an unbuttoned shirt. He was like a circus bear and Charlotte couldn't see the point of asking to see Samuel. She thanked the woman, but the door slammed shut before she even turned away.

***

1PM

Hobart's waterfront was no place for a lady to wander alone. But Charlotte felt she had little choice. This Ahab, a sailor who possibly worked on a coastal trader was now very much a suspect. Charlotte had instructed Edward earlier; he was to enquire aboard all vessels and around the harbour's environs for an older sailor, maybe in his forties. Ahab, after all wasn't a popular name.

'He may even be American,' she told Edward. 'When asked, *what do you want with him,* say you are searching for Ahab on behalf of a Melbourne solicitor and that he has come into an inheritance,' Charlotte said.

'Inheritance huh,' Edward grinned. He loved Charlotte's shrewd mind. 'I hope this works.'

'So do I.'

The task proved easier than Charlotte could possibly have hoped. Crossing the wharves at the southern end of Salamanca Place a voice called out over the general din of maritime industry. Charlotte turned to see an older man squeezing between barrels and landed cargo. He had apparently been in haste. 'You the lassie lookin' for Ahab?' he managed to call out on the approach, his breathing laboured.

'Yes. Are you he?'

'Ahab? No Missus. But I knows where he's at?'

'Oh?'

The man wheezed. 'Hell's bells, I'm not as fit as I used to be.'

'Where then, can I find him?'

'He's got an inheritance comin.'

'Is that so?'

Charlotte was cautious. *So that's the only reason he ran to catch me.* Clearly, she had been pointed out to him by someone she had spoken to, not so long ago.

'Inheritance, yes. Something like that.'

'What d'ya mean, somethin' like that? 'e either does or 'e doesn't.'

Charlotte read the man like a book. She took a half crown from her purse. 'Will this help?'

He snatched the coin. 'He works the channel run on the *May Queen*.' Charlotte knew the seventy-foot trading ketch *May Queen* well, with her retractable centreboard and shallow draft for loading and unloading cargo without requiring a jetty or wharf.

'Is the *May Queen* in port at the moment? I haven't seen her.'

'Yes Missus. She's moored off Battery Point at the shipyards. They just delivered fifty ton of pine.'

'You seem to know what's what.'

'Yer, well I work with Ahab see. I'm crew as well. That's not his real name by the way, Ahab.'

'Oh?'

'His real name's Dugal. He loved the story of Moby Dick; you know the one about the white whale?' Charlotte nodded. 'Well, every time we see a whale down river or on the coast 'e goes on about the book, so the lads named him Ahab, after the one-legged captain in the story.'

Charlotte couldn't help it smile. So, Ahab was a sobriquet, she had thought it an unusual name. 'Dugal. Dugal who?'

'Dugal Bean. He's not too smart miss, bloody good worker but not too clever.'

***

Dugal Bean sat on the bow of a beached tender, his boots firmly planted on the rocky shoreline, enjoying a cold pasty, when he caught a pleasant sight from the corner of his eye. Charlotte approached with caution. Other lads had pointed out the older man; early forties, barrel chested, tall dark and handsome. However, she was aware the man was of low intellect, a fact, she considered, that must frustrate a man apparently so eligible, yet lacking the basic skills of courtship. 'Mr Bean? Dugal?'

'Aye.' Dugal straightened, smiling like the punter who had picked the winning horse. Charlotte introduced herself and explained her presence.

The smile faded. 'I knew she was killed,' Dugal confided without hesitation. 'The lads tell me. Such a shame. She was so pretty.'

'She was also very young Dugal.' Charlotte wanted to say, *what were you thinking, trying to court her? She wasn't much older than a child and you're old enough to be her father.* But said instead, 'You are one of the last to see her alive.'

'Was I?' Dugal said this as if it was an honour.

'The police are looking for you.'

'Aren't you the police?'

'No Dugal, I told you, I'm an investigative journalist.'

'Oh.'

'What exactly happened on Saturday night? What time do you think it was when you met Rosa?'

'It were dark. Maybe seven o'clock.'

'What happened?'

'We went to the Freemasons and drank some cider.'

'And then?'

'She told me she had to get home.' Dugal seemed to grow dark as if something bothered him.

'What is it?'

'She lied to me.'

'Oh?'

'I seen her later walking across the street with another man.'

'What did he look like?'

'Tall, white hair.'

Jarl, Charlotte knew. 'Did you see her after that?'

'No. I ...'

Immediately they were interrupted by two uniform police and a plain clothes detective. 'We'll be taking it from here,' the detective called out.

Charlotte turned, to be abruptly confronted by Senior Constable Toby Hutton. The two uniforms stood either side of Dugal securing an arm each before fitting handcuffs. 'Mr Ahab, you are under arrest for the murder of Rosa Esposito.'

Dugal was terrified. He glared at Charlotte accusingly. Charlotte held his gaze, shaking her head, disbelieving what was happening.

'You tricked me,' Dugal said, his voice quivering.

'N-no! No Dugal,' Charlotte turned on Hutton. 'What's the meaning of this?'

'Exactly my sentiment. What is the meaning of your interfering in police business, again? You just won't learn, will you?'

Charlotte was speechless. We've been following you the past hour or so. I had a feeling you'd lead us to the killer?'

'There is no evidence this man is the killer.'

'Oh, I wouldn't be so sure about that.'

'H-how did you ...'

'Know about Ahab?' Hutton looked proud as a prized cock. 'Why Jarl Haugen told us after he told us about your visit.' Charlotte bristled. 'And he told us you told *him* not to mention to the police that you had been to his home.'

Charlotte watched a moment as the uniforms led Dugal Bean away to a waiting police wagon.

'His name isn't Ahab.'

'Oh, what is it then?'

'It's Dugal Bean and you will find he is mentally impaired.'

'No excuse for murder.' Charlotte shot Hutton a disparaging glare.

'Look, Charlotte,' Hutton's cockiness had faded. 'I like you. I like you a lot. I wish we could at least work together rather than you undermine the police all the time.'

'It's Mrs.'

'Pardon?'

'It's Mrs Clarke, not Charlotte. You have to earn that privilege and so far, Senior Constable Hutton, you are way off the mark.'

'My apologies. How can I earn your respect? Take you to dinner maybe.'

'I'm betrothed, you know that.'

'Are you certain?'

'I told you so.'

'Then does your ... betrothed ... know you were enjoying high tea at the Imperial Coffee Palace recently, with your stable boy.'

'Have you been spying on me all this time?'

'No, not at all. You had a window table and were seen. Word got back to me.'

'I dare say some people have little else in their lives than to tittle-tattle. I pity them.'

'Well,' Hutton persisted. 'Are you betrothed?'

'As far as you're concerned, yes.' Charlotte could not believe the man's audacity. She moved closer to face him, spearing her parasol into the dirt at his feet. 'Dugal Bean is a simpleton, treat him civilly.'

***

Less than an hour later. Police Interview Room.

Dugal Bean was nervous and on edge. A characteristic of guilt, the police surmised. Dugal panicked, telling the police he hadn't seen Rosa the night of the murder, only to retract the statement and say he had. He lied about taking her to the Freemasons and drinking cider, but earlier investigations had a witness put him in the parlour with Rosa the night of the murder. The contradictions were damning his pleas of innocence.

He was placed in a holding cell and told to reconsider his answers.

Early evening became late evening. Dugal was denied food or water. The moment he fell asleep he was woken and dragged back into the interview room.

'We've searched your locker on board the *May Queen* and taken your clothes,' Hutton told him. 'And one of your crew told us you came back late on Saturday night with mud on your britches and what he thought was blood.' Hutton threw the garment on the table. 'And they're torn, how did that happen?'

'I were drunk. I fell in the mud. It'd been raining.'

'They have been washed. You were seen washing these britches in the middle of the night. Why?'

'They was dirty.'

'But in the middle of the night? You were drunk. I put it to you that you followed Rosa when she made her way home. Because you were previously acquainted, she trusted you and you convinced her to take a short cut by the water's edge where you attacked her. You hit her on the head ...'

'No!' Dugal wailed. 'I never ... I like Rosa, she was kind to me.'

Hutton raised his voice. 'She tried to escape, and you stabbed her several times in the back.'

'No!'

'I put it to you that she got tangled in wire and fell and then you raped her when she was down and dying or was already dead.'

Dugal's face was white. He was terrified. 'No. I didn't kill her ... you must believe me. She was a good girl. I liked Rosa, I ...'

'You wanted her so badly you killed her.'

'No!' The man broke down, crying like a child. 'I never killed her,' he sobbed through red watery eyes, his nose running, slobber dribbling down his chin. Hutton thought the man pathetic, yet he sensed a confession was forthcoming.

'What did you do with the knife you stabbed her with?'

'I didn't ... I never ... I liked Rosa, she's a good girl ...'

'Was a good girl! Where's the knife?'

'I never have a knife?'

'Oh, come now Mr Bean, all sailors wear knives. We found the empty sheath on your bunk.'

Suddenly Dugal grew silent. After several seconds he said softly, almost in a whisper, 'Rosa and I argued.'

Hutton turned his head as if hard at hearing. 'Say that again.'

'Rosa and me, we had an argument.'

'Louder please.'

'Rosa and me, we had an argument.'

'Oh, now we're getting somewhere. Where did you argue?'

'When we leave Freemasons.'

'What did you argue about?'

'I spend two shillings on cider to take with us, so I ask her to come back to the *Queen*.'

'The *May Queen*?'

'Yes.'

'And she said no?'

Dugal nodded. 'I drank all the cider. I was drunk. I went looking for her and that's when I seen her with another man.'

'What man?'

'Tall man with white hair.'

'We already know about him. So, you saw the two of them go into the Phoenix, didn't you?'

Dugal looked sheepish, guilty. 'Yes. I was angry with her, but I didn't hurt her.'

'So, you waited for her to come out, met up with her and somehow managed to walk her along the waterfront where you eventually stabbed her and left her to die on the swamp.'

'No. I did not do this ... this terrible thing.'

'Liar,' Hutton threw his chair back, towering over the simpleton. 'You're a bloody liar.' He called to the duty policeman outside the interview room. 'Guard! Take him back to the cell.'

'Please sir, you must believe me.' Dugal reached out with handcuffed wrists trying to catch hold of Hutton's arm. 'I am a sailor,' he pleaded. 'I work hard. I never hurt anyone.'

Hutton ducked aside before taking the restrained prisoner by the collar. He slammed him hard against the wall. 'Don't you ever, ever lay a hand on me again.'

***

Two hours later.
Dugal was denied any refreshment, no food or water. A guard outside the cell kept an eye on him through the spy hole. Every time he attempted sleep, the guard stepped inside shouting, banging a tin cup against an enamel plate. Meanwhile Hutton slept at the station. This was his moment to shine, to prove his worth to his superiors and extract a confession from a dastardly killer.

***

5AM.
Dugal Bean, his face blotched red and smeared with dried secretions, was dragged back to the interview room. Hutton was waiting, refreshed, sitting on the edge of the table, sipping at a mug of hot coffee. Dugal could smell eggs, black pudding and bacon frying. His stomach growled. He was sleep deprived and parched with thirst. His simple life was falling apart. He was on the verge of a nervous breakdown.

'Ready to confess?' Hutton slurped his coffee noisily, smacking his lips in a torturous display of satisfaction. Dugal said nothing, he was absolutely exhausted. As arranged, a large breakfast plate was brought into the room by a constable; fried eggs, fried bacon, fried black pudding, four thick slices of buttered toasted bread along with sugared pastries and a jug of milk. Dugal stared at the food, his belly growling.

'Hungry?' Hutton said in a friendly tone, smiling. Dugal salivated, his eyes fixed on the food. 'I asked you a question Dugal. Are you hungry?' No answer. 'Well? What's the problem? Has the cat got your tongue?'

Dugal's eyes hooded over; his head drooped in defeat. 'All this is yours Dugal.' Dugal licked his lips. It was an involuntary move, like a pet hound might behave when a fatty bone is presented. 'Well then,' Hutton persisted. 'What's it to be?'

Dugal's voice was laced with despair. He was on the edge of a cliff. All he had to do was step off the precipice. 'What-do-you-want-from-me?' he croaked.

'What do I want?' Hutton plucked a crispy bacon rash off the plate, biting into it. The crunch alone knotted Dugal's stomach. But the aroma was pushing him over the edge. 'Sign this confession.' Hutton pushed a one-page document to where Dugal could reach it. 'Here.' He placed a pen alongside. 'Get it all over with and you can relax, eat like a king.'

Dugal Bean had never been taught to read, not properly anyway, let alone write. He took up the pen and made his mark the way he had been taught in the past.

'X' marked the spot.

***

Late afternoon.
Inspector Benjamin Boothman at the station was ecstatic. 'Well done Hutton, well done.' The older policemen, who had made a satisfying career of chasing villains and putting undesirables behind bars, looked upon his new recruit, the smart lad from Port Arthur, and hero of the recent fires down on the Tasman Peninsula, as a son. He saw traits of himself in the young lawman; eager, willing, hard-working and above all, a ruthless and smart policeman.

'A signed confession from Dugal Bean, excellent work.'

Charlotte smelt a rat. Nellie Nichols, police archivist, came to Charlotte's cottage that evening with a sense of justice and a copy of Dugal Bean's confession she had copied in shorthand.

'There are gaping holes in this confession,' Nellie warned Charlotte. 'But Inspector Boothman can't see them or won't acknowledge them. The wrong man could hang here.'

The two women sat in the drawing room. Charlotte read in silence for a moment. 'For one thing the timing's out,' Nellie said. 'Rosa's body was dry and laying on wet ground where it *had* rained but the rain had ceased by 11PM. So, she had to have been placed there after eleven.'

'Dugal has said here, that he struck the girl as she ran,' Charlotte said. 'So, the knife wounds in her back would strike downwards, particularly as he is a tall man. However, Rosa's wounds are upward slashes.'

'Correct. Also,' Nellie noted. 'You will notice the coroner deduced that the wounds were from a double-edged blade.'

'Was the knife ever found?'

'There was an extensive search made for Rosa's handbag *and* the murder weapon. Neither were found at the site. However, Dugal's knife was found where it had fallen under his bunk. It is single-edged and there is no sign of blood on it anywhere.

There's one other thing Charlotte.'

'Yes?'

'Word around the police office is that the confession was signed under duress.'

'Who extracted this confession?'

'Senior Constable Toby Hutton.' Nellie locked eyes with Charlotte. 'They're his words on the confession, as transcribed by the police stenographer.'

***

Late next morning.
Charlotte's article for the newspaper stated that in her opinion the suspect had signed a confession under duress. Bold words without proof. But Rupert Craddock, editor, trusted his star journalist's judgement.

And so did George Davies the newspaper heir, who demonstrated his support by sending eleven roses to Charlotte's desk. Charlotte's face turned as red as the roses, while the gesture created a divide amongst her peers; those approving and those who did not.

George had been watching from somewhere, he must have been, for he swooned into the journalist's office as if on cue, like a star of the stage, a single red rose in his lapel.

'Mrs Clarke, ah … Charlotte. I must congratulate you on your controversial article.' Charlotte was lost for words. 'It sells papers, and that's what we're here for, after all.' George looked at the other journalists sitting at their desks. 'To sell newspapers, eh?' Eyes avoided contact. George propped on the corner of Charlotte's desk. 'Come to tea?' he said quietly, leaning in towards Charlotte, who was trying her hardest to stifle a giggle.

'Pardon?'

'Come to tea. You must be ready for a break.'

Charlotte leant around George discreetly, to look at her peers. *It wasn't her fault she was the smartest journalist in the room, the most sought after, by the man himself.*

'Why not?' she said.

'Why not indeed.' George slapped his knee, launching himself back to his feet and opened the door for Charlotte. 'As you were,' he told the onlookers. And Charlotte slipped through the door smothering a smile.

The *Tasmanian Coffee Palace* neighbouring *The Mercury* premises was a delightful Regency residence. It boasted a pair of two-storey high Norfolk Pines in the front garden and a large oil lantern on iron brackets over the arched front entrance. Nowadays it operated as a small family-run café. Its title, *the* Coffee *Palace, was* in widespread, if inappropriate use, about the colonies these days, with a proliferation of coffee houses offering affordable home cooked fare.

It was full. George wrenched the door open with enthusiastic verve and they stepped into a fug of brewing coffee, delicious aromas, sticky treats and burning log fires. The cheerful atmosphere was contagious and, Charlotte thought, even the most fastidious diner could not possibly resist its attractions. Eager patrons waited for tables, some annoyingly blocking the entrance. George brushed people aside, entering the moment a couple left their table, in George's favourite spot as it turned out, overlooking the front garden and main street. The small round intimate table was bathed in late morning sunlight.

George slid the bentwood chair free for Charlotte to sit, saw that his companion was seated, and sat heavily himself. Sighing with satisfaction he spread a starched serviette onto his lap. The waitress appeared, to wipe the table clean.

'My, you were on the ball today Mr Davies.' The waitress was a pretty young lass, maybe sixteen, with medium length black hair in tight curls covered with a maid's laced bonnet. Clearly George was a regular. She acknowledged Charlotte. 'I'll fetch the menu,' she said.

George took hold of the waitress's wrist. 'Don't bother. Bring us a large plate of pastries filled with sausage meat, what are they called?'

'Sausage rolls.'

'Of course, they are. And a large pot of Earl Grey. Thank you.' George looked at Charlotte briefly. It hadn't occurred to George that Charlotte may have liked to have seen the menu and chosen for herself. He recognised a face of silent contemplation.

'You *do* like sausage rolls,' he said. 'Do you not?'

'Y-yes,' Charlotte almost laughed.

'Have you had Earl Grey before?' George asked.

'Once. It's an acquired taste.'

'You think so? I'm most fond of it. Do you know how it derived its name?'

'No. Kindly enlighten me.'

'Well according to legend, it was an accident. Apparently black tea leaves were being shipped to the earl with a shipment of bergamot oranges and on the journey the tea absorbed the citrus orange flavour.'

'Really?'

'Apparently.'

Charlotte noticed James Paton of *The Clipper* cross the street and remembered her recent conversation with him regarding the General Post Office construction. 'It's going to get somewhat untidy around here soon,' she said.

'How's that?'

'Well with *The Clipper* building being demolished and the new GPO.'

'Oh that. Well yes. But it's all progress. We're next, you know.'

What do you mean, we're next?'

'Our humble premises will also be replaced with a modern building.'

'So, the rumour is true.'

'Yes. Father and I have just completed meetings with Messrs Saliert and Rickard, architects. The old bank building will be demolished, and a new brick and stone building rendered with coloured cement is to replace it.'

'When?'

'Father seems to think we can start next year. It should look very smart, next to the new sandstone GPO. We are already the premier newspaper in Tasmania so with the new premises we will be able to broaden our horizons with the latest linotype printing machines that can manage a line of type in one operation instead of one letter at a time. We will have modern technology at our fingertips, with the electric telegraph that can send news around the world in hours. I remember father telling me it took 117 days for news of the Crimean War to reach Hobart back in 1853.' George puffed out his cheeks. '117 days Charlotte!'

The sausage rolls arrived. 'Fresh out of the oven Mr Davies,' the waitress smiled. 'So be careful, they're hot. I'll just fetch yer tea.'

George tonged a pastry onto Charlotte's plate before he bit into the flaky buttery pastry and wished he hadn't.

'So, tell me more about this book you're writing,' George asked, making a poor attempt to disguise his discomfort. 'What's it called for starters?'

'*Beyond the Seas of Tyranny.*'

'*Beyond the Seas of Tyranny,*' George brushed pastry crumbs off his suit lapel. 'Gosh, I like that.'

Charlotte took a moment to admire the suit before her, ash grey pin-stripe, tight fitting to show off the man's athletic physique. 'Nice suit by the way,' before slightly regretting the remark.

'Why, thank you.'

'The rose in the lapel sets it off nicely. Is that lone rose the reason you sent me eleven roses and not twelve?'

'Ah, most women would not have counted them.' George grinned and for the first time Charlotte observed he had a gold tooth. George was aware. 'You noticed.'

'The tooth?'

'Yes.'

'Does that pain you? I mean, to have it fitted?'

'A little at first. What do you think?' and George forced a wide smile. 'Makes me look debonair, what?'

'If you like gold teeth.'

George's mouth slammed shut. He straightened his back while aligning his cutlery. 'I've done a little reading about your famous father,' he said, matter-of-factly.

'Oh. And?'

'Your father's book was first released in serial form in the *Australian Journal*, in 1870 I read, continuing on well into '72. The series was called *His Natural Life*.'

'That's correct.'

'But many agreed it would make a great novel and told your father so.'

'You have done your research.'

'Oh yes. So, your father started revising the story, making vigorous cuts, trimming 370,000 words down to 200,000, a far more manageable novel.'

'That was no mean feat, wouldn't you agree?'

'Absolutely. He removed a 40,000-word opening chapter dealing with the protagonist's adventures before he was arrested and transported for a crime of which he was innocent.'

'I am impressed.'

'He then wrote a more definitive opening scene with a murder on Hampstead Heath that leads to the protagonist's downfall. He also cut out the adventures at the end of the book where the two main characters, Rufus Dawes and Sylvia Vickers survive the shipwreck at sea near Norfolk Island.'

'Yes, he drowned them! And that is where my novel continues the story,' Charlotte smiled.

'Well, the best of luck to you Charlotte. You have your work cut out.'

'I noticed your father dedicated his book to Charles Gavin Duffy, a rebel Irish national politician, himself imprisoned by the British for his involvement in the Irish Independent movement.'

'That's my Papa, he was always the rebel himself.'

'So, your book. It's a continuation of your father's work you told me before.' He leant back in his lean bentwood chair so as to cross his legs. 'Tell me more.'

Charlotte explained her ideas over tea and cake. How her father's existing characters, became lovers, married and had a family ...

'I hate to be rude Charlotte, but it sounds like it could be a little tedious.'

'That is but the first three chapters,' Charlotte became defensive. '*Beyond the Seas of Tyranny* is the story of Richard and Sylvia's children. You must understand that Richard Devine is still an escaped prisoner. So, after they are assumed dead – drowned in the shipwreck off Norfolk Island – they escape to America.'

'Oh, so the adventures continue in America?'

'Yes.'

'I like that,' George dropped three sugar lumps into his tea, stirring noisily. 'An American connection. Charlotte you are a genius. That would help sell your novel.'

'That is what I have in mind.'

'I say,' George became animated and leant forward across the small round table for two. 'I've met Mark Twain.'

'Mark Twain!'

'You know of whom I speak?'

'Of course. The famous American novelist. He visited Hobart a few years back.'

'That's correct. Well, I met him at a publishers' lunch in Melbourne just before I sailed to London to work with *The Times*. I spent many hours with him actually. You know he told me he was apprenticed as a typesetter at a Missouri newspaper, I can't remember the name, but he contributed articles to the paper also, at a young age too. He was also a river boat pilot on the Mississippi River, that's where he got his inspiration for *Tom Sawyer* and *Huckleberry Finn*. We discussed publishing new works. He would love

Beyond the Seas of Tyranny I am certain. Especially as you are Marcus Clarke's daughter.'

Charlotte sighed. Would she ever be Charlotte Clarke, and not Marcus Clarke's daughter? She had spent years shadowing her famous father, and earning the recognition as an independent success sometimes seemed as distant as and illusive as voting for women.

'What was Mr Twain like?'

'Colourful, interesting and very intelligent. However, he is not the greatest businessman I have ever met. He made a fortune writing and lost most of it with poor investments. But, if we can get him to endorse *your* book ... well ... the sky's the limit.'

'Where is he now? America?'

'No. Last I heard he resides in Austria, in Vienna. He has a lucrative contract giving lectures and speaking at clubs which has taken him all over the globe.'

'That's why he was in Hobart?'

'Exactly.' George sipped his tea, having some difficulty not to protrude his little finger at an effeminate angle, while his giant hand held the daintiest of teacups. 'Of course, you'll need a publisher first.'

Charlotte. 'Of course.'

'And that's where good old George comes in.' The wide smile that followed this comment showed off his *precious* gold tooth.

Against Charlotte's better judgement, Charlotte found she was warming to this man, openly a playboy. *But a publisher? Was this George Davies offering to finance the project as well?*

'Can I assume sir ...'

'George, please.'

'Can I assume George that you are willing to invest in my project? I mean I have other stories I wish to write also?'

'Absolutely. Your father was fortunate to know George Robinson, a Melbourne publisher, who published his book in '74 and, on the strength of that, it was published in London the following year.'

'Under the same title of his series *His Natural Life*.'

'Yes. The better-known title of *For the Term of His Natural Life* didn't come about for another seven years when the first posthumous editions appeared. But you know all this of course.'

Charlotte. 'You *have* been reading up on Papa.'

'It's a better title, wouldn't you agree?'

Charlotte nodded.

'*For the Term of His Natural Life* was a very profitable novel,' George said. 'It was reviewed in London by the *Athenaeum, Spectator, Vanity Fair, The Graphic, The Standard and the Morning Post.* That's no mean feat Charlotte. So, I am thinking this, George,' and George poked himself in the chest, 'would like to follow in the footsteps of George Robinson in Melbourne and invest in your novel.'

Charlotte was cautiously thrilled – past offers had come to nothing. She kept a level head. 'Thank you. That is very generous. I won't let you down.'

'I know you won't.'

'I heard recently,' Charlotte said, 'from family, that Charles McMahon the theatrical entrepreneur in Melbourne, has been making enquiries to turn Papa's book into a stage play.'

'Goodness, that is exciting news.' George poured fresh teas from the pot. 'But tell me, how advanced are you in *your* story?'

'I'm forty pages into my first draft.'

'Excellent. Then I will have to read some of what you have written to get the feel of your style.'

Charlotte did not hesitate. 'Of course.'

'I suggest I come to your aunt's cottage.'

'My aunt's?'

'Yes. And the sooner the better.'

Morning tea, it appeared, came at a price. But Charlotte liked George. He was good company and a gentleman, if not a little 'footloose and fancy-free' man of the world. But if he could help her succeed in a writing career ...

Over second cups of tea and creamed sponge cake with raspberry jam, George told Charlotte of his plans to buy a rural property. He quite fancied living in Coal River Valley he told her, near Richmond, as he was attracted to the English-style village. He also mentioned how his mother and father were keen for grandchildren.

'Apparently', George laughed, 'it is time for me to settle down, become a country gentleman.'

Charlotte's article about Dugal Bean's confession in Wednesday's paper had a ripple effect. Those close to Dugal sought justice and, at their advice, he retracted the confession. Now Hutton was in the limelight for all the wrong reasons.

Dugal Bean was released on bail but ordered not to leave Hobart. With the *May Queen* now docked at New Wharf he was permitted to work at least, loading cargo for the return journey down the channel; cargo such as barley for the sawyer bullock teams, groceries and other daily necessities. With so little evidence against him, it now looked like he would be found not guilty. A date was set for his first hearing.

The case was bitterly contested from the start. Although forensics tests under Rosa's fingernails proved negative, traces of semen were found on her undergarments. Her pantaloons were missing. Charlotte also knew the outcome of modern investigation could still be severely incorrect. If a body was dragged from the river, it was assumed death by drowning. So was a mangled body discovered at the side of the road assumed to have been dragged behind a passing cart or galloping horse. One of the most profound theories to aggravate the practical minded Charlotte was the belief a murderer's image could be extracted through photographing a deceased person's eyeballs; the killer being the last person the victim saw.

Charlotte was a realist. She was an advocate for the more recent science of fingerprinting. But unfortunately bringing criminals to justice through fingerprinting was in its infancy, although Mark Twain himself had recently published a book, *Life on the Mississippi*, where the murderer was convicted through fingerprint identification. However, this was fiction.

The courtroom erupted when it was realised Hutton had embellished a crew member's comment that Dugal washed his trousers that night. He *did* wash them, but the next day. The policeman had also fabricated information, like the fact a crew member told him Dugal came in late Saturday night with blood on his trousers.

'I said mud,' the witness yelled at Hutton in court and the furious crew member had to be escorted from the courtroom until his anger subsided.

Jarl Haugen came forward and told the prosecutor that Rosa had spoken of a man she called Ahab harassing her. Jarl himself had his own alibi. His friend and his friend's sister, whose cottage he stayed at in town that night, both testified that Jarl was home at their cottage in West Hobart by 11PM. He often stayed with them, they told the courtroom, when he came to town at the weekend.

More damning against Hutton was the stenographer who transcribed Hutton's rendition of the confession. Under questioning by the court-appointed defence lawyer for the accused, the stenographer told the court she had never met the prisoner. The room was made aware that the interrogation went on for twenty-four-hours and, according to other officers present at the time, the accused told Hutton the truth throughout. It was only through duress at the end of the 24 hours – when the prisoner was exhausted – that Dugal Bean broke down and told Hutton what the police officer wanted to hear, finally signing the *confession*.

Without a murder weapon and without blood stains on the accused clothes it seemed difficult to convict Dugal Bean. Then Dugal's mother arrived from Dover, a days ride south of Hobart, to testify that her son was a simpleton, bullied at school and had a child-like fear of pain and violence. He could not possibly have committed such a violent crime.

But the prosecution wasn't buying, and the judge had his doubts. After the first hearing Dugal was remanded in custody until the next hearing the following week.

The Caledonian Hotel and single men's lodgings. Elizabeth Street.
Mrs. Audrey Schuster ran a tight ship. The no-nonsense landlady rented five rooms above the hotel for single gentlemen, and woe betide any gentleman

who stepped out of line. Slight inebriation was tolerated, after all the lodgings *were* above her taproom and parlour. Mrs Schuster understood the necessity for men to imbibe alcohol, so if her lodgers were to spend money on drink, they may as well spend it in her establishment. However, female companions were strictly forbidden in the rooms.

The sixty-year-old woman had sailed to Hobart with her parents when the town was known as Hobarton back in the '50s, and the family had prospered ever since. Audrey married a German immigrant and bore him four children. The eldest, a daughter, and her husband had died in a coaching accident twelve years ago. Maybe it was this tragedy, those that were close to her thought, that had turned her into a bitter woman.

Shortly after *the girl in the swamp* murder made headlines, Nicholas Calonne, a twenty-four-year-old lodger, came to Mrs Schuster with a complaint. Someone had been in his room and his silver fob watch, a family heirloom no less, was missing. As no one except lodgers were allowed upstairs, it had to be another guest.

'Thank you for coming to me Mr Calonne. Because you are the third person to make a complaint the past week. Leave it with me.'

Mrs Schuster waited until midday when all lodgers were out for the day, and with the aid of one of her barmaids to keep a watchful eye, she searched first the room of Jake Crewe, a surveyor assistant with the railway. The room was neat and tidy, the washstand clean. The landlady had no hesitation searching the man's luggage.

'Nothing,' she muttered to the barmaid, stepping onto the landing and closing the door behind her. William Fowler's room was next to Crewe's. Fowler was a loner, a fifty-year-old accounts clerk at government offices. His window was closed tight, and the room smelt of stale clothing, soiled socks and the like. The landlady searched the room. The man was certainly not as tidy as Jake Crewe, with clothes discarded on the floor, the wardrobe doors open and other garments hanging skew-whiff and disorderly. A travelling trunk in one corner proved to be just an innocent bystander, but a bible book-marked at the beginning of the New Testament gave the woman confidence in the man's integrity. A good Christian would not steal.

'That only leaves Mr Culpepper, but I can't for the life of me imagine him stealing from other guests.'

The barmaid had other ideas. 'His father *was* a transportee mam.'

Edward's room smelt of rum scented tobacco where he had enjoyed his morning pipe before leaving. The window was left ajar. The room was tidy and everything in order. There wasn't a lot to search. A leather suitcase had been emptied and stowed under the bed, its contents either hanging in the wardrobe or neatly placed in a chest of drawers. Personal items seemed minimal. Exasperated, the landlady pushed the case back beneath the bed when she observed a second, much smaller suitcase, shoved against the wall, hidden. Kneeling awkwardly, Mrs Schuster reached under the cot and dragged the well-travelled case free. She flicked open the flimsy locks and looked inside and gasped. What was Mr Culpepper doing hiding a woman's handbag, clothing, a pair of pantaloons? She stared in horror, confusion and disgust before calling to the barmaid, 'Go fetch a constable, smartly now.'

CHAPTER EIGHT

Charlotte was feeling great about herself. She had certainly disturbed a wasp's nest with her article. Dugal Bean was innocent, she just knew it, and Senior Constable Toby Hutton should be made accountable for misrepresentation, for extracting a confession from a terrified man under duress.

However more pressing was the situation involving Mrs Hyacinth Hambleton. A preliminary court hearing had the judge throw the charge of murder out of court. The most damning evidence was the missing poker from the kitchen fireplace at the victim's home. It was found propped against a jardinière at the front entrance to Hyacinth's home in Richmond. Hyacinth claimed she had used it to jemmy open the coal cellar door at her husband's house, to check water damage in the cellar, and accidentally brought it home with her. However, the coroner was not convinced the murder weapon *was* a fire poker.

Also damning was the witness friend of the deceased who came forward and declared that Mr Hambleton had told him, quote. *I think Hyacinth is trying to kill me, to get me out of this house so she can sell it. If I am found dead, then you know what has happened to me.* But Hyacinth's defence lawyer asked the court the question: *if Mr Hambleton was on such bad terms with his estranged wife, do you really think Mr Hambleton would have opened the locked door to her.* And he reminded the court that only the housekeeper Eleanor Hark knew where the key was hidden outside. The judge agreed. He insisted there simply was not enough evidence to waste the court's time. Hyacinth was understandably ecstatic.

'Then who did kill the old scholar Osbert Hambleton? Who bludgeoned the man in his own home?' Charlotte asked those who'd listen.

No one wanted to point the finger.

Innocent of murdering her husband or not, Charlotte thought, she's still guilty of fraud and stealing her demented aunt's property from her Bellerive mansion.

'That'll be as 'ard to prove as the killin',' Edward had said. But Charlotte had a plan.

***

7.10AM. Mercury Newspaper offices.
George Davies was first into the journalists' workspace, which he passed through to reach his own office on the first floor.

'Charlotte.' George had an immediate spring in his step. 'You're early this day.'

The newspaper executive witnessed the most unusual sight. On Charlotte's desk were three typing machines, not one, but three, and all were in various stages of dismemberment. Cylinders, paper edge-guides, carriage-releases, ribbon spools, loosened shift keys, screws, knobs, levers and clamps sat alongside their respective machines in what appeared orderly mayhem. Charlotte looked up, clearly in deep concentration. She was armed with a screwdriver in one ink-stained hand, a magnifying glass in the other and a look of positive victory.

'My word!' George was astounded. 'Do you mind if I ask what you are up to, or would that be a doltish question?'

'George ... I ... ah. I'm just doing some sleuthing.'

'Sleuthing? It looks more like you have created a giant mechanical jigsaw puzzle.'

Charlotte instantly saw the humorous side of what, to George, must appear crazy. 'I suppose it does look a little strange.'

'Strange?' George peeled off his kidskin gloves and unbuttoned his coat. 'Please enlighten me.'

Charlotte explained the situation with the Hambletons and their nefarious activities. She finished by explaining how she paid a visit to the manager of the Savings Bank of Tasmania.

'You met old Cecil Winthrop huh? I'll wager you frightened the daylights out of him with your revelations.'

'Yes, well,' Charlotte tried not to blush. 'So, I have a theory about typing machines having similar irregularities as human fingerprints,' Charlotte's words, it seemed, spilled from her mouth as fast as the very machines before her could type them.

'Oh,' George removed his beaver fur top hat, nursing it gently under his arm. 'And how's that?'

Charlotte explained. Finally, she drew George's attention to the various letter shift-keys from different machines, and then paper samples, all spread out on her desk. 'I am confident that if I can get hold of Mrs Hambleton's typing machine, I will be able to prove that it was she who forged letters from her dying aunt Mrs Sayer, to appropriate her finances in the Hambleton's favour.'

'Are you absolutely certain Mrs Hambleton has a typing machine?'

'Yes. A Remington. I saw it on her bureau.'

'My!'

'Yes, I am convinced it is she, Mrs Hambleton, who has typed the letters and then forged the old lady's signature.'

'Incredible.'

'Yes. Incredible.'

'You really believe you can prove this?'

'Yes. Even a machine fresh from the factory will have some minor imperfections, but during their lifetime other identifying *fingerprints* appear.'

'Such as?'

'Each letter is a metal casting, made of pewter by the way, and they become chipped and unevenly worn, see here.' Charlotte demonstrated by comparing the letter 'F' on a colleague's disassembled machine with the same letter on her machine. 'This one is worn at the base of the letter where the shift key strikes on a slight angle favouring the bottom of the letter first. Yet this one,' Charlotte lifted the loosened 'F' key between 'D' and 'G' on her own machine with the point of her screwdriver. 'This one is a neat and complete letter 'F', clear as daylight.'

'I see.'

'And both machines are the same model manufactured by *Underwood*.'

'Well, I would never have thought.'

'Woman's intuition George.'

'Yes, well.'

Now Charlotte blushed. Had she been too bold? 'Some letters are used more than others,' she continued. 'Like the vowels for example. I've discovered alignments are disturbed or the shift key will become so worn, capital letters no longer align with the lower-case letters. To be honest, I would put typing machines in the same category as fingerprints and ballistics. They are all different.'

'Charlotte Clarke,' George grinned. 'You are quite the sleuth.'

'I would even go further and estimate the chances of two typing machines being identical would be ... say ... three billion to one.'

'Good heavens, just three billion huh? And how on earth did you come up with that number?'

'I made a few calculations. It is a wild guess nonetheless.'

'My.' George propped his backside on the corner of Charlotte's desk, stroking his chin in serious thought. 'So, ah, where is this leading us ... ah, leading you?'

'Well, I have copies of typed letters here, sent to the bank from Langley Home, and supposedly signed by Mrs Genevieve Sayer, authorising money transfers into Ashley Hambleton and his wife Adelaide D'Boville's accounts.'

George inspected one of the letters and his face became serious. 'Where did you get these?'

'Please don't ask.'

George returned the letter.

'Now I know these are fraudulent,' Charlotte said. 'But what I need to do is compare the typed information with the Hambleton's machine, which I can only assume is at their Richmond property.'

'And how do you suppose to do that ...?' Suddenly George stopped dead. 'Wait a minute. You mentioned the name Adelaide D'Boville.'

'Yes.'

'How is she connected to the Hambletons?'

'Like I said, she is Ashley D'Boville's wife, and a serpent, I might add. I met her once and ...'

George interrupted Charlotte mid-sentence. 'But I have been corresponding with her.'

'What? How?' Suddenly Charlotte remembered her station. 'If you don't mind me asking.'

'Well, I do believe I told you I am looking to buy an estate, preferably in the country.'

'Yes, the country gentleman, I do remember.'

'Well, I have correspondence from this woman. She is acting as the agent, so she informed me, for the sale of an estate near Richmond. I am to meet her at the property for an inspection. We are yet to set a time.'

'So, you have typed correspondence from *The Oaks*?'

'That's what I said.'

'Where?'

'In my office.'

Leonard McShan – Charlotte's unwelcome chaperone at Port Arthur – was the first journalist to walk through the door. He looked at his desk. His typewriter was missing. He looked at a sheepish Charlotte. 'Ten minutes Leonard, ten minutes is all I need to put your machine back together, and then you can write up your theatre review, or the weather or the football or whatever other article of importance that occupies your precious life.'

***

George Davies' office.
At the far end of the Literary Department an oak door led to a flight of stairs. George's office was situated on the floor above. As a rule, his secretary, Miss Juliana Haughton, vetted all visitors. They had first to pass through her

small office, so it was of no surprise to Charlotte when the fifty-year-old spinster, tall and straw thin, scowled at Charlotte, hurrying along in the company of the man himself.

George ushered Charlotte into his own office and stood with his hands on his hips staring at his neat roll top desk, temporarily confused by the efficiency of his thorough secretary. George rolled open the desk lid and sighed. 'Juliana,' George called out. He never knew where to start looking. 'Juliana.'

'Sir.'

'I'm looking for that correspondence for the property I am to inspect at Richmond.'

'That's in your personal file sir. Under 'R'.'

'R' ...' George tugged at a bottom drawer within a ten-tier blackwood filing cabinet. Everything was orderly. 'R', for real estate?'

'No sir, 'R' for Richmond.'

'Oh, of course ... here.'

George passed Charlotte a long descriptive letter with plans of the homestead's interior attached. A second letter was an authorisation signed by the owner of the property, Mrs Genevieve Sayer, giving Mrs Hambleton authority to sell the property on her behalf. Adelaide D'Boville was listed as the agent.'

Charlotte sat in the boss's chair and switched on an electric desk lamp. The instant light never failed to fascinate her, although it was extraordinarily bright and one of the reasons her Aunt Jocelyn thought she would keep her spirit lamps. The secretary, Miss Haughton, shuffled uncomfortably.

George noticed. 'It's alright Juliana,' he said. 'As you were please.'

'I can prove my point immediately,' Charlotte allowed her magnifying glass glide over the typing. 'Here. The '*D*' in *Dear Sir...* the bottom quarter of the key is worn or damaged. See?' Charlotte offered George the glass. 'It is subtle, but it is a defining anomaly.'

Charlotte ran an experienced eye over the letter. 'And without a thorough inspection I can see dozens more. It looks as though the ribbon got twisted here also.' Charlotte pointed out a blurred word on the fifth line down. 'And you've kept the original envelope – perfect.'

'Yes, Juliana doesn't throw anything away.'

Charlotte noted an immediate irregularity with the typed address. 'Because it looks to me that the *card and envelope* guide on the typewriter is out of alignment. That is a fingerprint right there. All we need is to compare this letter with the typing machine at *The Oaks*.'

'Oh, and how should we do that?'

'Don't know. I'll think of something ... may I?' Charlotte retrieved her magnifying glass. 'Now, the signature on the second letter. If we can prove this has been forged, well, that's a major felony right there.' Charlotte studied the signature, supposedly of a sick old lady with only weeks to live. *Mrs Genevieve Sayer.*

Charlotte sat back in George's swivel, jerking her chin up smartly to capture George's attention. There was no doubt, Charlotte was enjoying herself. 'Do you want my opinion?'

'That's why you're here Charlotte.'

'These plans of the interior of the property,' Charlotte said. 'They have been copied from the original using tracing paper. Right?'

'I suppose so.'

'And I will wager Mrs Sayer's signature has been traced also, traced from other documents the old lady has signed in the past, no doubt at *The Oaks* also.'

George studied the signature. 'It looks alright.'

'Maybe I'm wrong, but there are some telltale signs.'

'Like what?'

'The thickness of the lines. When you sign a document, you apply pressure to some parts more than others. Maybe you favour the loop on your letter 'G' for George and not the down stroke with your pen. If you trace a signature this could easily be missed. Then, do you dot your 'Is' and cross your 'Ts' after you have completed signing?'

'Never thought about it.'

'It's subtle but it could make all the difference in detecting a forgery. Then, after the original is copied onto tracing paper the perpetrator may have the alignment all wrong, different from that of the real signature. Then there is the pressure used on the paper.'

'Pressure?'

'Yes, you see when tracing, the forger would use a pencil, then go over it in ink.' Charlotte re-applied the glass and studied the letter. She ran her finger gently over the writing. 'This is a forgery! Yes, I would stake my reputation on it.'

'What did you feel?' George asked, leaning closer over Charlotte's shoulder.

'When you look really carefully you can see a reasonable amount of pressure has been used when the tracing was done using tracing paper. Then the forger wrote over the impression with ink. There is the slightest of a misalignment there, when you sign a document, you don't go over now do you?'

'No, of course not.'

'Feel that George.' Charlotte directed the end of George's finger gently between her own, guiding him over the impression. The act was so subtle, so innocent, yet electrifying for the habitual lothario.

'Run your finger gently over the signature,' Charlotte said. 'You can feel the indentation. It's very faint. And the ink signature is not exactly over the tracing.'

George was momentarily distracted. He turned his head slightly, taking in Charlotte's natural scent. He was so close, close enough to nibble her ear, to kiss her cheek. Charlotte felt his warm breath and suddenly remembered her position. From Miss Haughton's office a stifled cough signalled disapproval. Charlotte stood suddenly.

'We also need to acquire a sample of Mrs Sayer's signature to compare with this,' Charlotte said, a slight croak in her voice. 'There will be overlaps between letters or dramatic flourishes on others ... I know what!'

George straightened. 'What?'

'The bank will have many originals.'

***

Later in the day.
Florence had problems with her typing machine's carriage release. Hers had been one of the machines dismantled for Charlotte's experiment. Charlotte

loosened the screws, made suitable adjustments and set the release back in order. 'Sorry about that Florence. It's all good now.' Charlotte was about to return to her own desk when Florence took her by the wrist and lowered her voice. 'Edward Culpepper,' Florence flushed as she spoke his name.

'What of him?'

'I think he's keen on you.'

'Oh, nonsense Florence. We're just friends.' Charlotte knew this wasn't true. There was more. Lots more, but truth be known she wasn't quite certain what.

'He's awful handsome,' Florence said.

'Yes. I suppose he is.'

'And I've seen how he looks at you,' Florence looked around the room. 'We all have.'

Now Charlotte felt her face turn pink. Charlotte's colleague's tongues were wagging. Some saw Edward as a suitable catch for Charlotte; a widow four years now and they liked Charlotte. Other gossips suggested Mr George Davies had shown interest in Charlotte of late.

Surely not, most argued. *He's fighting below his weight*, they contended.

But they all agreed that Charlotte needed a man in her life. All except Leonard McShan.

Edward though, was handsome, tall, fine figured and intelligent. Certainly, he was a little rough around the edges. A rough diamond some commented, and to Charlotte's chagrin, others, like Leonard, mocked Edward's lack of etiquette behind his back. But most agreed if anyone could refine Edward Charlotte could.

Edward appeared at the office door, peered through the window and grinned. Charlotte was at her desk. Pushing open the door several pairs of eyes looked up, Florence amongst them. She flushed. Edward scanned the room. 'Afternoon all.'

Edward smiled at Charlotte and held up his leather purse. He rattled coins. 'Got me first remuneration,' he said quietly. 'I'm thinkin' we oughta take 'igh tea at the Palace. My treat. What d'ya reckon?'

Charlotte looked at the paperwork on her desk, not too much that she couldn't take time off for a meal. She looked to Florence and shrugged. The fellow journalist, smitten with Edward, smiled. 'You go,' she sighed, her shoulders sagging. 'I'll hold the fort.'

'High tea is not served until 4PM,' Charlotte told Edward. 'But you can take me to lunch next door.'

Next door of course, was the Tasmanian Coffee Palace. Charlotte also knew Edward had only earned nine shillings for the week and Elia Dell, who ran the *Palace*, gave generous discounts to *The Mercury* staff.

They both ordered the day's specially prepared rabbit and swede pie, boiled potatoes and cabbage, served with a pot of tea. One shilling and six-pence each customer.

'This 'ere pie's delicious,' Edward forked in a morsel of meat and licked gravy from his knife blade. 'I'm glad we come 'ere, cos I seen rabbit pie advertised on the winder yesterdee.'

Charlotte smiled. Edward always made her smile, and sometimes for the wrong reasons. So, how difficult would it be to educate the man? Teach him elocution, table manners and the ways of gentlemen that would see him better accepted by her peers and not give them the opportunity to laugh behind his back. Charlotte swallowed politely, placed her fork tines downwards at the eight o'clock position on her plate, her knife at the four o'clock position. 'Edward,' Charlotte started.

'Charlotte,' Edward felt uncomfortable. 'You sound serious.'

'Well ...' Charlotte chose her words carefully. 'I am being serious, but I do not wish to offend you.'

'Offend me? Why? What 'ave I done?'

'Done! Nothing Edward, you've done nothing wrong.' Charlotte suddenly felt more awkward than she expected. 'Ah, how would you like me to teach you elocution?'

'Elo ... what?'

'Elocution. Correct pronunciation ... to ... ah ... to speak like a gentleman.'

'Ah ... I get it. You think I talk like a ratbag, a country bumpkin.'

Charlotte flushed. She thought she had overstepped the boundary, when Edward smiled.

'It's all I know Charlotte. I don't know any better way o' talkin'. It's the way I were raised.'

'I understand. But would you like to improve your English?'

'What d'ya have in mind?'

'Well, with your blessing, I will correct you when you use incorrect English … like …' Charlotte looked at the blank wall behind Edward for inspiration. 'Like a moment ago you said to me "I'm glad we come 'ere, cos I seen rabbit pie advertised on the winder yesterdee.".'

This repeated sentence from the lips of his mentor struck Edward as being derisive. It sounded so crude. Was Charlotte being cruel, surely not?

'The correct English would be: *I'm glad we came here, because I saw rabbit pie advertised on the window yesterday.*'

Edward repeated the corrected sentence. It sounded refined. 'I know what yer sayin'. That were much better.'

'*Was,*' Charlotte corrected. 'That *was* much better. Not that *were* much better.'

'Got yer.'

'Got *you*, not *yer.*'

'Got *you.*'

'That's correct. Are you keen to do this?'

'Yes Charlotte.' Edward lowered his voice. '*How now brown cow,* and all that, eh?'

'In a nutshell, yes.'

Edward looked about the busy dining room, eager to remain anonymous. 'I am keen. It's just that it might take some time.'

'Time is something we both have, I think.' Charlotte looked into Edward's eyes. They looked grey in this light; she had thought they were blue. For a man in his thirties he had smooth skin, except for calloused palms, and a youthful figure, both muscular and sturdy.

'Did yer husband speak proper?'

'Did my husband speak correct English? Well yes, he did. What made you bring him up?'

'I were just thinkin' 'bout him the other day. Must be pretty hard losing someone yer loved.'

Charlotte thought for a long moment. Truth was, Charles was not in her thoughts much these days. Finally, she decided to open up. 'My husband was a little strange.'

'Oh, in what way, if'n yer don't mind me askin'.'

'Don't get me wrong, the first two years of marriage were happy times. But slowly he changed. He grew morose ...'

'Morose?'

'Depressed. We started arguing. Or I should say he started arguing about everything. He became an angry person. It was like he had a change of personality.'

'Was he violent?'

'Sometimes.'

'Did he hit you?' Charlotte was silent a long moment. 'Sorry Charlotte, I shouldn't 'ave asked. It's none o' me business.'

'No. It serves me well to talk about it actually. He hit me once, with the back of his hand.'

'Bastard! Sorry ... excuse me language.'

'But only once mind.' Charlotte's eyes widened at the memory. Her face reddened. 'I hit him back so hard he fell over backwards. And I told him, don't you ever, ever hit me again.'

'Good for you.'

Charlotte's thoughts were distracted briefly, then she said, 'He drowned a week later.'

'Oh.'

Charlotte changed the subject completely. 'What are you like at breaking and entering?' she asked across the table, surreptitiously.

'What? I mean pardon.' Edward looked about nervously. But the café was noisy and packed with contented diners.

'Ever fancied committing a little burglary in the name of justice?'

'Hell's bells Charlotte, do you want to end up behind bars?'

'Not particularly. No. But I need to expose Hyacinth Hambleton for the charlatan and thief that she is.'

Charlotte went on to explain how she had learnt that the recently deceased Mrs Genevieve Sayer, sent by her relatives to Langley House Home, had left all her property to Edith Woodrow, her niece living in South Africa. Charlotte told Edward how a new will and testament had been written and the old lady tricked into signing it. 'And the new will is made out to Hyacinth's son, Ashley.'

'What's this got to do with ...' Edward leant in close across the table. 'Breakin' an' enterin'?'

'Breaking and entering.'

'All right, all right ... breaking and entering.'

'Mrs Sayer owned a large home in Bellerive. A home full of valuable items that I am certain have been stolen over the past months. I need to inspect the mansion for myself.'

'Golly, I dunno Charlotte.'

Charlotte slipped both hands across the table taking hold of Edward's. 'In the name of justice,' she said with determination and a hint of mischief, 'will you please help me?'

***

Bellerive. Hobart's Eastern shore.

Domus Casandra, named after the first ship built by shipbuilder Andrew Sayer, was a substantial faux Tudor mansion built on an acre of land on Victoria Esplanade overlooking the River Derwent. It enjoyed sweeping views across the water to Hobart. Built twenty years earlier for Mrs Genevieve Sayer by her husband, the home boasted five bedrooms, two bathrooms – both with running water, marble tiles, an open fireplace in every wood-panelled room, and wooden ceiling beams of Tasmanian oak. Every modern convenience had been installed, including indoor water closets. But over the last year or so life had dealt the woman an unfortunate hand. The once beautifully maintained gardens were now in disarray, the windows boarded, and ivy crept about the exterior like avaricious kinsmen.

Charlotte entered by the scullery door; the lock picked by Edward.

'And where did you learn that trick?' she asked.

'Me Pa. "e were taught by an ol' lag back in the day.'

Charlotte thought to correct his English but now wasn't the time, or the place. Immediately she sensed the stale, fetid smell of rotten fish lingering in the dark shadows of the musty rooms, made even more daunting by the fact the windows were sealed shut and boarded up. Had Ashley Hambleton with his wretched skin disorder been in the house recently?

'I don't mind tellin' yer Charlotte,' Edward muttered in a loud whisper, 'this place gives me the creeps.'

Charlotte had to agree. She pushed the door to the front drawing room open. The hinges, gasping for oil, resounded throughout the hall, accentuating the fact that the rooms were empty. Charlotte's eyes adjusted to what under normal circumstances would have been a room filled with sunlight. Her voice echoed slightly as if she were in a cave. 'Just as I thought, the house is near empty.'

'The old lady died, right?'

'Yes.'

Edward felt an uncomfortable shiver. After living with so many ghosts at Port Arthur he felt like someone was watching. Perhaps the dead owner. They moved back into the hallway.

'Look at the floorboards here,' Charlotte pointed to the floor. 'You will notice the dust pattern tells us there was once a hallstand there, but it has been removed. And the picture hook hanging from the architrave tells of a painting, now missing.'

'Stolen?'

'Undoubtedly. I'd say everything has been moved to Richmond. If we can prove the bank transfers made by the Hambletons have been illegal, then we can lead the police to the property at Richmond, because, mark my words Edward Culpepper, this family of Hambletons have robbed the beneficiary in South Africa blind. I'd also wager Hyacinth Hambleton killed her husband.'

'But you said the judge threw the charge outa court. Lack o' evidence.'

'Yes, I did. But the entire matter stinks.' Charlotte walked to the stairs, stepping on the first tread before turning back to Edward. 'Keep a sharp eye outside, I'm just going to have a quick look upstairs.'

Charlotte watched Edward disappear towards the back door and into the gloom of the shuttered hallway. She continued on, one tread at a time, wary that some of the old blacksmith-made nails were loose, creaking the timber as she ascended. Charlotte stepped onto the top landing, when the pungent smell returned. The stink of rotting fish. And it smelt stronger up here. Closer by ...

CHAPTER NINE

Constable Bluey Johnson was ecstatic. Of all the lawmen patrolling the streets of Hobart this post Easter week he finally had a purpose other than arresting drunkards. *Wait 'til I tell me Pa about this,* he treated himself to a smile hurrying back to the police station to fetch detectives.

How lucky was he?

He had been first on the scene for clues to the brutal murder of the girl in the swamp, and he was smart enough to recognise the importance of the find in the suitcase hidden under the bed by one of the lodgers at the Caledonian Hotel; a woman's handbag, a woman's undergarments, lewd literature and ... and did he catch a glimpse of obscene photographic images?

Inspector Boothman and Senior Constable Hutton were both at their posts when the alarm was raised. Poste-haste, the two lawmen followed Bluey Johnson back to the Caledonian, where Bluey was ordered to guard the door and keep sightseers at bay.

'Landlady,' Boothman said. 'What's the name of this lodger?'

'Edward Culpepper sir.'

'Edward Culpepper!' Hutton could not believe what he was hearing. 'Excuse me ma'm, did you say Edward Culpepper? A tall, tanned man? He would be around thirty-three, thirty-four years of age.'

'Yes.'

The realisation that the lodger in question was no other than Edward Culpepper gave Hutton enormous pleasure as he conducted a thorough search, starting in the wardrobe.

'Why do you ask Hutton?' Boothman said. 'Do you know the man?'

'Yes Inspector,' Hutton took pleasure in tossing Edward's shirts on the floor. 'He was a guide at Port Arthur, showing curious visitors around the old prison.' Hutton dropped to his knees, searching under the bed.

'How long has he lived here?' Boothman asked the landlady.

'Bit over a week, thereabouts.'

'Is there anything else of interest in this room?' Boothman queried. 'I assume you searched it thoroughly.'

The woman's disgust was palpable. 'No sir, just the ... *that* suitcase.'

Hutton stood, taking a last look about. The room was small, Culpepper's possessions sparse. 'We need to arrest this man immediately.'

'Indeed, we do Mr Hutton,' Boothman said. 'Indeed, we do. Mrs ...'

'Schuster sir. Mrs Audrey Schuster.'

'Mrs Schuster, do you know, perchance, where this fellow is at this present moment?'

'No sir. But I believe he was recently hired by the newspaper.'

'That's correct,' Hutton said. 'He found service with *The Mercury*.'

Boothman thanked the landlady for her vigilance. 'Should he return before we are able to make our arrest, I implore you madam, to keep silent about this situation. Act as though all is normal and send for a constable immediately. Above all, be aware, the man is dangerous.'

'What if he misses ... *that*?' The landlady alluded to the case sitting on the bed.

'Madame, if he returns unexpectedly fetch the police immediately. However, we will do our utmost to arrest him before he has a chance to return to his lodgings.'

Boothman stopped a moment with Hutton in the downstairs foyer to the hotel. The senior-constable held the incriminating suitcase.

'We better make ourselves scarce in case he comes back suddenly,' the inspector said. 'Get that suitcase back to the station, smartly now. I want all the contents carefully inspected and a full report by tonight.'

***

Bellerive. Sometime after sunset.

Charlotte regained consciousness. It was dark. Panicked she sat bolt upright and wished she hadn't. In the stygian blackness her head spun. She felt nausea and inert.

Where am I?

The floor beneath her was flagstone. Cold. She began to shiver. Her head ached. Charlotte touched the back of her head and felt something sticky. Blood!

Where the hell am I?

Bellerive? Yes ... Bellerive.

Fighting her fear, Charlotte called out. 'Edward!' No answer. She rolled onto her hands and knees groping about in the blackness. *Why is it so dark?* She felt what seemed to be a post to one side. Then bannisters. She was at the bottom of a stair. Had she fallen? Charlotte now remembered she had been upstairs in the Bellerive mansion when she heard someone approach from behind. Yes! And the smell of rotting fish. Ashley Hambleton?

Charlotte stood disorientated. 'Edward!' she called out. All was silent. 'Edward!' she shouted. Suddenly Charlotte heard muffled footsteps overhead. Boots on floorboards. She must be in a cellar. But how ...

The cellar door opened. Lantern light spilled down the treads surrounding her with confusion. Had her attacker returned?

'Mrs Clarke ... Charlotte? Is that you?'

Charlotte shielded her eyes against the approaching light. Senior Constable Toby Hutton hurried noisily down the wooden steps. Two uniforms followed. 'Toby Hutton?'

'Oh, thank the lord, you're alive.' Charlotte was shivering. Hutton took off his jacket, throwing it about her. 'What are you doing here?' he said. 'You're hurt. Wounded. What happened?'

'I don't know. Someone hit me, I think.' Charlotte's dizziness returned. She wobbled drunkenly.

'Here,' Hutton caught her before she fell. 'Sit.' He helped her sit on the stairs.

'I'm at Bellerive,' Charlotte managed to ask. 'Right?'

'Yes.' Hutton grew more serious in front of his colleagues. 'You've some explaining to do I'm afraid. This is private property, and it appears you and Edward have entered without permission.'

'Edward. Where's Edward?' There followed an awkward silence. 'Toby, where's Edward?'

'Sorry Charlotte.'

'Sorry for what?'

'Edward's in the watch house.'

'In the watch house. Why?'

'He's been arrested for the murder of the girl in the swamp.'

'N-no! Don't be ridiculous.'

'Sorry to have to tell you. But evidence was found in his lodgings connecting him to the murder.'

Charlotte listened in dazed silence, speechless. *It could not possibly be true.* Hutton sat with Charlotte on the ferry. He placed an arm about her shoulder on the pretext he was comforting her. But Charlotte was too preoccupied with the unfolding drama in her life to notice. A southerly blew upriver from Storm Bay, making the ferry crossing back to Sullivan's Cove less than calm. Hutton explained what he knew so far ...

'We went to *The Mercury* office seeking Edward to arrest him for the murder of the girl in the swamp. The stable hand, what's his name ... Jim? Jim told us you were headed for Bellerive. We came here immediately, arriving in time to discover the Bellerive watch house had just had a complaint from a neighbour that there was a drunkard trying to break into the *Domus Casandra* House. The drunkard turned out to be Edward. He wasn't drunk, he was drugged on chloroform, his own.'

'That's impossible.'

'He's clearly accidentally doped himself.'

'I've never heard of anything so ridiculous. And as for him murdering ...'

'Like I said, we have evidence incriminating him.'

'Evidence? What evidence?'

Hutton explained the discovery of the suitcase.

'No ... I don't believe you. It's impossible.'

'I'm sorry Charlotte. But it's fact.'

'No Toby, you have this all wrong.' Charlotte's head ached. She touched her wound where her hair was matted with drying blood. 'It is completely impossible. Edward would not hurt a fly.'

Hutton refused to agree. 'It must have been Edward who attacked you.'

'Now you are going too far.'

'No,' Hutton's face grew serious in deep thought. 'He chloroformed you. Yes, that's it. He chloroformed you and dragged you from the first floor to the cellar. I put it to you, Charlotte, that he probably dropped you down the stairs, that part was an accident, hence the cut on the back of your head. I also put it to you that he planned on doing to you what he did to the girl in the swamp. He drugged you, locked you in the cellar of a deserted house and was planning to come back for you when it was dark.'

'Why ... *why on earth* would Edward want to harm me? We are friends.'

'You're also a journalist, asking questions around town when you shouldn't. Maybe he suspected you were onto him.'

'Onto him for what?'

'The girl in the swamp murder.'

Charlotte's head was spinning with confusion. 'I ... I was attacked and I'm telling you now it was not Edward. It's ludicrous.' Charlotte argued. 'Edward would never harm me.'

Hutton turned cold. 'I wouldn't be so sure about that?'

Charlotte shook Hutton's arm free. 'You say Edward was drugged also?'

'He must have knocked himself out with his own chloroform.'

'How on earth could he do that?'

'I don't know. Maybe he used his handkerchief to drug you and minutes later he's absentmindedly used it.'

'Ridiculous.'

One of the other officers said, 'I must admit his clothes smelt of chloroform.'

Charlotte. 'There has to have been a third party?'

Another officer weighed into the conversation. 'Culpepper claims he doesn't recall much either, other than waking up in the garden.'

'Yeh, but that's only *his* story,' another constable said.

Charlotte. 'This is all too much.'

'His story is that when he came to, he went looking for you Charlotte,' Hutton said. 'But the house was all boarded up once more, and the door locked. And that's when Officer Dyson here from the Bellerive watch house turned up and arrested him.'

'You should have seen the look on his face. And he *was* really disorientated,' the officer said.

'Where, exactly,' Charlotte asked, 'is Edward now?'

'In the Bellerive lockup. He'll be transferred to Campbell Street tomorrow morning.'

'Edward could have easily unlocked the door again and come looking for me,' Charlotte said.

'It doesn't make sense. Why? And why would he try and kill me in the first place? It is preposterous.'

'Like I said, maybe you know too much,' the accompanying officer reiterated. 'And you aren't letting on.'

'Balderdash!' Charlotte remembered the rotting fish, the creaking floorboards behind her in the gloom, the hit to her head. 'It was Ashley Hambleton. He tried to kill me because, yes, I know too much about *him* and his mother Hyacinth. It was Ashley who left me for dead. He threw me into the cellar, and I am guessing he plans to come back after dark and get rid of my body.'

Hutton. 'Now, *that* is balderdash.'

'You do realise the Hambleton's aunt, Mrs Sayer, who died recently, is the owner of *Domus Casandra* I am talking about the family of Osbert Hambleton, the old man who was also found bludgeoned to death recently.'

The look on Hutton's face told Charlotte that the senior constable had not made the connection. 'We have pretty much established that that was a botched burglary,' Hutton tried to save face.

'Botched robbery! Huh! Poppycock!'

Hutton. 'Why were you in that house in the first place anyhow?'

Charlotte, blank-faced, remained silent.

'You're going to have to make a statement sooner or later, Charlotte,' Toby said.

Charlotte took a deep breath, finally explaining the missing furniture and her suspicions.

'You really must learn to keep out of police business,' Hutton said, but his words lacked conviction. He was growing to understand Charlotte's methodology – her hands-on approach to criminal investigation - and as much as she irritated him at times, he desperately wished to win over Charlotte's affections.

'We found this upstairs,' one of the uniforms said. He presented Charlotte's parasol.

'It's yours I told these gentlemen,' Hutton added. Charlotte reached out to take her umbrella when it was pulled away. 'Sorry, evidence,' the policeman said.

'Evidence?'

The other lawman opened a cheesecloth wrapping to expose the bloodstained stiletto. 'Unless *you* have cut yourself,' the officer said, 'it looks like you wounded someone else, Edward maybe.'

'Edward? Don't be ridiculous. I vaguely remember now. I stabbed Ashley.'

'You still want to blame Ashley Hambleton?'

'Yes, who else? I had already pulled the stiletto free from the parasol when I was struck from behind. I stabbed blindly before I was registered unconscious. I remember hearing a gasp.' Charlotte's face whitened. 'Now I remember. The chloroform. Yes. I *was* drugged.'

***

The Oaks, Richmond.

Morton Dunbar lay stretched across the bare slats of the four-poster bed stored in the barn, once the property of the deceased old lady, Genevieve Sayer. Ashley's wife Adelaide D'Boville lay next to him, both were naked, sharing a lone blanket. China, the white Friesian was restless, mooing, in the dairy next to the barn. It was time for the evening milk.

'Your husband came in late last night,' Morton fished. 'He was trying to be discreet but, well it's difficult around here.'

'He had business in Bellerive,' Adelaide said.

'At the old lady's house?'

'Yes. And he stopped at a few inns on the way home by the smell of him. He woke me, looking for bandages and ointment. He cut himself.'

'Oh?'

'Yes, it was only superficial, a cut to his leg, but deep enough to become septic. So, I attended to him.'

'Like you would one of your hounds, huh?'

'That's all he deserves.'

Morton grew serious. 'Ashley's lost everything hasn't he?' The jackaroo's intimacy with Adelaide had allowed a glimpse into her financial affairs also.

'Yes, he's lost the lot.' Adelaide turned onto her side, to be closer to the man she feared she had fallen head over heels in love with. Her white body, curvaceous and with the firmness of youth. Her breasts not too large, but pert. She ran a long fingernail down *her* jackaroo's bushy chest, loitering at his navel, before continuing onto his pubis, where she curled his bristled hairs around the point of her petite finger.

'But we have a plan to regain our fortunes,' Adelaide whispered in Morton's ear before nibbling.

'We?'

'Hyacinth, Phillipa, Ashley and me.'

'Oh. How? By selling off all this furniture?' Morton alluded to the barn crammed with antique and modern furniture. 'The four of you will hardly get rich on this lot.'

'No. Aunt Genevieve was a wealthy woman. Her husband was a shipbuilder and when he died ten years ago, she sold up. Over a hundred thousand pounds. Plus, Mr Sayer had several properties around the state, most bringing in high rents. Genevieve was also a savvy woman and made wise investments.'

'You're going to inherit, right?'

Adelaide considered her answer. 'Not exactly,' she said, an impulsive smirk curling the corners of her mouth. Love, it seemed, was blinding her to caution. 'In fact, the entire estate has been willed to a niece in South Africa.'

'So, what do you mean then?'

'Well, if I tell you, you must promise you will never tell anyone.'

'Tell me what?'

'Promise?'

'I promise.'

***

The following day.

Ashley Hambleton woke with a screaming toothache, an excruciating pain that had woken him abruptly. The morning was still dark. He needed professional help but his fear of visiting the dentist was exactly what put him in this distressing situation in the first place. He had left it too long.

Adelaide slept soundly, pouting softly. Quietly Ashley moved to the bathroom where he applied oil of cloves to his gums for temporary relief. He looked in the mirror. He had aged. But he had other problems. Ashley had returned to Aunt Sayer's mansion in Bellerive to release that troublesome bitch journalist from *The Mercury*. He had caught her breaking and entering with some yokel whom he managed to subdue with chloroform. This was chloroform he had purchased that morning from a pharmacy in Bellerive Village for his own pain relief; an addiction he had acquired of late.

In a panic, Ashley had locked the inquisitive journalist in the cellar – the plan being to release her with the threat of filing burglary charges against her. But it all became so messy. The *bitch* had stabbed him. It was superficial, but still, the bitch stabbed him. *She had pulled a knife on him for Christ's sake!*

Ashley managed to chloroform the journalist. He dragged her downstairs, only to let her slip the last few treads and crack her head. At first, he thought he had killed her, but she still breathed. Locking the woman in the cellar Ashley was planning his next move when he heard voices outside. Constables had arrived.

How? Why?

He watched them arrest the yokel, who was staggering around the garden, drugged. With the doors to the mansion locked, the windows all boarded up, Ashley had slipped away minutes before more police arrived.

He returned late the next morning. The back door had been breached, then re-boarded. The journalist had been freed. Discreet enquiries told Ashley the police had taken her away. Now it would be her word against his, after all she *was* trespassing. But the *pièce de résistance* – from the gossip about the village – was that the yokel found trespassing was wanted for the murder of the girl in the swamp. Now that *was* most fortuitous.

If Ashley suspected his wife and the jackaroo Morton Dunbar were having an affair, he certainly didn't show it. In fact, he treated the man warmly. Dunbar was a good worker, obedient and cheap. Very cheap. Frank, the help and yard hand who had been with the family for years, however, was no fool. He may be old and lazy, but he wasn't stupid. He had caught their secret glances, seen the intimate brushing of hands in passing and their familiarity. Why, he could almost smell the chemistry between them and it certainly smelt sweeter than his master's skin malodour.

Frank was a lonely man, but not too old to fantasise. He had covertly admired Adelaide since his master brought her back to the family home after they had married in secret. Frank liked that. *In secret*. He enjoyed secrets and had been quite the voyeur over the years he had watched Adelaide grow from twenty-two to twenty-seven. Why, he had on occasion spied on her in her bath. He had watched the woman undress; he had viewed her nakedness. Now this, *this damned jackaroo bastard* had come along and was doing the very things to his master's wife that he fantasised about. It was all too much.

So Frank wasn't surprised when Morton was adamant about remaining at the property this day – he had repairs to make to the farm dray for starters – while Frank escorted the master to Hobart.

Like a torture chamber the dentist surgery waited out of sight in the basement of a retail merchant, two doors west of the Ship Hotel in Collins Street. It smelt of chemicals, cloves and trepidation.

Balding Doctor Mulligan with his grey tufts of hair at unruly odd angles on his head reminded Ashley of an aging god, Mercury, with fixed wings upon his head. 'Disastrous Mr Hambleton. Your teeth are in a terrible shape. And I hate to tell you sir, but your breath is abominable.'

'I am desperate doctor. Can you help me?'

'Some of my colleagues insist on extracting all troublesome teeth but I pride myself in filling cavities.'

'Filling with what, I might ask?'

'Well in days gone by we used tree resin, but resin-based fillings aren't strong enough to sustain constant chewing. Today, my good fellow, I am pleased to inform you that I use gold foil. Any dentist worth his pound of flesh uses gold these modern times.'

Doctor Mulligan went on to explain how he had recently acquired a delivery of several bottles of *Doctor R. B. Waite's Local Anaesthetic*. 'You are fortunate Mr Hambleton that this cocaine-based anaesthetic will render the operation painless.'

Had Ashley known, the same dentist was recently forced to compensate one of his patients when he broke a rib by resting one foot on the man's chest as he extracted a bad tooth by pulling rather violently with pliers. But Ashley was suffering so badly he cared not.

'I will extract these troublesome molars today,' the dentist decided. 'And there are three teeth with cavities that I can fill also. But this will be temporary sir, I recommend you make an appointment, and we will fit you with dentures.'

While Mulligan's female assistant held a new-fangled portable battery to power the drill, the troublesome teeth were hollowed clean and filled. But eventually, as Mulligan explained, he used the electric grinder to grind his teeth off at the roots in order to fit the custom-made dental plate.

The dentist was fortunate to be blessed with a large hand, with which he clamped upon Ashley's head from behind, grasping his patient in a kind of headlock. The extraction and fillings took more than two hours by which time the effects of the cocaine were wearing off.

'In the meantime, I suggest you take a sea trip Mr Hambleton,' was Mulligan's final advice. 'To Melbourne maybe. The sea air will help you mend.'

Ashley wasn't lost for words; he just couldn't speak. His answer came out as a slurry groan. The dentist then handed his patient a small cardboard box. 'And may I suggest you suck on these sir, for the breath.'

Ashley was barely coherent. 'What are they?'

'Comfits. They are anise, caraway and fennel seeds, each seed sugar coated so when chewed the seeds are crushed open, freshening your breath for up to half an hour.'

Doctor Mulligan watched his nurse help the patient into his jacket and see the man to the door. *Comfits,* he considered with serious consideration, *may assist in perfuming the man's breath, but what was that awful, bad-fish smell that permeated the surgery?*

***

Agapanthus Cottage, Macquarie Street.
Charlotte's Aunt Jocelyn saw Doctor Finch to the door and thanked him for his visit.

'She needs rest,' the handsome forty-year-old doctor told the woman. 'Charlotte's concussion *will* subside. But her brain needs time to recover. She must rest. She will more than likely suffer dizziness, maybe vomiting, double vision and, possibly, severe confusion. That was a nasty blow she was dealt. Limit her activities and restrict social engagements. No visitors.'

'How long will this take?'

'Absolute rest for two days at least, and it could take two weeks before she is back to normal. Oh, and here, give her these.' The doctor remembered a small bottle of tablets he meant to leave behind and took them from his leather Gladstone bag. 'These are cephalic pills for headache relief.'

Aunt Jocelyn saw the doctor to the gate before she returned to Charlotte. Charlotte was propped on cushions in the conservatory at the rear of the cottage where the north-facing glasshouse caught the sun throughout the day.

'I must get to Edward,' Charlotte said, frustrated at her situation.

'You heard the doctor. You must rest.'

'And I say I must see Edward.'

'Charlotte ...' aunt's words trailed off.

'You've gotten to know Edward the past weeks,' Charlotte told her aunt. 'You know his background; I've told you all about him. He did not commit this ghastly crime.'

'I hate to remind you, dear girl, but the evidence is damning. That suitcase under his bed.'

'He's been falsely incriminated. He didn't do it Aunt Jocelyn. It is ridiculous to even contemplate that Edward might be guilty.'

Aunt Jocelyn sighed. 'All the same, it doesn't look good Charlotte.'

'Someone else put it there, I know they did. He's been set up and I will prove it. Please, will you help me dress?' Charlotte tried to stand but the dizzy spells floored her. She fell back into the armchair.

'You're going nowhere,' Jocelyn said. 'Not today at least.'

'Then I must send Edward a letter. Send him hope. God knows what rubbish they have told him at the watch house about my side of the story.'

Aunt Jocelyn knew her niece only two well. 'Then you write that letter, and I will see he gets it.'

Charlotte woke from an afternoon sleep. Outside the autumn day was crisp, but in the warmth of the conservatory Charlotte imagined she travelled to the South Pacific, sharing the peace and serenity with her aunt's orchids and the season's remaining tomatoes – fat red and juicy, ready to be picked and made into relish.

The hall bell rattled on its coiled bracket for a second time and Charlotte realised what had woken her. Jocelyn wiped flour on her apron and hurried down the passageway muttering something about impatience. One moment later. 'You have a gentleman caller,' Jocelyn said, from the open end of the conservatory.

'Oh?'

'Looks very swish too.'

'Oh? Who?'

'Said his name's George.'

'George! Oh god Aunt, where is he, in the drawing room?'

'No, I told him you are convalescing, but he already knew that. I left him on the doorstep.'

'Oh golly Aunt, that's my employer.'

'Oh. Then what shall I tell him?'

'Send him through.'

'But you are not dressed suitably to entertain gentleman.'

'Don't be such a prude, aunt.'

George Davies looked handsome as ever, his long thin legs filling grey and black tartan trousers with a coat and short tails to match. Aunt Jocelyn took his top hat at the door. In his spare hand George carried a dozen red roses. Aunt Jocelyn was more than impressed. She stood in the doorway gaping until Charlotte appeared in the hallway, breaking her aunt's reverie.

Charlotte introduced them. 'This is Mr Davies from the newspaper.'

'Call me George, please.'

'Davies?' Aunt specified. 'As in Davies the newspaper?'

'Yes madam. Charlotte and I are colleagues.' George noted the woman's eyes drop to the bunch of roses. 'Oh, here, they may need a vase,' he said with a flirtatious smile that held the room.

'Oh, thank you.' Aunt Jocelyn took the roses as if they were intended for her. 'Thank you very much.'

Charlotte was half embarrassed. 'Did I hear you ask, *do we want tea,* Auntie?' she said without an ounce of subtlety.

'Of course.' Charlotte's aunt returned to the kitchen. Charlotte led George through the cottage to the conservatory. It was when they were alone George said, 'I've been so worried for you, you dear, dear girl.'

George pulled up a wicker chair to sit close. It was then that Charlotte realised George carried her parasol.

'My parasol!'

'Oh yes,' George immediately relinquished the umbrella. 'The police dropped it off at the office, said it was no longer an item of interest. I thought you'd be happy. But pray tell, what were they doing with it in the first place?'

Charlotte told George everything. There was no reason to hold back. She felt it was in Edward's interest to have someone as influential as George Davies on their side.

'I've been thinking,' Charlotte finally said. 'So, I was chloroformed also, like Edward, and thrown down those cellar stairs, that's how I hurt my head.'

'*Thrown* down the stairs?'

'Well man-handled anyway, I have bruises and my limbs are stiff.'

'The mongrel.'

'Ashley was spooked by the police turning up at the property you see. Thank god they did, otherwise I might not be here to tell the tale.'

'I don't know what to think,' George took Charlotte's hand in both of his in a comforting gesture. 'You seem pretty determined it was this Ashley Hambleton fellow.'

'Of course it was. And I recall smelling something sweet and strong, like ether,' Charlotte said. 'Like a hospital smell.'

'That is disturbing,' George frowned. 'Most disturbing. And Edward! I only met the man a few times. He certainly doesn't seem the type who would commit such a dastardly crime.'

'Edward didn't murder that girl found in the swamp. No way, George. Edward simply is not capable. He is kind and … I need to see him. Can you pull a few strings for me, get me into the watch house?'

'I heard he's been moved to Campbell Street gaol,' George said. 'In an isolation cell, on remand.'

Charlotte shook her head. 'Oh, poor, poor Edward.'

'The evidence against him is damning, Charlotte.'

'He didn't do it George. I know Edward.'

George felt a twinge of envy. 'He has only been in our service a few weeks.'

'I knew him from Port Arthur. He saved my life, in a way.'

'Oh, how is that?'

'The fires that devastated Port Arthur. I was there, as you know. Edward had taken me into bushland to interview an old man who was once a Port Arthur prisoner and had met my father when he was researching *his* novel. The fires struck so suddenly, and Edward led me to safety.'

'Oh, I see. I wasn't aware. Well, that's all very commendable, but there is a good chance he will hang for the murder of that girl.'

Charlotte fought back a tear. She was tougher than that. 'Can you organise a visit to the prison for me?'

Charlotte was determined.

'If he means that much to you, then I will see what I can do.'

CHAPTER TEN

Tasmanian Steamship Navigation Company arrivals. Hobart Docks.
Paolo Esposito was a ruined man. His only child, sixteen-year-old daughter Rosa was dead. And what a horrific death she had suffered at the hands of some deranged deviant; her petite body left to be eaten by insects and rats in open swampland. Gaunt, defeated and distraught, fifty-one-year-old Paolo disembarked the cargo-passenger ship SS *Corinna*. He travelled light with a canvas kit bag containing a change of clothes for a week and his bible. Paolo wanted to see the man who murdered his little princess, and he recently heard that the killer had been arrested. The five-foot-four Italian, who worked at the Holzer Brick Company in Melbourne – and was built like a circus strongman – wanted to see the killer face to face, to see justice done. In his mother country Italy, the death penalty had been abolished nine years earlier. The guillotine's last beheading was back in '89. But Tasmania, Paolo was pleased to learn, this *bastardo* would hang for his crimes. And Paolo wanted to be there to be certain he died. Now his sister-in-law, Francis Francesco, had sent him word that preliminary hearings in the courtroom should be scheduled soon.

Paolo was a simple man. Hardworking and very private. Introverted many would say. Choosing not to stay with his sister-in-law, Paolo took cheap lodgings at a waterside inn. And although Francis had sent a letter to Melbourne, she had no idea her brother-in-law was in Hobart.

***

The Oaks, Richmond.

Ashley heard the cottage back door slam shut. His health had deteriorated lately, and it may have been a knee jerk reaction, but he had recently terminated the employment of Maryanne the cook. She was becoming a nuisance, a busybody. He dragged himself to the bedroom window on the first floor to see if it was Maryanne leaving. Instead, he was in time to catch Adelaide crossing the field towards the barn. The two Irish Wolfhounds, Bernard and Barry, playfully bounded about her in circles, dutifully retrieving sticks thrown in all directions. Adelaide carried a notebook and pen. Ashley smiled; as ill as he felt, he smiled. He had been neglecting his wife of late and wanted to make amends. He decided to make an effort although the pain his teeth were causing made this difficult. For now, though, Adelaide should be busy making a list of all the furniture they had gathered. Ashley had arranged for an auctioneer to come and fetch the older pieces first, followed in a week's time by the modern blackwood furniture Aunt Genevieve had so loved.

Ashley was about to crawl back into his bed when *that infernal music* started again in the drawing room downstairs. Then he heard singing. *Singing for Christ' sake! Mother was drunk on gin again* and playing that damned gramophone taken from Genevieve's Bellerive property. Now, the *Admiral Dewey March* from the flaring horn filled the house with its awful melody.

Adelaide found Morton Dunbar in the stalls at the stable next to the barn. He groomed Bessie the Clydesdale. Morton, of course, had observed Adelaide leaving the cottage, spying on her progress through a gap in the stable wall, lest he be noticed by his master. Bernard and Barry bounded over to the jackaroo who knelt to greet them, rewarding each with a vigorous chin scratch. Adelaide took a surreptitious glance back towards the cottage. Assured she wasn't followed, she disappeared from sight. Adelaide stood in the doorway a moment. Each day their love grew stronger. Morton stared back, hardly disguising his pleasure, admiring Adelaide's figure silhouetted by the morning sun. She lifted her skirt high. Morton swallowed hard. The siren was naked beneath her dress, her dark-haired womanhood bewitching.

'Bonjour mon amant,' she purred.

Morton stood his full height. He felt like a stallion in the company of this most desirable, insatiable woman. They met halfway and kissed. Kissed passionately. The touching of lips so aroused the stallion he grasped her by the hips and effortlessly hoisted Adelaide onto a hall table. She wriggled herself into a comfortable position where the jackaroo threw back her skirt and had his wicked way with his Flemish femme-fatale.

Bessie the Clydesdale neighed. Something disturbed the enormous horse. She whinnied. Old yard hand Frank jerked back from the gap in the wall. He had been spying, again, on the side of the barn out of sight from the homestead. Panicked, terrified he would be caught, Frank hurried along the outside of the building. But his progress was noticed by Morton. The sunlight appeared to blink as Frank passed each gap in the vertical timber wall.

Adelaide tidied herself. 'What is it?' she asked Morton, her ardour sated, her thoughts misty.

'Nothing, my love. It was nothing.' Morton had a moment to think about Ashley. 'At least we know your husband is not in any mood to venture over to the barn. How is he this fine morning, anyhow?'

'He is ill. He does little but complain. The dentist suggested he take a sea voyage. The fresh air will do you good, he was told.'

'Oh, and?'

'I don't know. I told him he should go. But he is insisting I go with him.'

'Where to?'

'Melbourne. But I couldn't Morton, I'd be away for weeks, a month even. I simply could not bear to be away from you.'

'What did you tell him?'

'I told him we should sell off this furniture first. Anything to stall him.' Immediately Adelaide looked serious, almost distraught. She took both his hands in hers. 'Morton my love. Let's run away together?'

'Adelaide. Darling, darling Adelaide. I couldn't think of anything in the entire world I'd rather do.' Morton looked about. There was no sign of

Frank, if it had been Frank he had seen. He dragged Adelaide between wardrobes and said softly. 'I have no money my love.'

'Money!' Adelaide's eyes darkened. 'Money. Are you serious?'

'Yes, I ...'

'We will be rolling in it soon. We will have more money than you have ever imagined.'

'Oh?'

Adelaide dropped her voice to a whisper. 'But I need your help.'

***

Agapanthus Cottage, Macquarie Street.

Charlotte managed to send a note to her good friend Nellie Nichols, the police department archivist. 'I came the moment I received word,' Nellie said, dragging a wicker armchair in the conservatory next to the day bed in which Charlotte reclined. 'You poor thing Charlotte, how is your head?'

'Fine thank you.' Charlotte placed her writing paper and pen on the side table by the recliner.

'I'll be up and about in no time.'

'I see you have been working on your novel.'

'Yes, although I must confess, I am struggling to concentrate with Edward in prison. What news have you?'

Nellie took a deep breath. 'It's not good Charlotte.' She took out a note pad. 'As you requested, here's a list of contents in the suitcase found in Edward's lodgings.'

Charlotte read in silence: 1. One brown leather handbag, quite large, with pewter clips and a long strap. Empty. 2. Women's blouse, cream. 3. Women's pantaloons, cream with traces of semen. 4. Three copies of *The Pearl* ... 'What is *The Pearl*?'

'It is an erotica magazine, published monthly in London. But it is out of print now.'

'Erotica! Goodness. Have you seen these magazines?'

'Actually, I have, yes.' If Nellie blushed at the confession, Charlotte put her friend's pink face down to the warmth in the conservatory.

'And?'

'Well, it published obscene literature, usually set in the boudoir and most often stories about high society, incest and flagellation with obscene parodies, poems and limericks. That's a quote by the way, legal documents I read describing the publication.'

'My.'

'You sound like you would like to see a copy.'

'Ra-ther.' Charlotte continued to read, aloud. 'Number 5. *The Romance of Lust?*'

'That's an erotic novel.'

'Number 6. *Nunnery tales! Volume one* ... Goodness, if this wasn't so serious, I could laugh.'

But it was beyond a laughing matter. Charlotte read on in silence. Number *7. Erotic photographs. Fornication, bestiality.* Now she sickened.

Edward. This can't be the real you! I thought I knew you well ...

Later that day Charlotte received a note delivered from George Davies office.

Dear Charlotte,

I trust this communication finds you in good health and peace of mind and hope to see you at your desk sooner than later. After much deliberation, discussion and the request for payment of favours owed to me, I have managed to secure you a pass to visit Edward Culpepper at Campbell Street. Although I must admit I do not understand your determination to visit this man, you have my utmost support.

You are expected at the prison tomorrow, sometime between the hours of 8AM and noon. So, I have arranged a carriage to fetch you at 11AM. Should this arrangement not be suitable to you, kindly send word by the end of the day.

Signed your most humble servant,

George.

***

Agapanthus Cottage. 11AM, next day.

The cottage was permeated with Aunt Jocelyn's bubbling relish. Stewing tomatoes, onions, sugar and vinegar with *that secret* ingredient in the recipe that Jocelyn handed to anyone who asked – Keen's curry powder. Jocelyn knocked on Charlotte's bedroom door. 'Your carriage awaits.'

Charlotte looked at her watch. 'Goodness. Where has the morning gone?'

'Oh ...and Charlotte,' Auntie lowered her voice.

'Come in Auntie.'

Jocelyn poked her head into the room. 'Mr Davies is here also.'

'What!'

'Yes, he told me he had decided it best if he chaperoned you to the prison ... said something about it's not a place for a lady.'

'Oh bother!'

'Why, he really is a most delightful man.'

'Yes. But I need to see Edward alone.'

'Are you certain that's a good idea?'

'Yes,' Charlotte said flatly.

'Then tell George so.'

Newspaper executive George Davies stood at the fireplace in the drawing room, elbow on the mantle and holding a large stone jar of Jocelyn's tomato relish, still warm from the first batch this morning.

'My, you look beautiful if I may say so,' he said, taking the opportunity to admire Charlotte.

'Thank you. You look rather fetching yourself,' Charlotte said, before realising she was encouraging unwanted attention. 'And Aunt gave you a jar of her relish, how lovely.'

'Yes. I smelt the relish cooking out on the street as the carriage approached.'

Merrill Childers, Aunt Jocelyn's daughter, bowled into the drawing room from the dining room.

'Found it,' she cried out, pleased with herself. 'Oh, there you are.' Merrill acknowledged Charlotte. 'I was telling George ...'

Charlotte shot Merrill a look.

'It's alright Charlotte,' George said. 'I told Merrill here to call me George.'

'Yes, well,' Merrill continued, 'I was telling George we have a first edition of your father's book here and George asked to see it.'

Charlotte smiled awkwardly at her cousin's familiarity.

Merrill opened the novel to the first page. 'It's signed, see. *For my little princess, Charlotte, from Papa, October 4th, 1874.*'

George was impressed. 'First edition huh, that must have great sentimental importance to you.'

'Yes, Papa gave that book to me for my third birthday. He passed seven years later.'

'Yes. I'm sorry.'

'I did not read the novel until I was fifteen.'

'And I'll wager you have read it more than once.'

'Maybe half a dozen times. That is why I am so excited about writing a continuation of the story, I feel father would approve.'

'You ready?' Merrill asked George. He looked blank a moment. 'Mother's orchids.'

'Oh of course.' George looked back to Charlotte. 'Merrill was telling me about your Aunt Jocelyn's prize orchids. She has won awards at the agriculture show I am told.'

'Come along then,' Merrill was behaving like the belle of the ball. 'The conservatory awaits.'

George looked back to Charlotte and smiled. 'Will you excuse me a moment?'

'O-of course.' Charlotte was piqued at this sudden interest in orchids. Edward's situation was far more important. But on the other hand, was Merrill blatantly showing interest in this handsome bachelor? Charlotte grabbed George by the wrist. 'There is one more thing I wish to ask ... before we leave.'

'Fire away.'

'I know this is a huge favour to ask, but could you recommend a good defence lawyer for Edward?'

'I ... ah. You're serious, aren't you?'

'Of course I'm serious. If nothing else, I wish to give Edward hope today.'

'I'll see what I can do,' George said. Merrill poked her head impatiently around the door. 'Excuse me one moment while Merrill shows me the orchids, and then we'll ride together.'

'I can do this alone, George.'

'No, I insist. The prison is no place for a lady, even one as resilient as yourself. I will escort you to the prison and wait at the gatekeeper's while you go to the cells. I'd be more comfortable that way.'

***

The Oaks, Richmond.
Adelaide maintained a loving wife's persona. But under the façade, unhappiness brewed. The clock was ticking. Time flew by. But Ashley lived.

Why wouldn't the bastard die?

Adelaide, who had a sound knowledge of medicines and drugs learnt from her veterinary manuals, nursed Ashley through his ailments. On the surface she appeared to care. But dysentery followed bouts of vomiting. The week passed by. Ashley's health continued to deteriorate. He suffered depression and found it difficult to sleep. Due to his twitching leg muscles Adelaide organised an iron cot for her husband, next to the matrimonial bed, where he slept alongside her.

At the end of the third week Ashley complained of a metallic taste in his mouth. Light pained his eyes and he suffered from diarrhoea. On the Sunday night he collapsed with an internal haemorrhage.

Adelaide sent Morton to fetch the local doctor from Richmond in the dead of night. Doctor Alfred Wheatley, a lumbering Welshman in his late fifties with long disorderly red hair, smelt of whiskey. *Medicinal, one would hope.* Somewhere in the cottage, a clock chimed three. 'You have gastritis,' Wheatley diagnosed Ashley. 'Your ailments have been brought on by the pain in your gums and teeth,' he continued. 'For which I will leave you a bottle of laudanum.' Wheatley took a small bottle from his satchel, passing it to Adelaide. 'Let me see your teeth while I'm here.'

Ashley opened wide. Even this action pained the patient. 'What's this?' Doctor Wheatley looked closer, his face an ugly grimace when he caught

Ashley's foul breath. A fine blue line traced around the gums. 'He has signs of mercury poisoning.'

'I'm not surprised doctor,' Adelaide said, unfazed. 'My husband took several of these pills before I noticed.' She spoke softly, while Ashley closed his eyes trying to sleep. Adelaide presented the box.

'When?'

'He stopped yesterday.'

Doctor Wheatley recognised the pills to contain mercury, albeit a small dose. 'I suggest the mercury in those pills has reacted with your husband's rotting teeth to produce acute mercury poisoning.'

To Adelaide it seemed impossible, but she readily agreed. 'What do you recommend we do then, doctor?'

'A good purgative should do the job nicely.'

Adelaide showed the doctor to the door. 'How serious is it, doctor?'

'Oh, I think he will mend just fine.'

'Really, because I must tell you, doctor, that my husband has become a hypochondriac,' she fabricated. 'Taking this, drinking that. He tells me every day that he believes he is about to die, and he makes me sleep at the foot of the bed holding his toe, he says that is the only way he can sleep.'

'Yes well, most unusual. I'll call back tomorrow morning and see how he's doing.'

Adelaide bid the aging medical man a good night and locked the front door, when a figure appeared in the candlelight behind her.

'Makes you hold his toe, eh?' Hyacinth scowled, stepping from the drawing room, a large Geneva in her right hand. 'That must be nice for you.' Her words were slurred. Hyacinth swayed but grabbed the door frame in time.

'You're intoxicated.' Adelaide's tone was harsh, bitter even. Her relationship with her mother-in-law had also deteriorated. 'Go back to bed.'

'I might be intoxicated,' the older woman's eyes bulged. 'But I'm not stupid.'

'Stupid?'

'You don't think I know what you've been up to?' Spittle ran down Hyacinth's chin. 'Like my dead Osbert used to say, you're nothing but a continental hussy.'

'And you are a drunkard!'

'Bah! I'm warning you now, if I didn't need you, you'd be out that door immediately.'

Next morning. Doctor Alfred Wheatley inspected the roundworm in the Ashley's bed pan and screwed his face in amazement. 'This is most irregular,' he muttered. '*Ascaris lumbricoides* is a parasitic worm commonly found in dogs. Although they can infect humans they are rarely found in the human body and when they are it's usually in the warmer climates and amongst people of poverty.'

Adelaide, who enjoyed reading veterinary books, felt she knew as much as Doctor Wheatley. 'That maybe so, Doctor, but Ashley passed that this morning.'

'Yes.' Wheatley passed the pan back to Adelaide. 'All I can recommend is a purgative to flush the terrible things out.'

Adelaide couldn't agree more. 'Then a purgative it will be.'

***

Noon next day

Hyacinth was already inebriated. It was barely midday. She blamed the stress from her financial woes as she sought solace in the gin bottle. Slumping onto an ornamental garden seat she watched McRae Auctioneers load the last of the furniture stored in the barn onto a bullock dray. This was their third and last trip. Whilst Genevieve's furniture should fetch over a thousand pounds it was the final will and testament Hyacinth wanted settled smartly, and then she would travel to warmer climes, New South Wales most likely. And there live incognito and in luxury. Ashley and his continental hussy wife Adelaide D'Boville could rot in Richmond for all she cared. Her youngest, Phillipa, had already moved to lodgings in Hobart.

The laden dray passed through the property gateposts turning west on the road to Bellerive, finally trundling out of sight behind a large hedge. Morton Dunbar had been discreetly watching Hyacinth soaking up the autumn sun, and gin, for an hour now. Now alone on the garden seat the woman's head slumped forward in blissful sleep. He smiled to himself. Morton liked her this way, at least the woman left him alone as he potted about the property looking for things to repair or put in order.

Thirsty, Morton made his way across the field to the cottage where he was greeted by Bernard and Barry the wolfhounds contentedly gnawing a bone each. He found Adelaide in the kitchen, cleaning vegetables at the sink. He crept up from behind slipping his arms about her, cupping her breasts. Morton breathed in Adelaide's ear, whispering, 'God, I miss you ... what do the French say? *Mon petite choux ...*'

Adelaide turned sharply pushing him away, but gently. 'Careful ... Hyacinth ...'

'Hyacinth is sleeping off Madam Geneva over near the barn.'

'Really.'

'Snoring like an old drunkard.'

Adelaide smiled. 'Despicable woman.'

'So, it's just me and you, *mon petite choux*.'

'That's French. I'm Flemish remember.'

'Oh, so what do they say in ...'

Ashley's croaky plea for help from upstairs disrupted their tête -a- tête. Adelaide slipped herself free from Morton's embrace. 'I must see to Ashley.'

'How is he this fine day?' Morton asked, his tone devoid of the slightest empathy.

'Sick. He is terribly ill. I fear I shall have to call the doctor once more.'

A second cry descended upon them. 'A-Adelaide!'

'I must go to him.' Adelaide turned for the stairs. 'Make yourself useful my love, and fetch water from the well.' She nodded to the wooden pail on the sink. Morton listened to Adelaide's hurried steps to the attic bedroom when Bernard and Barry the Irish Wolfhounds rushed into the kitchen looking for scraps. Old Frank the yard hand was directly behind them.

'You an' me gotta talk,' Frank looked angry.

Morton flinched. 'Oh, about what?'

'I knows what yer up to, you and Mrs D'Boville-Hambleton-Hambleton.'

'What on earth are you talking about?'

'I seen youse two. Carryin' on in carnal sin, out in the barn.'

'Now listen here old man ...'

'Don't old man me, I could whip your arse in any fight.' Frank stepped to the doorway leading to the hall. He listened up the stairs and heard soft voices. He and this cocky bastard jackaroo were alone. 'I'll tell yer what's goin' to happen. You're goin' to bugger off outa here, tonight when everyone's asleep, exceptin' me, you're goin' to walk outa that front gate an' never look back.'

'Who the hell do you think you're talking to?'

'A rat! That's wha' I'm talkin' to. A damned rat. So did yer take it all on board, yer goin' to bugger off never to be seen again, savvy?'

'You know what you can do, don't you?'

Frank crossed the kitchen floor faster than Morton had seen him move since he started work on the property. 'Master Hambleton is gravely ill and here yer are takin' advantage of Mrs D'Boville-Hambleton like yer was married to 'er.' He dared push his face even closer. 'I won't have it, savvy?' Spittle speckled Morton's face and he caught the sour breath of an old man with an empty belly.

Morton wasn't backing away. 'Adelaide might have other ideas.'

'Why you insolent bastard? I should cut yer guts out an' feed 'em to the dogs.' This aggression fired Bernard and Barry. Both dogs started barking.

Adelaide called down the stairs. 'What is it?'

'Nuthin' mistress, 'tis only me, ol' Frank, come to fetch the water pail.' Frank faced Morton once more. 'So what's it to be,' he hissed. 'Bugger off quietly, or shall I tell the master and Mrs Hambleton what yer been up to.'

Morton looked at the man long and hard. His eye twitched. He was angry. Frank had him pressed hard into the sink bench, but Morton managed to salvage some pride by pushing the old man back an inch or two, out of his face. 'Fine. I'll go.'

Frank smelt defeat.

He collected the bucket by the handle and walked outside crossing the yard to the well where he hooked it to the rope and lowered the pail into the deep shaft. Pleased with the outcome, he listened to the splash and waited for the bucket to sink and fill with water, before winding the pail back to the surface.

Suddenly Morton stood behind the old man. 'Oh Frank.' Frank turned. 'There's one thing I meant to tell you.' Frank made to open his mouth when the jackaroo pounced. He punched the old man in the gut. Frank doubled over, winded. Morton brought a knee up into his face with a sickening crunch. Frank's broken nose gushed blood. But Frank was resilient in a fight. For a sixty-year-old he was a tough bastard. He clamped his hands about Morton's wrist. He twisted, locking one arm behind his assailant. Morton stifled a cry. The pain shot up his arm. Frank hauled about, slamming the jackaroo's head into the well wall. But Frank lost his hold. Morton straightened as Frank made to grip the other arm. Morton jerked his head back, violently managing to smash the yard hand's nose completely. Frank had a momentary blackout. The pain was excruciating. His eyes filled with blood. Blinded he threw wild punches. But Morton ducked each swing with the skill of a pugilist. Trounced, Frank turned to run but Morton snatched the back of his britches. He spun the old battler about, frogmarched him to the well and threw him into the dark abyss.

Frank sank.

The water was well over his depth.

Morton waited for him to surface. Took aim, and dropped the bucket filled with water. Frank didn't stand a chance. His head split open, and he sank into the fresh cool water, taking his secret with him into the afterlife.

Morton met Adelaide at the back door. 'Oh, dear lord, I fear the man is dead!'

'Who?'

'Frank. He was fetching water when he lost balance, fell into the well and the bucket dropped in after him. I think it killed him. There's no movement.'

Adelaide hurried to the well. 'Frank! Frank!'

No answer.

Morton joined her. 'He's gone, isn't he?' The water was dark. There was no movement. Morton Dunbar's performance was worthy of a theatre critic's praise. 'Just like that. I was talking to him in the kitchen, and he insisted on fetching you water and ... well I came outside the moment he disappeared over the edge.'

'What! He fell in?'

'Yes, it was awful, he struggled with the pail and over-balanced and ...'

'This is most unfortunate.'

'Unfortunate!' Morton was shocked at Adelaide's response. 'I think it's a little more than unfortunate.'

'It means we'll have the police here making enquiries. This could not have happened at a more inopportune time.'

'Then I'll fetch his body out and we'll bury it somewhere. Who needs to know?'

'No one.'

'What about Hyacinth and Ashley?'

'Ashley doesn't need to deal with this right now, he's too ill. Hyacinth doesn't have to know either. We'll bury him.' Adelaide noticed the fresh cut on Morton's forehead. 'What happened to you?'

'Oh, that. It's nothing. I fell when I rushed out here.'

The morning after Frank's death Doctor Wheatley visited Ashley. As requested, the day before, Adelaide had preserved a sample of Ashley's bowel evacuation in the bedpan. Exposing the excrement, the good doctor examined it carefully. 'Nothing. No sign at all of *Ascaris lumbricoides*. I don't understand. Should your husband have intestinal worms, the purgative should have flushed something out.' The doctor sighed, exasperated. 'And your husband is deteriorating,' he told Adelaide. 'I am seriously uncertain about his future.'

'Isn't there anything you can do?' Adelaide was at pains to sound convincing. 'Please Doctor.'

'Give him laudanum for the pain,' Wheatley had no other answers. Ashley Hambleton was fading when he should be recuperating. The doctor pulled on his coat, hooking his arms through his coat sleeves, when he remembered. 'Where's Frank?'

'Frank?' Adelaide immediately looked like a rabbit freshly snared in a trap.

'Yes. I was talking to him yesterday and he asked me to look at a nasty cut on his leg.' Wheatley took a small pottery pot from his Gladstone bag and Adelaide recognised *Holloway's Pills and Ointments*, a common cure-all. 'Where is he?'

'Frank ... ah ... he's not here.'

'Well, I really should examine that leg of his once more before I go. I fear infection.'

'Frank has chores in Sorell,' Adelaide lied.

'Oh, very well.' The doctor passed Adelaide the ceramic pot of ointment. 'Tell him to rub this into the wound and change the bandage regularly will you.'

'Certainly.'

'And tell him I want to see him tomorrow about the same time when I return to see your husband. Good day to you Mrs D'Boville-Hambleton.'

Morton appeared from behind the scullery door. He had listened to their conversation. 'Do you think he suspected anything?'

'About Frank?'

'No.' Morton pointed to the bedpan. 'That. Your husband's sample looks nothing like Bernard's sample,' he nodded to the bedpan. 'That you so masterfully collected from the field.'

'My, you are the observant one.'

Morton's smile was mischievous.

'Ashley is gravely ill,' Adelaide said. 'Why shouldn't his evacuations vary day to day?'

'Fine.'

Adelaide took Morton's hands and looked at him with her puppy dog eyes. 'I need more chloroform.' Truth was the pharmacist in the village would be suspicious if Adelaide was to purchase more. Morton had been sent for a second bottle on the pretext he needed it for removing grease stains from clothing. Due to its dangerous possibilities chloroform was sold in limited small amounts. He had already purchased a small amount in

Richmond. 'I will have to ride to Sorell and maybe even Bellerive to acquire more.'

'Then do it.'

Morton was no fool. Adelaide had told him a week earlier how she needed chloroform to splash in small amounts on a pad to hold to Ashley's nose to calm the pain. In small amounts this was a reasonable, temporary cure. But Adelaide required more, much more. And Morton Dunbar was only too happy to oblige.

Morton found a pewter wine funnel in the scullery and poured the contents of three small chloroform phials – purchased from three different pharmacies – into one unlabelled bottle. He then discarded the small narrow bottles. With Ashley's health appearing to improve slightly, Hyacinth travelled to Hobart to see her solicitor about Genevieve's last will and testament. Now Morton and Adelaide had carte blanche to do as their heart desired. Hyacinth, who seemed in high spirits when she left, would be staying the night with her daughter Phillipa, in her ladies' lodgings in Sandy Bay. 'She may even stay two nights,' Adelaide told Morton. 'As she adores to play bowls at the Beach Tavern where there are lawns behind the inn.'

Morton couldn't disrobe quickly enough. The two undressed in the guest room, kicking off loose trousers, hopping clumsily, tangling in undergarments in a frenzied foreplay to their passionate love making. The jackaroo, man of all trades, threw Adelaide onto the mahogany four-poster with the energy of a professional wrestler. Their groans carried through the cottage. Totally uninhibited. If Ashley heard them, he was too ill to act.

They were insatiable, selfish and heartless.

Morton had lit a fire in the guest room grate earlier, but their intense lovemaking had left them in a lather. They lay across the bed, sweaty and naked, sharing a cheroot. 'My god!' Adelaide panted. 'You are a stallion.'

'You aren't too bad yourself.'

A bell rang from along the first-floor landing. Adelaide propped on one elbow and listened. Ashley's bedside bell rang a second time, more urgent, louder.

'Damn the man's eyes,' Morton cussed. 'What does he want?'

'I better go see.'

Hastily dressed and barefoot, Adelaide found Ashley sitting on a chair at his dressing table. Somehow, painfully he had managed to drag his weakening body across the room.

'What do you want my love,' Adelaide could barely disguise her dark thoughts. 'Is everything alright?'

'Where's mother?'

'She has travelled to Hobart, to see the solicitor.'

Ashley coughed into a handkerchief and Adelaide noticed spots of blood. 'When will she return?'

'Tomorrow dearest. She is staying the night with Phillipa.'

'Who else is here? I heard voices.'

'Oh, that would be Mr Dunbar, he has been mending the step at the front veranda, you know the one that was rotting.'

'I'm hungry.'

'Hungry? Oh ...'

'What do you mean, oh?'

'Oh, I meant that is a wonderful sign my darling. We have jugged hare from last night and mother baked a lemon cake before she left.' And, as an afterthought, Adelaide said, 'And she iced it.'

'Then I will have both.' Ashley watched his wife pad to the door barefoot. 'Where are your shoes?'

'I was about to change clothes when you rang your bell.'

'Dunbar? ... Why can't Frank fix the step?'

'Frank ... ah ... Frank is ill my love. He has a bad influenza and I've ordered him to stay in his quarters. We can't have you catching the influenza on top of your current illness, now can we?' This moment, Adelaide thought, was not the time to launch into an explanation regarding Frank's death.

Forty minutes passed. Adelaide carried a tray of food into the bedroom. 'This should make you feel better.'

It smelt great and tasted even better. Ashley showed signs of improvement. Evening approached and much to Adelaide's chagrin, Ashley had perked up. He even managed two glasses of burgundy and a brandy. Adelaide fluffed his pillows and burnt incense in a vain attempt to disguise the odours of her husband's illness and the rotting fish syndrome that plagued the man's skin.

'I've been thinking my love,' Adelaide said. 'You need rest. I think I should sleep in the guest room tonight, let you convalesce.'

'If you insist. But I fear my health deteriorates once more. Can you at least be within reach, should I ring the bell?'

'Naturally, husband. I shall always be at your beck and call. Now I will prepare your chloroform, it will help you sleep.'

Adelaide soaked the cotton pad with three times the normal *dab*. True to its reputation the chloroform had an immediate soothing effect and Ashley dropped drowsily, back onto his pillow. Laudanum for the pain. Chloroform for slumber.

Blissful sleep ... But a sleep from which he would never awake.

Next morning Morton woke first. The lovers had slept in, their first night sleeping together. Even the rooster crowing in the yard had not woken them. Morton stretched, feeling about in the dark for Adelaide, thoughts of morning passion clouding his thoughts.

'Adelaide?' he whispered in the dark. Adelaide said nothing as she lay awake in the dark. Suddenly Morton pulled open the curtains. The bedroom flooded with sunlight.

'Ah, there you are,' Morton grinned.

Adelaide was lost in bedclothes and blankets. He bounced back onto the bed, his eyes bright with romance. But Adelaide ignored the gesture, gathering her clothes about her.

'Strange that Ashley hasn't rung for attention,' she said quietly.

'What's the time?'

'It's after seven. Get dressed and meet me in the kitchen ... and quietly now.'

Less than two minutes later Adelaide found Morton down in the kitchen stoking the wood stove alive and feeding the fire kindling.

'He's dead!'

'What?'

'Ashley's dead.'

Morton wasn't surprised but it was all happening too soon. This was not how *he* wanted it. Not yet anyhow. Adelaide stood by the kitchen table, clutching her heart. It was beating fast. She looked flushed. It was disturbing to see her husband lying in their bed, dead. Yet she was excited, anxious and suddenly terrified of repercussions all at the same time.

Morton closed the oven fire door. 'Are you certain?'

'Oh god. Yes. He must have died hours ago; he is quite cold.'

Morton hurried up the stairs. Adelaide followed. She had never been a religious person but at this moment she felt a dark spiritual presence. Adelaide felt watched, accusing eyes following her, staring back from the afterlife. Adelaide experienced guilt she hadn't expected. Morton looked at Ashley's body. His choosing this particular estate to find work had not been random. Ashley had been a part of Morton Dunbar's past and, unbeknown to Adelaide, Morton had unfinished business with the man. A man who was now a corpse, cold, grey and waxlike.

Morton Dunbar grew angry.

'W-What are we going to do?' Adelaide's words were frayed with panic.

Morton's was less than supportive. 'Isn't this the outcome you wanted? ... Well, isn't it?'

'Yes ... but ... oh god!'

'Get it together woman.'

Suddenly Adelaide was experiencing a side to this travelling jackaroo she had not seen before.

'Oh Morton ... what have I done?' Adelaide grew hysterical. She put her arms out for comfort, for assurance, for a sympathetic hug. Instead, Morton shook the woman.

'Listen Adelaide. Now listen to me. We have come this far. Don't lose it now.'

Adelaide's tears flowed. 'But I ...'

'Stop wailing. Stop it now. Unless you want to hang, get yourself together. Now, it's nearly 7.30. He's been dead for hours. We must ... listen to me ... we must go and fetch the doctor immediately. Get the doctor over here and have a death certificate authorised. Then arrange to have the body removed.' Morton softened his tone. 'Your husband died of natural causes, understand me? Natural causes.'

Adelaide nodded her head vigorously. 'Natural causes ... yes.'

'Here, wipe your eyes and blow your nose.' Morton handed Adelaide his handkerchief. 'Save the tears for the doctor.

Now! ... Adelaide.'

'Yes, my love,' Adelaide answered weakly.

'Get rid of any evidence. I'm going to ride into the village and fetch Doctor Wheatley. I should return in under an hour, so watch out for us, and prepare yourself. Have your answers ready for any questions the man may ask. I can't be by your side all the time; I am hired help remember. And a few tears for the doctor would be to your advantage.'

Doctor Wheatley had the hangover of a habitual alcoholic. While he felt parched, red eyed and dusty, his experienced years with the bottle did not affect his ability to operate as a medical practitioner. In fact, he had only momentarily quenched his thirst with a glass of porter and brushed his teeth with Cherry Tooth powder when he heard a horse neigh outside his cottage.

Morton knocked on his door.

Wheatley's clock chimed eight.

'Doctor Wheatley,' Morton held his Akubra in front of him with both hands, playing with the brim and trying not to look over theatrically serious. 'Mrs D'Boville-Hambleton-Hambleton has sent me to fetch you sir, Mr Hambleton has passed during the night.'

'Oh.' The doctor was not surprised. Mr Hambleton had been gravely ill when he saw him last. 'Right then, I'll ah ... I'll just fetch my coat and bag.'

Doctor Wheatley was not all that fond of dogs. So, when the wolfhounds came bounding, barking, down the driveway to meet him on his trap, spooking his horse, he was less than impressed. Morton rode up ahead.

Adelaide took a deep breath and steadied herself. She had been aiming for this outcome some time. Now she would have to hone her mettle. Her highest hurdle right now was to convince the doctor that her husband had died of natural causes. Have the man sign *that* death certificate. Then she could deal with her mother-in-law when the woman returned from Hobart. Adelaide also knew, with Ashley gone she would have a legal battle on her hands. Hyacinth and Phillipa would do all in their power to prevent Ashley's widow from claiming her share of this inheritance. The plan had been for Ashley to live long enough for the settlement. But now that was dead she would simply have put on her best performance.

'Damn dogs!' Wheatley cursed. He climbed from his buggy only to be set upon by amiable excited dogs with muddied paws. Morton dismounted, taking control. 'You really should control these animals,' the doctor grumbled.

He was considering another verbal broadside when Adelaide appeared. She was wearing a mourning dress, modestly concealing all flesh, neck to ankle. With high collar, ankle high boots and a widow's veil, the couture hugged her shapely body. She looked stunning. Morton did a double take.

Immediately the doctor reminded himself why he was here. 'I'm sorry Mrs Hambleton, it's just that … the dogs you see …' his voice trailed off. 'I'm awfully sorry about your loss.'

Adelaide caught the hint of beer on the doctor's breath. 'Thank you,' she said behind a veil she hoped would disguise any sign of guilt.

'I'll tend to the horses madam,' Morton sounded suitably subservient, while managing a rakish wink behind the doctor's back.

Although it was a pleasantly sunny morning and the day was shaping up to be warm for autumn, a well stoked fire raged in the master bedroom grate. The room was uncomfortably hot.

'Would you mind opening the window?' Wheatley asked.

Adelaide complied. Wheatley may have been suffering a hangover, but he had his wits about him. The first thing the doctor noticed was the bedroom smelt of the deceased's malady and that peculiar affliction, *rotting fish syndrome* that Wheatley knew Ashley suffered. The resulting fug in the room was quite unbearable. But there was also the unmistakable smell of what he thought was ether. On the mantle, Wheatley noted a wine glass containing dregs of some foreign liquid. He sniffed the glass and identified what smelt like brandy … and ether.

'Ashley seemed in such good spirits last evening,' Adelaide said, turning from the window in time to catch the doctor replacing the glass on the shelf. 'He ate a hearty meal, drank some wine and even enjoyed a brandy ... well most of it.'

'Why the fire? It's so hot in here.'

'Initially I thought Ashley was cold doctor ... I ... I had no idea ...' her voice trailed off.'

'Yes well,' Wheatley sighed. 'Your husband has been deceased some time madam. I would hazard a guess at around three o'clock in the morning. Were you not sleeping with him?'

'No. I slept in the guest room.'

'Oh?'

'Yes. To give him peace and rest you understand. He has a bell, there next to the bed. And he could call for me whenever he needed.'

'There will have to be an autopsy done.'

Adelaide felt her heart skip. 'An autopsy!'

'Yes madam, the coroner will be requiring a report on the cause of death.'

Adelaide felt the fear return. She channelled the panic into tears. 'But he passed in his sleep.'

'Yes madam. But all the same.'

'Oh, poor, poor Ashley.' She rushed forward taking her dead husband's hand and wailed. 'Why, why have you gone? So young. I'll miss you so my love.'

Wheatley gave Adelaide a moment's grief then asked, 'Mrs D'Boville-Hambleton. Would you mind fetching your yardman, what is his name, Dunbar I do believe? And maybe Frank. I would like to wrap your husband's body in a blanket, and I will have to transport him to the Richmond Arms for an inquiry.'

'Frank!' Adelaide looked suitably alarmed. 'I'm afraid Frank isn't here doctor.'

'Oh? He's not still in Sorell, surely?'

'No doctor, he travelled to Hobart with Mrs Hambleton.'

'With that infected leg of his?'

'Yes.' If Adelaide looked flustered, the veil hid it. 'He was more than comfortable with that jar of ointment you so kindly gave him.'

'Oh, that is good to hear. Then, madam, it … ah …' Doctor Wheatley looked awkwardly uncomfortable. 'I am afraid I will have to ask you to aid in the conveyance of your husband's … ah, cadaver. Onto my cart, that is. I am sorry madam, but we have little other choice.'

There would be no avoiding an inquiry. Adelaide knew only too well that her husband's body would be put on public display in the inn, as was the custom. Whilst death of a relatively young person was not uncommon, a death certificate must be produced, officially recorded and signed for the coroner, and the coroner would want to know the cause of death. In Ashley's case, Adelaide could only hope for *died of natural causes*, or as some liked to claim, *died from the visitation of god*.

Ashley's waxy white body was stretched out on a table in the hotel parlour. As was the law, a jury of *good and lawful men* was selected. This was to validate the inquest itself. The body could be viewed also by any number of witnesses who may wish to come forward and view the body and these people were free to ask questions and make suggestions. This practice was encouraged by the law to ensure the death had been a natural one and to keep others honest. No wonder Adelaide was nervous.

Doctor Wheatley refused to make a decision. He had his suspicions, as did some of the townsfolk. The next day Ashley Hambleton's body was removed to the morgue at St Mary's Hospital in Davey Street, Hobart, to await the coroner's pleasure.

***

Coroner's Laboratory, Davey Street.
Coroner and divisional police surgeon Doctor Edwin P Jones worked with medical officer Nicholas Cutts, an experienced surgeon from Sydney. The two men had more than fifty years' experience between them. Ashley Hambleton's cadaver lay cold, grey and rigid on the marble slab. Arranged on the wooden bench behind Doctor Edwin were several sterilised glass jars with glass stoppers for preserving body parts as they were removed for

examination. A photographer's developing tray sat on the slab, awaiting Ashley's stomach and its contents.

Doctor Jones examined the mouth and lips for corrosive signs caused by poisons. He lent in to smell if there were any tell-tale odours given off around the mouth. Doctor Cutts watched on. He pushed his wire rim glasses back into position, the better to focus. 'Anything?' he asked.

'Nothing obvious, no,' Doctor Jones held up a scalpel. 'Do you want to do the honours?'

'That's alright Edwin,' Cutts said. 'You go ahead, I'll record.'

Jones made the primary incision through the abdominal parietes and again, both men sniffed the cadaver for outward signs of poisoning.

'See that?' Jones asked his colleague. Cutts also noted the inflammation of the peritoneum and tissue surrounding the stomach. Severing the oesophagus and the duodenum, Jones removed the stomach, placing it in the developer's tray. Jones then opened the stomach along the lesser curvature and the two men carefully poured the stomachs contents into one of the larger glass jars. Now it was possible to inspect the lining of the stomach.

Cutts scraped samples onto glass slides and proceeded to examine them under the microscope for fragments of leaves, berries, and particles of pigments such as indigo used to colour certain poisons, like arsenic or strychnine that were used to poison vermin. The two men examined the intestines and oesophagus for the same clues.

The autopsy proved inconclusive but both doctors agreed that they detected a trace of chloroform. The two doctors deduced two or three ounces had been ingested. Also traces of acetate were finally found in the dead man's jaw. 'Possibly the result of prolonged exposure to poison,' Cutts noted for the court.

Doctor Wheatley had already recorded his own suspicions, writing his own report for the coroner. Adelaide D'Boville was duly arrested and officially charged in the Hobart Criminal Court with the wilful murder of her husband, thirty-three-year-old Ashley Baxter Hambleton,

Grieved at the loss of her son yet panicked by the thought of Adelaide exposing the truth, Hyacinth threw all her energy and what money she could raise, without drawing unwanted attention, into securing her daughter-in-law the best defence lawyer available in the colonies.

Inspector Benjamin Boothman sent uniforms to arrest Morton Dunbar as an accomplice. But Adelaide needed all the support she could muster on the outside. She refused to talk and declined to implicate the man she had fallen for in any wrongdoing.

***

Campbell Street Gaol, Hobart.
Morton sat on the side of his bed in his tiny remand cell trying to figure out what the hell had gone wrong. The only other furniture in his cell was a small desk, a stool and a soil bucket. He was permitted a pad and pen for correspondence and the only reading material was the Holy Bible. Morton was in dark spirits. This was not where he wanted to be right now. Surely, *they can't charge me with being an accomplice* to *murder. They don't have any evidence. Do they?* Certainly, he had purchased chloroform from three different pharmacies but that was under orders from his master's wife. He was innocent. Morton Dunbar was innocent of aiding and abetting. But what about old Frank buried in the yard? Now that *was* murder.

Days passed.

Morton sat and sweated, even though the cell was cold, especially at night. Any activity outside the cell drew the prisoner's attention. Anything to kill the boredom ...

A woman's voice had Morton on his feet. The scent of a woman's perfume drifted through the gaps in his cell door. The woman approached, talking seriously, urgently to the warder ushering her along the corridor. She said something about illegal incarceration.

He heard her words. 'The man is innocent.'

Of course he is, lady. We're all innocent.

Morton pressed against the door to peer out through the peephole – a voyeur in confinement. The shadowy figures grew close. Suddenly Morton jumped backwards. He swung the peephole closed. Fearful he had drawn attention to himself, Morton threw his back against the cell wall, refusing to take a breath. He waited for the key in the lock, the cell door to open. The inevitable. But the voices passed by. Morton pressed an ear back to the door. He heard the warder's fading words. 'Your father ... 'e were Marcus Clarke the novelist, weren't 'e?'

But by the time the woman answered, their steps were far away.

Locked in a tiny prison cell was not how Edward Culpepper wanted Charlotte to see him. 'Yer only allowed five minutes Missus,' the warder locked the door behind him. 'I'm outside in the corridor if'n yer want me.'

Edward Culpepper hadn't washed for days. His hair was greasy and matted and he looked gaunt and frightened. He rose from where he sat on his miserable cot and held Charlotte's gaze. Charlotte was speechless a moment. She wanted to hold a perfumed handkerchief to her nose but thought that would be offensive. Finally, Edward strained a smile.

'Char ...' he was forced to clear his throat. 'Charlotte.'

'Edward.' Immediately Charlotte let her guard down. 'Oh Edward!' She wanted to hug the man but held back. 'What is happening to you?'

'I didn't do it Charlotte. You must know that. I didn't do this evil thing.'

'Edward ... Edward ... I ... the suitcase ... it ...'

'I've been set up Charlotte, you must believe me.'

And believe Edward she so desperately wanted to. 'What was that suitcase doing under your bed?'

'One of the other lodgers put it there. It had to be, and there is only one man I can think who would stoop so low?'

'Who?'

'Jake Crewe.'

'Who is he?'

'He's a surveyor's assistant with the railway. 'e come over from Victoria some weeks ago.'

Charlotte wanted to believe this was the man. 'Jake Crewe. How old?'

'Twenty-five I'm thinkin'.'

'What's he look like?'

'He's a tall solid cove, curly dark hair an' skin, an' 'e always dresses nice.' Edward suddenly remembered his grammar. 'Nicely ... he always dresses nicely.' This brought a smile to Charlottes otherwise strained face. 'Oh yes, and he has a malformed hand.'

'Oh?'

'Yeh, his left hand is sort of ... what would you say? Sort o' maimed.'

'Well, that should help in identifying him.'

'You do believe me don't yer?'

'Oh Edward, I was so sickened when I heard you were arrested.'

'But you don't think I done ... I did it, do yer?'

'No, Edward.' Charlotte stepped forward taking Edward's hands in hers. 'No Edward, I don't think you did it. I never did. We now have to find a way to prove your innocence.'

Charlotte threw caution to the wind and hugged Edward. He smelt of stale sweat and fear, but the embrace meant more to Edward's mental well-being than she could imagine. 'I am arranging a lawyer for you.'

'What? A lawyer? How? I can't afford a lawyer Charlotte.'

'George is helping me.'

'Mr Davies?'

'Yes.'

Suddenly Edward felt a twinge of jealousy. 'But ... but why would Mr Davies wanna help me.'

'Because I have asked him to Edward. Besides you are innocent, and George is a man of justice. Together we will prove you innocent.' The sound of the key in the lock signalled their time was up. Charlotte raised herself on her toes to kiss Edward on the cheek. 'Take care. I'll be back soon.'

'Thank you. Thank you so much. Your visit means a lot to me.'

Charlotte was about to step through the cell door when she remembered two books she had brought with her. 'I nearly forgot. Here.'

'David Copperfield,' Edward smiled. 'Really? I've always wanted to read this book.' The other book was dog-eared, well read. 'Christmas Carols.'

'Yes. Charles Dickens. It should give you cheer.'

***

Next day. Agapanthus Cottage, Macquarie Street.
With a late start rostered at the newspaper, Charlotte spent the morning working on her novel. But Edward was foremost on her mind. In need of a break, Charlotte made her way downstairs when she saw the under stairs cupboard was open and heard her aunt in the dining room opposite.

'So, there you are.' Aunt Jocelyn was sorting through old newspapers and magazines. The dining table was strewn with papers.

'What are you up to Aunt?'

'I was having a little tidy up when I found these in a box under the stairs. I forgot I had them,' Jocelyn said.

'What are they?'

Charlotte's curiosity put a smile on Jocelyn's face. 'I'm happy you asked. Take a look.'

Charlotte picked up a copy of the *Australian Journal, September 1881, His Natural Life.*

Others read *Holiday Peak and other Tales, 1873. Four Stories High, 1877.* 'These are all written by Papa,' Charlotte said.

'Yes. I kept them all. Look,' Aunt Jocelyn pointed out one neatly sorted bundle. 'Here's the full collection of *Old Stories Retold* published back in 1870 and I also have *Old Tales of a Young Country* here somewhere, they were the short story pre-runners to *For the Term of his Natural Life* published in '71 after he visited Tasmania.'

'Here's one in French,' Charlotte said. '*La Beguine.*'

'Your father spoke fluent French you know.'

'Yes, he taught me a little but ...' Charlotte's voice faded. 'He died before I really learnt much.'

'Yes, it was so sudden. Your father fell sick with pleurisy and within a week he had passed.' Aunt Jocelyn smiled at more pleasant memories. 'He lost his voice but that didn't stop him from wanting to write. I heard before he died, he sat up in bed, pulled the sheets tight and made hand motions over them as if he was writing on paper.' Charlotte had a vision of exactly that. Feeling emotional Charlotte flicked through more papers. 'Did you know Papa well?'

'Not really. The first time I met him was at your mother's sister's house in Melbourne. That's your Aunt Rose, she was my second cousin. He was about thirty, if my memory serves me correctly, but I remember thinking at the time, he was good looking man with grey searching eyes.'

'Searching? You mean licentious?'

'No not at all, although he liked the company of ladies. I think your Aunt Rose was infatuated with him.'

'Oh?'

'There were whispers ...' immediately Aunt Jocelyn regretted her poor choice of words.

'Whispers?' Charlotte's face pinched.

Jocelyn shuffled papers. 'It was nothing dear.' Although she was thinking where there was smoke there was fire.'

'Aunt Jocelyn ... what whispers?'

Jocelyn had heard rumours at the time that Marcus Clarke's marriage to actress Marian Dunn, Charlotte's mother, was a rocky one, and that the whispers spoke of an affair with Rose and even talk of them running off together, and to America of all places. Aunt Jocelyn straightened and looked Charlotte in the eye. 'It's nothing to worry yourself about Charlotte,' she lied. 'It was a woman's infatuation that came to nothing.'

Charlotte wasn't so certain.

'Your father was always inquisitive,' Jocelyn said. 'He was bright and intelligent and took note of his surroundings. I had the impression he eyed everyone as potential characters in one of his imaginative stories. You know, he had a stammer.'

'Yes, I do recall that.'

'Really?'

'I was *ten* when Papa died.'

'Of course,' Aunt Jocelyn said. 'I remember his arm; your father suffered from a disease that affected the bones in his left arm. He had an operation when he was a child, but he never regained full strength in the arm.'

'Yes, ankylosis it's called. I remember he had difficulty picking up us children.'

Aunt Jocelyn tidied more bunches of papers into some sort of order. 'I hope you don't end up like your father.'

'In what way?'

'Oh, don't get me wrong. I meant as a writer. Marcus was prolific, wrote many articles, short stories, sketches and books, but *His Natural Life* overshadowed everything else and posthumously he became known as the novelist who produced only one great novel.'

'That's unfair.'

'Yes, it is. And they changed the title too after your father passed.'

'*For the Term of His Natural Life* is a better title though,' Charlotte said. 'Do you not think?'

'I suppose. How *is* your novel faring, anyhow? What's it called ... *Beyond the Seas of Tyranny.*'

'Oh, it is coming along. A little slower than I would have hoped.'

'Well, it's a brave move,' Jocelyn said. 'Continuing your father's popular novel. Did you know that in the serialised version of *His Natural Life* the two main characters ...?'

'Protagonists we call them.'

'Yes, well Rufus Dawes and Sylvia Vickers, *the protagonists*, did not drown off Norfolk Island but they lived on.'

'Yes.'

'But Rufus Dawes, who was originally Richard Devine before his arrest, was still an absconder and wanted by the law. He changed his name once again to Tom Crosbie, opened a general store on the goldfields in Victoria and became a rich man, finally becoming a man of property in Melbourne.'

Charlotte was impressed that her aunt knew so much of the story. 'You're well-read Auntie. Yes, I've studied both versions of the novel. Papa threw everything into his extended version, even the Eureka Stockade debacle.'

'That's right. In the final chapter in your father's extended original, they end up back in England. You were saying in your story, they go to America.'

'That's correct.'

'Well good luck with it all my dear.' Aunt Jocelyn pondered the collection momentarily, spread out on the dining room table. 'I saved these for you, really. I'll stack them back in the box and you may as well store them in your room.'

'Thank you.' Charlotte was genuinely grateful. She cast one last curious eye over the papers. 'Many, I know, I haven't read before.'

Aunt repacked, placing the lid back on the box. 'Here, you've some reading to do then.'

Charlotte stood staring at the box; her mind elsewhere. 'What's on your mind?' Jocelyn asked, but she already knew the answer.

'Oh, it's Edward. I can't get him off my mind.'

***

The Oaks, Richmond.

The police were frustrated and angry. All inquiries were leading nowhere. Now, due to lack of evidence Morton Dunbar was released from his remand cell. He bought a threepenny ticket on the steam ferry *Kangaroo*, crossed the River Derwent and caught the first available coach from Bellerive back to Richmond. From the village he walked the mile to the homestead. Hyacinth Hambleton, it appeared, was in his sights.

Hyacinth was seething, furious. Morton, *this, this jackaroo mongrel* who had ruined her life walked back into her homestead kitchen and her life like he owned the place.

Like a dammed rooster.

'How dare you!' Hyacinth ranted. 'You've got a nerve. What are you doing here? Get out of my home, now!'

'Take it easy Hyacinth.'

'Hyacinth! Hyacinth! It's Mrs Hambleton you wretch.'

'Wretch huh? I'll thank you to be more respectful from now on. We're partners now Hyacinth,' Morton was calm and collected. '*Equal* partners.'

'Partners?' Hyacinth was so deeply entrenched on the wrong side of the law, so guilty, she had the sense to listen. She managed to calm herself. 'What are you saying? What are you talking about ... partners?'

'I know all about your deceit, your dishonest dealings, forgery and fraud ...'

'What? Don't be ridiculous.'

'I know about the second, fraudulent will ...'

'How dare you.'

'Be quiet. Shut up and listen. I know all about the Mrs Hyacinth Hambleton's version of Mrs Genevieve Sayer's will. The one you managed to have signed while she lay on her death bed. While she was mentally incapable of understanding its contents, leaving everything to your eldest, Ashley. And I know about other documents and letters you have forged. But now Ashley's dead it all goes to you. How convenient.'

Hyacinth's face turned the colour of molten lava.

Morton looked Hyacinth in the eye. 'So now I want my share.'

Hyacinth flew into a rage. 'Why you insolent mongrel.' She ran at Morton with her fists balled, pounding on his chest.

'Easy, easy I say.' Morton clamped his huge hands about Hyacinth's fists and effortlessly pushed her away, forcing her against the kitchen wall. He held her hands above her head, pinning her helplessly, pressing his body against hers. Hyacinth struggled but the seventy-two-year-old was defenceless against the much younger man. Pinned bodily to the wall Hyacinth sensed Morton pushing into her. His sweat fresh and not unpleasant. His breath sweet. She looked into his eyes, stopped struggling, yielding to his demand. There was no point fighting. She was his prisoner, and he could do with her whatever he desired.

'Is that what you want?' Hyacinth said in a calm soft voice. 'You want to rape an old woman?'

Hyacinth may have been an attractive woman in her youth, but *this* was not Morton's intention. All the same Morton enjoyed preying on the weak. He savoured the smell of fear. He drew his face closer. Hyacinth turned her head to one side. Morton nibbled her ear and ran his tongue down her neck. Hyacinth felt his whiskers, like sanding paper, across her soft wrinkled skin. Her stomach churned. She felt nauseous. The jackaroo lowered Hyacinth's arms to her side, continuing to press her bodily against the wall. Hyacinth felt anxiety catch in her throat. She had never felt so vulnerable, so humiliated and defenceless. Until now Hyacinth Hambleton had always been in charge. But not now. Morton released her hands, taking the old woman's hips in his. He pushed harder against her.

'Is *this* what *you* want?' he answered her question with a question. Hyacinth surrendered herself completely. She had switched to self-preservation.

'Do what you must then leave me be,' she said, trying her utmost to maintain courage, yet the quiver in her voice betrayed her.

Morton slapped the wall hard, close to her face. He pushed himself away. 'I'm not here to satisfy your fantasies,' he said coldly. 'I just want what's mine.'

Hyacinth felt her chest tremble as she fought back tears. But her relief was palpable. She had experienced what this man was capable of and decided subserviency was her best defence. For now.

'Wh-what do you want?' she said, her words quivering.

'I told you, I want what's mine ... and with interest.'

CHAPTER ELEVEN

Agapanthus Cottage, Macquarie Street.

Charlotte was vexed. 'It is sickening Nellie,' Charlotte had barely ushered her friend and police archivist through to the kitchen before she was describing Edward's dire situation. 'Locked in a tiny cell like some animal, waiting for a hearing. It's criminal. And he's innocent, there is no question about it.'

'How can you be so certain?'

Charlotte shot her friend a dark look. 'I'll pretend I didn't hear that,' she said and continued to tell Nellie Nichols all about her visit to the prison.

'Has he a defence lawyer yet?'

'I'm trying to find him one Nellie. George Davies said he would try and help, but I'm yet to hear from him. I'm trying to help Edward find someone who knows what they are doing.'

'It's going to be difficult with such damning evidence found in his possession.'

'Let's get something straight Nellie, it wasn't *in his possession* as you say, it was planted under his bed, probably by another lodger named Jake Crewe.'

'Who is he?'

'Like I said, he is a lodger at the Caledonian Hotel. Edward told me about him and swears he is the only one capable of doing such a thing.' Charlotte looked Nellie in the eye. 'I need your help.'

'My help?'

'We need to follow this Jake Crewe, to watch his every move.'

'We?'

'Yes Nellie, *you* are all I have.'

'How's your head?' Nellie enquired, totally unexpected.

'My head?'

'Yes, where you were wounded at Bellerive, or had you forgotten?'

Is Nellie querying my sanity?

'My head is just fine, thank you for asking.'

Nellie sat at the kitchen table where a teapot – her aunt's favourite Spode – steeped a fresh brew. She sighed. 'So, who is this, Jake Crewe again?'

'He is a surveyor's assistant with the railway who lodges in a room next to Edwards'.' Charlotte sat. 'Tea?' She poured without waiting an answer.

'And why him?'

'Because Edward thinks it could only be him, out of the four other lodgers in the hotel.'

'So then, what is your plan?'

'We, that is, you and I, are going to the Caledonian Hotel for a glass of sherry.'

'Are we now?'

'Yes. It is a respectable establishment and two refined young ladies like you and I will be accepted in the parlour without question.'

'When?'

'At 5PM when this Jake Crewe returns to his lodgings.'

Aunt Jocelyn walked into the kitchen, struggling to close the back door, while holding an extremely large pumpkin. She greeted Nellie, settling the large vegetable on the table with a thump, rattling the tea pot and cups in the process.

'Nice to see you Nellie,' she said. She liked Nellie, one of her niece's better friends she thought. 'Are you staying for lunch?'

Nellie hesitated. She looked to Charlotte. 'Of course, you must stay, we have much to discuss. And Aunt has made her favourite grilled lamb kidneys.'

'Thank you. I would love to. I wondered what smelt so delicious.'

***

The Oaks, Richmond.

Hyacinth struggled with her awkward situation but managed to speak calmly. 'How am I supposed to help you,' she asked Morton, 'if I don't know what you are talking about? You say you want what is yours, and with interest. But what *is* yours?'

'Your son,' Morton Dunbar seethed. 'The bastard Ashley Hambleton the so-called investment banker, defrauded me out of one thousand pounds. I worked hard for that, and he lost the lot.'

'If you are talking about the collapse of the Bank of Van Diemen's Land back in '91 then I must inform you many people lost their investments at the time.'

Morton walked to the kitchen sink staring out the window and across the field towards the outbuildings. He leant, with both hands, on the Huon Pine trough, careful to keep Hyacinth's reflection in the glass. *God knows what this woman was capable of,* he thought.

'I told your son to withdraw my investment as early as 1889. But he kept making excuses. Told me my money was tied up. *Don't worry* he said. *It's invested in the building boom going crazy in Victoria. You are going to get a return tenfold.* All the while he was gambling with my money. Gambling in Chinatown's illegal gambling houses, gambling on the horses and he lost the lot. Me and others … my thousand pounds.'

Of course, Hyacinth knew this was true. There was no point in arguing and she knew the jackaroo had her cornered. 'I concede my son made some foolish decisions.'

'Foolish decisions!' Morton turned, his face bitter. 'That's an understatement.'

Hyacinth was the award-winning actress when it came to finances. 'And I will rectify it.'

'My bloody oath yer will.' Morton stepped to the larder and fetched a bottle of Artillery Brewery beer from the shelf. He unwired the cork from the black glass bottle and warm froth bubbled over the lip as he drank straight from the container. He was thirstier than he thought, drinking most of the contents in one gulp.

'I have a question,' Hyacinth said. 'Why did my son not tell me about you when he hired you? I mean, if he had lost your money the two of you would have had an altercation on the first day, would you not?'

'We never met before, that's why.'

'What?'

'All our correspondence was through the mail. I lived in New South Wales at the time. We never met. He didn't have a clue who I was.' Morton sat heavily at the kitchen table. 'Sit,' he ordered Hyacinth. She sat and his malty breath reached out to her across the table.

Refreshed, Morton mellowed. 'I know you are about to receive a fortune,' he said. 'To the tune of one-hundred-thousand pounds.' Morton whistled. 'Now that is a lot of money.'

Hyacinth was being attacked where it hurt most, in her greedy pocket.

That stupid woman Adelaide. Her infidelity was about to cause me ruin. Hyacinth had suspected her daughter-in-law of being untrue to Ashley of late. But now ... the truth was exposed. *Was it possible Adelaide really did poison her son?* At first Hyacinth thought not. She thought it a terrible mistake, but then Adelaide was arrested. Maybe the continental hussy did murder her son. Hyacinth remained calm. She adopted the rhetoric of a businesswoman. 'Shares have to be cashed. Properties sold. It is going to be a long process and there may be repercussions and holdups from South Africa.'

Of course, Morton knew of the true beneficiary, the cousin living in South Africa. 'Oh, that's fine. I have plenty of time. I'll wait for my share, say twenty-five-thousand ...'

Hyacinth wanted to scream, *twenty-five thousand! Over my dead body.* But remained phlegmatic.

'But for now, I'll be taking a share of the auctioned furniture money, a little sampler to get me through. I've made enquiries, the first part of the auction fetched you six-hundred and eighteen pounds which has recently been deposited into your Savings Bank Account. So, you will start by signing a withdrawal note for me for two hundred pounds. I need new clothes to start with, especially if I'm to look the country gentleman.' Morton was starting to enjoy himself. 'Don't look so worried Hyacinth, I won't see you stranded, castaway from your own cosy cottage. You can stay in your room and I'll be sleeping in the master bedroom.'

'And Adelaide?'

'Well,' Morton shrugged. 'Adelaide is being held on a murder charge.'

Such coldness, Hyacinth thought. 'I have heard on good authority that Adelaide will beat those charges.'

'Oh, and how do you feel about that?'

'About what?'

'That Adelaide killed your son, and she may get away with it.'

'There is no evidence to charge the woman. I'm sorry to say, my son was a fool, even a bigger fool than I expected when he married that ... that hussy. But for now, we are stuck with each other.' Hyacinth's bitterness returned. 'Like you and I, so it seems.'

'Then,' Morton said with a wry smile, 'should Adelaide be released she can stay with me, in the master bedroom.'

Hyacinth said nothing, she didn't have to, her face said it all.

'That doesn't bother you?' Morton asked the woman.

'Like I said, she is a hussy.'

Morton changed the subject back to finances. 'Something else Adelaide told me; you will benefit from the sale of your murdered husband's house in Hobart. You'll do alright.'

Morton helped himself to another beer and placed the decanter of Geneva on the table with a tumbler. 'Let's drink to a prosperous future.'

He poured a large gin for his reluctant hostess. Hyacinth raised her glass, but not in salutation. Simmering, she drained it in one mouthful ... while planning retribution.

***

Agapanthus Cottage.
Charlotte spent a fascinating and fruitful afternoon with Nellie, poring over papers Nellie had copied from the police department archive. It appeared

the police were amassing enough evidence against Mrs Hyacinth Hambleton to make an arrest for fraud. All these documents were pertaining to complaints made against the woman in the past months. There was evidence of at least five cases of fraud and forgery.

'The last will and testament is under scrutiny also,' Nellie told Charlotte. 'The woman is a charlatan, a thief and a liar.'

'Harsh words Nellie Nichols,' Charlotte said. 'Have we got enough to hang the woman?' Of course, this was figuratively speaking. But a lengthy prison sentence wasn't out of the question.

'And look at this list.' Nellie presented a list of cashed cheques to businesses in Hobart, from merchants to pharmacies, drapers to general stores. 'Several thousand pounds there, not to mention cheques exchanged for cash to the value of three thousand pounds.'

'Three thousand!' Charlotte tried to whistle but her lips were dry.

'Mrs Hambleton has forged her signature on each and every one. And there's something else.'

'What?'

'The old lady's funeral was weeks ago and the funeral fee hasn't been honoured. Mrs Hambleton, now the executor, hasn't even paid off Langley's, the poor people's home, for a pauper's funeral.'

'She's a piece of work.'

'She certainly is. Now here's a copy of a letter Hyacinth sent to her own solicitor a year ago. She wrote a letter complaining about the frustration of her husband's refusal to sell the family home.'

'Osbert Hambleton.'

'Yes. She claims she is starved and destitute. Nellie quoted from the letter. *I am in need of his removal from the house painlessly, cheaply and above all with haste.* There is another interview report here that records Osbert telling a friend, I quote again. *Osbert Hambleton confided in me that he thought his wife was planning to kill him. He told me, if I am ever murdered, you know what happened and by whom.*'

'Well, what are the police doing about this?'

'They just don't have enough hard evidence against her Charlotte. Not yet anyhow.'

Hard evidence. Charlotte's thought returned to Edward. 'Tell me something Nellie.'

'What's that?'

'Fingerprints. You must know how human fingerprints are unique to each and every one of us. How the patterns on the outer skin, named the epidermis I seem to recall, are unique to all of us, therefore leaving behind evidence of foul play.'

'Of course. You are talking about the patterns left behind on smooth surfaces at a crime scene.'

'Yes.'

'They are called arches, loops and whorls.'

'Very well, so you know what I'm talking about?'

'Yes.'

'Well, I read recently how police departments, in India of all places, are taking impressions of criminals' fingerprints to be used in criminal cases.'

'Yes, it's been happening in England too,' Nellie said. 'But it has yet to stand up in court. No one has been found guilty of a crime and convicted due to this process.'

'Not yet anyway.'

Nellie lifted the tea pot, but there was only enough remaining for one cup.

Charlotte. 'You finish it.'

Nellie poured, putting two lumps of sugar into her cup before stirring noisily. 'So how can this help Edward? The suitcase was found under his bed, his fingerprints are bound to be on it.'

'Exactly my argument. What if they are *not* on the suitcase? That would have to prove it isn't Edward's. And then this Jake Crewe could be made to give the police an imprint of his fingers, and then compare them with what *is* on the case. If he is innocent, then it will clear his name.'

'You have a valid argument there.'

***

The Oaks, Richmond.

Days passed. It was in Hyacinth's and Morton's interest to have Adelaide released from remand. If she was to face a murder charge, then god knows what she would tell the authorities. Hyacinth contracted the finest legal firm in Hobart. Morton even agreed to share expenses. But there was something even more worrying bothering Hyacinth. Where was old Frank the yard man? Morton and Adelaide, both told her how, disgruntled, Frank had left for the north of the island.

After years of service, without saying farewell to Hyacinth. I think not.

And the more Hyacinth thought about it the more she felt murder was afoot. She would have to be careful. Damned careful. Once settlement was finalised, she would move to warmer climes.

For now, each night at *The Oaks* as the lamps were turned down for the night, Morton and Hyacinth both locked their doors.

***

Police Headquarters.
In discussions at the police station it was suggested Mrs D'Boville-Hambleton-Hambleton was not the only person using chloroform at *The Oaks*.

'It has been argued that Mr Hambleton, that is Ashley Baxter Hambleton, used the chemical as well as his wife,' the inspector told Senior Constable Hutton. 'Supposedly used as a solvent in the chemical preparation of compounds used on the property, in floor polishes, lacquers, adhesives and resins.'

'How do we know this sir?' Hutton asked the inspector.

'Because a preliminary search of the master bedroom by an astute officer found a sweet smelling, ether-like substance hidden in airtight jars in the deceased's wardrobe. It has been identified as chloroform. This fact, apparently, his wife Adelaide was not aware of. And it appears it was this chloroform that was used to drug Edward Culpepper, that afternoon he was illegally entering Genevieve Sayer's Bellerive property. The very same day you arrested him for the murder of the girl in the swamp.'

'How can we be certain it's not the same chloroform used by the wife on her husband?'

'Would you hide poison in amongst your spouse's private belongings, should you intend to kill her?'

'Point taken. But can we prove it?'

'With Ashley Hambleton dead we will never know the answer.'

Meanwhile Adelaide was held in remand at the Campbell Street Gaol in the women's section, annexed to the main prison, when she was informed her hearing was inexplicably to be fast tracked.

***

The Caledonian Hotel, Elizabeth Street.
Charlotte and Nellie arrived at the Caledonian Hotel some ten minutes after five that evening. The taproom was busy. Publican Audrey Schuster mingled with her customers, smoking a large Meerschaum pipe – the bowl suitably carved in the shape of a Bavarian beer stein. She worked the room, chatting amicably, acting the perfect host. But under that veneer of civility the woman was fiercely protective of her establishment. With the Caledonian enjoying a respectable reputation, Charlotte and Nellie felt comfortable enough to be seen in the parlour where they were served at a smaller horseshoe-shaped bar by an attractive and efficient bar maid whom they learnt, was named Sally. They were the only patrons in the parlour. They ordered two small glasses of Spanish sherry.

'How are we going to do this?' Nellie asked, as two long stem glasses were put before them.

Charlotte shot Nellie one of her standard *watch and learn faces*. She took her purse from her oversized satchel, placing a half crown on the bar.

'I wonder if you can help us?' she asked the maid.

'How's thart?' Sally's Londoner accent was easily recognisable.

'You have a lodger here, lives upstairs I do believe, by the name of Jake Crewe.'

'Jakey, aye.'

'Is he by chance here this evening?'

'I can't be tellin' you thart I'm afraid. Mrs Schuster would 'ave me guts for garters.'

'Dear me, we can't have that now, can we?' Charlotte pushed the coin across the bar towards Sally, keeping her finger firmly on the disc of silver. 'Maybe if you keep the four shillings change that might sway your decision.'

The bar maid looked over her shoulder back into the taproom. Mrs Schuster was busy. "e's here alright.' She made to take the coin. 'Walked in ten minutes ago.'

Charlotte's finger remained firm. 'What's he look like?'

'You can see for yourself, 'e's right behind me.' With the main bar noisy with happy patrons, the woman leant closer to Charlotte. 'The big bloke with dark skin and the deformed hand.' The bar wench then stepped aside surreptitiously, sponging the counter, allowing Charlotte and Nellie a clear view into the taproom.

Jake Crewe had already been observing the two young women who had just arrived in the parlour opposite. He caught Charlotte and Nellie staring and lifted his beer in a silent salute. Charlotte granted him the hint of a smile. That's all the man needed. He fetched his flat cap from off the bar, stood, drained his glass and made his way around to the parlour. The bar maid took the half crown. 'Youse be careful,' she said. "e's a bit of a lad that one.'

'Bit of a lad?'

"e likes the ladies. Don't say you weren't warned.'

'Well, well,' Crewe said as he walked through the door from the corridor and into the parlour where he stood strategically at the end of the booth in which Charlotte and Nellie now sat. 'If I didn't know any better, I'd say you were talking about me.' The man, in his early thirties, was tall and powerfully built with short dark hair and the tan of a man who worked outdoors. He wore dark trousers, a white shirt with a tartan waistcoat. One sleeve was rolled up to the elbow while the other was pulled down in an attempt to conceal a deformed hand, hanging to one side.

'Talking about you? No sir,' Nellie said straight-faced. 'You have got that all wrong. My friend was merely asking the bar maid questions of another matter.'

'Another matter eh,' Crewe answered with a lascivious smile, licking his bottom lip, planning his next move. 'And what would your friend's name be then?' Clearly Crewe had his eye on Charlotte, who appeared to be doing her darndest to avoid him.

'I don't believe that is any of your concern, sir,' Nellie said.

Crewe was about to say *oh don't you now?* when Charlotte cut him short. 'I'm Scarlett Parker and this is my friend Emilia Pickle.'

The man was taken aback. 'Well, ah … I'll be blowed. You do have a voice, and what a pretty one it is too, I might add.' He plucked at his bottle-brush moustache in a grooming manner. 'I'm Jake. Jake Crewe. Mind if I take a pew?' The man didn't wait for an answer, sliding into the booth seat next to Nellie where he could face Charlotte.

With the light of late afternoon fading outside, Sally stepped from behind the bar, lighting gas lamps each side of the parlour on their wall sconces. The extra light gave Charlotte a chance to take a writer's note of this man they suspected to be a killer. He was older than her, about Edward's age she guessed, maybe thirty-three, quite good looking in a rugged way, he was clean shaven and well groomed – smelling slightly of lavender soap. Charlotte had to check herself. If her hunch was right, she was sitting opposite a brutal murderer. The thought terrified her and thrilled her at the same moment.

'What do you do?' Charlotte heard herself ask without thinking.

'What do I do? Well, that's nice of you to ask pretty lady. I work with the railway. I'm a surveyor … well surveyor's assistant. But I'll have me papers soon and be a fully qualified surveyor.' Crewe pushed his chest out grinning like he expected an accolade.

'Nice,' Charlotte said.

Nellie kicked Charlotte under the table. *In the name of god, what are we doing here?* Nellie's serious eyes stared into Charlotte's.

'And what do you two lovelies do?'

'Seamstress.'

'Cook.' They lied in chorus.

'Oh, which is it then, seamstress or cook?'

'Scarlett's a cook and I'm the seamstress,' Nellie said. If Crewe suspected they were lying he didn't care. *Who cares if they lie, as long as I can have me way with one of them, preferably the little redhead.*

'Goodness,' Charlotte feigned surprise. 'You haven't got a drink.' Charlotte squeezed out from behind the booth, collecting their empty sherry glasses. 'What are you drinking Jake?'

'You buying?' Crewe asked. *This is getting better and better.*

'Of course.'

Nellie shot Charlotte a look of horror.

'Then I'll have a pint of pale ale.'

Charlotte made her way to the bar. Jake Crewe showed no discretion following her figure with a licentious eye as she walked away. Sally served Charlotte in silence, having lost her respect for the two lone ladies. *Ladies! Huh! They were warned.*

Charlotte brought the pint of ale to the booth first. 'There we are,' she handed Crewe the pewter tankard by the handle. The man reached to take the drink. 'Both hands now Jake, we don't want to drop it now do we?' Dutifully Crewe grabbed the tankard with his good hand. 'This 'ere mitt's not much use.' He alluded to his deformity and took a long deep draw on its contents before placing the mug on the table.

Charlotte sat with the sherries. 'Tell us all about yourself Jake,' Charlotte said. 'To begin with, what happened to your hand?'

This was a sensitive subject. But when asked by a pretty woman Crewe explained that it was a deformity he had been born with. 'It were caught in me umbilical cord, so me ma said the nurse told her, but it grieves me none. I'm used to it.'

'Oh. Where are you from then?'

It took three pints and fifty minutes of listening to the mundane life story of Jake Crewe before he excused himself to visit the latrine. 'I'll be right back ladies,' Crewe's voice was slightly slurred. 'Then I'm thinking maybe it's my turn to buy youse a drink, but we might go somewhere a little quieter, eh?'

'That sounds lovely Jake,' Charlotte touched the back of the man's hand as he stood.

'Charlotte!' Nellie was mortified. What are you doing?' she said as Crewe disappeared out the door.

'What am I doing? Quickly, let's get out of here.' Charlotte carefully picked up the empty pewter tankard by the lip and dropped it into her satchel.

'Charlotte! What the …'

'Quickly now, before he returns.' Charlotte wasn't hanging about to argue. She rushed into the passageway leading to the front foyer. Men's voices and laughter followed them from the men's latrine. 'Hurry Nellie.'

Nellie couldn't decide what she was more terrified of, the suspected killer catching them departing or being caught stealing hotel property. It was all happening so quickly. Nellie was on Charlotte's heel when the taproom door flew open and the proprietor, Mrs Schuster, barred their path. 'Not so fast young lady,' the large no-nonsense publican slammed an open palm against Charlotte's chest, stopping her in her tracks. 'I'll be having my tankard back thank you very much.'

'Pardon?'

'That mug you just stole. The mug in that bag of yours. Hand it over or I'll be fetching the constable.'

'I don't know what you're talking about.'

The hotelier lost her temper. 'Give it here.' She grabbed at the bag. Charlotte struggled. She had to keep the tankard at all costs. It was possibly Edward's ticket to freedom.

'Let go!'

'Why you little thief.'

The commotion was attracting unwanted attention. Charlotte didn't hesitate. She stamped on the feisty woman's foot. The ruse worked. The woman screamed in pain, letting the bag slip from her hold momentarily. Jake Crewe appeared from the latrine. 'What's happening?'

'Thief!' Schuster shouted. Charlotte had her bag. She had her evidence. She snatched Nellie by the wrist and led her onto the street where they ran for their lives. The publican turned her attention on her lodger Jake Crewe, down the corridor. 'Mr Crewe,' she yelled. 'A word if you please.'

Charlotte and Nellie did not stop running until they reached Liverpool Street where they continued east towards police headquarters. Finally, satisfied they had not been followed, Charlotte stepped into a laneway. Nellie joined her.

'I get it, I get it!' Nellie was snatching breaths. 'Fingerprints huh?'

'Yes.'

'You are crazy, but you know that don't you?'

'Uh-huh.' Charlotte carefully took the tankard from her bag. 'This is the biggest favour I'll ever ask of you Nellie,' Charlotte panted. 'Please be really, really careful with it. Take it to the police laboratory and they will take Crewe's prints from it. It's paramount you do not let it out of your sight.'

***

Next day. Hobart Courts.

Adelaide D'Boville's defence barrister and criminal lawyer, Terrence Makepeace, was on fire, shredding the prosecution like slow stewed pork for the soup pot. The prosecution lawyer, Herman Fairbairn, claimed that Adelaide had given her husband chloroform in a disguised form, say, in his brandy, just like the wine glass Doctor Wheatley had warily sniffed in the deceased bedroom. Adelaide readily admitted she administered small amounts of chloroform in the way of a soaked pad to help relax her anxious husband. But she emphasized the amounts were minuscule.

Charlotte sat in the public gallery, busily making notes in shorthand.

'Or,' barrister Makepeace stated, 'the deceased drank the liquid himself.'

'Ridiculous!' Fairbairn boomed across the courtroom, holding both lapels of his coat with his chest pushed out like the prize cock he was. 'Your honour, that is the most ridiculous statement I have ever heard. I have already heard from Professor Charles Dumbarton of Melbourne University, and he is an expert in forensic science, that it would be impossible to ingest chloroform in that manner. If the deceased tried to swallow the chloroform himself, even diluted with brandy, the liquid would have burned his throat so fiercely the man would have gagged and thrown up immediately. If the liquid was dripped down his throat the burning would be obvious in the mouth and oesophagus, and, I have been assured, it would also have scarred his windpipe.'

The coroner, Doctor Edwin P Jones was cross examined, and his inconclusive examination leant in favour of the defendant. However, he stipulated the internal organs smelt slightly of chloroform.

'Well of course they do,' Makepeace argued. The man had recently undergone extensive dental surgery and chloroform played an important part in his expected recovery.' Makepeace addressed the jury. 'As we have already established to the court, it is no secret the deceased stored bottles of chloroform in his wardrobe. I put it to you, members of the jury, that the man was financially broken and took his own life.'

The jury of ten men and two women listened with interest. The judge, Justice George Dyson, concluded that impossible or not, the fact remained that chloroform was found in the deceased's stomach.

The jury deliberated for an hour and a half. Although suspicion pointed to Adelaide poisoning her husband, there was insufficient evidence to convict her.

'What say you?' the judge asked the foreman of the jury.

'Not guilty your honour.'

Adelaide's knotted stomach unravelled. *Not Guilty, not guilty.* The words resonated inside her head. She would remember this moment for the rest of her days. But there was little cheer from the public gallery, whose trial by hearsay and gossip had seen her destined for the gallows. Defence lawyer Terrence Makepeace congratulated his client. He cheered, albeit silently.

Prosecutor Herman Fairbairn slumped back in his seat the moment the judge left the bench. He looked across at Adelaide D'Boville, a fixed smile stretching ear to ear across her beautiful face. *The face of a siren,* he thought, *you poisoned your husband, I know you did. You've been slowly poisoning him for some time, with acetate or maybe mercury vapour administered on a gauze pad. You even planted a worm from your dog's faeces into your husband's bedpan to confuse the doctor and his diagnosis, to accentuate your husband's ailments. And you have a motive. Money, your husband's inheritance. What kind of woman are you?*

Fairbairn rose again, collecting his notes and tidying them before placing everything in his leather satchel. He was sickened by the verdict and had difficulty holding his tongue.

'Congratulations Terrence,' Fairbairn said in passing the bar table. 'Another victory. I envy your court record old chap.'

'Thank you, Herman.'

Fairbairn faced Adelaide. 'Tell me Mrs D'Boville-Hambleton, now that you have been declared innocent, maybe you could tell us how you did it, being impossible as our learned judge said. Please reveal all, if not in the name of science at least.'

'Careful Herman. I'm certain you don't want a charge against you, now do you ... old chap.'

Fairbairn forced a thin smile.

***

The Mercury Newspaper offices, Macquarie Street.
The door to the journalist office slammed open hard against the wall. 'Mrs Clarke!' The young messenger shouted. 'Mrs Charlotte Clarke. I have a message for Mrs Charlotte Clarke.' The office stopped. The messenger's enthusiasm was commendable. Charlotte had been deep in concentration using her typing machine ... until now. 'That's me.'

'"ere you go luv.' The boy dropped an envelope on her desk.

'New on the job are we?' one of the desks nearby asked the boy.

'Yes mate. First day today.'

Charlotte. 'Thank you.'

The lad was going nowhere. He may have been new on the job, but he knew enough to know delivering messages was worth a penny or two both ends.

'Here.' Charlotte slipped a threepence from her purse. 'Thanks luv.' The door swung shut with another bang.

The envelope, headed Police Department, was from Nellie Nichols;

My dear Charlotte, I want you to be the first to know. The few fingerprints that the forensics laboratory managed to find on the suitcase found under Edward's bed are not Edward's. They match the fingerprints taken from the beer tankard. Yes, the suitcase was handled by Jake Crewe, therefore proving he must have planted the case under Edward's bed.

This information is being handed to the detectives in charge.

I suggest you buy a ticket in Mr George Adam's Tattersall's sweep while your luck is in. We must meet soon.

Nellie.

Miss Juliana Haughton did not like surprises. And she certainly disliked anyone breaking protocol. So, when Charlotte enquired ... no, demanded, to see her boss, George Davies, in his office on the first floor, the senior executive's secretary was beside herself. 'Mrs Clarke, Mr Davies is very busy. You can't go in there.'

'This is very, very important, urgent even. A man's life depends on it.' *And Charlotte had that part right.*

Charlotte knocked. Miss Haughton pounced, grabbing the doorknob and pulling the door firmly closed. George's voice reached out across the room. 'Enter.'

Charlotte pushed the door. It opened an inch before being slammed shut.

'Would you please stand aside?' Charlotte hissed at the secretary.

'This is most irregular.'

Charlotte knocked again. 'It is me, Mr Davies, Charlotte Clarke.'

'Charlotte!'

Charlotte wrenched the doorknob. The door opened and jerked shut again. George investigated. 'What is going on here?' he said pulling the door open. 'Miss Haughton?'

'I'm sorry sir ... Mrs Clarke here insisted ...'

'That'll be all Miss Haughton, thank you. Mrs Clarke, do come in.'

Charlotte entered the executive office, having only been here once before. Sharpened daggers from the secretary followed her every move.

'Please accept my apologies Mr Davies,' Charlotte said.

George made certain the door was closed and Miss Haughton was out of earshot. 'George, please.'

'Sorry George, but this is really urgent.'

'Fire away then.'

Charlotte explained the latest news and the fingerprint evidence. 'This certainly changes things. But why the urgency? The police will handle this matter and Edward should go free sooner than later.'

'It is not as simple as that.'

George frowned. 'Oh?'

'I ... well, let us just say I have a contact who passed this information onto me, not exactly legally.'

'What do you mean?'

'Well, I have a contact in the police department who leaks information to me.'

'Really? Who?'

'I cannot say.'

'Goodness me Charlotte.' Secretly George was impressed. 'So why come to me?'

'You have contacts. You can say ... ah ... a little bird told you ... blah, blah, blah. Get the ball rolling. I fear for poor Edward's mental and physical well-being, locked up in that awful cell.'

George considered his options, after all he really wanted to help. 'Inspector Boothman would be our best shot,' George agreed. 'Like me, he's a member of the Royal Society and I play Royal tennis with him once in a while as well.'

'Thank you, I do so appreciate this. I'll repay you some day, I am certain.'

There followed an awkward moment of silence. George was clearly contemplating his next move. For a man of the world, this feisty red head had him lost for words.

'I have the inspector's telephone number here somewhere,' George fumbled at his desk. 'I'll give him a courtesy call first. I think that the best approach.'

Charlotte took the opportunity to look about the office. It was spacious with its oak roll-top office desk covered with a green leather writing top. At one end of the rectangular room a six-legged table groaned under the weight of dozens of back issues of the newspaper – going back to 1854, George had informed Charlotte earlier. The walls were sparsely decorated with a calendar and, opposite, an oil portrait of the paper's founder, John Davies, George's grandfather, hung on a wire from a picture rail. Charlotte couldn't help herself, she straightened the picture, standing back to inspect her handiwork. George had a discreet chuckle to himself. The other wall was hung with a group photo, George and his shooting club comrades. George caught Charlotte looking at a brass and iron model cannon used as a large paperweight.

'Father gave me that. It's a model of a Crimean War cannon, Russian I believe.'

Boys and their toys, Charlotte thought. *There will be model soldiers somewhere.* And almost as if they had been summoned onto the parade ground George pointed out his little army of hand painted lead soldiers. They saluted back from behind the glass doors of a cedar bookcase.

'There *is* something you could do for me,' George finally gathered confidence, twisting his waxed moustache pinching the ends into needle-like points.

Oh!

'Oh ... and what is that?' Charlotte was wary.

'Invite me to dinner.'

'Dinner!' Charlotte smiled, but she really wanted to laugh. 'Dinner?'

'Yes. Is that forward of me? Presumptuous. You seem alarmed.'

'Oh no,' the last thing Charlotte wanted was to appear ungrateful. 'You would be most welcome.'

'How about Saturday then?'

My, the man is keen.

'Sat ... Saturday. Hmmm ... why not? I'm certain Aunt Jocelyn will be most willing.'

***

Saturday evening. 8PM.
George stood at the drawing room mantelpiece admiring Aunt Jocelyn's knick-knacks. With his hands behind his back in a most gentlemanly manner he took time to inspect Charlotte's wedding photograph mounted in a carved folk-art frame. 'So, this is your husband, Charles Claiborne?'

'Yes.'

'I am so sorry for your loss Charlotte.'

'Yes ...' Charlotte looked vague; her voice trailed off. There seemed, to George, to be a vulnerability surfacing.

'He was a good-looking man,' George said.

'He had different coloured eyes you know.'

'Oh?'

'Yes. It was a rare condition that I read the scientists call heterochromia iridum.'

'I'm not even going to try and repeat that,' George smiled. 'Different colours. Interesting.'

'Yes, the left eye was blue and the right eye brown. It was quite endearing actually.'

'You must miss him.' The moment these words escaped George's lips George thought how hollow they sounded. 'Sorry. That was a stupid comment.'

'No, that's fine.' Charlotte was composed. 'To be honest, the marriage was failing the past year before he passed. Charles was suffering a disease of the mind.'

'Oh?'

'Yes. A mental disorder. Apparently, so the doctors told me, the condition was always there, it just took time to manifest itself later in our marriage.'

Charlotte offered George another glass of sherry. He studied Charlotte as she poured from the cut glass decanter. He had to admit he had been attracted to the intelligent redhead since the day they met at the newspaper offices. The fire in the grate grew warmer and he stepped away, taking the sherry. The sweet wine had gone straight to his head and he realised he hadn't eaten lunch.

'Charlotte,' he finally managed. 'I ... ah ... I ...'

'My, George, you sound serious.'

'Do I?' George fumbled clumsily. 'I was about to say ... ah ...'

Charlotte was saved by the bell. Literally. Merrill bowled into the drawing room with a small dinner bell, clanging the thing vigorously and making fun of the situation. 'Dinner is served,' she cried out. Merrill's smile vanished. 'Goodness me, you two look serious.'

'Oh, we were just talking about Charles,' Charlotte said.

'Were you now? Well cousin, he's not with us anymore. It's time to move on,' Merrill said, winking at George in an unexpected and most unladylike manner. She spun on her heels and hurried off back to the dining room.

'Please excuse her,' Charlotte said. 'But Merrill never did get along with Charles.'

The joint of roasted beef was well cooked, too well cooked in fact. 'Oh dear,' Aunt Jocelyn fussed. 'I seem to have overcooked the meat.'

'The vegetables are nice though Mother,' Merrill said. They all managed a laugh.

The four sat around the blackwood dining table with tall-backed chairs where George felt very much at home. This relatively humble setting was what he had often craved, having been pampered by servants all his life. With George at the head of the table, Aunt the other end and the two young women either side sitting opposite each other, George entertained his hosts with stories of his time in London.

'Did you meet the Queen?' Merrill asked.

'Actually,' George sawed through a piece of dry meat keeping his audience in suspense, 'I did not. I invited her for high tea at the Ritz but Her Majesty sent her apologies, said she was too busy ... having tea with Kaiser Wilhelm I believe.'

'Really?' Merrill had always been gullible.

'Really.'

They all laughed.

***

Police Headquarters.
Senior Constable Toby Hutton was lost for words. 'What do you mean Edward Culpepper has been set free?'

'Charges have been dropped,' fellow Senior Constable Miles Broadfute told his angry colleague. 'Inspector's orders. We're to arrest Jake Crewe, a fellow lodger at the Caledonian Hotel instead.'

'How could he be freed? The suitcase was found in his possession.'

'Fingerprint evidence. It's the way of the future Toby. If this is proven, then it could be the first case of its type in Australia using fingerprints as evidence. We're a part of law-and-order history making, my friend.'

Surprised at colleague Toby Hutton's attitude towards Edward Culpepper's release and subsequent freedom, Senior Constable Broadfute, dressed in plain clothes, recruited two uniforms to accompany him to arrest Jake Crewe.

Crewe was finally located at temporary surveying offices north of Bridgewater along the railway line. He did not resist arrest, if anything the man was smug and confident.

'You've got the wrong man' was his only comment, saying it over and over, mainly for the benefit of his workmates as they watched on in silent shock.

***

Two days later. North Hobart.
Paolo Esposito listened to fellow Italian, Teresa Cortellezzi, savouring her every word. The woman translated the newspaper article on Paolo's daughter's killer's release in *The Mercury*. 'Release?' Paolo did not believe what he was hearing. 'What this word, release? He let out from prison?'

'Si. Thees paper, it say he ees innocent.' Teresa slapped the newspaper on the table and pointed to the relevant sentence; words Paolo could not possibly read. 'It say another man ... he been arrested for the ....' Theresa's voice faded away when she thought of the words on her mind ... *For the death of your daughter.*

Paolo was confused. Teresa took a small pot of thick stewed coffee from the stove and poured the two of them fresh coffees. She had found Paolo difficult the past week. But he was *Italiano, family,* and she felt an obligation towards him. Paolo had learnt of the small Italian community in Hobart, most of whom had come to Tasmania ten years earlier, brought over from Italy by Diego Bernacchi the entrepreneur. Bernacchi had settled Maria

Island off Tasmania east coast, as a winemaker, orchardist and cement manufacturer, of all occupations. Now, here in the back room of Teresa's Bakery, Paolo had found sympathetic patriots.'

'Thees man, what his name?'

'Jake Crewe.'

'When he be in courtroom?'

'Tomorrow Paolo.' Sympathy had crept back into Teresa's voice. 'The paper, it say one week. He be here.' Once again Teresa pointed to the article, *Court Notices. Preliminary hearing.* 'Now drink coffee, ees hot.'

***

Five days later. Hobart Criminal Courts.

Charlotte took a seat in the public gallery of the criminal courts at the Holy Trinity Church on the corner of Brisbane and Campbell Streets, part of the Campbell Street Gaol institution. Charlotte had witnessed many cases here and knew the building well. It was built in the early 1830s out of necessity due to overcrowding at Hobart's only Anglican Church, St David's in Murray Street. Governor Arthur ordered the chapel built on the northern wing of the Campbell Street Gaol. The design never failed to humour Charlotte. This house of god was built to house prisoners as well as the good citizens of Hobart. Below the nave (there was no sanctuary) was thirty-six solitary confinement cells as an adjunct to the penitentiary. The design was cruciform with east and west transepts once having tiered floors sloping towards the central pulpit in the nave. This allowed the free citizens to worship without being gazed upon by convicted felons. However, it was doomed to fail. A new Trinity Church was built in North Hobart and the old Trinity Church, which was never consecrated, was converted to criminal courtrooms, associated offices, judge's chambers and jury rooms. That was back in '59.

Charlotte could hear the muffled cries and curses of the prisoners in holding cells beneath the courtroom. She thought she could smell the fear. She definitely caught the fetid sour smell of unwashed bodies amongst the public gallery. *Ghouls*, Charlotte thought. Here to be entertained, most of them, entertained by the ruination of others. However today was different.

This was the first hearing for Jake Crewe, the *Monster of the Swamp* as he was being touted.

Paolo Esposito, the victim's father, sat two rows back from Charlotte. He sat in pained silence staring at the dock, waiting – waiting to see the face of the man appear from the cells beneath them. The face of his daughter's killer.

Jake Crewe was ushered up from the cells in handcuffs and ankle irons. The gallery booed. They were immediately silenced; however, murmurings continued. The man had already been found guilty by public opinion. Crewe stood forlorn in the dock, facing the judge, but staring at the floor. His confidence had evaporated. At first Charlotte considered hiding her face, should the accused recognise her. But then thought otherwise. *So what if he does see me? I was instrumental in catching the monster.*

The victim's father, Paolo Esposito, watched in silence.

The judge, Sir Richard Arledge Watchorn, entered the courtroom from his chambers, immediately commanding respect and silence. He was a short man, seemingly misplaced to command such power Charlotte thought. Of course, she had watched Sir Richard at work on many an occasion. His rhetoric never failed to amuse her. He occasionally made impassioned speeches if he thought the defendant innocent.

All in the room stood until the judge was seated at the bench. The room remained deadly silent while Watchorn arranged his notes and took a moment to uncap a scent bottle and dab some perfume on a handkerchief. He too, apparently, caught the unpleasant aroma emanating from the public gallery.

Charlotte listened as the charge of wilful murder was read out in court, as drawn up by the prosecution. Charlotte knew that decisions taken at this stage of the legal process were important, since the severity of the crime would eventually affect the punishment, when, hopefully, the defendant was found guilty.

'Is there sufficient evidence to try the case before a trial jury?' the judge asked. 'If so the prosecutors and their witnesses will be able to testify.'

'Yes, your honour.'

Jake Crewe was formally charged and asked to plead to the charge now formally read to him. 'Defendant,' the judge ordered, 'You are accused of a most heinous crime. You must make a plea, what say you? Guilty or not guilty?'

'Not guilty!'

***

Agapanthus Cottage, Macquarie Street.
'We've got him,' Charlotte paced the drawing room of Agapanthus Cottage while Nellie read up on court procedures. 'And it's your insistence, Nell, that forensics dust for fingerprints on the suitcase that will hang him,' Charlotte said.

'I can't take all the credit Charlotte. You are the one who managed to secure the man's fingerprints.' They shared a giggle.

'Which reminds me,' Charlotte said. 'We must have that tankard returned to Mrs Schuster at the Caledonian when the case is over.'

'You know,' Nellie grew serious studying the court papers. 'The trial process, as it stands, places defendants at a disadvantage.'

'Oh, and how's that?'

'Well, many can't afford legal assistance and must organise their defence cases on their own, and this is while they are still locked up without access to aid, like books or advice,' Nellie said. 'Also, the defendant is unaware of the evidence the prosecution is going to use against them until the actual trial.'

'Yes,' Charlotte said. 'And you know why?'

'Why?'

'This way they are forced to be spontaneous, answering the prosecution's questions unrehearsed. This is the best way of ascertaining the truth. Spontaneity,' Charlotte said. 'It's not so common now, but in felony cases the accused often appeared at the session immediately after the committal.'

'Yes. But this could be only a day or two before the actual trial and they were given no rights, not even to demand extra time to prepare their case.'

'In Jake Crewe's circumstance, we know he is guilty.'

'True. But this spontaneity could work in the defendant's favour,' Nellie said. 'If the prosecution goes ahead without counsel, the judges sometimes choose to sympathise with the defendant, especially if they feel the defendant is innocent.'

***

Hobart Criminal Courts, Corner of Brisbane and Campbell Streets.
A preliminary hearing was scheduled ahead of plan, due to new evidence the defence lawyer told the court. New evidence that proved it was impossible for the defendant Jake Crewe to have committed the murder.

The Railway Union threw their weight behind one of their own, Jake Crewe. Jake, it appeared had forged many bonds with his colleagues, and some in positions of authority in the company, particularly in the union.

Barrister Edsel Beardsley QC was sixty-six and sharp as a razor. He was also man of books, learned with court procedure and smart. His first comment was that the prosecution had no reliable witnesses.

'You talk of compression marks on the deceased's throat,' Beardsley articulated in a deep clear voice, 'showing clearly a deep bruise on the right side of the voice box. That appears to be made by a thumb while three lighter bruises in a fine line on the other side made by a right hand. They are four inches across. There are no curved fingernail impressions related to these marks, but there are scratches on the neck that could have been made by the victim struggling to prise away the killer's grip.'

The prosecution agreed.

'But there's one major flaw in your hypothesis.'

'Oh?'

'The first two joints of all four fingers on the defendant's left hand are missing.'

'This has been noted,' the prosecution concurred. 'However, medical inspection agrees that the pressure of Crewe's deformed hand would still be strong enough to kill his young victim. This would also explain the absence of fingernail indentations.'

Beardsley QC brought forward his first witness, a prison doctor set the task of ascertaining the strength in Crewe's deformed hand, and he strongly believed the accused didn't have the strength to strangle the girl.

The prosecution argued this point vehemently. With the judge's permission Crewe was ordered to display his hands to the jury. Crewe was a well-built man with powerful arms, yet his deformed hand, minus its two joints on four fingers, did not appear to be a formidable weapon capable of strangulation.

Next the prosecution made a valid point about Crewe's jacket worn the night of the murder. Every single button had been torn free. 'Why? Because when the defendant returned to his lodgings that night,' the prosecutor suggested, 'he realised he was missing one button, so he pulled all the others off and threw them away.'

'Fiddlesticks.'

'The suitcase,' the prosecution continued. 'Would the accused kindly explain to the court what he was doing in possession of the incriminating suitcase and why did he plant it under another lodger' bed, namely Mr Edward Culpepper, who subsequently was incorrectly arrested as the killer.'

Embarrassing for the defence lawyer and those at Tasmanian Railway who funded the barrister, Jake Crewe was forced to admit he had a record for petty theft – a fact not many were aware of. He explained to the court how he stole the suitcase from a man who left it unattended at Page's Coach Depot in Collins Street. And that he did not know what was in it until he forced the lock back at his lodgings. Then, that same day, police came to the Caledonian Hotel to talk to Mrs Schuster the proprietor. As it turned out it was about something else entirely. However, Crewe told the court, 'I panicked and shoved it under Mr Culpepper's bed.'

'That sounds a highly unlikely story Mr Crewe,' the prosecutor said. 'A fabrication if I have ever heard one.'

The case against Jake Crewe was weakening when, finally, his defence barrister pulled the ace from his sleeve. Miss Harriet Simpson was an exotic dancer and to those that knew her, she was also a prostitute. Miss Simpson, whose address was given as The Ocean Child Hotel in Argyle Street, swore under oath that Jake Crewe had spent the night with her.

'*All* night?' the prosecution asked.

'From nine sir, until seven the next morning.'

'You realise madam, that you are under oath, that you swore to tell the truth and nothing but the truth, so help me god.'

'Aye, o' course.'

'Your Honour,' the prosecution roared. 'Is the court to take the word of a common prostitute?'

The courtroom booed and sneered.

'Silence!' Sir Richard Arledge Watchorn's gavel came down so hard the handle nearly snapped. 'Silence I say!' The judge frowned at the prosecutor. 'Mr Beardsley you would do well to curb your tongue sir, should you not end up in the dock yourself under a charge of libel.'

At 4.30PM precisely the judge completed his ten-minute summary with the warning to the jury that they should carefully weigh any doubts in the matter. The jury retired to consider their verdict. It took less than half an hour.

'And what say you?' the judge asked the foreman of the jury. 'Do you find the defendant guilty or not guilty?'

'Not guilty your honour.'

Instantly disruption followed. A disturbance of shifting bodies and urgently exchanged whispers as mixed feelings filled the courtroom.

Charlotte was astounded, lost for words. For the first time she realised Jake Crewe had recognised her sitting in the public gallery. He turned to her and smiled, with a one finger to forehead salute. Suddenly Charlotte felt vulnerable.

Paolo Esposito was mentally drained. He felt an empty vessel. He was confused, not angry, yet puzzled. The anger would come later. He spilled out onto the footpath with the rest of the gallery rabble and watched the man accused of killing his daughter being congratulated. Yet as he listened to the banter outside the courthouse, a majority seemed to feel justice had not been served. Paolo walked to the bakery in North Hobart and wrote to his wife Maida a letter. She too would be devastated.

I will not return until Rosa's killer is found and punished, he wrote in their native language. *Then I shall return to you my love.*

***

Princes Park, Hobart Waterfront.

Charlotte bit off more sandwich than she intended. 'Aunt Jocelyn makes the best bread,' she said in a most unladylike manner, her words incoherent, vying for clarity around the corn beef and mustard pickle she had just sunk her teeth into. Charlotte and Edward shared a small picnic basket in the park where the old Prince of Wales Battery once defended Hobart against a possible attack by the Russians. That was the threat anyway, back in '54.

Edward laughed. 'What did you say?'

Charlotte swallowed. 'Please excuse me. I'm just so hungry ... I said Aunt Jocelyn makes the best bread.'

Edward had to agree. The two had grown even closer since Edward's release from prison. Hardly a day had gone by when the two weren't seen together. Although the day was cool the sun was out and the sky turquoise blue, all in all the perfect autumn day.

Edward was forever grateful for Charlotte's intervention. Some branded her foolish for confronting Jake Crewe, but to Edward the woman was a hero. He had fallen in love and he knew she felt the same way, but their situation had made things awkward. Edward worried that they were becoming just good friends.

Also, a darkness lingered. Since Jake Crewe was acquitted Charlotte was always looking over her shoulder, expecting retribution from Crewe. The two had discussed Edward facing the railway surveyor, man to man. But Charlotte argued that Crewe was unlikely to risk his freedom with an assault charge. 'We're just going to have to prove his guilt another way.'

'Yes, but how?'

'I don't know, I'm working on it.'

In the meantime, Charlotte spent evenings in her room writing. *Beyond the Seas of Tyranny* was coming together. The ideas flowed. The adventure continued for her characters, with doors opening and doors closing on her various twists and turns. Charlotte would daily regale Edward with her story. He proved to be a great listener. She also read him excerpts from her previous night's writing.

'Yer father done a lot o' writin' didn't he?'

Charlotte looked serious and gave Edward *that* schoolteacher look she had perfected lately, and Edward corrected himself immediately. 'Your-father-did-a-lot-of-writing-did-he- not?' he articulated.

'Now that was easy, wasn't it?' Edward's English improved daily and although to outsiders it may appear condescending, belittling even, Edward was adamant he wished to be corrected.

'Easy? Yer ... yes. But old habits die hard, me mum used to say.'

'*My* mum used to say,' Charlotte corrected. 'I suppose she also said you can't teach old dogs new tricks.'

Edward feigned utter surprise. 'How did you know that?'

They laughed. They locked eyes. 'Oh Charlotte,' Edward started. 'I ...' Immediately the mood sobered. 'I ... I think of you all the time ... I ...' He reached out and Charlotte took his hand in hers.

'And me you,' Charlotte returned the compliment. From where they sat on a blanket on the park lawn love was in the air. Nearby other couples strolled by, making the most of the pleasant afternoon. Edward wanted so much to lean over and kiss Charlotte. To hug her, to throw her back on the rug and make love to her. Clearly it was not the place. The moment was lost when a dark cloud moved across the sun, spoiling the mood.

'Best we be movin' on eh?' Edward said, standing.

'Best we be moving on,' Charlotte said.

'Oh! And how-now-brown-cow,' Edward answered.

CHAPTER TWELVE

The Oaks, Richmond.
Weeks had passed since Adelaide's acquittal. She sniffed the country air. Her time incarcerated while on remand had put the fear of god into her. Now she valued freedom more than anything, even money. *Well almost.*

Hyacinth Hambleton, Morton Dunbar and Adelaide Hambleton D'Boville dined in silence around the cedar dining table of the rural homestead. Ashley's sister Phillipa, who had not been seen since her brother's funeral, chose to remain in Hobart. It was agreed that all who were party to Hyacinth's fraud, would take their share of the money and run as soon as the settlement came through. This equated to twenty-five per cent of one hundred thousand from the estate alone. Then there was the sale of property. But as expected the will was being contested by the deceased Genevieve Sayer's niece, Edith Woodrow, residing in South Africa. Modern communications by telegraph had sped up the legal process. However, word had arrived that the woman was sailing to Tasmania to settle the matter in the courts, in person.

'Damn the woman. Damn her eyes,' Hyacinth was furious. She was also worried. 'This could go on for months.'

'Oh, I don't know, Hyacinth,' Morton spoke from the head of the table pouring himself a generous glass of Burgundy. 'Life's not that bad. We've all done nicely from the auctioned furniture, and we have deeds secured for several properties we can sell at leisure.' Morton reached across and took Adelaide's hand. He had taken to being master like a duck to water. He felt a measure of security for his future. And to make him feel safer still, he had found a gentleman's pocket derringer amongst Ashley possessions, along with a box of fifty bullets. Now he kept the pistol on him day and night. 'And I don't mind lording over the manor until we sort this business out,' he grinned.

This comment alone made Hyacinth want to retch.

The three had already planned Edith Woodrow's future when she arrived, and it was bleak. The legal beneficiary to the old aunt's will was herself in her sixties …

And there were all manner of ailments or accidents that might befall her for her troubles.

Mrs Audrey Schuster of the Caledonian Hotel in Elizabeth Street had lost two lodgers through this incident. Edward Culpepper's faith in a landlady who snooped through his belongings had vanished and he found new lodgings, while Jake Crewe sent a friend to collect his belongings. Crewe took a temporary room in the Saracen's Head in Barrack Street.

Paolo Esposito first smelt a rat when he followed Jake Crewe into the Telegraph Hotel on the docks and observed him meeting with the foreman in the jury. They took care to sit quietly in a dark corner. Paolo knew this just wasn't right as he spied on the two men, deep in intense conversation.

Days had passed after Jake Crewe's acquittal. And Paolo Esposito knew the man's every move. The stocky fifty-year-old was like a dog with a meaty bone. He knew Crewe was his daughter's killer. He just had to prove it. The main reason for his acquittal was the strength in Crewe's deformed hand. Although the man was missing two joints on four fingers on his left hand, a deformity from birth Paolo had learnt, he was certain the man had more strength than he let on.

'Meester Crewe.' Paolo appeared like an apparition the moment Crewe stepped from his lodgings and onto Barrack Street. As difficult as it was, Paolo forced a wide smile. 'Meester Crewe, what pleasure is for me to meet you.' Paolo feigned surprise. 'Fancy I meet you in street … si … I would like very much to be one of the first to congratulate you.'

'Congratulate me?'

'Si, si, I was at the courthouse. That man, what he called, prosecutor? He was so wrong.' Paolo did not give Crewe the opportunity to back away. He knew he had only one chance at this. The Italian's left hand shot out, and instinctively Crewe took it. The two men shook hands. Paolo gripped firmly. Crewe squeezed back ...

Eureka!

The moment was bittersweet for the grieving father, for at that very moment Paolo knew this man had the strength to strangle his daughter.

Edward decided to wait for Charlotte on Macquarie Street at the main entrance to the newspaper offices rather than disturb her at her desk. He pulled his coat collar up about his neck, for a chill breeze swept up from the harbour. The afternoon light had grown dull. Rain threatened. It was 4.05PM when Charlotte stepped through the front entrance doors and onto the busy street. 'Edward! Are you waiting for me? What a pleasant surprise.'

'It's important Charlotte. Do you remember Daisy Mather?'

'From Port Arthur ... at the general store?'

'Aye ... I mean yes. Well, she's in hospital, at St Mary's.'

'Is this to do with her anorexia?'

'If that's what that skinny disease is called, well yes. She's real sick Charlotte, but she sent me a message. She wants to tell us something she learnt about Annie.'

Daisy lay in her hospital bed, one of twelve iron cots, six down each side in her ward. There was little privacy, and although seclusion curtain rails had been installed around each bed, there were few curtains. Charlotte and Edward took the opportunity to talk to the matron, Matron Spencer, before visiting Daisy.

'Short of force feeding her there is nought we can do,' the large-portioned woman told them, freely admitting that her tolerance for what appeared such an unnecessary ailment was limited.

'How sick, exactly, is she?' Charlotte asked.

'She simply will not help herself. This morning we made her eat a mutton chop.'

'Made her?'

'Yes, we sit with them, hand feed them, hold them down if we have to. It was a nice juicy chop with plenty of fat, but she vomited it all up moments after she ate it.'

Electric lighting illuminated the ward, however the chill outside meant all the windows were closed creating an unpleasant atmosphere from the stink of human waste and other by-products of illness.

Daisy snoozed. Charlotte took the patient's hand. 'Daisy.'

Daisy's eyes sprung open. 'Mrs Clarke, you came. Edward ... oh this is lovely to see you.'

Edward. 'You sent for us Daisy.'

'Yer I know, but I didn't think you'd come, like.'

'Nonsense Daisy,' Charlotte said. 'Of course, we'd come. How are you feeling?'

'Tired. Always tired, an' I have headaches on an' off.'

'Oh, I'm sorry Daisy.' Charlotte wanted to say. *Just eat and all this will go away,* but she knew enough about anorexia nervosa to know those words would fall on deaf ears. Charlotte said instead, 'You wanted to tell us something.'

'Yes.' Daisy struggled to sit up. 'Please, can you help me?' Once the sixteen-year-old wax propped upright on pillows she started. 'I know who killed me best friend Annie Smith.'

Edward and Charlotte listened in silence. They were surprised, yet not shocked ...

***

Friday 13th

Dusk crept along Old Wharf docks around 5PM. By six it was dark. At 9PM the General Post Office clock chimed through blackness. There was no moon and the sky was heavy with cloud. Only a single streetlamp lit Jake

Crewe's path as he stumbled from the Steam Packet Tavern and made the fatal mistake of turning down the narrow laneway alongside the inn. The docks were quiet for a Friday night. Whilst the inns were full of warmth and cheer, the wharves were deserted.

Crewe started to whistle. If Paolo was familiar with songs of the sea, he would have recognised the tune as the shanty, *Blow the man down*. Crewe was drunk, but not so drunk that he did not suspect he was being followed. More than once he stopped to search the darkness behind him for any sign, anything suspicious. Paolo dived into deepening shadows, cursing himself for his clumsiness. Crewe walked faster. But drink also gave him courage. His rendezvous with his friend Miss Simpson at The Ocean Child Hotel would have to wait. Crewe decided to avoid Wapping. He crossed the rivulet and, passing the old slaughterhouse, he headed for the Queen's Domain where he could lose his tail before taking the short cut over the parkland to Argyle Street. But first ...

Who was following?

Paolo pushed into the bushland that made up the Queen's Domain, fuelled by determination and retribution; the last words he read in his bible repeating themselves over and over ... Romans 12:19 *Vengeance is mine saith the lord!*

There was no sign of Crewe. He stopped to listen. Nothing. Paolo hurried along a dark path. Visibility was minimal. He broke into a jog ...

Crewe pounced. He took Paolo by the throat, slamming him against a eucalypt. 'You followin' me?' Crewe unsheathed a small fish knife from his belt. Paolo remained calm. Relaxed. He did not resist. Crewe eased his grip, when the slightest of moonlight exposed Paolo's face. 'You!' Crewe said. 'I know you. You're the bastard what congratulated me outside the Saracen.'

Paolo fumbled in his trouser pocket where he carried his only defence – a sailor's cosh. The ten-inch baleen handle was double-ended with solid lead neatly held with woven string. A formidable weapon prized by seamen as it was easily concealed inside the trouser leg pocket.

'What's it all about then?' Crewe put the knife point to the Italian's back. 'Why yer followin' me old man?'

'Why you do it?" Paolo's heart was racing, but he wanted answers.

'Why I do what grandpa?'

'Why you kill my Rosa?'

'Rosa! Jesus! Is that what this's all about? Rosa, Rosa.'

'My little girl,' Paolo thought he was stronger than this. But now the moment had come his emotions were interfering. 'My little Rosa. She sixteen and you ... you did what you did ... you are animal.'

'Nar mate.' Jake Crewe was starting to enjoy himself. *This short arse Italian must have come all the way from Melbourne to do this ... do what ... piss his pants?* 'That little Rosa asked for it.' Crewe used his deformed hand to grip Paolo's throat while he toyed with the knife in the other. 'She begged for it she did. Tasty little bit she was an' all, you know she ... Fuck!'

The cosh slapped Crewe's skull just above the left ear with a nauseating crack.

'Fuck!'

Crewe's deformed hand instinctively touched the wound. His shortened fingers came away sticky with blood.

'Fuck!'

His eyes narrowed, his nostrils flared, and spittle ran down his chin. Paolo stepped backwards for leverage and brought the cosh to bear a second time. The next wound far outweighed the first. Crewe slashed out with the knife slicing Paolo's shirt, opening a shallow wound in his chest. But Paolo's adrenalin powered his hatred.

Romans 12:19 *Vengeance is mine saith the lord!*

Paolo struck again. The wild thrust splintered Crewe's bone above the right eye. Crewe speared his blade towards his attacker, but Paolo was seething with energy and loathing.

The pig must die.

Romans 12:19 *Vengeance is mine saith the lord!*

The fourth blow had Crewe staggering. He was fighting consciousness. He lashed again. This time wounding Paolo's arm. But it was nothing. Nothing compared to what Paolo would do next.

***

Days later.

George Davies was in the enviable position of having access to information before it was put into print and distributed to the general public. Real estate for example. Now aged twenty-nine with his training in London behind him and the security of a future in the Tasmanian newspaper industry, George was keen to marry and buy a rural estate, and not necessarily in that order.

Prospect House on the north side of the road heading into Richmond was perfect. The twenty-three-acre property was manageable for a gentleman whose main income was not reliant on farming, and the sale price of seven and a half thousand pounds was reasonable. After the pleasant hour and a half ride from Bellerive, George's mount crossed the short wooden bridge over a boundary creek and onto the property, and he was instantly smitten. Even with dark skies brewing a storm, two storey Prospect House was a sight to behold. Indeed, a gentleman's manor, with its portico entrance, Palladian windows, large chimneys and neat quoined corners. Built during the reign of King George IV six decades earlier, the mansion would need some restoration, especially since it had been rented the past fifteen years to a sheep farmer, and clearly little money had been spent on its upkeep. George also knew the landlady, a shipbuilder's wife, Mrs Genevieve Sayer, had recently died, and the property was to be sold by the new owners who had recently inherited the property.

Morton Dunbar whipped the horse into a fast trot. Ahead of them, already waiting at Prospect House was their prospective buyer, a young gentleman of wealth from Hobart. Adelaide D'Boville sat in the buggy behind her *livery man*, honing her charm. Hobart was a small community where most wealthy citizens knew each other and Adelaide was certainly aware of Mr Davies pedigree, and would respond accordingly.

George heard the carriage approach and watched from the portico steps as the owner's transport rattled across the bridge and onto the gravel turning circle in front of the old property. With ever an eye for the ladies, George was instantly impressed with this most attractive woman before him, following her form discreetly as Morton helped Adelaide alight. With her hair tied in a chignon the woman wore a wide brimmed velvet hat on a rakish angle. Beneath the hat, hiding in the shade was a beautiful woman, clearly continental, with large devilish hazel eyes, a small, curved nose and a wide sensual mouth.

'Mr Davies,' Mrs D'Boville-Hambleton's accent was immediately obvious but her English perfect. 'It is a pleasure to meet you.'

'Likewise, madam.'

Their communication, for what was intended as a private sale, had been via mail. Now, finally, George could put a face to their exchanged letters. 'You are much younger than I expected, Mrs D'Boville-Hambleton.'

'Flattery will not alter the selling price Mr Davies,' Adelaide smiled cheekily. She took a set of iron keys secured on a large ring from her satchel. 'The tenants are out on the field so, shall we?'

Adelaide slipped the antique key into the front door lock. Somewhere in the distance a low rumble herald approaching storm clouds. Morton felt spots of rain.

'I'll take the trap to the barn, madam,' he told Adelaide. Morton gathered the loose reins and started off. George looked to his own mount and passed Morton his rein. 'Be a good chap would you.'

Morton took the rein and the two men exchanged glances. There was a moment of recognition and George was taken aback. George made to comment, *have we met before? I know you, don't I?* But Morton took the strap and, with head bowed, went about securing the horses.

***

Queen's Domain, Hobart.
Senior Constable Toby Hutton was the first of the detectives to the murder scene on the Domain. He had not long eaten a hearty breakfast of grilled

black pudding, bread and dripping, all washed down with steaming tea. White, three sugars. Now he lost the lot. Vomiting on the crime scene and any evidence the killer may have left behind.

The mutilated body had been dragged several yards into thick bushes from a pedestrian track where he had been attacked. It had been a man walking his dogs that had discovered the body. Hutton took a second look at the victim. Male, Caucasian, early thirties, powerfully built.

'Whoever did this musta been a strong devil,' one of the uniformed officers accompanying Hutton said.

'Or he was ambushed,' Hutton said. 'Has he got a wallet on him?'

The police officer looked back at the body. Death had occurred several days earlier, and he certainly did not want to interfere with the rotting corpse. The head had been battered and the torso slashed. But the most disturbing wound was the groin. The victim's dark trousers were pulled down to the knees and his penis appeared to have been severed. In fact, there was so much congealed blood in that area it was difficult to tell if the penis was still attached to the body at all.

'Wallet, man?' Hutton said. 'Is there any sign of a wallet or purse?'

The second policeman joined the search, poking at the remains with a stick and disturbing a thousand blowflies. Hutton retched again.

'Here,' the second officer eased a coin purse from the front left pocket of the dark trousers. He tipped the coins into his palm displaying gold amongst the silver and copper. The lawman whistled. 'Three half sovs.'

'He weren't robbed then.'

Suddenly the first man noted the missing joints on the left hand. 'Say, isn't that the cove in court last week for the *girl in the swamp* murder? The cove who was found not guilty. Look at his left hand.' He looked to his colleague. 'Tom, you escorted him to the courthouse did you not. That's him, isn't it?'

The three men studied the face. The *girl in the swamp* case had had a lot of publicity and the missing finger joints couldn't be mistaken. 'Yeh, yer right.'

Approaching policemen caught their attention. 'Here's the inspector.'

Inspector Boothman arrived on the scene. He put a hand in the air for the accompanying uniforms to fall in behind him. 'Inspector,' Hutton greeted his mentor. Hutton counted six officers.

'Hutton,' Boothman said solemnly. Toby saw colleague Senior Constable Daniel Haynes join them. 'Dan.'

Daniel nodded. He looked awkward.

'Brought an army with yer huh?' Hutton smiled at his friend.

'Senior Constable Haynes will be taking over this investigation,' Boothman said.

Hutton smile vanished. 'Why?' Instantly he remembered his place. 'I mean ... sorry ... ah, why is that sir?'

'Senior Constable Toby Hutton,' Inspector Boothman voice was official, 'you are under arrest for the murder of Annie Smith in Port Arthur on the thirty-first of December 1897.'

***

The Mercury Newspaper Offices.
Edward ignored protocol, barging into the journalist office where he knew he would find Charlotte. 'Heard the news?' Edward said without greeting.

'About Toby?'

'Yes.'

'Yes, I just heard. They finally believed us Edward. Inspector Boothman's gone ahead, and Toby Hutton's been arrested.'

Edward and Charlotte's thoughts returned to Daisy's bedside at the hospital ...

'I know who killed me best friend Annie Smith,' Daisy had told them. *'Senior Constable Toby Hutton.'* Edward had flinched at the name. *'It were his baby what Annie was havin'.'*

'Hutton's?'

'Yes. He got Annie pregnant while she was having relationships with the reverend.'

'Are you serious?'

'*Yes, absolutely serious. The reverend couldn't 'ave children, see, that's why 'e was childless. Annie was seduced by the reverend who promised to make an honest woman of her when his wife Beverly died. She was sick you must understand.*'

'*Yes, we knew that.*'

'*But Annie was having a relationship with Mr Hutton at the same time also.*'

'*So how did you find this out?*' Charlotte had asked.

'*I heard the reverend and my master Mr Gill talking about it one afternoon a few weeks back when they thought I had gone home after the store closed.*'

'*I knew the reverend wouldn't kill Annie just because she was with another man.*' Charlotte had said.

'*No, it's the other way around. The night of the fire Constable Hutton came to see Annie while the reverend was away. He was there when the fires swept through. It was Constable Hutton what killed Annie.*'

'*Why, on earth?*'

'*Oh, it weren't deliberate,*' Daisy had pushed her back against the bedhead to sit up even higher. '*My sister is friendly with Constable Hutton's friend, William Beacon, 'e told my sister that Hutton told him he wanted to take Annie away from the reverend, but Annie refused for one reason or another. They argued. Had a big fight. And Hutton struck Annie, and she fell down the stairs and died. It was a horrible accident. So, Hutton tried to make it look like she was burnt to death when the fire come through. 'e told William Beacon the back of the rectory burned and miraculously went out, so 'e put paraffin on 'er and was goin' ter burn Annie's body further but someone come along, and he took off.*'

'*That must have been us,*' Charlotte had told Edward. '*We turned up late that night and found Annie.*'

'*Then that mongrel Hutton came along with Reverend Finch just after we got there.*'

'*He must have run off to fetch him,*' Edward had said. '*Knowing we were there.*'

It was at this moment Matron Spence joined them at the bedside. '*I will have to ask you to leave, Daisy needs her ablutions now.*'

Charlotte and Edward were forced aside by a nurse, looking particularly enthusiastic and wearing a navy and slate grey ankle length dress, white bonnet, white pinafore apron and a neck cloth tied in a bow. She wheeled an iron trolley with an enamel wash basin, sponge and towels.

'One last thing Daisy,' Charlotte had asked. *'Are you prepared to be a witness? You and William Beacon?'*

'I can't speak for William, but I'll do it ... I'll do it for Annie, of course.'

***

On returning to Hobart from his visit to Prospect House in Richmond, George rode directly to Agapanthus Cottage. He knew Charlotte was at the offices. Merrill opened the door. 'George,' she smiled. 'What a lovely surprise.'

George, ashen faced, asked, 'Is your mother in?'

'No, just me, Merrill,' Merrill's smiled faded. 'They've left me all alone. Do you want to come in?'

This was most inappropriate, but George had urgent business. 'Look Miss Childers ...'

'Merrill, please.'

'Merrill ... I ... ah ... I don't know how to put this.'

'My you do look serious.'

'I am Merrill, deadly serious. But yes, I do need to come in?'

***

Police Headquarters.

Inspector Benjamin Boothman walked out of a meeting with the manager of The Savings Bank of Tasmania, Cecil Winthrop, his assistant Humphrey, representatives from Anderson and Craige Realty, Charlock Stockbrokers, Franklin Gallery Fine Arts and Burns Auctioneers. He was appalled. The evidence against the Hambletons was damning. The paperwork the businesses presented was a trail of deceit and theft on a grand scale.

Arrests had been in the planning stage when Boothman received news about Senior Constable Toby Hutton. For a lawman who expected nothing but honesty from his subordinates he was nauseated – one of his own on a murder charge. He sent a telegram to his cousin Mary in Launceston to inform her that her only son Toby had been charged. *He* was devastated. And he knew Mary would be a broken woman.

'If it don't rain it pours, eh Inspector?' Sergeant Geoff Broadmoor read the inspector's angst. Right now they needed to have their wits about them and strike while the iron was hot.

'Arrange a carriage and I want four good officers, sergeant. Fetch side arms for you and me and rifles for the men.'

'Expecting trouble?'

'Not particularly, but I'll not take risks.'

***

Two hours later.

The journey through Coal Valley along the road to Richmond was solemn, filled with mixed emotions. *What if George was right?* Charlotte thought. She had taken some convincing. But finally, after offering indisputable evidence, George Davies had Charlotte where he wanted her – in a carriage and heading for Richmond.

Rain had started as they crossed the River Derwent on the ferry. It had been relentless ever since. Winter was only weeks away and George was forced to hire a covered carriage for their journey, leaving their newspaper buggy at stables in Bellerive. Country lad Edward, as liveryman, was quite comfortable with the weather, up on the driver's seat in his oilskins. But he was concerned for Charlotte. Everything had turned upside down. And so quickly.

Charlotte's brain was scrambling.

'This rain has settled in,' George said, attempting to divert Charlotte's thoughts. With the road turning to a quagmire from the persistent rain, Bellerive to Richmond took almost two hours. George pointed out Prospect

House in passing. Fifteen minutes later they passed through the township, crossed the Richmond Bridge and rode a mile east to *The Oaks*.

George was insistent and had told the other two earlier, 'Surprise is paramount. I will knock on the door, apologise for visiting unannounced, and explain I am very keen on purchasing Prospect House and wish to have a second inspection. They will have to comply.'

Edward parked the carriage thirty yards from the cottage under the shelter of a huge oak tree, its decades old branches supporting enough greenery to provide excellent shelter.

Charlotte was shaking. But it was not from the cold.

'Do you think they have seen us?'

They did not wait long for an answer. Hyacinth appeared at the drawing room window. Another face appeared. 'That one's Adelaide,' George said, recognising the dark-haired woman instantly.

Immediately the front door opened, and a man appeared in the doorway, his face masked with an umbrella against the pelting rain.

'Right, here we go. Plan A.' George had discussed his plan earlier, to tell Mrs D'Boville-Hambleton he was very keen on seeing Prospect House a second time and would ask for their livery man to come with me for the inspection.'

Their livery man. Charlotte studied the man on the threshold. With thirty yards between them and the heavy rain, it was difficult to tell. 'Is that him?'

'Yes,' George said. 'Now you wait here, I'll go and explain that I have brought my wife also, to see the house.' George paused, studying Charlotte's face. 'Are you alright with that ... wife?' Charlotte nodded. There was no smile.

Wife? For the first time Edward suspected he may have a rival for Charlotte's affections. Edward alighted, taking a position alongside the carriage and out of sight. Charlotte's nerves were shattered.

'Are you alright?' Edward asked. Charlotte indicated that she was, but her performance was less than convincing.

At the cottage entrance Morton Dunbar called out over the rain. 'Can I help you?'

'Yes, yes!' George yelled back. With an umbrella in hand, he dodged puddles to the front door of the cottage. 'It's me again,' he sang out on the approach. 'George Davies.'

Adelaide joined Morton at the door, standing behind Morton, just out of view.

'He's keen,' Morton said over his shoulder. 'Looks like you have sold Prospect House my dear.' Adelaide placed a hand on Morton's shoulder.

Waiting at the carriage Charlotte studied the man at the door. What if her *dead* husband Charles Claiborne *was* masquerading as hired help for Hyacinth Hambleton in Richmond?

Hyacinth for heaven's sake!

Charlotte had visited this property, *The Oaks*, recently. Had *Charles* been there at the time? But why? Why the deceit? Worse still ... how? His body was found washed up at Adventure Bay on Bruny Island.

It's impossible!

But his body was badly mutilated in the storm, washed over rocks, the face was shredded. Was it possible Charles survived, swapping his clothes for those on his friend's body? The body that was never found.

But why? Is he tied up with Hyacinth's fraudulent activities?

If so, how?

Charlotte was frozen in thought.

As Charlotte and Edward watched George making conversation, George pointed to Charlotte in the carriage. Morton lifted his umbrella, the better to see.

'Oh god,' Charlotte felt sickened. 'It-is-him!'

Edward. 'Are you certain?'

'Oh Edward ... yes ... oh god no. It *is* Charles.'

Charlotte felt faint.

George made his excuses. He looked back for a sign from Charlotte. Charlotte stared back. Her face cold. She was in shock.

Now George knew he was right. He just knew it.

As he watched Edward comfort Charlotte in the carriage, George had a flashback to earlier in the day with Merrill at Agapanthus cottage.

'It's most important that I inspect Charlotte's wedding photograph on the mantelpiece,' he had told Merrill.

'You had better come in then.'

'That's him!' George studied the groom in the sepia photograph, Charles Claiborne. *'He calls himself Morton Dunbar now.'*

Merrill was confused. *'Who does? Charles?'*

'Yes.'

Merrill had looked completely bewildered. She shook her head vigorously. *'He's dead George.'*

'Oh no! No, he's not.' George tapped the glass. *'He's older and a little thinner but he certainly isn't dead. Tell me everything you know about this Charles Claiborne.'*

Merrill explained the rare abnormality. *'Heterochromia iridum.'* Merrill even knew the scientific terminology. *'That is eyes of two different colours. It's one in a million ... probably more.'*

At the cottage threshold Morton Dunbar sensed George's scrutiny. This prospective buyer for Prospect House was staring into his eyes.

The eyes!

One blue, one brown. George was certain even in the poor afternoon light. George opened his mouth to speak. He opened his mouth to ask the truth. But before he could speak Morton Dunbar's real name was yelled across the yard. 'Charles Claiborne!'

Claiborne recognised his widow immediately as she jumped from the carriage and, with parasol overhead, made a dash for the cottage.

Behind the homestead Inspector Boothman heard the voices. He caught the name called out, Charles Claiborne. Strange. The name rang a bell. The inspector and five officers had approached *The Oaks* from the north, crossing fields near the outbuildings. Using the heavy rain for cover they were out of sight of the front of the building. Their target, Mrs Hyacinth Hambleton, might not be arrested for her husband's murder, but, thanks to Charlotte and Nellie, she was certainly going to be found guilty of fraud.

Charlotte stopped dead. She stood in the mud, her parasol overhead, barely stopping the deluge from washing over her. Charlotte didn't know whether to scream, cry or strike the man on the threshold. Her *dead* husband Charles Claiborne. The man she had grieved over. The man she had buried for Christ's sake. The man whose grave she had visited the past four years. Instead, Charlotte's voice was breaking. 'Charles?' she said, her voice croaky, yet brewing with rage. Tears welled. 'Is that really you?'

'Charlotte ... I ... I ...'

Adelaide D'Boville pushed past Charles into the rain. 'Morton? Morton?' She stared down at Charlotte. 'What's going on?' She looked at Charlotte with utter contempt. 'You know this woman, this ... this journalist?'

Charlotte's voice returned and anger brewed. 'He's my husband.'

Hearing shouted threats, Boothman drew his .38 Smith and Wesson service pistol. He rounded the henhouse. Without warning he was stopped by two large Irish wolfhounds. But the dogs were pre-occupied. They were gnawing bones.

Meaty bones!

And Boothman immediately recognised a lower leg – a human calf with a boot. Boothman moved back against the henhouse wall and raised his pistol. Beside him, a fifty-gallon barrel, propped on a rotting wooden stand collecting rainwater off the roof, overflowed.

'Charles!' Boothman heard the woman's voice cry out once more over the battering rain. The dogs continued tearing meat from the bone. Clearly hungry they were totally absorbed. Boothman was joined by two other officers. 'Jesus Christ!' one said. 'Is that what I think it is?'

Boothman nodded, his clothes saturated. The human leg suddenly gave this arrest more gravity. 'Now lads, we need the element of surprise. I want someone at the backdoor, one each side of the cottage while I approach the front door.' Boothman looked skywards. 'This bloody rain's getting worse.'

Why didn't we wear waterproofs?

'I think we have company sir,' one of the officers noted.

'Yes. The situation's becoming awkward,' Boothman said.

'I saw a carriage approaching minutes ago.'

'There's no room for error,' Boothman told the officers. 'Sooner we make this arrest the sooner we can get out of this bloody rain.'

'I'll take the backdoor,' the first officer turned, avoiding even more water pouring off the henhouse roof. He tripped and kicked the barrel stand, the cask overbalanced, and fifty gallons of water crashed to the ground. The sudden surge washed over Frank's shallow grave exposing the remaining body. 'Oh, Christ!'

'This is even more serious than we thought,' Boothman said. 'Get the others. Move it, quickly now.'

Adelaide D'Boville was seething with the realisation she had fallen for an imposter. Hyacinth stepped into the open.

'Now what have you done you dirty whore?' she shouted at Adelaide. 'I warned Ashley. I ...'

Adelaide screamed back, 'Oh, shut it you wretched woman.'

George had stood on the periphery, pleased to have exposed Charles, yet mystified and shocked. 'You've got some explaining to do old boy.'

He reached out to take Charles by the arm. No one saw the tiny derringer. Charles drew Ashley's pistol from his pocket and fired off a wild shot. The bullet hit George in the right shoulder. Stunned at the unexpected outcome, George staggered backwards. Blood soaked through his jacket. Thinking the wound worse than it was, George collapsed against the cottage, sitting heavily on the ground. Instantly police appeared from three sides, surprising even Charlotte.

'Put down your weapon!' Boothman shouted.

Charles fired another shot towards Boothman, who was hesitant to fire back. Charles snatched Charlotte and he pressed the short muzzle into the side of her head. He dragged her inside, taking Charlotte hostage. The door slammed shut. All outside heard the door being bolted.

'Jesus no!' Boothman now had a hostage situation. How could everything go belly up so quickly? He turned to Hyacinth and Adelaide left in the pouring rain, their clothes saturating, their faces in shock while the deluge washed away tears. 'Arrest these women,' Boothman ordered the officers.

Edward of course had seen everything. With everyone preoccupied at the cottage, he had made a run through the vegetable garden to the rear of the building. From its west side, he watched the police and was about to walk into the open when he heard the first gunshot. Edward remained hidden. He heard shouting, watched the police appear ...

Then Charlotte was taken hostage.

Edward threw his back against the wall. Crouching low beneath the windowsills he hurried to the rear of the cottage in time to hear the backdoor bolted. Edward heard voices inside.

'Charles!' It was Charlotte's voice. Edward pressed an ear to the door. Charlotte remained calm. Calm but angry. 'What have you done? I thought you were dead. How could you? What are you doing with these people?'

'Shut it Charlotte!'

Charlotte remained stoic. 'But Charles ... why?'

'I ... I said shut it.'

Edward recognised fear in Charles' voice. A dangerous situation and he knew Charlotte's life was in peril.

Inside Charlotte took note of her situation. She had been into the hallway and drawing room before of course, but the cottage homestead was now sparsely furnished, not crammed with furniture like she had seen it weeks earlier. Charles shoved her into the dining room, ostensibly the most fortified room in the homestead with only one window. He forced Charlotte onto a chair, throwing her parasol to the floor. She fought back but was slapped hard for her trouble.

'You're pathetic, hit a woman, go on ...'

Charles slapped Charlotte a second time. This time harder. 'I always wanted to do that,' he hissed through a dark smile. Charlotte glared into the man's eyes. 'You did it once before, hit a woman. Coward!'

With the pistol aimed at Charlotte's head Charles stripped the curtains of their cords, securing Charlotte so she could barely move.

Outside Edward ever so carefully tried the door. *Yes, it was bolted.* He approached the kitchen window as Charles appeared. Edward ducked. Immediately wooden louvres were slammed shut. Edward knew the shutters were fitted back in the '30s when roaming bushrangers were a threat. Edward hurried along the west side. Shutters slammed. In less than a minute the farmhouse was fortified.

Charles burst into the front drawing room and as a measure of his determination he fired a loose shot through the glass at a police officer slow to make himself scarce. Another armed officer momentarily had Charles in his sights through the window. But Boothman caught him in time. The inspector struck out knocking his pistol aside. 'Are you mad? There's a hostage in there.'

Immediately the drawing room shutters slammed closed.

'I don't know what on earth you think you are doing,' Charlotte said quietly. 'But you are trapped. You cannot possibly escape.'

'I told you to shut it.'

'There's police out there, everywhere.'

Charles turned on Charlotte with the coldest eyes, blue and brown. Both dark.

Charlotte persisted. 'They'll shoot you. Charles ...'

'Then we'll go together. Me and you. Just the two of us.' It was then that Charlotte smelt the oily pungent odour of spilt kerosene. She saw the one-gallon stone crock lying in the hallway, the remains of its contents spilling, soaking into the runner, dripping through cracks in the floor. Charles must have splashed the kerosene about the cottage. He rattled a box of matches in Charlotte's face. 'Just me and you.'

Charlotte was fighting fear, fighting back tears, battling to remain calm. 'Why ... Charles? Why did you fake your own death?'

'What? You haven't worked it out yet. You were always the savvy sleuth. Miss Charlotte Clarke, the daughter of the famous novelist.' Charles grew even darker. 'Yes. Charlotte Clarke. I noticed you don't call yourself Claiborne anymore.'

'Charles ... I ... you died. Drowned at sea. Your body was washed up. I *did* miss you. But life for me had to go on. Reverting back to my maiden name was a professional move. It made sense.'

Hammering on the door stopped the conversation. Charles stepped into the hallway. The front door was being rammed, but it was solid oak and he had put the crossbar in place, designed for this very purpose sixty-five years earlier. Charlotte heard Charles run down the hallway into the kitchen. He returned seconds later and from where she was secured, she watched him take to the stairs. He was now armed with a shotgun. Upstairs in the master bedroom Charlotte heard the dormer window thrown open on its sash. Charlotte heard an explosion. Not one but two. Outside police scattered.

Charlotte heard Charles screaming at the police, 'Move back or I'll shoot her. Back ... back, the lot of you.'

Charlotte struggled in her chair. The cords were tight. She managed to rock the chair. But the cording seemed to tighten further. Another shotgun blast exploded from the floor above. Charlotte heard shouting outside. Men scrambled. But then someone fired back. She heard glass shatter. Charles cursed. Reloaded, fired both barrels and reloaded again. 'I said back you bastards.'

The stink of raw kerosene filled Charlotte's nostrils. She managed to hook a boot behind the table leg. She found leverage. Rocking the chair Charlotte picked up momentum. Finally, the chair tipped back, overbalanced and Charlotte fell heavily onto the dining room rug. But still she was trussed like a pig about to be placed on the spit.

With the shooting increasing, Edward dropped to the ground and crawled through the mud. At the corner of the building, he could just make out four uniformed police officers through the driving rain. One guarded the prisoners Hyacinth and Adelaide, and another attended to George who had been dragged to safety behind the carriage. The other two uniforms were now armed with rifles, trained on the upper windows. Then Edward caught sight of their inspector. But to expose himself now would be suicide. Edward looked to the henhouse when he saw what appeared to þe a body. It was half buried. Nearby two large dogs watched on, clearly disturbed by the gunshots.

Charlotte floundered on the floor. Struggling only made matters worse. With her hands tied behind the chair she was in a dire situation. Lying on her side, strapped to the chair, Charlotte twisted, pushing her body along a few inches whenever she found traction on the floorboards. Then Charlotte felt something familiar lying on the floor behind her. Her parasol. She wriggled her fingers, managed to grasp the handle with one hand, and the shaft with the other. Charlotte pulled, and the stiletto came free.

It's now or never ... now or never ... hearing gunshots from the upper floor Edward decided to try the scullery shutters ... but then he noticed the cellar door.

Rarely used these days the hatched door, level with the ground, was overgrown with grass and weeds. The rusted latch wasn't locked. Edward lifted the cover, dropped through the cobwebs into total blackness and closed the door behind him.

Charles shouted a final threat. Fired off one barrel scattering the armed police near the carriage and shuttered the upper floor window. He hurried back downstairs. He was about to check on Charlotte, but a sound at the rear of the cottage disturbed him.

With some difficulty Charlotte wedged the stiletto handle against the hearth. She backed closer to the blade and blindly commenced sawing the cord securing her wrists. It parted. With bloodied hands Charlotte then tackled the knot securing her legs to the chair. Footsteps approached. Charles was returning.

Edward fiddled about in the dark. His eyes adjusted ever so slightly, but with the hatch closed and such a bleak day outside progress was limited. It appeared only floorboards were between those upstairs and himself. Edward heard muffled voices. Threats. Threats deadened by the floorboards, but threats none-the-less.

Where's the damned stair? Edward asked himself. Edward stumbled in the darkness and walked into a crate of empty bottles. The noise would have woken the dead. Edward froze. He heard a man's voice. The words were muted but he understood ...

'What was that? That was in the cellar.'

Damn!

Edward prepared for a fight. There was no way he was going to be shot dead down here in the dank and darkness. He felt in his pockets, his pipe, tobacco, his matches ...

Matches. Excellent.

Heavy boots crossed the floorboards overhead. They were headed to the cellar stairs. Edward struck a match against the side of his matchbox. Edward's immediate surrounds were awash with welcome light from the flame. Edward looked about for a weapon. He saw a coal pick as the cellar door opened from the hallway upstairs. Charles stood silhouetted in the doorframe. Edward recognised the murderous outline of a loaded shotgun. He flicked his match aside. Darkness would now be his saviour.

Without warning the cellar exploded into blue flame. Kerosene had dribbled through the floorboards. The flames rushed up the stairs where the fuel had leaked, licking across the wooden steps saturated only moments earlier. If it wasn't so deadly it was almost beautiful to behold.

Charles wanted his revenge. But not like this. The flame licked at his boots. Tongues of flame rose up each side of his trousers. Panicked, Charles jumped backwards. He rushed to the kitchen in search of water. Edward dodged flames, hurrying up the cellar steps. In the hallway the flames took hold. The house was doomed.

'Charlotte!' he called out.

'Edward?'

The dining room filled with smoke, acrid from burning carpet, drapes and furnishings. Charlotte struggled with the stubborn knot securing her ankles to the chair. Flames quickly spread and from where Charlotte lay on the floor the flames spread at an alarming speed.

The homestead was on fire. Hyacinth broke down in tears, collapsing next to the carriage where she and Adelaide had been handcuffed. With police now surrounding the property, Boothman and one uniformed officer attempted to breach the back door. Charles, in the kitchen, fired both barrels. Fortunately the uniformed officer was protected by the thick wooden door. Boothman had no course of action other than to drag the officer to safety. Charles heard Edward call out for Charlotte and hurried back along the passageway ...

Only to be chased by a serpent of fire.

Edward burst into the dining room pirouetting, dancing, skipping to avoid the fire spreading at his feet. 'Charlotte?'

'I'm here!' Charlotte reached behind her, frantic to locate the stiletto. Finally, she managed to slice the cord. 'Watch out!' she screamed.

Charles loomed up behind Edward. As Edward turned, Charles, with his weapon spent, slammed the shotgun, butt first, into Edward's chest.

Winded, with cracked ribs, Edward dropped to his knees. The pain was worse than the threat of fire.

'Edward!' Charlotte rose to her feet. Edward swayed on his knees. He fought consciousness. Charles struck out a second time connecting with Edward's shoulder. Edward crumbled to the floor.

'Who's he, your lover?' Charles yelled over the fire, his blackened face turning demonic, his heterochromia eyes now black satanic spheres. Flames licked about him. Charles had become a fiend ... a ghost.

And he wasn't passing over to the other side alone. He fished two last shells from his trouser pocket, jamming them into the breeches. He snapped the barrels shut, planting the muzzle at the back of Edward's neck where he lay. Charles cocked both hammers. Charlotte leapt forward ploughing into Charles. She struck out at the shotgun the moment both barrels were discharged. The recoil sent Charles staggering back. But he caught his balance and grabbed Charlotte in a bear grip. He was now on fire. Flames licked up at Charlotte, now about to suffer the same fate. She swung her stiletto, burying the polished pointed blade deep into his thigh. Charles screeched in pain. Falling back into the blazing hallway, he groped frantically to extract the knife.

'Edward! Edward!' Charlotte shook her friend. She slapped him. 'For god's sake. Edward.'

Edward's coat caught fire. Edward's eyes opened. He looked up at Charlotte, her hair smouldering, her face black. 'Get up.' Charlotte tugged at Edward. She tore his coat free. Finally, Charlotte managed to put Edward's arm about her own shoulder and the two staggered into the hall.

Flames now took a firm hold on the house. The stair was well alight, and the spilt kerosene was now a river of flames. The atmosphere was toxic and the black smoke pungent. Even with the heavy rain the building was rapidly becoming engulfed in flames.

Struggling to breathe, Charlotte and Edward staggered towards the exit. Suddenly the front door crashed to the floor and gust of wind rushed into the hallway feeding the fire. Boothman appeared through the smoke. Behind him broken guttering showered him with water. He met Charlotte on the threshold and threw Edward's other arm around his own shoulder and between the two of them, Charlotte and the inspector dragged Edward out into the open.

Police officers rushed forward. 'Where's the gunman?'

'Still in there,' Boothman shouted over the crashing timber and the shattering glass. 'He's a dead man.'

With Edward safe Charlotte turned back. She stepped under the waterfall of spilling rainwater, throwing her arms towards the heavens until she was soaked. And then ran back into the burning building.

'What's she doing?' someone shouted. Police rushed after her. Edward, fighting the pain, pushed Boothman away. He staggered back towards the blaze.

'Charlotte!' he screamed out. 'Charlotte!'

Inside Charles flaming body crashed against a window. The shutters collapsed. 'The gunman's still alive!'

'Charlotte!' Edward mounted the steps, but a blast of flame pushed him back.

Instantly Charlotte reappeared in the doorway. She stumbled through blackened smoke, coughing, gasping breaths but with a contagious smile. Under her arm she carried Hyacinth's typewriter.

'I got it!' she shouted. 'Hambleton's Remington. It was in the front room.'

'By Jove,' George grinned, holding a cloth to his bloodied shoulder. He too rushed to meet Charlotte. But another explosion and resounding rumble pushed everyone back as the hall wall collapsed into the cellar. Brick dust and smoke billowed from the broken windows and main entrance.

'Look!' one of the police shouted. 'It's him!'

Charles appeared in the doorframe, his blackened fist still gripping the shotgun.

But he burned like a body on a pyre. His hair crackled like straw while his mouth opened in a crooked scream. His handsome face melted like hot wax while his once colourful eyes blistered into white orbs. There was nothing anyone could do to help him. Resigned to his fate, Charles collapsed across the threshold and gasped his last, agonising breath.

Sickened by what she was seeing, Charlotte turned her attention to Edward who now lay stretched out on the carriage floor with painful cracked ribs, an aching shoulder and burns. But he was alive. The homestead was ablaze. All present were forced further back when the roof caved in and flames reached for the blackened clouds chased by a galaxy of sparks.

Inspector Boothman was joined by the local constabulary from the village who took Hyacinth Hambleton and Adelaide D'Boville off to the lockup.

George watched on with his bandaged shoulder. He was amazed at the resilience of this woman.

'Charlotte Clarke,' he said with sincere reverence, 'you will never cease to amaze me. And you saved the typewriter. Well done. We'll have the evidence we need to lock those two up for some time I should imagine.'

'How's the arm?' Charlotte asked.

'Well,' George looked to Edward who was in far more pain. 'I've got nothing to complain about like our hero there. The bullet passed clean through the flesh under my shoulder. But a little sympathy wouldn't go astray – it hurts a little.'

Charlotte looked back at Edward; he certainly needed medical attention.

George conceded, 'Tell me Charlotte, is there anything you aren't capable of?'

Charlotte suddenly realised she must look like something the cat dragged in, as her Auntie would say. She was soaked through, her clothing torn, her face soot black, but miraculously, she had only superficial burns, scratches and bruises. This was the second time this year she had been threatened by fire. But she was alive. She had a duty to complete, and a novel well on the way. Yes, life was good.

'Is there anything I'm not capable of?' she repeated, turning to the horses still harnessed to their transport. 'Well, we need to get Edward to a doctor to start with, and I've never driven a two-horse carriage before. Have you?'

CHAPTER THIRTEEN

Agapanthus Cottage, Macquarie Street. Sometime after 8PM
Fifty-six-year-old Aunt Jocelyn looked stunning. She wore a tight bodice hugging her comfortable breast, with a white skirt gathered at the waist and falling naturally off the hips. Her curly red hair was tied back into a large bun on the top of her head. Charlotte also noticed her editor, and mentor, Rupert Craddock, exchanging discreet glances with her aunt when they thought they were not being observed. *Love is blind,* Charlotte thought.

Of course, Charlotte knew Rupert and Aunt Jocelyn went back a way, to their youth in Melbourne, and looking at them now Charlotte wondered if there hadn't been more to their relationship all those years ago.

At Jocelyn's suggestion, the celebratory dinner took place in the dining room of Agapanthus Cottage two Saturdays after the Richmond debacle. Jocelyn insisted Charlotte invite her friends and colleagues and now Charlotte realised why her aunt had proposed she invite her mentors at the newspaper. Like her editor Rupert Craddock and George Davies who had become close to the family also; in particular, close to Merrill. Other guests were Edward, naturally, and Nellie Nichols from the police archive.

Outside, winter had arrived on the island. Hobart's guardian, Mount Wellington, kept watch over the city under a blanket of snow, while a chill, gathering about the doors and windows, was kept at bay by a blazing log fire warming the entire cottage. Inside, the convivial company dined on roast venison (shot by George's friends on a recent club outing) served on a vast china platter with all the winter vegetables available from the market and bottles of wine from South Australia.

Edward sat opposite Charlotte. His health had improved tenfold but cracked ribs would take time to heal. Both had superficial burns. But these also were healing nicely.

George, cutting a fine figure dressed in green tweed suit, tweed waistcoat and pale pink tie, carved the roast. He made suitable faces from time to time to remind the table he had a bullet wound to his shoulder, and he made it clear that occasional sympathy was totally acceptable.

One item not in short supply at the table was conversation. There had been so much to discuss.

Toby Hutton was the first surprise. 'Who would have guessed?' Charlotte said.

But Edward wasn't shocked. 'I knew 'im from Port Arthur and 'e was always a bit of a dark 'orse ... *horse*, I meant,' Edward remembered his place. 'Dark ... horse.' He reiterated.

The table laughed. It was common knowledge Edward was being taught to speak 'proper'. Charlotte smiled her approval.

'He confessed to pushing the loose carving over the edge in the Port Arthur church the night of the fire,' Charlotte told the table. 'Trying to scare us he said.'

'Well, 'e could've killed us,' Edward muttered.

'Charles was the *real* dark horse,' Aunt Jocelyn said. 'Managing to find work with Hyacinth Hambleton as a jackaroo just to get close to Ashley, who had stolen his money.'

'Charles could always put his mind to most things,' Charlotte considered. 'I'll give him that.'

'And he wanted Ashley dead also,' Nellie said.

'That's right.'

'Why was that?' Merrill asked.

Charlotte explained how Ashley, as an investor, had misappropriated Charles life savings.

'Yes, but to the point of killing someone?'

'I put it to you,' Charlotte said sounding more like a lawyer than a jour-nalist 'that that was the true nature of Charles Claiborne. I just didn't recognise it at the time.'

'Love is blind they say,' Merrill chirped, looking at Edward for support, when she realised what she had really done was open her mouth to change feet. Merrill blushed.

'It was Charles,' Rupert said, 'masquerading as Morton Dunbar, who purchased the chloroform from various pharmacies was it not?'

'Yes,' Nellie said. 'And he decanted the small phials into one jar.'

Aunt Jocelyn asked. 'Why?'

'Over twenty years ago, in '76, an Act was passed that all poisons had to be clearly labelled as hazardous,' Nellie explained. 'Strychnine and arsenic, for example, are not to be sold as a clear liquid. They must be coloured with soot or indigo to avoid accidents. Purchasers are made to register when they purchased poisons and the vendors must record the poison purchased and the quantity. This was why Morton Dunbar, Charles, had to ride to Sorell and visit multiple apothecaries to acquire the quantity Adelaide requested.

'Surely he was suspicious early in the piece?'

'Of course he was. Don't forget he wanted Ashley Hambleton dead also,' George said.

'The law also now stipulates that one must be over the age of eighteen to purchase poisons, and all vendors must be registered,' Charlotte told the others.

'But,' Nellie said, 'I have noted loopholes in the law.'

'Oh?'

'Yes. If the poison is to be used in the manufacture of medicine, like ar-senic, then the same rules did not apply. Or poisonous and hazardous chemicals used in photography. Veterinary surgeons are also exempt from the above laws. Animals, it seems, do not matter.'

'Didn't I hear someone say Adelaide D'Boville was an amateur veteri-narian?' Aunt Jocelyn asked.

'That's correct. And poisons available for exterminating vermin are also exempt. One can easily acquire poisons from the grocer,' Nellie said. 'All one has to do is explain to the vendor that they have a pest problem with mice or rats.'

'And arsenic is the foundation for rat poison,' George added.

'Exactly.'

'I'll not forget Charles standing in the doorway of that burning house,' George shuddered. Possibly not a suitable dinner table conversation. But all seemed to agree.

'I'd like to have seen Charlotte stepping from the fire with the incriminating typing machine under her arm,' Merrill said with youthful enthusiasm.

Aunt Jocelyn. 'That was very brave of you my dear.'

'Or foolish,' Nellie said.

'Foolish it may have been. But I'm proud of you Charlotte,' Craddock said. 'It was the single most important piece of evidence to nail that evil woman.'

'I fear she may have got away with murder though,' Charlotte said. 'She must have killed her husband. And for what, money?'

'I heard she always cried poor, but she had thousands salted away.'

'I have it on good authority,' George said, 'that she'll be well into her eighties before she is released from servitude.'

Nellie nodded. 'And she'll be a pauper.'

'Well, that's justice for you.'

'And Adelaide D'Boville,' Edward said. 'Now there's a piece o' work.'

'She'll be locked away for at least ten years also.'

George caught Charlotte admiring Edward. Certainly, he had had desires on the intelligent young lady when they first met. But tonight, in particular, he was convinced the two had found true love.

'But he is the son of a convicted felon,' insipid Leonard McShan had unwisely complained to his employer only recently.

'May I remind you, Mr McShan, that the founder of this great newspaper, Mr John Davies, my grandfather, was also a transportee.'

McShan found alternative employment not long after his wayward comment.

Edward stood awkwardly with bruised ribs. 'Well, I'd like ter make a toast to Charlotte,' he said, his eyes warm with wine and love. The others held their glasses high.

'If it weren't fer Charlotte, we'd not be together this 'ere night ... sorry ... this evening. An' may she have great success with her novel.'

'Hear hear.'

They all drank a salute to Charlotte.

Merrill. 'It's almost finished isn't it, Charlotte?'

Charlotte nodded. 'I've finished the first draft.'

'I'm so proud of you dear,' Aunt Jocelyn said. 'I must confess I didn't expect you to complete it.'

Edward didn't agree. 'Oh, I knew she had it in 'er the first time I seen 'er. I mean the first time I saw her.'

Edward looked to Charlotte for approval, mouthing silently, *how now brown cow* ...

EPILOGUE

Part One

'I have some copies here of lesser-known articles your father wrote for *The Australasian.*' Rupert Craddock told Charlotte on one of his visits to Aunt Jocelyn. It had been two months since the dinner and the editor's social calls were becoming more regular, with Jocelyn's blessing. In fact, Agapanthus Cottage seemed to have had the same effect on George and Merrill, and Charlotte and Edward.

'Oh,' Charlotte took the papers and laid them out on the kitchen table. 'Where did you find these?'

'Well, some were in *The Mercury* archive and others I found amongst old papers of mine. There are one or two written in your father's hand.'

'What are they about?' Aunt Jocelyn asked.

'They are essays on Marcus's visit to Tasmania, and in particular Port Arthur, when he researched his material for the series, *Old Tales of a Young Country*, which as we know was the prelude to his famous novel. They are really very interesting.

Rupert pointed out a folder of hand-copied quotes. Charlotte read with interest, the words of her famous father, Marcus Clarke …

You will find it difficult to get down to Port Arthur unless you've got friends there!' said the genial landlady of the Ark Hotel. 'Of course, I mean friends in the Government,' she added, seeing that I looked askance.

'You can see your father had a sense of humour,' Aunt Jocelyn smiled. Charlotte agreed, turning to a page dealing with the horror of the penal settlement ...

To me, brooding over stories of misery and crime, sitting beside the ironed convicts, and shivering at the chill breeze which whitened the angry waters of the bay, there was no beauty in those desolate cliffs, no cheering picturesqueness in that frowning shore. I saw Port Arthur for the first time beneath a leaden and sullen sky; and as we sailed inwards past the ruins of Point Puer, and beheld it barring our passage to the prison and the low grey hammocks of the Island of the Dead, I felt that there was a grim propriety in the melancholy of nature.

Charlotte was clearly sentimental. 'So beautifully written.'
'Yes. He wrote this after his visit in 1870, seven years before the prison was closed. Read on.' ...

I know that I thought to myself that I should go mad were I condemned to such a life, and that I caught one of the men looking at me with a broad grin as I thought it. I know that there seemed to me to hang over the whole place a sort of horrible gloom, as though the sunlight had been withdrawn from it, and that I should have been ashamed to have suddenly met some high-minded friend, inasmuch as it seemed that in coming down to stare at these chained and degraded beings, we had all been guilty of an unmanly curiosity.

'The last article deals with solitary confinement,' Rupert said in a respectful voice.

The warder drew aside a peephole in the barred door, and I saw a grizzled, gaunt and half-naked old man coiled in a corner. The peculiar wild-beast smell which belongs to some forms of furious madness exhaled from the cell. The gibbering animal within turned, and his malignant eyes met mine. 'Take care,' said the gaoler,' he has a habit of sticking his finger through the peep hole to try and poke someone's eye out!' I drew back, and a nail-bitten hairy finger, like

*the toe of an ape, was thrust with rapid and simian neatness through the aper-
ture. 'That is how he amuses himself,' said the good warder, forcing-to the iron
slot; 'He'd best be dead, I'm thinking.'*

Charlotte eyes moistened. 'Most poignant.'

'Yes.'

'Where did you find these again?' Charlotte tapped the folder. There seemed hundreds of cut-outs and newspaper clippings.

'They were mostly in the newspaper archive. You know, we are all aware of the atrocities that occurred at Port Arthur, and in the colonial prison system on the whole. So, your father, Charlotte, was a brave man. A brave man indeed to open such wounds by being so descriptive and honest in his story. I mean, we know all about these atrocities now in 1898, but your father wrote his novel when Port Arthur was still occupied and functioning as a prison. He studied court records and royal commissions and used these true events in his writings.'

Charlotte said, 'He did put poor old Rufus Dawes through the mill, did he not? I mean the man was tortured no end throughout the story. It suggests that there were people in real life who were falsely imprisoned, punished and god forbid, hanged on the gallows.'

'It's so sad that you never got to grow up with him,' Aunt Jocelyn said. 'He could have taught you so much.'

'He told me he witnessed a flogging once,' Craddock said.

'A real flogging?'

'Yes. And it thoroughly sickened him.'

'I should think so. Where did this barbaric act occur, Tasmania?'

'No, Melbourne actually. He and other journalists were invited by the prison governor to witness a prisoner receiving fifty lashes for one misdemeanour or another. It was at the Melbourne Gaol, in the early '70s.'

'How awful.'

'Yes, he wrote about it saying, quote, *I do not believe in its efficacy as a rule.* He later told me he was often lashed at his school back in England. Struck with a birch. And he felt even then as a student, there was no place in modern society for such punishment.'

Editor Rupert Craddock thought back to the day Charlotte first told him of her ambitious plan. He was concerned at Charlotte's persistence to finish and publish a sequel to her father's famous novel, lest her career be compromised, and he had taken her to task. The editor had a copy of her father's book opened at the last page.

'What I want to know is how can you possibly continue your father's novel, write a sequel, if his protagonists died in the end?' he stabbed a finger on the words of the last page.

'Ah,' Charlotte had smiled back. 'But did they die?'

Surprised at her answer Craddock argued. 'Yes Charlotte, they died. Let me read aloud, your father's epilogue …

At day-dawn on the morning after the storm, the rays of the rising sun fell upon an object which floated on the surface of the water not far from where the schooner had foundered.

This object was a portion of the mainmast head of the Lady Franklin *and entangled in the rigging were two corpses – a man and a woman. The arms of the man were clasped round the body of the woman, and her head lay on his breast.*

The Prison Island appeared but as long as a low line on the distant horizon. The tempest was over. As the sun rose higher the air grew balmy, the ocean placid; and, golden in the rays of the new risen morning, the wreck and its burden drifted out to sea …

I repeat … *the wreck and its burden drifted out to sea.* The End!'

Charlotte would not be swayed. She had a novel to write. She had a story to tell. And now, strangely enough, there were actions in her own life that paralleled her own book, like her husband Charles Claiborne feigning his own death, so all thought he had drowned in a shipwreck and been washed up on a beach.

'So, I put it to you sir, what if Rufus and Sylvia actually survived.'

'That was your father's original plan you know, for them to survive and sail to America.'

'Exactly. What if the bodies drifting at sea after the storm were so badly damaged, they were misidentified?'

'Are you by chance using parallels in your own life here?'

'If you mean my husband Charles faking his own death by using the body of his friend Harry washed up on a beach, well it is but a coincidence. I have had the idea of father's characters surviving on my mind for some time.'

'Then I speak for all your father's thousands of readers, good luck my dear.'

EPILOGUE

Part Two
The pen danced across the paper and words appeared in ink; ideas spilling from Charlotte like a composer might write a sonnet for a stage version of Pied Piper of Hamelin; with the one difference – the infamous rats were replaced by the author's words, and the melody for the play was created by a brass nib scratching on paper ...

Beyond the Seas of Tyranny

By Charlotte Clarke

Chapter One

Birds of the sea flew around the castaways, passing over the splintered spars of the wrecked ship. An albatross appeared. Was this a portent of good fortune or, as many sailors believe, an omen of approaching evil?

Rufus Dawes opened his eyes to the brightness of a burning tropical sun. His movement disturbed Sylvia. They had weathered the tempest, survived the most terrific storm. Now they floated on wreckage in the middle of the Pacific Ocean, drifting with the current. Clinging to a fragmented mast and secured by rope, they had survived a most horrific shipwreck.

There was no sign of their ship the Lady Franklin. *Their ship had sunk with all hands. Rufus and Sylvia were now alone on a vast ocean, all seemed lost, their very existence doomed, when Sylvia sighted a sail on the horizon ...*

Four hundred and thirty pages later, Charlotte finally completed her manuscript. Rupert Craddock was the first to read it. He was impressed. *Beyond the Seas of Tyranny* proved to be more than he could possibly have envisaged and finally, the old editor conceded, Charlotte Clarke was qualified to walk in her famous father's footsteps.

THE END

ACKNOWLEDGEMENTS

Damian Bester, Tasmanian historian, thank you for sharing your knowledge of The Mercury Newspaper, of which surprisingly little has been published.

Marcus Clarke: Novelist, Journalist and Bohemian. Michael Wilding. 2021

Marcus Clarke's own writings for *The Australasian* and *Austral Edition.* 1873

Thank you Editors: Warren Boyles and Penny Cocker

ABOUT THE AUTHOR

After decades in the hospitality industry and the best part of forty years since opening the Drunken Admiral Seafood Restaurant Craig hung up the apron to leave family at the helm and indulge in his other passion, writing fiction.

Craig was born in Hobart, Australia, in 1952 and travelled extensively giving him the experiences and escapades he so enjoys putting into print. This includes working as a chef for a restaurant owned by Sydney underbelly figures in the early 70s and cooking in Darwin when cyclone Tracy destroyed the city. Life has been busy and interesting to say the least.

In the 90s Craig independently shot two feature films, a murder mystery set in Southern Tasmania which aired on television and a splatter comedy still available online. He wrote, produced and directed both.

Having led a 'normal' life of work and duty Craig Godfrey decided to follow his real passion of writing fiction. And with Tasmania's fascinating past he has plenty to write about.

Using Tasmania's history as a blank canvas Craig loves nothing more than to weave adventure, mystery and mayhem involving colourful characters from all walks of life. He has published 9 previous novels.

Craig has nine previously published novels.

PENMORE PRESS TUCSON

1814

Taken to the Grave

Silent from the Shadows

Coral Moon

BLACK ROSE WRITING

Prisoners of Fate

On the Devil's Knee

Poveglia Island

Vatican Ruby

Cap'n Jonathon Bourke.

PRISONERS OF FATE

CRAIG A. GODFREY

NOTE FROM CRAIG A. GODFREY

Word-of-mouth is crucial for any author to succeed. If you enjoyed *The Novelist*, please leave a review online—anywhere you are able. Even if it's just a sentence or two. It would make all the difference and would be very much appreciated.

Thanks!
Craig A. Godfrey

We hope you enjoyed reading this title from:

www.blackrosewriting.com

Subscribe to our mailing list – *The Rosevine* – and receive **FREE** books, daily deals, and stay current with news about upcoming releases and our hottest authors.
Scan the QR code below to sign up.

Already a subscriber? Please accept a sincere thank you for being a fan of Black Rose Writing authors.

View other Black Rose Writing titles at www.blackrosewriting.com/books and use promo code **PRINT** to receive a **20% discount** when purchasing.

9 781685 133566